The Gentleman's DECEPTION

The Gentleman's DECEPTION

a regency romance

KAREN TUFT

Covenant Communications, Inc.

Published by Covenant Communications, Inc.
American Fork, Utah

Printed in the United States of America
First Printing: December 2017

23 22 21 20 19 18 17   10 9 8 7 6 5 4 3 2 1

ISBN-13: 978-1-52440-431-4

For Stephen, always

"I do love nothing in the world so well as you—is not that strange?"

—William Shakespeare
Much Ado About Nothing, Act 4, Scene 1

Acknowledgments

THIS NOVEL WAS VERY LITERALLY a labor of love. The idea for it was conceived, developed, and eventually birthed during an active and turbulent year, which saw, among ups and downs too numerous to list, the arrival of five—count them, five—grandchildren in quick succession. And that doesn't include the fact that my wonderful editor, Samantha Millburn, gave birth during this same time frame. I couldn't have done it without Sam, and I'm not sure how she got it done either.

So, here's to you, Sam, and the new life that joined your family. And here's to the Tuft Fab Five: Malcolm, Venna, Tessa, Porter, and Nora, who keep their parents and grandparents on their toes and have stolen our hearts.

Chapter 1

THROUGH THE WINDOW OF HER hackney carriage, Lavinia Fernley caught sight of the boisterous crowd that had gathered once again in front of London's Orpheus Theatre. It was becoming a common occurrence these days: the curious onlookers, the young Corinthians and old roués who were her most ardent admirers, and the small congregation of people off to one side, holding hands and singing hymns.

Today she'd worn a pale-pink muslin adorned with yards of delicate lace and a matching pelisse and fashionably tiny bonnet. The pink should have clashed horribly with her signature red locks but, instead, made for quite a dramatic picture, and the late afternoon sun would set her hair ablaze, she knew.

This would be the last time any of these people saw Ruby Chadwick, The Darling of Drury Lane, and like any good actor, Lavinia intended to give them a truly memorable performance.

The hackney driver, aware he'd had the privilege of escorting a celebrated personage to the theatre, adapted perfectly to his role. He jumped from his seat, made a show of straightening his dirty neckcloth, opened the carriage door, and dropped the steps. The crowd took a collective breath.

Oh, but she would make them wait and allow the suspense to build.

She stretched one gloved hand out the doorway and laid it on the driver's arm and then allowed a single foot, clad in soft kid leather, to extend from beneath her petticoats to the step.

"Ahh," a few of the onlookers sighed.

The group singing hymns sang louder.

When she finally emerged on the top step of the hackney, she looked over the crowd, making sure to give eye contact to as many of them as possible, then turned her gaze to her now-smitten hackney driver and offered him a beatific smile. All watched, mesmerized, as she glided down the steps, nodded her thanks to the driver, and raised her parasol.

"It's her," someone whispered. "It's Ruby Chadwick!" The name rippled through the crowd, creating a groundswell of both awe and derision.

"Ruby, Ruby Chadwick. The Darling of Drury Lane."

"The actress who wears men's clothes and shows her legs on stage."

"The incomparable beauty."

"The trollop."

Ah, yes. She'd heard it all before, and she was hearing it all again today.

She took her time making her way through the crowd, which parted before her like the Red Sea before Moses. When she successfully reached the theatre door, she turned to face her audience. Smiling demurely to admirers and haters alike, she lowered her parasol and raised her chin ever so slightly. "Thank you all for coming today," she said in a low voice, expertly pitched to carry over the crowd. "You have blessed me more than you can ever know."

They had made her a fair amount of money, in fact.

At the age of twenty-four, Lavinia Fernley, known by her stage name as Ruby Chadwick, had accomplished something most young ladies her age had not: in the three short years since she'd arrived in London, she had managed to become both a popular success and financially independent. Oh, there were plenty of young misses in London and elsewhere much wealthier than she, to be sure. Lavinia saw many of them in the audience of the theatre each night, but they undoubtedly had received their fortunes from their papas, not by using their own wits, as she herself had done.

She could hear the theatre door being unlocked behind her, right on cue. She raised a hand in farewell to the crowd and stepped through the now-open door only to have it lock behind her again.

Act 1, scene 1, and exit.

"Well, Ruby," Alfred Hinchcliffe, owner of the Orpheus Theatre, said as he pocketed the keys to the door. "Once again, your many admirers have shown their devotion to The Darling of Drury Lane." He rubbed his hands together in avaricious glee. "It's always a good sign when the crowds gather, especially so large a crowd this late in the Season. Means money in the coffers. Ticket sales are still going strong."

"Speaking of which, Alfred, darling, you do remember you still owe me for last week's receipts," she said sweetly. "I keep a close account of things, you know."

"That I do, Ruby dear; that I do," Hinchcliffe said. "Never met a better businessman than you, if you'll pardon my expressing it in such a way to a member of the fairer sex."

Alfred Hinchcliffe was as tightfisted a theater owner as there was, and she'd met many theater owners over the years, but he was always ingratiating with her since they both knew she was his golden goose. Lavinia patted his arm reassuringly. "We females do have our expenses. I would be happy as a lark if you were to bring me my share of the last week's receipts. Perhaps you can save time and bring me my estimated share of this evening's receipts as well." She leaned in and gave him a peck on the cheek, then went in for the kill. "I should *so* hate to fall ill with worry before tonight's performance after waiting on edge all week for my earnings—you know what a sensitive nature I have," she whispered.

"This evening's too, Ruby? You aren't aiming to ditch me and run, are you?" He chuckled at his little joke.

Lavinia raised a delicate eyebrow.

"Fine, then." He sighed. "I'll see what I can do."

"You really are a dear man, Alfred. You're *so* good to me." Maintaining her smile, barely daring to breathe, she watched him lumber toward his office, where he kept the safe that held the theatre's revenue, and disappear inside. For three long years, she'd watched him like a hawk and used her wiles to make sure he didn't cheat her out of her agreed-upon share of the receipts. Alfred was no fool—the crowds showed up to see the sensation that was Ruby Chadwick, and he knew it. He was no better and no worse than any of the men she'd encountered in her twenty-four years—as far as Lavinia was concerned, they were all greedy and unprincipled, to a man.

Act 1, scene 2 was over.

She had to keep up the pretense for only a few more hours, and then she would be *free*. Ruby Chadwick, The Darling of Drury Lane, would vanish forever. And Lavinia Fernley, who'd been safely hidden away for the past three years, could emerge and live as she chose, away from the audiences and naysayers and ardent suitors.

It all hinged on everything going as planned tonight, Lavinia reflected as she hurried to her dressing room—a few more such scenes that she must play, in addition to her performance onstage, before freedom was truly in sight. She needed all her wits about her if she were to be successful in those scenes. She must be more believable than ever if she was to have the life she'd always hoped—*dreamed*—of having. It would also take a miracle.

Oh, please send a miracle, she prayed after she slipped inside the door and leaned against it, her eyes clenched shut, her hands clutched at her breast.

* * *

It was as if a curtain had fallen, Lucas Jennings thought as he watched his best friend, Anthony Hargreaves, the Earl of Halford, dance with his new countess. The end of a chapter, the conclusion of an act.

He and Anthony had known each other at Cambridge. Anthony, however, had earned his degree, while Lucas had left university after his first year, choosing to enlist in the infantry instead. It had been an impulsive decision, perhaps, but he'd had his reasons at the time.

In the meantime, good fortune had eventually brought Lucas and Anthony together again. Anthony had achieved the rank of captain and had arranged for Lucas to be assigned to him as his personal assistant and valet.

The arrangement had been beneficial to both men. Indeed, each had saved the other's life on more than one occasion while fighting Napoleon in Spain. Anthony had been at death's door earlier this very year, wounded after a night of battle in the town of Badajoz, Spain. Lucas had worked fiercely to keep him alive and then to help him recover from the nightmares resulting from the experience. It was gratifying to see him now, today, smiling at his good fortune of both health and happiness.

Lucas had played a part in that and was not sorry he had delayed his own homecoming in an effort to first see Anthony whole again. In fact, it had been a relief to stay in London with his friend, as it had allowed him to delay the inevitable. Now it was time for him to move on. Return home to his family, his parents and brothers and sisters and their families. He would begin his journey today. The wedding ceremony was over, and Lucas had eaten his fill at the banquet that had followed. His belongings were already packed.

Anthony and his bride made their way to Lucas's side. "I can see that you are keen to be on your way," Anthony said with a twinkle in his eye. "Even from a fair distance, I can spot your restlessness."

"You are wrong, my friend. If you see restlessness, it is only because you are now married to the most beautiful woman I know, and I am envious and determined to find such a prize for myself."

Amelia, the new Countess of Halford, laughed. "What a flattering rogue you are," she said. "Actually, I believe a wife would do you a great deal of good." She placed her hand on Lucas's arm. "Oh, Lucas, how we will miss you."

"I won't," Anthony said. "I have found someone with whom I would much rather spend my time. She does not lurk in my dressing room or hover about me constantly, fretting if I am well or ill."

"I did not and do not hover," Lucas said with mock indignation. "Or fret. Not much, anyway. Only a bit, on the rarest of occasions. Besides," he continued once Anthony and Amelia ceased laughing at his humorous confession, "I am leaving my friend in competent hands, milady, and for that I am grateful. I would hate to see all my good work go to ruin." Anthony had been haunted by the specter of war, much more so than Lucas himself had been, and he had worried his friend may never recover. Lucas may have saved Anthony's life, but Amelia had done much to heal his soul.

"You make light of the situation, Lucas." Amelia took both of Lucas's hands in hers and looked him squarely in the eye. "In truth, I cannot imagine my life without Anthony, and I owe you a debt of gratitude I can never hope to repay."

"Not at all, my dear," Lucas replied gently.

"You must promise me, if there ever comes a time when either of us can be of service, you will let us know," she said. "I would do anything in my power for you, and Anthony feels the same. Don't you, Anthony?"

"It goes without saying, my love."

Lucas raised one of her hands and kissed it. "I shall remember that, milady, and thank you."

A guest who wished to congratulate the newly married couple interrupted them, which served to end the conversation. Lucas watched his friend a few minutes more, then discreetly left the banquet hall, trying to put the dread he felt at returning home out of his mind.

He returned to his room and dressed in clothing suited for travel, tucked a couple shirts and clean changes of linen into his saddlebag, and rang for a footman.

"Please have my horse readied and arrange for my trunk to be sent to the coaching inn at Stamford," Lucas told the footman upon his arrival. Stamford was a two-day journey north of London and a half-day's ride from Alderwood, the Jennings' family estate in Lincolnshire. The innkeeper could arrange to have his trunk sent to Alderwood from the inn.

"Certainly, sir." The footman hoisted the trunk onto his shoulder and excused himself.

Lucas had written his parents, informing them he would be arriving sometime within the week, unwilling even now to commit to a specific day. It was foolish to be so reluctant to return home. He loved his family and truly wanted to see them again—and yet he was also loath to do so. One would think he was going into battle. Devil take it, but he'd gone into more than one battle in Spain with more enthusiasm than he was currently feeling.

He eventually descended the staircase leading to the front hall, expecting to slip away unnoticed, having already said his goodbyes to Anthony and Amelia.

Before he could get away, Lady Ashworth, Anthony's mother, hurried toward him. "Mr. Jennings! I have been waiting for you to come downstairs. I see that you are intending to leave us now, but it is nearly evening. You could just as easily stay the night and depart in the morning."

"Thank you, but I am determined to begin my journey today, milady. I have friends awaiting me." He always had a friend or two—old army associates—in any number of pubs and taverns in Town and who were willing to pull up a chair for him, so it wasn't an outright lie. If he stayed, he'd only be tempted to find more reasons to delay his return home.

"At the very least, allow me to have Cook prepare some food for you to take with you."

"You are kind to offer, but that won't be necessary, I assure you."

"I wish there were some way I could thank you more fully," she said. "You have done so much for my Anthony and for Ashworth and me too, by extension. I cannot do enough to show my gratitude."

"I did nothing he would not have done for me, ma'am. It was the nature of things, you see, and I was fortunate to be in a position to assist."

He bowed over her hand and turned to the door. The groom would have Hector prepared and waiting for him by now, and the horse wasn't known for his patience.

"Mr. Jennings."

The marchioness's voice was commanding, so Lucas immediately turned back to her. "I would have you know unequivocally that you always have an honored place with us in our home."

He nodded his head in acknowledgment. "Thank you, Lady Ashworth."

"See that you remember it."

"I shall, ma'am."

And that was that—the end of a chapter, a very large chapter in Lucas's life. There had been a certainty that had come with serving in the military, beyond the variables thrown at them by the weather and the enemy. An order of command. Structure. A sense of purpose.

This new chapter in his life was a blank slate. There was opportunity, yes, but at present Lucas could see only uncertainty and unfulfilled expectations, with the barest glimmer of optimism. He felt oddly like the poor chaps who volunteered to be the first to charge during battle. The forlorn hope, they were called, and not without reason.

There was nothing for it now, however, but to move forward and write his destiny as best he could.

"Time to go, old friend," Lucas said to Hector as he secured his saddlebag and patted the horse's neck before hoisting himself into the saddle. "Time to face our future." He took Hector at an unhurried pace away from Ashworth House and on through the streets of London. It was dusk, and the grayness of the atmosphere around him matched his mood entirely.

He eventually found himself in front of White's club and could see several gentlemen of his acquaintance through the large bow window. Lucas, however, had not become a member, despite being the son of a viscount. Such things had not been foremost on his mind as a youth when he'd enlisted in the army, and during the past few weeks, while he'd been back in London, he'd been more concerned about seeing to Anthony's health than socializing. Other than making arrangements for a basic wardrobe and the occasional night out with old army friends, he'd done little else.

The scene through the window at White's left Lucas feeling even more melancholy, so he rode Hector several blocks north to the Hissing Goose, a local pub he'd visited on a few occasions, to fortify himself before continuing on his way. Dusk had descended into full darkness now, with only the occasional streetlamp offering a weak respite from the gloom.

Upon entering the pub, Lucas immediately saw Sir Michael Foresby, with whom Lucas had a passing acquaintance, playing cards with a few of his friends. "Jennings, well met. Come join us," Sir Michael said with a welcoming gesture. "You look to be ripe for the plucking this evening."

Lucas picked up the ale the barman had poured and wandered over. "Sorry to disappoint, but I'm only here for a quick drink before continuing north."

"North, eh?" the fellow to Sir Michael's left said. "Had your fill of the debutantes and their meddling mamas, have you?" He laughed as though he'd made a tremendous joke.

"Returning home from an extended vacation in Spain," Lucas said.

"Ah," another fellow, a man named Harris, said. "Been off fighting the Corsican, then. Well done. Join us, sir, do. The next drink is on me." He gestured to an open space at the table. "A few hands and some agreeable company before you go on your way, eh?"

"Rumor has it you've been hidden away at Ashworth House since returning from the Continent," Sir Michael added. "Since you've waited this long to return home, a few rounds of cards won't make much of a difference, will they?"

Lucas sat, banishing the thought that he was procrastinating once again, and he sent the accompanying guilt along with it. One of the men at the table proceeded to collect the cards and shuffle them, dealing to Lucas along with the others.

"It's fortunate you and your money came along," another gentleman said as he studied his cards with an inscrutable face. "I've won nearly all my friends can afford to lose. Are you in?"

"I'm in." Lucas tossed a few coins on the table.

The men got down to the serious business of card playing, and Lucas won and lost right along with them.

"You've got the luck tonight, Jennings," another fellow, Pinckney by name, said. "I daresay you're a few quid richer than you were when you entered the Hissing Goose a few hours earlier."

A few hours? Lucas checked his pocket watch.

Blast, it was later than he'd realized.

He stood. "Gentlemen, it's been a pleasure, but I truly must be on my way." He would barely make it out of London tonight if he didn't go now.

"That's quite all right," Sir Michael said, his words a little more slurred than they had been earlier in the evening. "I was about to leave for the Orpheus Theatre anyway. Who's with me?"

"Now, *there's* a bet to wager on," Harris said with a sly, somewhat drunken grin. "And how is The Darling of Drury Lane these days, Sir Michael? Taken you up on your generous offer now, has she?"

The others at the table laughed and guffawed. Lucas had no idea who or what they were talking about; apparently, he'd been a little *too* solitary since his return to Town. "The Darling of Drury Lane?"

All eyes at the table turned in his direction. "You haven't heard of The Darling of Drury Lane?" Harris asked. "Where have you *been*, old man? Oh, right. Spain." He sat forward, placing his forearms on the table in anticipation of the tale he obviously planned to share. Lucas sat back down. "One would *have* to be in Spain not to have heard of Ruby Chadwick."

"And even there, I'm sure her name has made the rounds of the officers' quarters," Pinckney added. "There are, uh, *illustrations* of her for purchase at some of the gentlemen's bookshops. I wonder . . . do you suppose she posed for them in person—"

"Miss Chadwick," Sir Michael interrupted, raising an unsteady arm to make his point, "is the most exquisite of females to grace God's green earth. Her beauty is unparalleled: fair of face, with eyes like storm clouds, lips like rose petals, hair as fiery—"

"Breeches roles," Pinckney whispered loudly to Lucas behind his hand. "Legs on display. Lovely ones they are too."

"Ah," Lucas said. It explained much more about Sir Michael's raptures about her than gray eyes and rosy lips did.

"She has her choice of admirers, so she can afford to be picky. And picky she is, by thunder," Pinckney continued. "Surprising that she hasn't taken a protector from among the lot of them already; but no one has bragged about it so far, and you can bet the lucky man would."

"So our Sir Michael here hasn't lost hope yet," Harris said.

"She claims to be betrothed," Sir Michael explained. "Won't talk about him much, always manages to change the subject. I've yet to see the man materialize, however. And there isn't a man living I can't best if given half a chance."

"Speaking of which," Harris said.

"Right," Sir Michael said, struggling to his feet. "I better be off if I'm to reach the theatre when the first play of the evening finishes. Must be quicker than her other admirers to get backstage, y'know."

"You'll be lucky to stay atop your horse in your state," another of the fellow gamblers, a man named Berbrooke, said. He hadn't spoken much this evening, this Berbrooke fellow, and even now was only stating the blatantly obvious.

"The Orpheus does two short plays each night," Harris explained to Lucas. "Musical productions, they are, to an extent. Ruby Chadwick has a leading role in the first one but holds court for her gentlemen admirers during the second play. If she performed in both, people would be at the theatre all night long. Theatre owner thought better of it. Ruby brings in plenty of money as it is, although it doesn't make the actors in the second play very happy." He chuckled.

"She sounds intriguing," Lucas said politely.

"Aye, she's that but too rich for my blood," Harris replied. "The betting books are full of wagers about her. She flirts with all and sundry but hasn't let any gentleman get too close—I imagine it's because of this mysterious betrothed of hers. A heroic figure, apparently. Only makes her admirers that much more determined, from what I hear."

"Odds are against you, Sir Michael," Pinckney said. "Sorry, old chap, but you know it's true. The Earl of Cosgrove has the best odds anyway, last time I checked at White's."

"Cosgrove is like all the others—he's only interested in her as a mistress," Sir Michael exclaimed. "Everyone knows he'll only marry the bluest blood—and only when he can't avoid the parson's mousetrap any longer. He's avoided it longer than most already."

"Of *course*, he's only interested in her as a mistress," Harris said. "She's an *actress*. That's all any of her admirers are interested in. What gentleman in his right mind would marry her?"

"I would," Sir Michael said indignantly.

"Only because you're drunk," Berbrooke said.

"I am, at that." Sir Michael sighed, slumping back into his abandoned chair. "But I would still marry her. She's a goddess."

"As enlightening as this conversation is," Lucas said, standing again, "I must be on my way if I'm to make it any farther north than the Hissing Goose tonight. Thank you all for your company—and your money—and I congratulate you on your pending nuptials, Sir Michael."

The others laughed, and Sir Michael gave him a wobbly salute. "I shall invite you to my wedding, if there ends up being one," he said.

"Enjoy your trip northward," Harris said. "Don't get lost in a bog on your way."

Getting lost in a bog was a delay tactic Lucas hadn't considered before. He'd keep it in mind if he happened to feel increasingly desperate en route. His mood was decidedly lighter than it had been though, thanks to his winnings at cards and the jovial banter.

He mounted Hector and turned northward. He was starting his journey too late to make any real progress this evening, but he'd continue for a while longer. His thoughts returned briefly to the conversation regarding Ruby Chadwick, the supposed Darling of Drury Lane, and apparently the talk of all the gentlemen so far this Season, not that Lucas had heard of her. He really had been more reclusive than he'd realized during his stay in London. He might have enjoyed seeing a dashing young actress cavort on stage, playing a breeches role.

What kind of bravado would it take, he wondered, for a young woman to appear onstage dressed in such a manner?

He had heard of other such actresses, some achieving great recognition. And yet he knew that even with that recognition, the *ton* would not condone such an actress joining their illustrious ranks. Actresses were, by and large, part of the demimonde, fringe members of society known for their libertine lifestyles and not accepted by the best of families. Sir Michael wasn't the highest of sticklers, but the Earl of Cosgrove, with whom Lucas was somewhat familiar, most assuredly was. Cosgrove would never marry someone like that. Dabble with, yes. Marry? No.

Fog had settled in and grown thick during the time Lucas had been playing cards. He kept Hector at a walk as they carefully made their way toward the northern limits of the city. He passed a night watchman who called out the time.

Nine of the clock.

Nudging Hector to quicken his pace, he continued on his way.

Chapter 2

Lavinia, dressed in men's breeches, her red hair a tumble of curls down her back, stood center stage after the final scene of *The Highwayman's Prize* and bowed along with her fellow actors while the audience roared its approval, cheering and tossing flowers onstage.

Lavinia's heart pounded within her chest like a wild thing trying to escape.

It was a physically demanding role, with intricate swordplay that she and Nicholas Randall, who played the hero, and George Babbitt, who played the villain, had rehearsed down to the finest detail: Lavinia's character enters stage left just as the villain is about to finish off the wounded hero with a final sword thrust, her arrival distracting him from his evil deed. She fights valiantly against the villain as the hero struggles to his feet . . . and she strikes the villain down just in time. During all of this, Lavinia's carefully hidden hair comes unbound in a glorious fall of red curls, and the hero realizes who she is at last and what she has done to save his life. In the end, they have saved each other, collapsing into a loving embrace . . . And curtain.

It was always a challenging scene to perform. George had been perfectly cast as the villain; he was a rake and a bully in real life, and Lavinia was constantly on her guard when he was around. On stage, he tended to be intentionally aggressive toward her.

Nicholas, on the other hand, was a little long in the tooth to play the romantic hero, but he was one of Hinchcliffe's cronies, so there was nothing Lavinia had been able to do about it. The swordplay was too strenuous for him, and by the end of the scene, he was sweating and breathing hard and stinking of the onions he'd invariably had for supper. Lavinia's best acting skill was always required at that particular moment, when she was to kiss Nicholas and look madly in love rather than repulsed as the curtain fell.

It was not the demanding nature of the scene and dealing with her fellow actors that caused Lavinia's heart to pound now, however. It was the anticipation she felt knowing that after tonight, she would never have to kiss Nicholas Randall or dodge George Babbitt again.

The only safe place to kiss an actor, her father had always warned her, *is on the stage. And there isn't a safe place to kiss any other man.*

The applause continued, so Lavinia, although in breeches, dropped into an elegant curtsy while George and Nick bowed alongside her.

"You best hurry along to your dressing room, Ruby, love," George purred at her when they rose. "It would appear your admirers are in a particularly boisterous mood tonight. Best not to keep them waiting."

"If it weren't for Ruby's admirers, George, the show would have closed and you'd be doing two-bit parts in the Cotswolds." Nick sniffed. "I don't see the ladies congregating outside your dressing room door."

"They aren't flocking outside yours either."

Lavinia ignored them. Bickering like this was a common occurrence between the two men after each performance. There was always something one of them did to set the other off, considering the fragile egos at work here.

She hurried backstage to her dressing room. She must prepare for her next performance, the one in which she entertained and flirted and played coquette with the gentlemen who gathered outside her door with flowers and gifts each night.

Telling herself to be calm, she slipped into her dressing room.

"There you are, finally," Hannah said. The older woman hurried over and assisted Lavinia out of her tailcoat. Lavinia had been but a child in leading strings when Hannah had come into her life. "I'm that glad you won't be wearing these gent's clothes again after tonight." Hannah folded the tailcoat and placed it in the small bag that sat nearby as Lavinia worked at the buttons of her waistcoat. "What would your papa have said if he'd seen you dressed this way? Sit now so I can help you with them boots."

"Papa would have said, 'Hear, hear, my girl,' especially as it has kept us from the poorhouse these past three years." She sat in the chair and grabbed hold of the dressing table while Hannah crouched and tugged on the heel of Lavinia's boot.

Hannah shook her head and grumbled under her breath as she set the first boot aside. "Not likely he would, despite what you said about the poorhouse bein' true enough. 'Tisn't right for a young miss to be prancing about in men's breeches for all and sundry to see, lovey, and your papa would agree with me."

"Oh, Hannah, I'm an *actress*, the daughter of an actor. He wouldn't have batted an eye at this costume, and you know it." She wriggled out of the waistcoat and began unbuttoning her breeches.

"Five minutes, Miss Chadwick," a voice called following a brisk knock at the door. "And then I'm lettin' 'em backstage."

"Miss Chadwick this, Miss Chadwick that," Hannah muttered as she folded the waistcoat and put it in the bag with the tailcoat. "I'll be that glad to see Ruby Chadwick gone forever, and there's a fact. I want my Livvy back, and it can't happen soon enough for me. Hand me them breeches now."

"And that time has arrived, has it not, Hannah? Ruby Chadwick will disappear after tonight. Poof! Just like that." Lavinia snapped her fingers as she stepped into the burgundy velvet gown she'd chosen to wear tonight and wriggled into the sleeves and bodice. At least Hannah had made the gown with the fastenings in front for convenience. "Be a dear and help me fix my hair."

"'Twon't be a done thing until we're well away from here." Hannah picked up the brush from the dressing table and began running it through Lavinia's curls while Lavinia finished with the fastenings and reached for her ruby earbobs and put them on. "And you with all them gents what won't leave you be. I'm that nervous."

Lavinia would *not* think about all that could go wrong tonight. "We'll be fine; you'll see. You remember the plan?"

Hannah nodded. "O' course. I pack up what's here, then I meet Artie out back round the corner away from all them gents gathered outside. Delia and Artie will have our belongings loaded into the rented post chaise at the house, and we meet you at the White Hart on the way out of London."

"Not the White Hart, Hannah, the White—"

"Two minutes, Miss Chadwick," the voice outside Lavinia's dressing room door called again. "Then I'm unlocking the door for 'em."

"White *Horse*, Hannah. The White Horse. Quick now, the necklace."

Hannah stuck the last pin in Lavinia's hair, creating a loose collection of curls around her head. Then she removed the ruby necklace that matched the earbobs from their box.

Lavinia checked her appearance in the looking glass while Hannah fastened the clasp of the elaborate necklace. She hoped wearing the burgundy gown and jewelry wasn't overdoing it, but it was important that she look *memorable* in her final performance as Ruby Chadwick, The Darling of Drury Lane. Her admirers—not to mention Alfred Hinchcliffe—would be less inclined to suspect her to make a dash for it if their last image of her was as the glittering darling of the theatre welcoming her many admirers.

Lavinia could hear movement and the low hum of conversation increasing outside her dressing room door. The gentlemen were on approach. She took a deep breath to settle her nerves, which, like Hannah's, were on edge. Not that she would let Hannah—or the gentlemen outside the door, for that matter—suspect it.

"Livvy!" Hannah held up the finishing touch for the costume. It was a ring with a large ruby set in it, and Lavinia never went out in public without it. It was one of her greatest defenses against the ardor she constantly fended off from all her admirers, supposedly given to her by her make-believe betrothed, who was serving as an officer in Spain.

Whenever an admirer attempted to seduce her—and it had happened frequently since arriving in London—she would delicately dab away tears and claim she could not betray her betrothed, who was serving King and country so heroically.

The admirer in question would immediately remember he was somewhat honorable and beg her forgiveness. Most of the time.

Lavinia suspected that part of her overall attraction in Town was the fact that none of her gentlemen admirers had been successful in their pursuits of her so far. Unfortunately, a few of the more ardent ones were becoming impatient, especially the Earl of Cosgrove. Lord Cosgrove was a man in his late thirties, tall and blond, who could have been handsome had he not spent the last decade or so indulging himself in a variety of vices.

He'd been getting more and more aggressive the last few times he'd been to the Orpheus to see her perform, and Lavinia had begun to feel threatened. It didn't help that Alfred Hinchcliffe, greedy bounder that he was, encouraged these attentions to her, especially from wealthy, titled admirers like the Earl of Cosgrove.

Even thinking about the earl gave Lavinia the shudders.

She snatched up the ring and hurriedly slid it onto her finger. She could tell by the rumble outside the door that her admirers were getting restless. "You have the receipts I got from Hinchcliffe?"

"Yes, Livvy."

"Good. And you remember the plan?" she asked Hannah once more. "Most importantly, you remember that if I don't make it there by midnight—"

"We goes on to the next post stage without you. I don't like that part, Livvy, and I mean to tell you—"

"I'll be there, don't worry. It's only a contingency plan. Now, go!"

Hannah picked up the bag and opened the door. "Move back and let me through," she grumbled to the group of men gathered there. They groaned and booed when they saw it wasn't Ruby Chadwick finally making her appearance. Through the crack in the door, Lavinia could see Lord Cosgrove standing amongst the other men.

She shut the door, leaned her back against it, and gritted her teeth.

Perhaps she should have kept Hannah here with her after all, but Lavinia had been certain she could manage her entourage for one final evening, and it was important that Hannah and the others leave Town ahead of her. Lavinia was their decoy while they left, and the disguise she'd chosen for later would work better if she was on her own while she slipped out of Town.

What Lavinia hadn't counted on was Lord Cosgrove being here tonight. *Again.* He'd mentioned he had other plans for this evening.

Oh, but she was tired of it all.

Stupid, stupid, arrogant man. Stupid, stupid men who wanted the illusion of Ruby Chadwick but knew nothing of the real woman. It was Lavinia's own fault. She had created Ruby Chadwick in the first place, who was no more real than any of the other characters Lavinia played onstage, not that any of her admirers cared to recognize that fact.

But Ruby had been essential to their survival, providing Lavinia—and by extension, Hannah and Delia and Artie—the financial means to begin a new life. Ruby's larger-than-life theatrical presence and flirtatious ways had been the reason for their success. Lavinia could not hate Ruby; she owed her too much, and yet it was Ruby who now held her captive.

Lavinia had only to get through this next scene.

Ruby Chadwick's final scene.

She could do it. If it meant having a quiet life in the country, free to plant flowers and raise a few chickens and sew and read—in other words, live like a *normal person* did for the first time in her life—she could do it. She *would* do it.

Lavinia took a deep breath, straightened her spine, pasted a sultry smile on her face, and opened the door. "Gentlemen," she cooed as she floated out into their midst.

* * *

When Lucas reached the outskirts of London, he took a room at the White Horse Inn, deposited his belongings therein, and then settled at a corner table in the public room to eat a late supper. While he waited for the serving girl to bring him his food, he retrieved the two letters he'd received during the past week from his coat pocket.

The first letter, from his mother, was a lengthy epistle written in her usual loose, flowery script that filled two sheets back and front. She'd also added postscripts in the side margins, so there was hardly any blank space to be found anywhere.

"Lucas," it said in part, "it has been too long since we saw you. If it weren't for the small portrait of you we commissioned before you left for the Peninsula, we should never know how you look. I know you will say we saw you briefly when you were on leave three years ago and that more recently you owed it to your commanding officer to see him returned to health. It is what you have written and explained to me before. But surely you have fulfilled that obligation, and your earlier brief stay can hardly imprint your changed appearance into our memory as fully as we would wish."

The portrait to which she referred was a ghastly thing his father had coughed up the money to commission due to his wife's constant pestering, only relenting when she had exclaimed that it would be their only remembrance of their dear Lucas were he to die on the battlefields of Spain.

On that happy thought his father had capitulated, hiring a fellow from a neighboring village who claimed to be a portrait painter. After seeing the finished product, it was obvious the man had exaggerated his abilities; although, considering what his father had paid the man, they'd probably gotten their money's worth. The person in the painting had the same hair and eye color as Lucas, but beyond that, the similarities were difficult to discern.

Still, the argument his mother had put forth in her letter was a valid one. Lucas had changed a great deal since he'd enlisted in the army at age nineteen. He was a man now, not a youth, and his countenance undoubtedly reflected the past seven years of his experience, especially as it related to the harsher aspects of war.

"You will not believe it," her letter continued, "but James has written to say he will take time away from his duties as a barrister to visit once you arrive. Martha and Albert, sadly, cannot, as Martha is in the family way again and too close to her confinement for travel. Isaac, as you already know, is vicar at St. Alfred's nearby, and Thomas and Isobel and their brood live here at Alderwood, of course, along with your other siblings, excepting Simon."

Simon, three years younger than Lucas, was living in London, his mother's previous letters had informed him. Lucas felt a pang of guilt over that. He hadn't been inclined to get in touch with Simon when he'd arrived back in London from Spain. His mother would have presumed he had since he and Simon were close in age; Lucas hadn't had the heart to tell her he had not yet seen his brother.

And there it was—the entire Jennings family. They would almost all be at Alderwood, the family home, and Lucas must face them with a smile and a hearty greeting.

He refolded the letter and returned it to his pocket.

The second letter was from his sister-in-law, Isobel. In contrast to his mother's, this letter was brief and to the point. "My dear brother Lucas," it began. *Brother*, she'd written, when Lucas had expected it to be so much more than that.

"We are all looking forward to welcoming our hero home," the letter said. "For that is what you are. Our hero. It has been too long, Lucas. Your parents and your brothers and sisters yearn to see you, as do your nieces and nephews, some of whom you have not even met. I yearn to see you too, my dearest brother and friend. Let us put history firmly behind us. Alderwood is your home. It is time to return to that home, Lucas. With affection, your sister, Isobel."

He had told himself for seven long years that Isobel was now his sister-in-law and that he needed to think of her as such. He had even managed that visit home three years back when he was on leave and had been able to behave civilly toward her and his brother Thomas when he hadn't been able to avoid them completely.

This time was different, however, he reflected as he sipped his ale. He was no longer in the army. He had no profession to return to, no home, no solid plans for his future beyond enduring his reunion with his family. To face Isobel again after she'd so easily transferred her affections to his eldest brother—who would become Viscount Thurlby and possess Alderwood one day—would be like a knife blow to his manhood. It had been a knife blow to his heart, a betrayal, seven years before.

Perhaps he'd spend a second night at the White Horse.

He wadded up the letter and tossed it onto the table, then gestured to the serving girl to refill his glass.

* * *

Lavinia batted her eyelashes as she tapped naughty gentlemen on the arm with her fan and sweetly declined expensive gifts—small tokens were one thing, but expensive baubles implied she owed the gentleman more than mere flirtation—and sighed over bouquets of flowers until she thought she would scream.

Lord Cosgrove, of course, then insisted upon escorting her home. On the one hand, his offer discouraged the other men and sent them on their way more speedily. On the other hand, it meant she would be alone with him in his carriage since she'd sent Hannah home earlier so she and Delia and Artie could be on their way.

Lavinia tried to keep distance between herself and the earl on the carriage seat, though it was nearly impossible since there wasn't much room to begin with and he'd deliberately planted himself in such a way as to take up as much space as possible.

"You look breathtaking tonight, my dear," the earl said. "A glowing, lustrous ruby of a woman, full of fire within. Your performance onstage tonight was particularly riveting and—dare I say it—passionate."

"Thank you," Lavinia purred, praying he wouldn't notice how tightly she was pressed against the side of his carriage.

"My pleasure, Miss Chadwick. It would be even more to my pleasure if you would allow me to kiss you and not merely compliment you."

She smiled demurely and extended her hand—with the betrothal ring in full view.

"That is not what I meant," he said, chuckling. "And you know it, you little vixen. I would have you, Miss Chadwick; I am determined in this. And I have been more patient in pursuing you than any other woman."

"And yet, I am not yours to have, my lord," she said, her heart pounding in her chest. She glanced surreptitiously out the window behind his back to see how close they were to her little rented house—the house that would be empty and without her friends there to assist her if the earl got out of hand. "I cannot believe you would ask me to betray my betrothed when he is so valiantly fighting against Bonaparte."

"And *I* cannot believe that a man who would betroth himself to an *actress* would be at all surprised to return home and discover his betrothed had added to their income by becoming a rich man's mistress. He might even be pleased."

"Such flattering words, my lord," she said, her voice dripping with honeyed sarcasm. She would not have him see the fear she felt in that moment for anything. "Perhaps you should stretch your imagination to believe that I am a maiden who wishes to remain so until I am married." The minute the words were out of her mouth, she knew she'd made a mistake. She'd only meant to imply that she intended to be faithful to her betrothed—make-believe though he may be—as a means of putting Lord Cosgrove off, but the earl, of course, presumed she was now dangling for a marriage proposal.

He already had her trapped in the corner of the carriage, and now he leaned over her, bracing his hands on the walls of the carriage on either side of her, his face next to hers, his lips against her ear. She bit the inside of her cheek to keep from shuddering in disgust.

"Forget marriage, my sweet. It'll never happen," he whispered, tracing kisses behind her ear and down her throat. Lavinia squeezed her eyes shut, frantically thinking how she could repel his advances without incurring his temper. It was a precarious situation; he was much larger and stronger than she and not known for being particularly reasonable when not getting his way. "Be practical, instead," he continued. "Think of the pleasure we can find together. I will be generous, you know."

Lavinia shamefully admitted to herself that she might have been tempted by such an offer a mere three years earlier. Her father had just died, the original members of the traveling theater company to which she and her father had belonged had gotten old, and the younger actors had splintered off and gone searching for greener pastures.

If she hadn't come up with the idea of Ruby Chadwick and if Ruby hadn't become such a success, Lavinia might have felt she'd had no choice but to accept such an offer as the one Lord Cosgrove was making.

She did have a choice, however. Lavinia placed her hand on his chest and pushed firmly. "While I am sure you are generous with your paramours, my lord, the answer is still no."

"I don't believe you," he said. "Or, rather, I believe I can change your mind."

The carriage stopped not a moment too soon. Thankfully, Lord Cosgrove had not as yet descended into the wholly undignified behavior she might have experienced at the hands of a rougher man. She'd dealt with such types during her time with the company and didn't relish contending with the earl in such a manner tonight.

Oh, but she was exhausted.

He sighed impatiently and drew away, then exited the carriage and extended his hand to her, assisting her with aristocratic dignity. He did not relinquish her hand, however, as he led her to her front door. The house was completely dark, and Lavinia prayed he wouldn't notice and that nothing else might appear suspicious to him.

She tugged her hand from his and turned toward him very deliberately. "Good evening, Lord Cosgrove," she said in a carrying voice while dropping into a formal curtsy, hoping her actions would put more emotional distance between them.

"I catch your drift; don't worry, my dear. I will not have it said that I forced a lady," he replied with an edge to his voice. He moved closer, and Lavinia tensed. "But I believe I have at least earned the kiss I requested." He took her chin firmly in hand and lowered his mouth to hers, using his vast expertise in an attempt to lower her resistance.

Lavinia endured the earl's kiss, despite the repugnance she felt. It was safer to do so than to resist, especially since he'd indicated he would leave afterward.

He eventually drew away from her and dropped his hand. "Well," he said. "Well, well, but you are a stubborn little thing, aren't you? Do not presume to think matters have been resolved between us, my dear Miss Chadwick. On the contrary, I believe the game is just beginning. I am a determined man—and I always get what I want. Do not doubt me on this score." He bowed to her. "Adieu, then. For now."

She watched him return to his carriage and climb inside before she turned and unlocked the door to her house. Once she'd closed the door behind her, she relocked it and rushed to the parlor so she could continue watching until his carriage retreated from sight.

With Lord Cosgrove finally gone, she made her way in the darkness to the back of the house, where Hannah had left a change of clothing for her. It was time for Ruby Chadwick to disappear for good.

But first she needed to catch her breath.

Lavinia's entire life had revolved around the theater. She'd been born into it, the daughter of an actor, who'd also been a drunken womanizer, and a mother who hadn't cared enough about her own daughter to take her with her when she'd left. All Lavinia had ever wanted was a normal life and a normal home, away from the clamoring crowds and predatory men she encountered every evening. And now she had the means to do it, if everything continued to go according to plan.

She hurriedly changed out of her red velvet gown, carefully folding the beautiful garment before putting it in her bag. The dress would never be the same after traveling in such a manner, she thought sadly. Hannah was gifted with the needle, and the gown was a masterpiece.

She tucked her earbobs and necklace into the bag as well, nestled into the folds of the gown. The jewelry was expertly made, but they were paste costume pieces created for the theater, as was the matching ring on her finger. They'd been created for her to wear while playing Anne Boleyn in *Henry the Eighth*—well, more like a shortened, somewhat musical version of *Henry* that the troupe had performed in Dorset a few years back. When the troupe had disbanded, they'd divvied up the props and costumes, and she'd kept these, along with a few other items. They weren't real, much like her life on stage and her identity as Ruby Chadwick weren't real. They had come in handy tonight though.

She quickly donned the drab gray dress and cloak Hannah had left and twisted her unmistakable red hair up and tucked it inside the oversized lace cap she would wear under her bonnet. Then she peered into the mirror and dabbed on theater paint to aid in her disguise, but there was no disguising her facial features from anyone who knew them well. She would have to hope she didn't run into any such person.

She left the house through the kitchen entrance in the back, quietly making her way through the garden gate and keeping in the shadows until she was several houses away from her own. As careful as she'd been, she had to be sure Lord Cosgrove hadn't sent one of his lackeys to spy on her. She wouldn't put it past him; the man was too possessive. Too *obsessive*.

Finding a hackney ended up being more difficult than she had expected, but she finally managed to get one and, after a long, tense drive, she was finally in the courtyard of the White Horse on the northern outskirts of the city, near the borough of Barnet, her bag by her side as she dug money from her reticule to pay the hackney driver his fare. All she needed to do now was find Hannah and Delia and Artie.

It wasn't quite midnight, which was good, although she really hadn't expected to be cutting it so close on time, drat the Earl of Cosgrove. He'd nearly ruined everything.

Despite the lateness of the hour, there was a surprising amount of activity at the White Horse. A group of passengers was exiting a stagecoach and hurrying inside the inn for the night while grooms busied themselves tending to the horses.

She handed the money to the hackney driver, picked up her bag, and crossed the courtyard toward the entrance of the inn. Once inside, she stayed near the door to survey things and search for her friends. At least one of them, if not all three, was supposed to meet her in the public area of the inn.

The large public room was still busy despite the lateness of the hour, the majority of its tables occupied. A group of local men sat at the bar, drinking. Serving girls wandered from table to table, refilling glasses and clearing away empty plates. The air was warm and heavy, and the smell of roasted mutton and potatoes filled Lavinia's nostrils as the low hum of conversation swirled around her. Her stomach growled; she hadn't eaten since luncheon, being too nervous to eat before this particular evening's performances—both onstage and off—but she needed to find Hannah and the others first before addressing her hunger.

She looked around the room but couldn't see them, which was troubling. Delia and Artie were dears, but they tended to leave the details up to Hannah, and Hannah had been worried enough about the details tonight to get them confused.

Hannah wouldn't have gone to someplace called the White Hart instead of the White Horse after all, would she?

Would she?

Lavinia frantically cast her eyes around the public room again, praying she'd simply overlooked her friends the first time. This go-around, she noticed a man sitting alone at a table in the corner. He didn't appear to be much older than herself, a few years at most, and yet there was a look about him that told her he was older than his years. He was intently studying a crumpled piece of paper that sat on the table next to his empty supper plate.

Even though he was seated, it was obvious he was taller than the average man. One long leg extended out from beneath the table, and the hand reaching for his glass of ale was large and competent looking. The fact that he was a lone traveler had also made him stand out from the crowd.

Her gaze moved on, although it became readily apparent that Hannah and the others weren't here. And then she spied a group of gentlemen who were familiar to her, seated at a table to her right, playing cards. She froze at the sight.

The gentlemen, eager to make their mark in London society, were frequently part of Lord Cosgrove's usual entourage. Lavinia had often seen them in the boxes of the theatre and outside her dressing-room door after performances. Why they were here, on the very outskirts of London, and not at one of their more usual haunts, was most likely a coincidence—but a worse coincidence she couldn't have imagined.

The night needed only this.

She had to avoid being seen by them. If they recognized her, word would make its way back to Drury Lane and Alfred Hinchcliffe and Lord Cosgrove and all the others. It was not vain of her to imagine she would be pursued by at least some of them, most notably Cosgrove—she'd deliberately created the character of Ruby to be intriguing and desirable to the opposite sex, and with demonstrable success.

She would not give up on her dream, not after all she'd done tonight to have it. She would *not*. She must leave the White Horse immediately. Hannah, Delia, and Artie were obviously not here, so there was no use staying anyway.

Oh, but she was tired and hungry.

In her tiredness, however, she waited a fraction too long to act. One of Cosgrove's minions looked up from his cards and spotted her. He half stood in recognition and opened his mouth. "I say—" he began.

There was nothing for it.

"Husband!" she exclaimed, hurrying across the room to the tall man sitting alone in the corner. She threw her arms about his broad shoulders and tucked her head next to his on the side facing away from the rest of the room. "Here you are!"

Chapter 3

WHAT THE *DEVIL*?

One minute, Lucas had been nursing his ale and staring at Isobel's crumpled letter on the table, and the very next, a gray bundle of femininity had fallen into his lap and called him *husband*.

He instinctively rose to his feet. Since the lady's arms were securely around his neck, she invariably came with him.

"Please," she whispered in his ear when he moved to set her on the floor—his head being drawn down to her height by the arms she'd slung around his neck. "Go along with my ruse."

Well, then!

He'd been perfectly content procrastinating his inevitable trek upstairs to his room, aware that in the morning he'd have no excuse but to get on his horse and be on his way to Alderwood. Had he not procrastinated, he wouldn't now be forced to deal with this . . . well, this unaccountable *surprise*, for lack of a better term.

"Er, you found me . . . my dear," he stammered aloud for the benefit of anyone who might be paying attention to them. "What is it you wish me to do?" he asked her in a whisper.

The lady seemed reluctant to show her face to anyone. Lucas had hardly caught a glimpse of it himself. She was still pressed tightly to him, her head tucked in close so the brim of her bonnet hid her face from the room. "I wish to retire, husband, after a long day's journey, if you don't mind," she said, not exactly answering the question he'd asked. Then she added, her voice again in a whisper, "Appear to be a normal husband, and get me out of here. *Please*."

"Very well, ma'am."

With his simple reassurance, she gradually lowered her arms to her side, keeping her head down, and turned away from the room. Lucas reached for his hat and scooped up the crumpled letter, then offered his arm to his mysterious "wife" and proceeded to escort her from the public room—whereto after that he wasn't entirely sure. But just as they were passing the group of young dandies Lucas had observed drinking and playing cards earlier, one of them came to his feet. "I tell you, it's her," the man exclaimed, pointing. "It's that—"

"If you don't mind." Lucas directed his words to the dandy in a tone he'd learned from his best friend, the Earl of Halford. The woman's hand had gripped Lucas's arm tightly. "I'm sure I don't know what you're up to, but I won't have you disturbing my wife in such a manner." He glared at the man, who was a good foot shorter than Lucas, making him shrink back into his seat.

"I beg your pardon, sir," the fellow mumbled. "I was mistaken."

"Come, my dear," Lucas said and led her from the room, sensing that all eyes were on the two of them. He was curious to know what the fellow had planned to say, but he'd assured the lady of his assistance, and he was a gentleman who would not go back on his word, so he played his part.

They continued on together, up the stairs and down the corridor toward his room. She still held his arm in a death grip.

Unfortunately, her impulsive move had created a dilemma for them both. Lucas didn't need a damsel in distress. He needed to figure out what he intended to do with the remainder of his life. He needed to reconcile himself to the uncomfortable situations in which he would find himself once he returned home. And while he *had* wanted to delay his return, he hadn't wanted a reason quite of *this* magnitude. He unlocked the door to his room and opened it wide.

"After you, *wife*," he said, gesturing theatrically for her to enter.

She glanced up at him from behind the brim of her bonnet and went inside without an argument. After he closed the door, she turned toward him, her face lowered. Why the devil was this woman so intent on hiding her face? "I suppose I owe you an explanation," she said.

"That would be helpful," he said with no little sarcasm.

She sighed and untied the ribbons of her bonnet and then removed it from her head. Underneath it, she wore a large lacy cap, so Lucas still had no idea what she looked like.

"May I have a glass of water first?" she asked.

"Certainly." He strode to the washstand that sat against the far wall and poured water from the pitcher there into a glass, then brought it to her.

"Thank you," she said, her face still lowered.

She took the glass and wandered away from him, toward the window that overlooked the stables in the back. "I suppose it's too much to hope that the men downstairs will pack up and leave anytime soon and I'll be able to see them ride away on their horses if I were to peek out this window."

"Undoubtedly," Lucas said. They hadn't seemed particularly inclined to move from their spot downstairs, even after Lucas's public rebuke of their friend.

He waited until she'd drunk her fill. "Let's begin with an introduction," he said. "You are . . ."

"Lavinia, er, Fernley," she replied. She paused briefly as though her name hadn't come naturally to her lips. Suspicious, that.

"Miss Fernley, how do you do?" he said. "I am Lucas Jennings, obviously at your service, it would seem."

"Yes," she said. "And I thank you for it."

She used her fingers to part the curtains and peeked out at the stable yard.

"See anyone?" he asked, already knowing the answer to his question.

"No."

Who were the men in the public room? They'd looked like normal enough chaps to him, although he hadn't really paid them much attention after deciding they were harmless. Yet Miss Fernley had wanted to be away from them—with *him*—as quickly as possible.

"So, Miss Fernley, it seems a bit of a paradox that you would rather run headlong toward a stranger than greet someone you know. Who is he? What is his name and his connection to you?" *And why were you so shaken by it?* he wanted to add.

She dropped the curtain. "I don't know his name. I know him only as someone who is frequently in company with . . . a person of my acquaintance."

"Does this person have a name?"

"I'd rather not say," she said.

"You must do better than that, Miss Fernley. You just proclaimed me to be your husband in front of a crowd of strangers in a busy inn. At midnight, no less."

"I am truly in your debt, Mr. Jennings."

"That remains to be seen, Miss Fernley. Leaving the question of this acquaintance of yours aside for the moment, I would ask you: Why me? Of all the people in the room, why did you run to me?"

"I don't know," she said. "I noticed you when I entered the inn, sitting by yourself, and you looked trustworthy. And I had to act quickly."

"Trustworthy," he mused aloud. "You could see my halo glowing where my hat should have been."

"You mock me, but yes," she eventually answered. "You were the safest alternative at the time." She parted the curtain and began looking out the window again.

Hmm.

Lucas hadn't been described as safe by anyone for several years now. He was tall, and rather than having a lean build like many tall men, he was muscular and proportioned to his height. He'd used his size to intimidate a lot of people, mostly enlisted men from the lowest dregs of humanity, who'd bullied those who were weaker than they.

He decided to use his size to intimidate this woman now, test her assumption that he was indeed safe. He needed to find out what her story was and if she was genuinely in need of assistance or was trying to trick him in some way. He crossed the room until he stood next to her, nearly touching.

She merely turned her head slightly in his direction, aware he was making a strategic action but calling his bluff and otherwise making no attempt to move, which surprised him.

"Miss Fernley," he said to her ugly lace cap since that was all he could see of her at this proximity. "You must give me more of an explanation than the fact that you are avoiding the unnamed acquaintances of an unnamed acquaintance if I am to assist you further. I have no desire to be embroiled in your troubles."

Her stomach growled in reply.

He sighed heavily. "And, of course, you're also hungry."

"I'm fine," she said.

Her face, what little he could see of it whenever she turned her head slightly, was sallow in color. If he was to guess her age based on his observations thus far, including the brief time his arms had been wrapped around her, he would place her near forty—a little worse for wear for that age, too, perhaps—and most likely a spinster well on the shelf.

Miss Fernley's stomach growled again, contradicting her answer to him, and she placed a hand firmly on her midriff to stifle the sound.

He sighed again. "Stay here, Miss Fernley. I'm going to get you some food."

"You don't need—"

"I expect you to be here when I return," he said, interrupting her. "I have several more questions I would like you to answer, but I would prefer you be fed and coherent when you do. I will warn you though—there is nothing here for you to steal, if that is your intent. My money is safely ensconced upon my person, and there is nothing in my saddlebag but a change of clothing."

She gave no reply, so he left the room—*his* room, he reminded himself as he made his way downstairs—that he was most likely going to have to share with a female. A total stranger. His *wife*, as far as everyone in the inn was concerned.

He spotted the owner of the White Horse behind the bar, counting the day's receipts. The man had shown Lucas to his room earlier and would know he had arrived alone, with no mention of a wife joining him later. Lucas would have to hope the man's many years as an innkeeper had taught him discretion.

"My lady wife is hungry," Lucas said with no other explanation, noting that the man Miss Fernley had specifically wished to avoid was still in the public room, drinking and gaming with his friends. "And have additional water and towels sent up as well, if you please."

"Certainly, sir," the man replied, a knowing look in his eye. "Right away."

Lucas wandered toward the men, who were a little deeper in their cups than they'd been a few short minutes ago, and casually seated himself at a nearby table. He drew his mother's letter from his pocket and pretended to read it so as not to appear to be eavesdropping on the men and their game. Lucas wanted more information if he was to determine the right approach to take with the new "Mrs. Jennings."

After several minutes, however, it became apparent that they were merely a passel of spoiled, wealthy young cubs who undoubtedly spent their time in pursuit of pleasure and entertainment and little else. During the course of their conversation, they did mention a few of England's elites, including Lucas's good friend Anthony, Lord Halford, but it was done mostly by way of idle gossip. The one who'd seemed to recognize Miss Fernley earlier looked at him suspiciously, Lucas noted.

Lucas tipped his head at him in greeting, making the man scowl, but he returned his focus to the game, which he appeared to be losing.

Nothing helpful to be learned from this pathetic lot.

"Last call, gentlemen," the innkeeper announced. "I'm locking up for the night."

The young men held their glasses out to be refilled, and Lucas returned the letter to his pocket and proceeded back to his room, arriving just as two maids did, one carrying a tray of food and the other holding a pitcher of hot water with towels draped over her arm. When Lucas opened the door for them, he saw that Miss Fernley had seated herself in the upholstered chair by the fire and appeared to have fallen asleep.

He held his finger to his lips, and the maids quietly set down the food and water and left. The tray included a loaf of bread, some cheese, and two apples—not precisely a sumptuous feast but enough to curb hunger until morning.

He shut the door with a soft thud.

She jolted at the noise and sat up straight, raising a gloved hand to her face before turning to look at him.

"You're back," she said in a voice husky from sleep. She cleared her throat. "I was just wondering when you would . . ." Her voice trailed off as she noticed the tray of food on the table near the door. "Oh. It appears I must have dozed."

"Yes," he said. He gestured toward the tray. "I suggest you eat. And then we are going to talk."

She moved to sit at one of the two wooden chairs next to the table and tugged off her gloves, revealing a large ruby ring. He pointed at it. "It appears I'm a rather generous fellow, giving you such a lavish betrothal ring."

"Not so generous," she replied before slicing a bit of cheese for herself. "It's paste."

It was a saucy answer from someone in a vulnerable situation, and the ring's appearance added another curious element to this already curious situation. "May I sit?" He gestured to the other wooden chair.

"Of course you can," she said. "It's your room."

"I'm glad you remember that." He adjusted the chair so it faced her rather than the table and then sat.

She ignored his actions, however, and, while still keeping her head down, tore a piece of bread from the loaf.

He reached over and tore off a piece of bread for himself, chewing and swallowing before speaking. "Your gentlemen acquaintances are still downstairs and don't appear to be in any hurry to leave," he said matter-of-factly. "So unless you plan on tying the bedsheets together and escaping through the window, it appears we are stuck here together, at least for the time being. Unless I simply invite you to leave."

She stopped chewing. "You wouldn't do that."

Whether she was telling him or asking him, Lucas wasn't sure, but he definitely had her attention. "That remains to be seen, ma'am, but certainly not before you have eaten and had your say."

She nodded and helped herself to more of the cheese while Lucas pulled out his penknife and sliced up one of the apples.

"Apple?" he asked.

She took the slice he offered.

Her dress, he observed, was a shapeless gray sack that hid her physical attributes. Since Lucas had briefly held those attributes in his arms, he was aware that she was slender but not thin. She still wore her cloak—also gray. Her hair was entirely covered by the ghastly cap she wore, which was overlarge with a huge lace ruffle that also managed to conceal a good share of her face.

From what little of her face he could see, it seemed the sallowness of her skin was due to the use of face paint, which was odd. She had a straight nose and full lips, nothing out of the ordinary, he thought, just the sort of features one would find on many females. Her eyes remained hidden by the cap.

How he, of all the other people in the public dining room, ended up being the one shackled to this drab gray goose of a woman for the night he could not imagine. It might delay his return home, but beyond that, it was simply a bother.

Eventually, she sat back in her chair.

"Have you eaten enough?" he asked her.

"Yes," she said.

"In that case, you may proceed with your explanation." He crossed his ankle over his knee and waited for her to speak.

* * *

"There is nothing untoward in what I am attempting, if that is what concerns you," Lavinia began. "Nothing of a sinister nature, that is. I haven't broken any laws, nor do I plan to." Heavens, but Lucas Jennings was an extraordinarily large specimen of a man. She hadn't realized how exceedingly tall and muscular he was when he'd been sitting, staring at a crumpled piece of paper downstairs. He'd seemed the safest choice to her then. Now it was taking all her acting ability to keep the unease she felt hidden from him. She didn't know the man at all, she was in his private room, and he looked like he could break a small tree in half.

He looked in the direction of his saddlebag, which sat on the floor near a corner of the bed.

"I didn't even *peep* inside your bag, Mr. Jennings."

He turned back to her. "I will take your word on that particular point, ma'am, and yet I have other suspicions I would have addressed. The cosmetics on your face, for example."

Her hands flew to her cheeks. When had he had a chance to notice? Their initial encounter in the dining room had caught him off his guard, she'd known it, and she'd been careful to keep her head down since then. Unless . . .

Her stomach dropped to the vicinity of her toes. What a reckless fool she'd been! She had no idea how long he'd been in the room before closing the door loudly enough to wake her. And yet he had acted the gentleman so far. "You watched me sleep," she said. "Yet you didn't touch me."

"I did *not* watch you sleep, just to be clear, but I am also not blind," he replied. He twirled his hand in the direction of her face. "I recognize a disguise when I see one."

Lavinia rubbed two fingers across her cheeks and looked at her fingertips. They were as gray and pasty as the dress she wore. "As you say. I used them to disguise my face a bit," she said. "I was to meet up with friends, but I was traveling alone until then. It was a means to help me feel safer on my own."

"You have no maid or lady's companion, then," he said.

Since that was clearly the case, his next deduction would be that she wasn't a lady, and he would be correct. Lavinia's roots were decidedly common. But being born and raised in a traveling theater troupe, she'd paid attention to the way people had spoken in the various parts of the country they'd visited and had trained herself as best she could to speak as a lady, as she was doing now, in addition to mastering several regional dialects. She was a good mimic, her father had always said.

"One of the people I was to meet serves as my maid when needed, although she is a friend rather than a servant. We are on our way north. I was to meet them here, at the White Horse, but I suspect they mistakenly went to an establishment called the White Hart instead." Blast the Earl of Cosgrove and all men like him! She would be safely on her way north to Primrose Farm with Hannah, Delia, and Artie right now if Cosgrove had not persisted in being such a nuisance.

There was nothing Lavinia could do tonight to locate them, however; she would have to begin her search in the morning. And if that failed, she would catch up to them at the next post-stage.

"I assume your—er—attire is part of the disguise as well?" Mr. Jennings asked, grimacing as he looked her up and down.

She tugged her cloak closer. "Yes."

"That was where you went wrong, Miss Fernley. I suspect it was your so-called *disguise* that drew the attention of the gentlemen downstairs instead of avoiding it. It's"—his hand was waving at her again—"too much. Almost theatrical."

Theatrical? That was the *worst* thing Mr. Jennings could possibly have said since looking theatrical was the last thing Lavinia wanted. She had been so concerned she'd be recognized she hadn't stopped to consider the possibility that she may have overdone it.

Would she have realized it anyway? Even her regular clothes were more like costumes than anything else. She was always playing a part, always on stage, no matter where she was: Ruby Chadwick, delightfully attired in sprigged muslin as she strolled through Hyde Park; Ruby Chadwick, a vision in gold satin at Lady Cowper's soiree; The Darling of Drury Lane, smartly dressed in a pale-blue day dress, shopping on Bond Street . . .

"Ahem."

Lavinia started. "Sorry."

"Drifting off to sleep again or woolgathering?" Mr. Jennings asked. "I must be frank, Miss Fernley. Having a woman in disguise running to me for assistance is unsettling. It also suggests a certain willingness on your part to deceive others. It makes one suspicious."

"I have not lied to you, Mr. Jennings," she replied, hearing her voice rise despite the hour and knowing the guests in neighboring rooms would be trying to sleep. But she was exhausted and worried about the others, and dealing with Lord Cosgrove had frayed her nerves. "My name is indeed Lavinia Fernley, sir. I was on my way to meet my friends so we could journey north to a small farm I inherited from a family member. Since I was traveling alone until then, I wished to avoid drawing attention to myself, although it appears, at least according to you, that my overly enthusiastic disguise accomplished the exact opposite, nearly resulting in my being recognized and requiring me to act quickly." Lavinia stood, picked up her bag, and strode to the door. "I apologize for my intrusion upon your privacy and thank you for your assistance downstairs and for the food," she said in a lofty tone. "Now, I shall bid you adieu and good night." She reached for the doorknob.

Behind her, she heard a slow clap. She turned.

"Brava, Miss Fernley," Mr. Jennings said. "That was quite a performance, I must say, however unnecessary. You are not the little gray goose your appearance would lead one to believe, that it certain. Now, please sit down. I'm tired; you're obviously tired, from what I saw when I returned to the room; and I'm satisfied that you aren't going to rob me blind during the night."

Lavinia dropped her bag with a thud.

"Sit, Miss Fernley," he said, gesturing at the empty chair.

She sat.

"That's better," Mr. Jennings said. "Tomorrow after breakfast, we will ask our host if there are any establishments nearby called the White Hart. Does that meet with your approval?"

"Yes." Lavinia let out a breath she hadn't realized she'd been holding and relaxed for the first time all day. "Thank you."

"Unfortunately, we do not know if your gentleman acquaintance and his friends have taken rooms here at the inn for the night, so we shall have to act the happily married couple for now. As such, we should get used to calling each other by our Christian names. You may call me Lucas."

"I am Lavinia, of course," she said.

"Now that that has been taken care of, it is time for us to retire—you to the bed, me to the floor by the fire. I, for one, am exhausted."

"You don't need to do that—" She stopped short when he gave her a speaking glance.

"What are you suggesting?" he asked in a low voice.

"Nothing!" Good heavens, he couldn't think she was insinuating some sort of romantic liaison with him! They'd barely reached a truce for the night—not to mention she hadn't kept all her admirers at arm's length for years for nothing. "What I mean is that I have inconvenienced you enough already. You may have the bed, and I'll sleep in the chair. It is really quite comfortable—"

"Miss Fern—er—Lavinia," he said. "I spent most of the past seven years fighting the French in Spain; the floor will be a luxury compared to what I am used to. As a gentleman, I will not sleep a wink if you are not ensconced in pillows and blankets and goose down and happily dreaming of your friends and your idyllic farm up north. Now, if you will excuse me, I intend to take a late stroll through the courtyard while you do whatever it is ladies do when they prepare to retire for the night. I will take the room key and let myself in when I return."

Lavinia was too tired to argue, and Lucas Jennings seemed an honorable gentleman—at least so far. One could never entirely let down one's guard.

"Thank you, Lucas," she said.

He picked up his hat and the room key. "Sweet dreams, wife." He left, and Lavinia heard the key turn in the lock and the sound of his boots fade as he walked down the corridor.

She let out a huge sigh and tugged off her cap. It was time to remove her disguise.

Chapter 4

LUCAS RETURNED TO THE ROOM and unlocked the door precisely twenty minutes after taking himself off to wander the stable yard. Lavinia Fernley had been exhausted enough to fall asleep sitting up earlier. He suspected that she wouldn't dillydally about preparing herself for bed.

He'd been correct in his assessment. By the dim light of the single lit candle she'd left for him, he could see her burrowed under the blankets, a huddled lump of a person with only the top of her head poking out. His curiosity about her appearance—*why* he was curious, he had no idea—would have to wait until morning to be satisfied.

He turned away from the bed and noticed, much to his surprise, that she had folded a blanket and laid it on the floor next to the fireplace, along with one of the pillows, for him to use.

He quickly stripped out of his coat and waistcoat and tugged off his boots and neckcloth. The rest of his clothing would remain on for propriety's sake. His good friend Anthony had merely been caught kissing a woman and had found himself thoroughly entangled in the parson's trap. Now, here Lucas was spending the entire night alone with a strange female who had announced to all and sundry that he was her husband. If he wasn't exceedingly careful, he could find himself similarly stuck. Anthony had been fortunate; he'd at least *seen* Amelia and had known he cared for her before being compelled to offer for her hand. Things had turned out remarkably well for them, considering the circumstances.

Lucas lay down on the blanket, setting his coat next to him in case he needed it for warmth come morning, and blew out the candle. He wasn't willing to bet that he would have the same good fortune, based on what he'd deduced about Miss Fernley so far. Her appearance, with her large cap, greasy face, and baggy sack of a dress, hadn't offered much information.

When she'd been in his arms, she had at least felt surprisingly normal, but that was the only positive he'd been able to discern thus far.

There was also more to the situation than she had told him. She was to meet up with friends, she'd said, traveling to a property she apparently owned. And yet she'd felt the need to travel in disguise. It had more to do with hiding her identity than merely keeping safe, Lucas was certain. Why would she feel the need to do that?

He bent one knee and braced his foot against the floor, then stared upward at the ceiling, not that he could see anything. Only a little starlight was making its way through the window, and there was no moon. He shut his eyes and tried to sleep. He could hear the evenness of Miss Fernley's breathing and knew she had fallen asleep already, but then, she was in a soft bed, wasn't she? The floor was hard under his back. It wasn't anything he hadn't endured before—he'd slept on the ground more times than he could count, but he'd obviously readjusted to the comfort of a bed since his return from Spain. He plumped the pillow beneath his head and shifted his position to get more comfortable.

The fire in the grate had been banked, the coals barely sharing their low red light and providing only the merest bit of heat along one side of his body. Blast it all. He'd meant to burn Isobel's letter, but he'd forgotten. He sat up and removed the letter from the pocket of his coat and tossed it in the grate, then watched as it gradually caught fire, flared briefly, and turned to ash before lying down again.

Isobel had called him "her brother and friend." The words still rankled. Of course, Lucas knew he was her brother. Brother-in-law, to be precise. And they had been friends growing up. The closest of friends.

But Lucas, in his youthful foolishness, had thought it more than friendship. When he'd gone off to Cambridge, he had thought there'd been an understanding between the two of them. Not many weeks after, he'd received a letter from his mother informing him of Isobel's betrothal to his eldest brother, Thomas.

They had celebrated a Christmas wedding. Lucas had attended the nuptials and had enlisted in the army the following day.

Miss Fernley let out a sigh and shifted on the bed.

Lucas shook his head at the irony of it all. He was returning home to his family, which now included the girl he'd loved his entire life but who was off-limits to him, and on the way, he'd gotten himself—through no fault of his own—"shackled" to a female of unknown origin, dubious motives, and questionable appearance. He finally managed to drift off to sleep, the image of Isobel's face his last waking thought.

Lucas awoke abruptly at dawn, as had been his habit in Spain, and it had not changed since his return. Miss Fernley—he really must remember to refer to her as Lavinia while they were here at the inn—was still asleep. It was just as well; he had several things he wished to take care of this morning before he must contend further with her.

He rose from the floor and donned his clothing, then built up the fire in the grate before taking himself to the stable yard, where he could wash and see to his basic morning needs.

If he was to free himself from his temporary wife and begin his journey home, he determined as he splashed cold water from the stable pump on his face, he must first reunite her with her friends. A gentleman would do no less. And that meant finding a nearby inn with the name White Hart.

* * *

Lavinia awakened with a start. It took only the briefest of moments for her mind to clear and for her to remember that she wasn't in the small house she had rented and shared with Hannah, Delia, and Artie. She was in a hostelry, after accosting a stranger and unwittingly pulling him into her plans.

He was not currently in the room, although he had taken the time—and the courtesy—to rekindle the fire before taking his leave.

She had heard him return last night. She'd barely settled herself in the bed when she'd heard the key turn in the lock. She'd pretended to be sound asleep—she was good at that, having played death scenes on stage numerous times. And feigning death in front of a large audience was infinitely more difficult than feigning *sleep*. Thankfully, the muffled noises she'd heard him making had told her he'd been settling down for the night and had no intention of disturbing her.

Perhaps he really was an honorable gentleman, although she'd never met one before, and he'd seen her only in disguise thus far, so she wasn't entirely convinced. She was reminded again how impulsive her actions from the night before had been—and how fortunate she was, considering he may have proven to be as bad and untrustworthy as every other man of her acquaintance had been. Excepting poor Artie, of course.

The soft light coming through the window told her it was still fairly early in the morning. She bounded out of bed and quickly washed and donned her gray dress, then sat at the small dressing table next to the bed and unpinned her hair.

It felt good to pull out the pins and loosen the braids after having her head assaulted by them all night long. She ran her fingers through her hair, separating the woven stands that reached nearly to her waist.

Too late she heard the key turn in the lock. She jumped quickly to her feet, pulling her hair over one shoulder in a vain attempt to twist it up and hide it.

The door opened, and Lucas Jennings stepped inside.

Lavinia knew the exact moment her appearance hit him—not the ugly gray dress and drab cosmetics this time but her own features, most particularly her hair. Her dratted, garishly red, unavoidably obvious hair. He inhaled sharply and took a step back, his eyes wide with shock.

Lavinia boldly returned his gaze while he stared at her, his mouth hanging open like a fish gasping for water. She crossed her arms over her chest. "Now you understand why the face paint and cap were necessary," she said.

"I—" he stammered.

"Precisely," she said, sitting again and picking up her brush. "If you think you are the first man to react in such a foolish manner, you would be wildly inaccurate."

She vigorously brushed and braided her hair, pinning it on her head and replacing the cap, ignoring him and allowing him time to return to his senses. When she was done, she tossed her brush in her bag and closed it. "Have you learned anything about an inn called the White Hart nearby?" she asked. She had to crane her neck in order to look up and see his face. Gracious, but the man was tall.

"About that," he said after clearing his voice. "I did make a few inquiries this morning. Apparently there is a pub called the White Hart a mile or so from here, not to mention an inn called the White Hart farther north on the way out of Barnet. Popular name hereabout, it would seem. I've arranged for us to have breakfast in a private dining room downstairs, after which we will assume your friends went to the inn, and I shall take you to them."

"I don't require—"

"But I insist, Miss Fernley," he said, holding up a hand to silence her. "After the unique circumstances that threw us together last evening, I feel honor bound to see you safely to your friends. A gentleman would do no less, nor would your nearest male relative allow you to continue on your way unescorted—even an honorary male relative such as I." He grinned briefly.

His words and humor squeezed Lavinia's heart. Her father had been the only real family she'd ever known, not that he'd been a good father— quite the contrary—and he'd been gone for over three years now at any rate. She could barely remember her mother. "I have imposed on you too much already, Mr. Jennings."

"Nonetheless, I will see you reunited with your friends." He picked up his saddlebag and slung it over his shoulder, then paused. "I do understand now why you chose to travel incognito last night; the cap alone is a definite necessity if you wish to remain anonymous. Your hair is . . . er, *vivid* and clearly recognizable. I am glad you chose to forego the face paint this morning, however. You are exceedingly lovely without it." He opened the door for her and then picked up her bag. "After you, Mrs. Jennings," he said.

Ruby Chadwick would have flirted and teased away his comment, but Lavinia, as herself, could not. "Thank you," she said as she passed him on her way through the door, and then they continued on along the corridor and down the stairs of the inn to the private dining room he'd arranged for them.

She hoped she wasn't making a mistake in choosing not to wear the cosmetics today. She was counting heavily on the fact that they would soon leave London behind them and that Mr. Jennings was correct in saying her disguise had drawn attention to her rather than maintain her anonymity.

She hoped she wasn't making a mistake in trusting Mr. Jennings's words. She had only his honorable behavior of the night before to go on, and if there was anything Lavinia had learned in her twenty-four years, it was that men in general were not to be trusted and eventually showed their true colors.

Chapter 5

LUCAS WAS STILL REELING FROM the vision he'd seen when he'd returned to his room. He'd literally rocked back on his heels at the sight of Lavinia and her exquisite face and glorious, fiery hair tumbling over her shoulders. His pulse still raced, even though they'd finished breakfast and were now on their way to Barnet and the White Hart Inn in search of her friends.

Miss Lavinia Fernley was no on-the-shelf spinster. Quite the contrary. And she was even more of a mystery now than she'd seemed last night.

Last night, a gray-faced woman of middle years had thrown herself into Lucas's arms and called him husband. She'd been alternately wary and bold, timid and defiant. She'd held her own with him even though he'd known she was intimidated by his size. She'd also been considerate. In the brief time she'd had to herself when he'd left the room, she'd still managed to make up a bed for him on the floor.

But the heart of it all was that she was the most dazzling creature he had ever beheld. Who in blazes was this woman?

She was currently sitting in front of him atop Hector, and Lucas had an arm around her waist to hold her steady. She remained silent, her head facing forward as they rode, the top of her ugly bonnet all Lucas could see of her, which was undoubtedly a good thing for them both.

He was feeling lighter this morning, he realized as they made their way along the streets, his dread over returning home having been replaced by diversion and a sense of curiosity.

"Who are these friends of yours you are meeting?" he asked her, wanting to learn more about her to put some of the puzzle pieces together. "I take it they aren't family."

"They are as near to family as one can be without actually sharing blood ties," she answered, still facing forward.

Interesting reply. "You've known them for a while, then."

"Yes."

"Are they childhood friends?" he asked.

"No," she answered.

Hmm. He wanted more from her than yes and no answers. He would try a different tack. "Perhaps you could tell me their names, for a start, and a little about each of them," he said.

She was silent for a time, and Lucas wondered if she was going to answer him. What could be so secretive about a few friends, especially when she'd allowed him to accompany her to them? He was just opening his mouth to prod her further when she finally spoke. "There are three: Arthur Drake, Delia Weston, and Hannah Broome. Hannah was my nurse when I was a very young child. Ah—I see the sign for the White Hart up ahead."

Lucas nudged Hector to a quicker gait. Lavinia had provided only the barest of bones for details, but it appeared he would now have to wait to question her further.

She straightened up and pointed. "There, over there. I see them."

Lucas looked in the direction she pointed. A plump, middle-aged woman was hurrying across the courtyard toward them, flapping her apron and clutching her bosom. Behind her, a gaunt elderly man and tiny elderly woman with fluffy white hair followed more slowly.

Lucas brought Hector to a halt, and before he could offer much assistance, Lavinia wriggled out of his arms and off the horse and went into the middle-aged woman's open arms. Lucas dismounted, tossed the reins to the stable boy who'd dashed over, and followed her.

"I'm that glad to see you; I was that worried, luv," the woman said as she hugged Lavinia. "I weren't sure what we was to do next, and poor Artie has been fretting and Delia too, but we couldn't leave you behind. We just *couldn't*, even though you told us to go on! And here you are now, and I fretted the whole night long. I thought, 'What if my girl has trouble and that terrible man—?'" The woman abruptly ceased her emotional rambling when she spotted Lucas. "Who's this?" she asked Lavinia in a low voice.

"This is my hero, Hannah, Mr. Lucas Jennings. It is quite a story, which I will share with you in a moment. Lucas, may I introduce my friends. Hannah Broome"—the woman begrudgingly bobbed a curtsy—"and Miss Delia Weston and Mr. Arthur Drake."

Mr. Drake offered Lucas a bony hand to shake. "Mr. Jennings, how pleased we are that our dear Lavinia appears to have been in safe hands all this time." The man, in Lucas's opinion, looked as if his next destination should be the church graveyard rather than Lavinia's little farm.

Delia Weston, the tiny white-haired woman standing next to Mr. Drake, looked as if she'd blow away in a puff of wind. "Yes, indeed," she said. For such a tiny thing, she had a clear, surprisingly resonant voice. "We don't know what we would do without our dear Lavinia."

"I told you all would be well," Lavinia said. "You needn't have worried."

"Of course we should worry, and rightly so," Mr. Drake said. "You were on your own at night in a strange place—a dangerous situation for any young woman, even one as capable as you, dear girl." He raised his fisted hands into boxing position and mimed a few good jabs. "I should have liked to be there though, you know, to defend you should you have required it."

Lavinia smiled affectionately. "You are a dear one, Artie. But it wasn't necessary after all, was it? I'm here now, safe and sound."

"Are you, luv? Safe and sound, that is?" the woman, Hannah Broome, asked. She had not stopped glaring at Lucas since their introduction. "And when exactly did this here *gentleman* decide he were going to be your hero, pray tell?"

"I'm willing to answer that question, madam," Lucas said, "if you will allow me to escort you all into the inn for tea. I'm sure we would appreciate some refreshment, and the discussion might be better suited away from the bustling courtyard."

"Excellent idea, Mr. Jennings," Miss Weston said. "I would enjoy a cup of tea after all this excitement."

"Come, Delia, allow me to escort you back inside," Mr. Drake said, offering her his arm. "Hannah?" He offered his other arm to her. "Since Mr. Jennings has brought our girl to us safely, we can trust him to escort her a few steps farther."

Hannah shot Lucas a dark look before begrudgingly taking Mr. Drake's proffered arm. Lucas watched Lavinia bite her lower lip in an attempt not to smile. He winged his elbow out for her to take.

"I have a suspicion, my dear Miss Fernley," Lucas said in a low voice, "that, once again, there is more to your story than you are letting on."

"And I find I must thank you once again, Mr. Jennings, for it is my suspicion that my friends have not broken their fast this morning. Your offer of tea was generous. Thank you."

"On the chance your suspicions are correct, we shall have food sent in with the tea," Lucas said. "Your two elderly friends in particular look as if they could use a hearty meal."

They were the oddest group of traveling companions he had ever seen: a devastatingly beautiful young woman with a cranky nurse and a doddering old couple haring off to live on a farm, of all places. It seemed absurd. How had this motley group been formed? Why were they so intent on going to the country when it was obvious none of them—except, perhaps, the maid—had ever set foot on a farm before, at least in terms of understanding the harsh physical demands of farm life?

Lucas realized he could not, in good conscience, leave them to their own devices yet, nor was he ready to part ways with the intriguing young woman who'd landed in his lap the night before.

Home could wait for his arrival a bit longer.

* * *

"Ah," the elderly Miss Weston said after taking a sip of her tea. "This is just the thing to soothe our anxieties away, Mr. Jennings. And ham and eggs too. Such a feast." She cut off a minuscule piece of ham from the slice on her plate and chewed delicately. With her wispy white hair, which was refusing to stay in its knot on her head, and her diminutive size, Lucas thought she looked unearthly, like an ancient wood fairy choosing to associate with humans for a time.

"Delicious," the elderly Mr. Drake added, dabbing his mouth with his napkin. "Dashed sporting of you to order breakfast for us all, Jennings, when some of us were less than grateful for your service to our dear Lavinia." He shot a speaking glance at the nurse, Miss Broome.

"Men has been all alike when it comes to our girl, Artie, as you well know," Miss Broome muttered back. "Who's to say this one's any different?" She glared accusingly at Lucas again.

"I am, Hannah," Lavinia said. "And I told you before, it was *I* who imposed upon Mr. Jennings, not the other way around. When I reached the White *Horse* late last night, there were complications, and Mr. Jennings came to my assistance. You owe him an apology."

"Thank you for helping our girl, sir, and I'm that sorry for any inconvenience I may have caused you," Miss Broome muttered, flushing red with embarrassment at the mention of the other inn.

"Apology accepted," Lucas replied as seriously as he could.

They were interrupted by a knock at the door before it opened. "Beggin' your pardon," a spotty-faced youth said, looking decidedly at the floor in front of his feet. "But I been sent to ask when you be plannin' to be on your way."

"Inform Mr. Grimes we shall be ready in a half hour's time and I shall be speaking to him directly, Garrick," Lavinia said. After the youth tugged on his forelock and left, she turned back to the others at the table. "Mr. Jennings and I broke our fast before we arrived, so if you'll excuse me, I am going to make sure everything is in order with the coachman; you can join me once you've finished eating. It will be a long journey, so a hearty breakfast is important. That means you, Delia."

The wizened fairy sighed and sliced off another minuscule piece of ham.

Lavinia set her napkin down and left the room. Lucas excused himself from the others and followed her.

"Lavinia," he said when he caught up to her again. He took her by the elbow and led her down the corridor toward the back of the inn and around a corner, away from listening ears. "I know it isn't my right to pry, but you are clearly no less vulnerable with your friends than you were last evening on your own. Who are they? And where is this farm you intend to take them to? You do understand that farming is hard physical labor, don't you? The only person among you who looks suitable for such work is your sour-looking Miss Broome."

"I'm stronger than I look," she said. "And Delia and Artie can certainly help in small ways. We shall be fine."

"I applaud your determination, but do you even have farming experience? Do your friends? Who *are* these people?" he asked again. Her loyalty to them was obvious—and admirable too, of course—but their association with her was baffling. "And where is this farm you say you possess?"

"I *do* possess it," she said. "I inherited it from my grandfather's spinster sister."

"Where is it located? What is its name? Have you even been to this farm of yours?"

She sighed. "You will not cease, will you? Very well. Primrose Farm, in Lincolnshire. And no, I have not been there yet, but—"

"Lincolnshire?" he asked. Here was a stroke of good fortune. He could legitimately continue toward home and still have an excuse for delaying his arrival there by playing the gentleman and escorting Lavinia and her friends. "As luck would have it, I am traveling to Lincolnshire myself. It would be my honor to accompany you and your friends on your journey and see to your safe arrival."

Her eyes were silvery slits as she studied his face. "Where precisely in Lincolnshire are you going?" she asked.

"Alderwood, my family seat, located northeast of Stamford. My father is the Viscount Thurlby. And where is Primrose Farm to be found?"

"The illustrious son of a viscount, hmm?"

"Indeed." More soldier than noble son, however.

"I'm not precisely sure where Primrose Farm is," she replied, grimacing. "The letter I received from my great-aunt's solicitor said only that it was near Sleaford."

"Sleaford is but a half day's journey north of Alderwood," he said. "I'm quite familiar with the area, although I've not heard of Primrose Farm. But in all seriousness, Lavinia, how do you plan to shepherd your eclectic little flock from London all the way to the northern part of Lincolnshire? No offense to Mr. Drake, but any highwayman you meet along the way would be more frightened of Miss Broome."

"I'm sure Mr. Grimes and his postilion will see that we are safe," she said.

"Perhaps," he said, although he didn't really think so. The coachman would be more concerned about himself and the horses, and that spotty young postilion, Garrick, looked afraid of his own shadow. Accompanying Lavinia and her friends to Sleaford would put him a few days behind schedule—a welcome few days behind schedule.

"I would feel much better if I were to stay with the four of you on your journey," he said. "Truly, Lavinia, as a gentleman."

She tapped her foot in thought. "Perhaps," she eventually said. "It might reassure the others to have someone—a tall and strong someone—join us as an escort. Hannah will not be pleased, but Delia and Artie will be, I daresay."

"Excellent," Lucas said, rubbing his hands together. "That's settled, then. Now, back to my other question: who are these people? Ease my curiosity just a bit for now."

She sighed. "Very well. Delia and Artie were associates of my father before his death three years ago. I have known them all my life. And Hannah took care of me when my mother left and has been with me ever since. Will that suffice?"

Her mother had abandoned her when she was young? That was the first real bit of information Lucas had gotten out of her.

But before he could respond, Artie interrupted them. "Oh ho! There you two are, hiding around the corner, having your own little tête-à-tête, eh?" he said as he made his way toward them. How a man could move at such a slow, stiff pace and still appear jaunty, Lucas didn't know. "We've been looking for you. The coach awaits."

"I have good news, Artie," Lavinia said brightly. "Mr. Jennings has agreed to accompany us on our way to Primrose Farm."

"Indeed?" Mr. Drake's grizzled eyebrows rose in surprise. "Well, well. An interesting development, I must say." He looked back and forth between Lucas and Lavinia several times.

"We will continue our conversation later," Lucas said under his breath as he offered his arm to Lavinia. "Let us be on our way, then, Mr. Drake," he said more loudly.

He'd given himself three, maybe four, additional days to organize his thoughts and plan for the future. Three days to find his purpose in life and save face, especially when it came to Isobel.

I yearn to see you too, my dear brother and friend.

"Is everything all right?" Lavinia asked him.

"Why wouldn't it be?" he asked.

"I don't know," she replied, frowning at him before returning her attention to Mr. Drake as they continued on to the courtyard.

He was returning home a former soldier, emphasis on the word *former*. He had no career upon which to build a life; he had no wife, no family of his own. Nothing to show for his years in the army, fighting Bonaparte. Nothing at all.

I shall miss you dreadfully while you're away, Isobel had said when he'd left for Cambridge. *You must write me every day, or I shall die of loneliness.*

And Lucas had written to her every day of Michaelmas term—until he'd received his mother's letter in late November.

You will be pleased to learn that Thomas proposed to Isobel Hewlett, and she has accepted him. She has spent so much time here at Alderwood over the years, I feel as though she is a daughter already.

The one time he'd returned home, he'd endured it because at least then he'd been a soldier—he'd *been* something the others would have viewed with a level of respect.

But enduring the terrible siege at Badajoz, the one that had nearly taken Anthony's life, had changed his mind regarding a career in the military. He was done with war. Done with death. But that had left him with a future of few options—precisely *not* the way he'd wished to return home this time.

* * *

"*Such* a nice man," Delia said to Lavinia as their carriage approached the village of Hatfield. "And a fine-looking one, as well. I don't blame you one bit for watching him through the window that way."

Artie chuckled, and Hannah narrowed her eyes and shook her head. After a lifetime in the theater, Lavinia wasn't a person prone to embarrassment, but she could feel herself blushing. "I'm *not* watching Mr. Jennings, Delia," Lavinia said primly. "I merely find I tolerate the movement of the carriage better when I look out the window."

"I'm sure that's the reason, dearie," Delia said with a twinkle in her eye. "It was very kind of him to arrange for additional cushions. My old bones are not feeling nearly so rattled as they usually do bumping along on these country roads."

"After so many years of riding in a dogcart from town to town, it's pure luxury to be traveling this way," Artie said, patting the cushion tucked comfortably between his arm and the side of the carriage.

Lavinia turned away from the window and the view of Lucas upon his horse. "Did you eat enough at breakfast, Delia?"

"Oh yes," she replied, although Hannah shook her head and Artie's buoyant mood dimmed noticeably.

"We shall take tea in Hatfield, nonetheless," Lavinia said.

"Excellent plan!" Artie said, patting Delia's hand. "Isn't it, Delia? A little more sustenance will do us all a world of good."

"Before we reach Hatfield, however," Lavinia said, "I want to stress once again the importance of down playing our connection to the theater. Mr. Jennings doesn't seem to know anything about Ruby Chadwick, and I would prefer it remain that way."

"I won't be talking to the likes of Mr. Jennings," Hannah said. "So you got nothing to worry about from me, luv."

"I'll certainly try to do my part, dearie," Delia said. "Although it will be something of a challenge. The theater is all Arthur and I know. Fifty years in the theater a piece, give or take. It's how we met your father, of course, and you know Mr. Jennings is going to ask about our connection to you sooner or later."

"Perhaps we should take the time now to invent a story, Lavinia," Artie suggested. "Something believable—not too exotic—that would explain how we all ended up together. It could be rather jolly, like acting without the limits of the stage. I rather like the idea."

"Oh, Arthur, how ingenious!" Delia exclaimed. "Let's think, shall we?" She tapped her forefinger against her chin in thought.

Artie's face brightened. "I've got just the thing. Delia can be an Austrian princess, sent to live in an English convent at birth to protect her from her evil uncle—"

"I don't think there were any convents in England when I was a girl, Arthur," Delia pointed out. "Church of England and Henry the Eighth and all that, you know."

"Well, perhaps not a convent, then. Raised by an English friend of the Austrian royal family; that's the ticket. You've got the elegant manners of the royal, my dear. Best to keep to our strengths, I always say."

"Thank you kindly for the compliment, Arthur, but—"

"And I shall have been your childhood friend and, like the knights of old, swore to be your protector all your days."

"Oh, Arthur," Delia said, patting his gnarled hand. "How sweet you are, and what an imagination you do have. But, my dear, Mr. Jennings has already heard me speak and will recognize that I have no Austrian accent."

"Easy enough to explain," Artie said. "You've lived all your life in England, after all."

"Good point. Austrian royalty, then. What fun! Let's say I was reared in Devon, since that's the truth anyway."

"I'm not playing a part," Hannah said, crossing her arms over her bosom. "No princess or knight or nothing else. I am who I am, and I do what I does—and that is to see my dearest girl safe and happy." She looked at Lavinia.

"No princess or knight, you will be happy to hear, Hannah," Lavinia said. "Nor any other part as well. We are to be honest in our dealings with Mr. Jennings . . . just perhaps not completely forthcoming. If he presses you, tell him the truth—that you were formerly with a theater company and that is where you met my father . . . and me. But don't elaborate. If he asks if I was an actress, again tell him the truth. But you needn't inform him of every detail—the breeches parts, for example, or my stage name."

"Very well, Livvy," Artie said. "Though you would have made a lovely princess, Delia."

"I played a queen once, you know," Delia said, a faraway look in her eyes. "Titania, queen of the fairies, back before you joined us, Arthur, or your father either, Lavinia. *A Midsummer Night's Dream*. We played to sold-out crowds outside Cheltenham for three weeks straight and then another week at Swindon. My fairy costume was a vision, Hannah, although I daresay you could have created something even more impressive. Unfortunately, our success encouraged three of our most talented young actors to leave and try their luck in London. And that was that."

"I should have liked to have seen you as Titania," Artie said.

"You would have been perfectly cast as Titania back then, Delia," Lavinia said. "You are every bit the fairy queen, even to this day."

"Thank you, dearest." Delia patted Lavinia's arm. "You're such a sweet girl."

"I guess we shall simply have to play Delia Weston and Arthur Drake for a while longer," Artie said to Delia with a wink.

"Precisely," Lavinia said. "For that is who you are." The ironic and sad thing about it all was that Lavinia had been Ruby Chadwick for so long, she wasn't entirely sure she remembered who Lavinia Fernley was.

Through the window, Lavinia spotted the spire of a church, which meant they were approaching Hatfield, their first stop on the way north. The carriage rolled to a stop, and Lavinia saw Lucas dismount and walk toward them. "Remember what I said now," she whispered.

"Don't worry, dearie. Ah, Mr. Jennings," Delia said cheerfully to him when the carriage door opened and Lucas stood ready to assist them from the carriage. "You are a sight for sore eyes and such a handsome devil too. Perhaps you would care to accompany me on a stroll around the courtyard."

Lucas's eyes briefly lifted to Lavinia's before returning to Delia. "I do find I have a need to stretch my legs after our journey thus far, ma'am. I would be honored to be your escort." He handed Delia down from the carriage and then turned to assist Lavinia and Hannah, who sourly placed her hand in his.

"She's up to something, and that's certain," Hannah grumbled as Lucas and Delia walked away.

Artie tutted. "Don't fret, Hannah," he whispered. "Delia is as clever as they come. She won't go off script; you can rest assured of that. Perhaps you would care to join me for a stroll, Lavinia?" Artie said, changing the subject. "And Hannah too, of course. These old bones of mine could use a bit of a stretch as well—although the cushions helped immensely."

"I'm going inside to order tea," Hannah said. "I'm already going to get my fill of the great outdoors today. I don't need extra, thank you very much." She turned and stalked off in the direction of the posting inn.

That left Lavinia to walk slowly with Artie while he gallantly tried to appear as though every joint in his body hadn't ceased to function during the carriage ride. He kept up a stream of chatter about nothing in particular, but Lavinia knew they were both watching Delia and Lucas, who had walked far enough ahead to be just out of earshot.

Delia's laughter wafted back to them on the breeze. "'With mirth and laughter, let old wrinkles come,'" Artie remarked. "The most beautiful sound in the world, her laughter, in my estimation."

"Indeed," Lavinia said, although she actually feared Lucas was charming Delia so she would speak more freely to him.

She was mightily glad when she and Artie finally entered the inn, where Hannah was already seated at a table with a tea service awaiting them. A hot cup of tea and a biscuit was just the thing to distract Lavinia from fretting. Lavinia wouldn't be completely at peace until they were well and truly settled at Primrose Farm.

Chapter 6

The weather, which, up to this point, had been cooperative, took a shift toward the inclement late in the afternoon, with storm clouds rolling in from the west.

Since Lucas's clothes were en route to Stamford and he was essentially limited to what he was wearing and what few items he'd stuffed in his saddlebag, he opted to ride in the carriage with the others when the rain began in earnest. After a bit of shuffling, he ended up sitting next to Mr. Drake, facing the ladies, who were pressed closely together on the forward-facing seat.

It was not a spacious carriage.

The elderly Miss Weston was seated in the middle between the two other women.

"Otherwise," the ever-grumpy-looking Miss Broome said, "I'll be constantly bumping into you with all the jostling that's bound to occur, Delia, and you'd be squashed like a bug against the side of the carriage, as sure as anything."

As a result, Lavinia had ended up seated directly across from Lucas.

He'd much rather it be Lavinia than Miss Broome, who had only ever glared at him since they'd met. He could appreciate Miss Broome's protective nature, especially after learning she'd essentially raised Lavinia, but, blast it all, she was making him feel like a villain when he was nothing of the sort. After all, who'd rushed into whose arms and begun this entire situation? Not he. He had been a perfect saint all night long—and would have been even if he'd known what an attractive guest he'd had—and perfectly amiable and gentlemanly the entire time since.

The downpour was making the roads muddy and slick; Lucas could feel the wheels of the carriage slip in the ruts along the way. The coachman,

Grimes, had slowed the horses considerably as a result. Lucas had gotten his fill of mud during his time on the Peninsula—marching in mud, digging in mud, fighting the French in the mud. Blood and mud. Mud did not generate pleasant memories in his mind, but today's mud meant something entirely different—it meant they would, of necessity, be adding extra time to their journey. And that was entirely fine with him.

He settled into his seat, with his shoulder resting in the corner of the carriage, then adjusted the brim of his hat to cover his eyes. He hadn't slept well lying on the floor the night previous. He'd been too aware of the strange woman sharing the room, not to mention the hard floor.

He'd almost succeeded in nodding off when the carriage suddenly lurched to one side. His eyes shot open, and he instinctively braced himself. Old Arthur Drake nearly flew into Lucas's lap; Miss Broome was thrown against Miss Weston, who cried out as she was crushed against Lavinia by the force of movement. Lavinia flung one arm against the side of the carriage and the other arm toward Miss Weston for balance.

The carriage rolled to a stop—upright, thankfully, but at a definite tilt. Not a good sign. Dealing with a carriage mishap in this weather meant trouble, especially when he could see that Miss Weston, contrary to the stoic look on her face, was in a great deal of pain.

"Goodness, is everyone all right?" Lavinia asked, pushing her bonnet back into place, while Miss Broome settled into her seat again and started fussing over Miss Weston.

"We all took quite a tumble there, Livvy," Arthur Drake said, checking himself over, "but I daresay poor Delia got the worst of it." He looked worriedly at Miss Weston.

"I'm fine, Arthur," Miss Weston said, although her voice trembled a bit. When she attempted to shift into a more comfortable position, her eyes fluttered and she moaned.

"Delia!" Miss Broome cried.

Lucas caught Miss Weston just as she slumped forward in her seat. He eased back carefully, cradling the elderly woman in his arms.

"Here, let me help," Mr. Drake said, gently arranging Miss Weston's legs across Lucas's lap so he could hold her more securely. Lavinia started fanning Miss Weston's pale, wrinkled face with her hands.

The carriage door squeaked open. "Everyone all right in here?" Grimes asked. Water poured off the brim of his hat onto the shoulders of his greatcoat.

"No," Lucas replied. "One of the women was injured in the mishap."

"Dash it all. Was afraid something like that might have happened. You're best off keeping her here in the carriage, guv, whilst I sees to the damage. We've a broken wheel, blast the luck and the weather."

Lucas was inclined to agree with the coachmen's assessment of the situation, including his colorful language.

"I've sent Garrick to the next town for assistance," Grimes continued. "Biggleswade's not too far from here—two or three miles, by my reckoning. Shouldn't take long, him all alone on a horse, like. An hour or two at most."

Mr. Drake began wringing his hands. "Oh dear," he muttered. "Oh dear, oh dear."

"All will be well, Artie," Lavinia assured him. She was now fanning Miss Weston's face with an actual fan Miss Broome had located somewhere. "We've been through worse. Look, she's coming to. Delia, my dear, you gave us a scare. How are you feeling?"

Miss Weston had indeed opened her eyes just a bit. "Where am I?" she asked faintly. She laid a limp hand on her forehead as though in pain and then realized she was lying across Lucas's lap. "Oh," she said. "Mr. Jennings." She reached up and patted his cheek, of all things, as though she was comforting *him*. When she tried to sit up straight, however, she moaned and looked as though she might faint again.

"Careful, now," Lucas said. "I've got you steady, so there's no need for you to move. Where does it hurt?"

"My neck, a bit," she said weakly. "And my side."

"Got you right in the ribs with my elbow, no doubt," Miss Broome said. "I'm that sorry, Delia. I was supposed to be cushioning *you*, not the other way around."

"It takes more than an elbow to get me down, Hannah. I only need a moment to recover; you'll see." Delia wheezed out a chuckle, but the effort made her wince in pain.

"I thought we was leaving all the drama behind us when we left old Hinchcliffe behind," Miss Broome replied.

Lavinia shot her a startled look, and Miss Broome's mouth snapped shut with a surprisingly loud clacking noise.

Hmm, Lucas thought. Miss Broome's slip of the tongue afforded the first real bit of information he'd gotten. Now he at least had a name: Hinchcliffe. It wasn't much, but it was a start.

The interior of the carriage had felt cramped enough before—and was even more so now that it tilted toward the broken front wheel. Lucas wasn't of a mind to sit holding elderly Miss Weston for the next hour or so while they all waited to be rescued, although he certainly would if the situation called for it. He decided on a different plan, though it meant his only suit of clothes was going to get thoroughly wet and muddy.

"I believe I'll step out of the carriage for a while so there will be room to lay Miss Weston on the carriage seat," he said. "She'll be more comfortable that way."

"Oh dear," Miss Weston said.

"Thank you, Lucas," Lavinia said. She stood and moved out of the way while Miss Broome placed a cushion at the end of the seat for Miss Weston to use as a pillow. Thank goodness for the extra cushions he had obtained for the journey. They would provide Miss Weston with a bit of comfort for the time being.

Then Lucas stood, slouching due to his height and the low ceiling of the carriage, and held Miss Weston against his chest, an arm under her knees. As he moved, the others all shifted positions in the cramped space— Mr. Drake into Lucas's spot, Lavinia next to him, and Miss Broome in the corner previously occupied by Mr. Drake. It all took a bit of squeezing and shuffling, but they managed it without bumping Miss Weston too badly in the process. When they were finally in place, he laid her gently on the seat.

Mr. Drake found space to place a cushion on the floor of the carriage and then managed to fold himself up and sit on it cross-legged, giving Lavinia and Miss Broome the entire bench to themselves. He patted Miss Weston's arm reassuringly with a solicitousness that bordered on affection.

Lavinia reached out and laid her hand on Lucas's arm.

"Thank you again, Lucas," she said. "It was indeed fortunate that you were here to assist."

A few strands of vivid red hair that had escaped their confines of the cap and bonnet during the mishap now framed her face, a perfect oval of fair skin. And her eyes . . .

For the briefest of moments, her eyes were luminous with something Lucas had not seen there before. She had beautiful eyes—large gray ones that were hard to ignore. He had already begun to wonder if she used her eyes as some sort of tool. He wasn't even sure what he meant by that, precisely, except that he'd observed her arch a brow, narrow her eyes, or shoot glances that seemed intended to elicit particular responses from others.

But just now he'd seen something deeper expressed in them. Honesty? Authenticity? He wasn't sure, for as quickly as he'd seen the look, it had disappeared.

He nodded to her. "At your service, ma'am," he said and then left the close confines of the carriage and stepped out into the deluge.

Chapter 7

LAVINIA WATCHED LUCAS TROMP THROUGH the mud, his wide shoulders hunched over in the downpour. The rain drummed constantly on the roof of the carriage and slashed at the windows.

He wore no greatcoat, only the traveling clothes he'd been wearing yesterday. He was going to be soaked to the skin in no time.

"Where is he now?" Artie asked from his position on the floor of the carriage.

Lavinia leaned closer to the window, using her handkerchief to clear away the moisture that had formed there so she could get a better glimpse of Lucas. He'd nearly reached Mr. Grimes, who had already unhitched the horses, including Lucas's, and had led them off to the side of the road where they could calm themselves and graze after becoming agitated by the mishap.

"He's speaking with the coachman," Lavinia replied, reluctant to drag her eyes from his receding figure.

"That's good, then," Delia said.

Lavinia heard shuffling and turned away from the window to look. Delia was propping herself up on her hands so she could sit up.

"What's going on?" Hannah asked.

"I say, brilliantly done, Delia," Artie said. "You were always the best, my dear."

"Hardly that, Arthur," Delia said, patting her fluffy hair back into place as best she could. "Although I do pride myself on producing quality work, if I must say so myself."

Hannah shook her head.

"Delia, what are you up to?" Lavinia asked.

"It should be obvious, Livvy," Delia replied. "I was ensuring that our escort remain with us until we arrive at Primrose Farm."

"She always was the best fainter onstage," Artie exclaimed proudly. "You are just as impressive a fainter up close, my dear. I was thoroughly convinced you were in agonizing pain, even though I was fairly certain I knew what you were about. Well done!" He clapped.

Lavinia rolled her eyes. "Next you'll be telling me you planned for the carriage to break a wheel."

"Don't be foolish, Lavinia," Delia said. "That was merely an opportune moment."

"Perfect dramatic timing," Artie added.

"I would have found another reason to faint if that carriage wheel hadn't broken as it did."

"You weren't injured at all, were you?" Lavinia said accusingly. "Mr. Jennings had already agreed to accompany us. I don't see that this little antic of yours was called for in the least."

"It wasn't any different than what *you* did," Artie said. "You threw yourself in his lap and called him your husband. In *public*."

"That was *entirely* different. I hadn't planned it ahead of time and only did it when it appeared I was about to be recognized by one of Cosgrove's nasty little minions."

"Now, dearie," Delia said. "It isn't as if I didn't get jostled and bruised a bit. I'll be sore for a day or two; Hannah does have a sharp elbow, but a good actor takes his—or her—lumps. It's all part of the craft. But have you taken a good *look* at that fellow, Lavinia? He's a tall, brawny, utterly splendid specimen of masculinity. *And* he's a gentleman with all his manners intact. These types don't show themselves very often, especially lurking backstage after performances, I'm sorry to say. Perhaps he did agree to accompany us to Primrose Farm, but a little insurance never hurt anyone."

"You're the cleverest girl I know, Delia, and your performance was first-rate—but surely he's too young for you?" Artie asked a bit anxiously.

Hannah snorted and shook her head again.

"Arthur," Delia said gently, "you're the dearest man in the world, and thank you for thinking I'm still capable of attracting such a handsome young man at my age. But, gracious, I'm not thinking of keeping Mr. Jennings around for *myself*. It's *Livvy* I'm thinking about."

"Ah, of course," Artie said.

"Delia, *no* matchmaking, and I mean it," Lavinia warned. "I've had my fill of men—the flowers and flirting and propositions . . . not to mention my name appearing in the betting books at all the gentlemen's clubs. Oh yes, I've heard the stories. We've worked too hard for this little bit of independence, and for the first time, we will actually have a place to call home and put down real roots. I'll not be tossing it all aside on the first attractive gentleman with whom I cross paths—"

"Aha! So you *do* find him attractive, then!" Delia said in a triumphant tone that couldn't help but irk Lavinia.

"Well, of course I find him attractive," she retorted. "What young lady wouldn't? And of course I'm indebted to him for coming to my rescue and for helping me find all of you this morning—"

"Could have sworn you said the White Hart," Hannah muttered.

"You know, a *hart* is a deer, Hannah," Artie said instructively. "Not a horse. Some very clever puns on the word in *Twelfth Night*."

"Artie . . ." Lavinia warned.

"'O, when mine eyes did see Olivia first,'" Artie quoted, gazing steadfastly at Delia, his arm outstretched dramatically. "'Methought she purged the air of pestilence! / That instant was I turn'd into a hart; / And my desires, like fell and cruel hounds, / E'er since pursue me.'"

Delia applauded. "Bravo, Arthur. Very moving."

Artie placed his hand on his chest. "Hart and heart, you see."

"Of course we see," Hannah grumbled. "We aren't daft, now, are we?"

"Give us a hand, now, Hannah, if you please," Artie said, shifting about so he could get his feet solidly under him. Hannah grabbed him beneath his elbow and helped support his weight while he rose shakily and settled next to Delia on the bench. "I daresay the rain has made my rheumatics act up," Artie said in an apologetic voice. "Blast this getting old business."

"Never you mind about that," Delia said. "Sing for us, Arthur. Otherwise I fear we shall be sitting here for an hour or so listening to the rain rat-a-tat-tat until we are like to go mad. And you have such a lovely voice. I always did like listening to you sing."

Lavinia turned her head to look out the window again. Lucas and his horse had disappeared from view. Part of her wondered if he'd decided he'd had enough of dealing with her and her friends and had ridden off in escape.

But another part of her thought he might just be the gentleman she'd told him he was last night at the inn. It was difficult for Lavinia to imagine a man who actually kept his promises—although Artie was a dear and was very loyal, so perhaps there were a few such rare men who existed.

Perhaps Lucas Jennings was such a man. Perhaps.

"'When that I was and a little tiny boy, / With a hey, ho, the wind and the rain,'" Artie crooned softly in his low baritone voice. "'A foolish thing was but a toy, / For the rain it raineth every day.'"

It was a sweet, melancholy little song Shakespeare had penned and wholly appropriate for the occasion, and not only because it was raining. The words spoke of a man's efforts to improve his station only to continually encounter hardships regardless. Lavinia felt that way—or, more precisely, she felt her life thus far had allowed her to be nothing but a toy—a whimsy, an actress who flaunted herself in breeches and whom men longed to treat as a plaything.

There had to be more. Life couldn't always be about the rain.

* * *

Lucas was up to his neck in water, but at least now it was steaming-hot bath water, not the cold rain that had been running down his neck and soaking through all the layers of his clothes. The tub was too small to accommodate his tall frame, so he was sitting with his knees poking out well above the water, but such had been the case since achieving his adult height at the age of fourteen.

He rubbed soap on a cloth and scrubbed his right foot and then his left. While he did, he could hear Mr. Drake puttering around on the other side of the privacy screen. They'd managed—barely since there were other travelers who'd chosen not to continue their journeys in this weather—to find two small vacant rooms at the Rose and Crown near the town of Stevenage, and the innkeeper had been good enough, despite the bustle of extra business the rain had caused, to send his servants up with the tub and pails of boiling water. They'd also lit and stoked the fire, which was blazing nicely now. Lucas's coat, waistcoat, and breeches were currently draped near the fire in the hope that they would dry sufficiently for Lucas to actually dress in them after his bath.

He still had his clean change of linen; last night, since circumstances had compelled him to share his room with a strange female, he had not shed some of his usual clothing.

On the Peninsula, a soldier slept in his clothes out of necessity because it enabled him to respond quickly and, therefore, more successfully during an attack. And although Lucas had spent the past several weeks enjoying a comfortable bed and the luxury of sleeping in nightclothes if he so chose, his encounter with the enigmatic Lavinia last evening had resurrected all his old precautionary military behaviors.

Now, for the second night in a row, Lucas was sharing a room with a stranger. This one, however, concerned Lucas significantly less. Case in point: presently, Mr. Drake was humming to himself as he moved about the room, occasionally letting loose a "heigh ho." Lucas had wondered during the coach ride today if the elderly man had all his wits about him, as he'd occasionally made comments that had seemed rather off-topic—that is, until right now, when Lucas finally had time to consider the words in retrospect.

For example, Lucas thought as he soaped up his chest and under his arms, there had been that moment when the others had been discussing their plans when they arrived at Primrose Farm. Hannah had been fretting over the condition of the house, while Miss Weston had been expressing her desires to create a flower garden.

And then Mr. Drake had opened his mouth and said he was looking forward to playing the butler. *Playing* the butler.

Lavinia and the others had given him a sharp look, which had caused the old fellow to withdraw into himself, mumbling something along the lines of using the word *play* because he'd never been a butler before and expected the challenge to be fun.

At the time, Lucas had considered Mr. Drake's words merely eccentric, but now he wasn't so sure, especially when added to the man's propensity to spout Shakespeare.

Lucas slid under the water to rinse his hair, causing the water to slosh over the sides of the tub.

"You all right back there?" Mr. Drake called when Lucas resurfaced and began sluicing the water from his face and head. "Sounds like you brought the storm inside."

"I'm fine." Lucas rose from the tub and dried off. "Are my clothes dry, Mr. Drake?" he asked.

He heard the man move across the room to the fireplace. "Not quite, but making fine progress. Not long now, I should think."

Blast. That was an inconvenience, to say the least, but there was nothing that could be done about it but attempt patience. He may as well use the time the best he could.

He wrapped the towel around his middle and secured it in place, then knelt by the tub and proceeded to wash his dirty linens in the bath water. It wasn't an ideal laundry setting, but he'd dealt with worse on the Peninsula, where his clothes washing had usually taken place in whatever river or stream they'd encountered. At least tonight he had soap, something that hadn't always been available while he'd been in the army, depending on where his regiment was and how near to a supply transport they happened to be.

There was a knock at the door, which Mr. Drake answered, and then the door closed with an ominous thud. "Goodness, but it's hot in here!" Lucas heard Miss Weston exclaim.

He froze.

"It's that way for a purpose, Delia," Mr. Drake explained. "'Tis the only way our friend Mr. Jennings is going to have a scrap of clothes to wear otherwise."

"Dear me," Miss Broome said.

Mr. Drake had let Miss Weston *and* Miss Broome into the room? And if those two were here, Lavinia was undoubtedly with them. Lucas quickly situated himself behind the tub as strategically as he could and silently berated Mr. Drake.

"No other clothes?" Lavinia called out, proving his assumption to be correct. "Is that true, Lucas?"

Lucas realized he was wringing the water from his drawers a little too vigorously. "Indeed," he replied as coolly as possible, considering he was trapped behind a privacy screen in his natural state. "You may recall, if you were to cast your mind back, that I had only my saddlebag with me when we were so suddenly thrust together." He set his drawers aside and began scrubbing soap into his shirt.

"Your poor coat," he heard Lavinia say. "It not only soaked up the rain, but it encountered a great deal of mud as well. And your boots! Well, there is only one thing to be done."

Lucas looked up in alarm, although, really, all he could see was the privacy screen—

"Hannah," Lavinia continued. "Collect Mr. Jennings' clothes, if you please—"

"No!" Lucas dropped his shirt into the tub and jumped to his feet, clutching his towel to keep it securely in place. He stumbled around the tub and poked his head around the side of the screen, careful to keep the rest of him well concealed.

"Ah, there you are, Mr. Jennings!" Miss Weston said cheerily, as though her earlier ordeal in the carriage had not occurred and greeting an unclothed male—however strategically hidden—was a daily occurrence for her.

"Miss Weston." He greeted her with a nod. What else was he to do? The entire situation was ludicrous. "I'm glad to see you have recovered from the accident this afternoon. Lavinia, I would ask that you not take my things, for the obvious reasons."

She, unlike Miss Weston, kept her eyes averted and directed her efforts toward inspecting his clothes, feeling them for dampness. She'd changed out of her gray traveling clothes, exchanging them for a dark-green dress that, sadly, wasn't any more flattering. She had left off her bonnet but had retained the cap. "Hannah is the most accomplished person you shall ever meet when dealing with any article of clothing. She can take the proverbial sow's ear and turn it into something even finer than a silk purse. Hannah shall have you looking better than ever. I guarantee it."

Lucas wasn't convinced since Miss Broome had never looked at him with anything more than wary mistrust. "All the same, I think I'd rather fend for myself in this regard."

"Nonsense. It's the least we can do." She began gathering Lucas's clothing and handing them to Miss Broome. "Artie, be a dear and run to the kitchen. I'm famished, and I expect everyone else is as well. And see if they've an iron we can borrow."

"And some cleaning rags too, Artie," Miss Broome said as she examined the items she now held. "These clothes is going to need some sponging up first." She reached for his boots.

"*Not* my boots," Lucas said, clutching at the privacy screen in frustration. "I draw the line at my boots."

"Very well; leave his boots, Hannah," Lavinia said, handing the rest of Lucas's clothes to her. "Let's get to work, then."

"I'm relying on your honor, *Miss Fernley*, to ensure that my clothing is returned to me within the hour. I may seem disadvantaged at the moment, but you are dealing with a seasoned veteran of war. I have very little actual modesty remaining as a result, and what there is at present is in deference to you ladies. But if you prove untrustworthy, do not doubt me when I say there will be retribution, regardless of my state of dress or lack thereof."

Lavinia arched her brows at him. "There will be no need for retribution, *Mister Jennings*." She'd returned his formal address to her with one of her own. "My claims about Hannah's skills are an understatement of fact. And as you have graciously accompanied us, obviously to your detriment, it is only fair that we return a kindness with a kindness." She turned with a flourish and left the room, with Hannah—her arms filled with Lucas's only clothes, heaven help him—trailing in her wake.

Miss Weston winked at Artie and followed, shutting the door behind her.

There was something odd about the old lady's wink . . .

He furiously cast his eyes about the room. Blast it all, they'd toddled off with his boots in tow after all!

Lucas's head felt perilously close to exploding. He stalked to the door and locked it before Mr. Drake could make a clean getaway, then turned and loomed over the little man. "*What in blazes* were you thinking?" Lucas practically roared. "Letting those women into our room like that, with me—" He gestured up and down his body with the hand that wasn't presently holding his towel in place. "Where is your *decorum*, man? Have you lost your mind?"

"Sorry, old boy; it's only that after so many years in the—um, well, never mind that." Artie straightened and struck an oratorical pose. "'Women speak two languages—one of which is verbal,'" he said.

"That makes absolutely no sense whatsoever," Lucas said, his frustration ratcheting up several more notches. He tossed his towel onto the bed and tugged on his remaining clean shirt and drawers, leaving his other shirt marinating in the tub. "For future reference, Mr. Drake, bathing and other private needs are to be accomplished without an audience."

"Audience, hah! That's a good one, sir. I'll remember that."

"They took my clothes *and my boots*, man! In the meantime, *you* are finding jokes in my speech that do not exist." He dropped his voice to a menacing tone. "If you do not wish to meet your Maker anytime soon, you will make certain my clothes are returned to me *within the hour, as I said.*"

"Hannah's good, but she doesn't like to be rushed, if you see what I mean, Mr. Jennings."

Lucas loomed even closer, forcing the old man to shrink back. "One hour, Mr. Drake. One. Hour."

Mr. Drake nodded his head vigorously. "I shall do my best, sir. You have my word."

"Just make sure that it happens," Lucas snapped. He felt as if he were acting in a farce at the moment. "Go see to the food and the iron," he said.

"Right. Food, iron, and rags."

"Now you're beginning to think straight," Lucas said. He pulled one of the chairs—the one his breeches had been draped across—a few feet from the fireplace and sat.

"I shall return shortly," Artie announced.

Lucas waved a hand in his direction.

"Decorum it is from here on out," Artie added.

Lucas said nothing.

"And privacy."

"*Goodbye*, Mr. Drake."

The key in the lock turned, and the door opened and closed.

Lucas slumped in the chair and closed his eyes. It had been an exhausting day after an uncomfortable night with little sleep. He wanted to crawl into bed but didn't dare—not while the women had his clothing. Lucas didn't relish waking up hours later to find his trust misplaced, his traveling companions gone, and his clothing missing in action.

Closing his eyes in an overwarm room was not a good idea, he thought drowsily.

A knock at the door awakened him with a start. Blast, he'd fallen asleep, he thought as he tried to clear the cobwebs from his brain. If he were still in Spain, he would be dead by now.

The person on the other side of the door knocked again. "Supper, as was ordered," a female voice called.

He lunged to his feet, grabbed a blanket off the bed, and wrapped it around himself before opening the door. He wasn't about to miss supper, regardless of his fatigue or lack of attire.

"Over there, please," he gestured to the red-faced serving girl, who hurriedly set down the tray and exited with the quickest curtsy Lucas had ever seen, not that he blamed her.

He quickly polished off the surprisingly decent mutton stew and bread, then placed his dishes outside the door, unwrapped himself from the blanket, and proceeded to make himself a bed on the floor.

Mr. Drake was an odd old duck—a fitting play on words—but he seemed harmless enough. Miss Broome huffed and puffed about but reminded Lucas more of his own old nurse than a sinister character. And while tiny Miss Weston definitely had a devious streak, she was too old and frail to be much of a threat.

Now, Lavinia, on the other hand . . . She was an entirely different matter. She was still traveling in disguise, for one thing. She was also much younger than Lucas had originally thought—most likely in her midtwenties, if he were to venture a guess—only a bit younger than himself. Despite her young age, however, she was definitely the leader of their little group. What had brought them all together was still a mystery, but he was developing a theory. And soon enough, he would put his theory to the test.

His traveling companions were an entertaining lot. And if they made off with his clothes? Now that he'd eaten and was feeling more rational, he realized that if they did abandon him, his situation wasn't the end of the world, for he still had his saddlebag, which now held his money, and there was enough to see him to some clothing and boots if necessary. He would get the innkeeper to assist him in the purchases.

At any rate, Lucas was fairly confident now that Mr. Drake would return soon enough with his clothes in tow.

He lay on one side of the blanket and pulled the rest of it over him on the floor, his saddlebag at his side for safety's sake; he wasn't an utter fool. He plumped the pillow beneath his head, sending a few goose feathers from their confines and floating past his eyes. How had he ever managed to sleep this way during all his years in the army? Even with the brief nap, he was exhausted.

He punched the pillow again and swatted more feathers from his face. The plain truth was that one simply learned to deal with one's circumstances. Just as he was going to have to do when he reached home and faced his family—and Isobel.

He had done everything in his power to suppress any thought of her during his years in the army. Isobel, with the golden, blue-eyed looks of a porcelain doll. She had gazed at him adoringly when they were children; she had made him feel strong and manly, even as a boy. Their childhood friendship had blossomed into youthful love, and they had vowed to love each other forever.

Oh, Isobel, he thought as his eyes drifted shut. And then he thought no more.

* * *

"What *on earth* were you thinking, Artie?" Lavinia stopped pacing the small confines of the room long enough to direct the question to him with a good deal of emphasis. "We're supposed to look like *normal* people, and a normal person does *not* allow ladies to enter a room where gentlemen are . . . are . . ." She waved her hand up and down, trying to come up with the proper word and failing—not that it mattered. They were all perfectly aware of what Lucas's state had been.

"I already got an earful from the man himself," Artie said morosely. "No need to lay it on further, Livvy."

"Don't be too hard on Arthur, Livvy," Delia said from her seat by the fire. "It is difficult to change one's habits after a lifetime in the theater. You know what it's like. Fifty years of backstage costume changes may have muddled Arthur a bit, but it's those same years of theater experience that got us out of the room without stumbling all over ourselves."

"You may think we extricated ourselves smoothly, Delia," Lavinia said, "but I'm absolutely certain our smoothness only served to raise questions in Lucas's mind. We should have been aghast and blushing and excusing ourselves. Instead, we were all politeness, as if nothing whatsoever was amiss. And *then* we took his only clothing with us."

"That part was your doing, dearie," Hannah pointed out.

Lavinia ground her teeth. "Perhaps so, but I was hardly expecting to find myself in such a situation, was I? The entire scene was absurd."

"How are his clothes coming along, Hannah?" Artie asked. Hannah was busy polishing Lucas's boots while his clothing dried. She was nearly done with the first one. "He was especially insistent on getting them back within the hour."

"A little polish and brushing and he'll be right as rain," Hannah said. "P'raps an hour and a bit."

"Closer to an hour would be better for my mortal existence, Hannah."

"Coat and breeches need more time to dry before I can brush them neat. His shirt and neckcloth could use some starch, but we can't have everything, now, can we? At least the innkeeper had an iron we could borrow. I'll see what I can do."

"That's all a fellow can ask."

"There. You see, Livvy?" Delia said. "An hour and a bit. Perhaps less. Tempest in a teapot, if you were to ask me. Mr. Jennings doesn't seem the sort to hold a grudge for long, and once he sees what our Hannah can do, he'll be over it in a trice."

"'And where two raging fires meet together, they do consume the thing that feeds their fury,'" Artie said.

"Rather out of context, Arthur, but I do believe you're onto something," Delia said. "Very observant of you."

Lavinia had no idea what Artie meant by his reference or what Delia meant in reply, and she refused to speculate. "Enough with the Shakespeare, at least for now, Artie. Normal language for normal people. Besides, the Bard doesn't have an answer for everything, you know."

Artie and Delia both looked at her as though she'd uttered blasphemy.

"Artie could try the Bible instead," Hannah suggested. "It would do him a world of good."

"I know the Bible as well," Artie replied archly. "'Wherefore I abhor myself, and repent in dust and ashes.' There. You see? The book of Job." He gazed off into the distance. "I should dearly like to play Job sometime. Such depth of character."

"You would make a wonderful Job, Arthur, but I think I still prefer Shakespeare, if you are to quote from anything, despite what Livvy says. Much less guilt attached overall," Delia said.

That led the two of them into a general discussion of the dramatic merits of the Bible versus Shakespeare, completely losing the thread of the original conversation, which was, ironically, how their behavior needed to be more normal and reflect less obviously on their theatrical background.

Lavinia began pacing again. This was the reason she'd put Hannah in charge last night. And Artie and Delia continued to prove her decision right time and again, despite their ending up at the White Hart.

Lavinia herself had reacted too theatrically by *not* reacting as a young lady would. How was she ever to find her way to a normal life if her ingrained instincts let her down?

She crossed to the window and looked out at a view of the inn's stable yard, although there wasn't anything to see. Had it really only been last night she'd sneaked away from the theatre and Mr. Hinchcliffe and Lord Cosgrove? It seemed a lifetime ago.

They needed to appear *normal.* How were they ever to be accepted by their new neighbors when they reached Primrose Farm otherwise? The people in all the towns and villages they'd performed in over the years had enjoyed their theatrical productions but had tended to be suspicious of them too, fearful that the theater troupe might be of a dishonest nature and steal their goods or their spouses or sons or daughters.

The suspicions hadn't been unwarranted in many cases. Her own father was an example of that, at least when it came to the daughters of the townspeople.

The same types of suspicions might arise when they reached Primrose Farm if they weren't careful. And then, there they'd be, relying on only themselves, with no practical knowledge about farming and no friendly neighbors offering advice and assistance.

A soft knock at the door heralded the arrival of their supper.

"'Mine eyes smell onions; I shall weep anon,'" Artie said, rubbing his hands together.

His Shakespeare repertoire was already back in full force. Lavinia sighed and turned away from the window.

Hannah ate quickly and resumed her task. In just over an hour, she had Lucas's clothes ready to return to him. She instructed Artie to carry Lucas's boots since she intended on carrying the other garments herself. "Livvy told the man his clothes was going to look even better than usual, and I intend for them to be that way. Artie would have them all wrinkled if I was to leave it up to him."

"I daresay I know how to carry a man's garments," Artie replied, all indignation. "I am a man, you know. 'For the clothing oft proclaims—'"

"Just grab his boots, Artie," Hannah said, carefully placing Lucas's neck-cloth on top of the other garments she'd laid out and then sliding her hands under them all to lift them. "And let's be off. Tomorrow will arrive sooner than later, and I've a mind to sleep before then."

"I'll accompany you so you don't have to return alone, Hannah," Lavinia said. She opened the door, allowing Artie and Hannah to precede her out into the corridor, leaving Delia in the room to prepare for bed.

"That Mr. Jennings, he's a clever one; you mark my words," Hannah murmured as they walked down the corridor. "He's taking in all we say and sorting the wheat from the chaff."

"I agree with you, Hannah, but so far, he has also kept a respectful distance. His presence can provide us protection and even respectability if we remember to play our part correctly. I don't agree with Delia's tactics—my own actions were purely a result of finding myself recognized and in need of a quick escape—but I can forgive her motives." Having a strong male presence around had given Lavinia a brief respite from the responsibilities she felt for the others, a chance to breathe before they encountered the next challenge upon their arrival at Primrose Farm.

"He's going to put the puzzle pieces together, and soon. You need to decide what you're going to tell him when he does," Hannah said.

"He most likely already has," Lavinia said. "But hopefully he'll be well on his way before he discovers he was playing escort to The Darling of Drury Lane."

"It's a right good thing I took my supper with you ladies," Artie grumbled as they approached the room, pointing to the serving tray on the floor outside the door, its dishes thoroughly emptied of their contents. "What if I hadn't? What if I'd returned to the room expecting to find my share of food, and it's gone? What then?"

"Then we would have sent to the kitchen for something more, Artie," Lavinia said soothingly.

"Still, you'd think a fellow would know it was a sharing thing we were about. And he ate every morsel."

"Never mind about that, Artie," Hannah said. "You aren't hungry now, are you? Open the door. These clothes is getting heavy, what with me trying to hold them careful-like and keep them from wrinkling."

Artie did as commanded and then stopped in his tracks just inside the doorway. "Well, would you look at that!" he exclaimed under his breath.

"No, thank you, Artie, considering Hannah has the man's clothes in her arms," Lavinia whispered back.

Artie shushed Lavinia and tiptoed into the room. "It's all right, Livvy. It's safe enough, after all," he whispered and proceeded quietly into the room.

Lavinia maintained her distance, despite Artie's assurance. She'd nearly given herself away when she'd been in the room earlier. She would be extra cautious this time.

Hannah peeked around the doorjamb and then followed Artie inside.

If cautious Hannah was willing to go in, it must be safe. Lavinia warily stepped inside. "Well, goodness," she whispered.

Lucas had taken a blanket and pillow from the bed and had made a place to sleep on the floor, and he was sound asleep, his torso and legs covered by the blanket, one muscular shoulder exposed by the light coming through the open door from the corridor. He lay facing the door, undoubtedly more evidence of that soldier training he'd mentioned to her, although it had failed him this time, as he hadn't moved a muscle at their entrance.

He'd left the bed for Artie to use.

"Come, Hannah," she whispered. "We have a long day of travel ahead. Let's get some rest." They bid Artie farewell and returned to their room.

Lavinia didn't know what to think. Lucas Jennings was proving more and more that he was different from all the other men of her acquaintance. Seeing him on the floor, leaving the bed for Artie, had stirred something inside her, and she found herself truly wanting to trust him.

If only she hadn't learned so early in life that wanting didn't necessarily make it wise.

Chapter 8

Lucas awakened, his muscles stiff from sleeping on the floor for the second night in a row. He sat up and stretched, taking a moment to knead a spot on his neck that was particularly tight. As he turned his head, he noticed with relief that his clothes had been returned, as promised, and were neatly laid out on a chair near the tables, clean and pressed, his boots polished to a decent shine. Miss Broome had done an excellent job, as Lavinia had assured him she would.

He rose from the floor, washed, and donned the clothes, all the while listening to the lump huddled under the blanket on the bed snore in a whistling, snuffling sort of way.

A quick peek through the window curtains showed the rain had stopped and the clouds didn't look threatening, which boded well for getting back on the road. The first order of business, then, was to find Grimes and determine the status of the broken wheel.

He nudged the lump on the bed. "It's time we got on our way, Mr. Drake."

The lump groaned and rearranged its shape a bit, then began to whistle-snore again.

Lucas nudged him less gently this time. "Wake up, Drake. Morning awaits."

"If you say it is morning, I'll believe you," a gravelly voice uttered from beneath the blanket. "But my bones are inclined to argue the point."

Lucas drew the curtains back, letting the early morning light into the room. "The roads will be muddy today, so we need to be on our way in order to make decent time. Please inform the ladies of this as soon as you can. I'm off to see if the carriage wheel has been mended."

Mr. Drake's head emerged from beneath the blanket, his thin gray hair mussed, his eyes puffy from sleep. "Haven't been the proverbial early bird for more than half a century now. Give a man a moment to wake up." He rubbed a hand over his grizzled face. "I'll tell them, assuming they haven't already figured it out for themselves."

"Good man. I'll meet you downstairs." Lucas grabbed his saddlebag and left Mr. Drake struggling to an upright position and sliding his bony legs over the side of the bed.

Much to his surprise, Lucas found all three women already in the dining room, eating breakfast despite the early hour. Miss Weston seemed in good spirits, and even Miss Broome looked a bit less sour of countenance this morning. And Lavinia . . . Now that he knew what she really looked like, he wondered at the fact that he'd not noticed before.

Her traveling clothes were the same, and she still wore the cap, but she seemed to be making an incremental transformation as they made their way north. Anyone who'd seen her arrive at the inn yesterday would see the same woman, but Lucas detected more of the real Lavinia beginning to emerge. After two days—had it been only two days?—she looked fresh and exquisitely lovely to him, and her gray eyes had flashed with intelligence just now when she'd turned her head to glance at him upon his arrival in the dining room.

There was something conspiratorial about the women's behavior, however, that made a particular spot on Lucas's sore neck throb anew. Their heads were drawn close together, and they spoke in low tones as they drank their tea and attacked their breakfast.

"Ah, Mr. Jennings," Miss Weston chirped when he approached. "Come and join us, won't you? I hope you slept well."

"I did, thank you," he replied. "But I must refuse your kind offer. I am off to learn the status of our carriage."

"The carriage wheel is mended, and we can leave as soon as we wish," Lavinia said, dabbing at her lips with her napkin. "I have already spoken with Grimes."

What an efficient person she was.

Lucas was surprisingly irked that she'd already seen to the task. "Excellent," he said. "Then I shall be pleased to join you ladies after all." He sat in the vacant chair next to Lavinia while Miss Weston motioned to the serving girl, who quickly returned with a hearty plateful of eggs, kidneys, beans, and toast and set it in front of him.

"When shall we arrive at Primrose Farm, do you think?" Miss Weston asked him. She sighed gustily. "Primrose Farm. Was there ever a more idyllic-sounding name? I can hardly wait to get there and spend my days walking through the gardens and sewing and reading for enjoyment and not out of necessity."

"It won't be long now, Delia," Lavinia assured her. "A couple more days at most."

"In answer to your question, Miss Weston," Lucas said, "with any luck, we'll reach Stamford by this evening, assuming the roads have dried sufficiently. By the end of the following day, we should arrive at Primrose Farm, assuming you are prepared for two long days of travel."

"Oh, I am," Miss Weston assured him. "We have traveled in much worse conditions than these, Mr. Jennings. Why, I remember a time—" She jumped a little in her seat. "Well, it doesn't bear repeating, now does it? But rest assured, Mr. Jennings, I am a hearty traveler, as are we all."

Lucas and Hannah both glanced at Lavinia, who was calmly sipping her tea. She set her cup back on its saucer. "I daresay you won't find any group of persons more eager to reach a destination than you find us, Lucas. I do wish Artie would hurry so we can be on our way."

As if on cue, Mr. Drake entered the dining room. "Fried kidneys, my favorite," he exclaimed, rubbing his hands together after viewing Lucas's plate. "I daresay it looks to be a grand day for travel."

"It took you long enough to get down here," Hannah said.

"Didn't want to wake up," Mr. Drake replied. "Haven't slept that soundly in years—all thanks to you, Jennings, my good man. These three can put a man to fretting, what with their headstrong ways. 'Care keeps his watch in every old man's eye, / And where care lodges, sleep will never lie.' Nice to have a fellow gent to share the burden for a time. Restful."

"Indeed," Lavinia said briskly as Lucas stood so Mr. Drake could take his seat at the table. The serving girl removed Lucas's plate and set a fresh one filled with food in front of Mr. Drake. "Now, eat quickly so we can be on our way. It does us no good to be sitting here waxing poetic if we are all so intent on getting to Primrose Farm."

"You have no worries on that score, Livvy," Mr. Drake said before picking up his knife and fork and putting action to his words.

Once again, old Mr. Drake had tossed a Shakespearean couplet into the conversation, and Miss Weston had assured Lucas they were old hands at traveling. The pieces all supported Lucas's theory that they had been involved to varying degrees in theater. But they weren't thieves or scoundrels; he'd been around enough of those types in the army to read a person's character well enough.

It was Lavinia who intrigued him most. She was the central figure in their charade, and it was more than obvious the other three were dependent upon her.

Who was Lavinia Fernley, the ravishing young woman traveling incognito from London to Lincolnshire? How could her countenance blend a look of innocence with one of such world-weariness? Where was the family that should have taken her in after her father had died?

He would find the answers, he resolved as he walked to the stable. He would see Lavinia and her friends to their new home, and during that time, he would put the remaining pieces of the puzzle together.

* * *

The roads were still muddy when the coach came round to collect Lucas's four traveling companions, but the clouds had cleared, leaving a blue sky that promised sunshine. Lucas opted to journey on horseback; the roads would be much better by midday.

If the weather continued thus, they should make it to Stamford by the end of the day, and if Lucas was fantastically lucky, he would find his trunks still at the inn there, still waiting to be fetched by one of his father's servants. He would be able to retrieve one of his smaller trunks and have additional clothes for the continued journey northward to Sleaford and then on to Primrose Farm. He would also be able to leave a note at Stamford for his family, explaining his unexpected detour and its resulting delay in his arrival at Alderwood.

He gave Hector free rein to pick his way along the road. Hector was a good lad and had been with him in Spain. The one thing Lucas had insisted upon for himself when he and Anthony had returned from the Peninsula was that Hector return with them. He and Hector had ridden through a great deal of muddy terrain together the past few years—muddy terrain, scorching heat, freezing cold. For the first couple years Lucas had been in Spain, he'd marched. As a lowly enlisted man in the infantry, he'd not had the luxury of a horse as the officers and cavalry did.

What a fool of a boy Lucas had been back then, to have impulsively enlisted in the army at the callow age of nineteen—and over a female, to boot.

And yet, it was this very female who, even now, created a pit in Lucas's stomach and whose presence at Alderwood was causing him to delay his return there. *Ah, Isobel*, he thought. He had faced the French with more readiness than he could muster for Alderwood at present.

Their travel northward went smoothly and was uneventful, which was a relief after the storm and broken carriage wheel the day before. They were able to make it to Stamford by early evening, and on Lucas's suggestion, they took rooms at the George, the owners having provided accommodations to the Viscount Thurlby and his family on many occasions over the years.

"So good to see you back from the Peninsula safe and sound, Mr. Jennings!" Tom, the robust innkeeper, said upon their arrival. "And, of course, only the best rooms will do," he added, motioning to his servants.

As blessed fortune would have it, his trunks had arrived on the mail coach shortly after their own arrival in town. "I'll be taking the small trunk with me, Tom," he said to the innkeeper. "Can you arrange for the others to be taken to Alderwood? I'll also be writing a letter to include with them."

"I'll see it done, Mr. Jennings."

"Thank you."

Lucas took his small trunk to his room. Luckily, he wouldn't have to share his room with Mr. Drake tonight, as Tom had provided their lodgings for the evening at a nominal rate. It was always good to do agreeable business with the local aristocratic families, Tom had assured him. Lucas hadn't felt inclined to argue the point. He was looking forward to sleeping in an actual bed tonight.

He removed a sheet of foolscap from the writing desk in his room and picked up the quill, dipping it in the ink bottle while he pondered his words.

Dear Mama, he began, for, of course, if he addressed the letter to his father, his mother would be at his heels, shaking her finger at him for not writing to her. His father, on the other hand, would merely expect his arrival to occur when he arrived—and would presume Lucas had a reasonable explanation for arriving whenever he did. So, "Dear Mama" it was.

> *I look forward to seeing you and Father soon, as well as the rest of the family. Would that it were today, my dear! However, my services have been required elsewhere for a few more days.*
> *All my love and regard,*
> *Your son,*
> *Lucas*

As letters went, it was a pathetic specimen. Perhaps he should have explained his reason for delaying a bit more or made mention of each family member rather than refer to them collectively. But then he would have had to list Isobel, and that he would not do. The less he thought about her, the better.

A knock at the door heralded the arrival of his supper. He thanked the serving girl, who bobbed a curtsy before leaving.

Actually, the less he thought about his siblings altogether, the better off he'd be, he thought as he dug into the steaming pork pie on his plate. It would only serve to remind Lucas of his own lack of fortune and vocation. He loved his siblings and truly wanted to see them again; he didn't begrudge any of them their accomplishments and happy lives.

If only he could arrive at Alderwood with a sense of accomplishment himself.

Chapter 9

THEY SHOULD BE NEARING PRIMROSE Farm if the directions Great-Aunt Mary's solicitor had given Lavinia were correct. Anxiety was making her heart race and stealing her breath. They would be facing the truth of their future any moment now, and she was keyed up with anticipation. Lavinia had seen Lucas ride ahead of the carriage until he'd disappeared from view, undoubtedly looking for the private lane that led to the farm.

Delia and Artie had managed to nod off during the carriage ride. It was amazing what a pair of old traveling theater veterans could sleep through. Hannah sat quietly to Lavinia's left. They had visited many parts of England during their years together with the troupe, but they'd never traveled to Lincolnshire. Lavinia suspected it was due to her father's efforts to avoid his family, thought he'd never said as much.

She looked now at the landscape that surrounded them: flat, green, lush. Marshy. Fens, as they were called: low-lying flatlands requiring drainage and flood protection to keep the lands dry and arable. It was rich, promising soil, but Lavinia suddenly understood how little she knew about the place. It wasn't quite the picture of genteel farm life she'd had in mind.

This morning she'd decided to set aside her ill-fitting clothes and cap and dress as she intended to dress going forward as a member of the community. She'd chosen a traveling gown of deep blue, with a tiny straw bonnet trimmed in forget-me-nots—nothing at all fancy. And while the innkeeper had initially stumbled over his words, he'd been able to collect himself eventually, as had Mr. Grimes, although poor young Garrick had tripped in his attempt to put down the steps of the coach.

Their overall reactions had been promising.

Lucas had been momentarily stunned, even though he'd already seen her without her disguise. His eyes had traveled up and down her person, but then his eyes had met hers and he'd smiled with warm approval, indicating that he'd understood what she hadn't verbalized—that she was neither hiding in disguise nor flaunting herself in her choice of dress. She was simply being Lavinia Fernley—whatever that meant.

She wished she had a better idea of who Lavinia Fernley was, in truth.

Through the window, she could see Lucas riding back toward them and hailing Mr. Grimes. The coach slowed until it rattled to a stop.

A knot formed in her stomach. She pushed the window open and leaned out until she could see Lucas, who was in discussion with Mr. Grimes. "What is it?" she called. "Did you find Primrose Farm, Lucas?"

He ended the discussion with Mr. Grimes and approached her window, his face blank. "Yes, I have located Primrose Farm, Lavinia," he said in a low voice intended for her ears only. "It isn't far, but I would speak to you privately before we arrive there."

"What's going on?" Delia asked, blinking as she awoke. "Have we arrived?"

"Dozed off there for a bit, I suppose," Artie said, stretching. "What news have we?"

"Lucas says we're nearly there," Lavinia answered in a cheery, matter-of-fact tone. She would not have the others sense her anxiety for the world. "I'm going outside to speak with him. It might be a nice opportunity to stretch your legs while I do."

"If we're that close, I'm inclined to think our legs can wait a while longer," Artie said. "What say you, Delia?"

Delia had covered her mouth with her handkerchief to stifle a yawn. "I believe I'm quite cozy at the moment, thank you, Artie."

"As you wish," Lavinia replied. The door opened, and Lucas held out his hand to assist her down. "We'll return shortly," she said, hoping she sounded more reassuring than she felt.

"You go on, dearie," Hannah said. "We'll be fine here."

Lavinia smiled in thanks before turning to place her hand in Lucas's, certain Hannah had sensed something amiss just as Lavinia had and grateful she hadn't said anything to alarm Delia and Artie.

Lucas led her to an old post at the side of the road where he'd tied Hector. "I'm taking you to see it before the others do, Lavinia." He grabbed the reins and swung onto his horse. "Place your foot on my boot."

"Tell me what's going on first."

He looked off in the distance and then returned his gaze to hers. "I'm afraid it isn't the idyllic place you and the others were counting on," Lucas said. "Although there is a farmhouse, of sorts."

The knot in her stomach grew. "Is it that bad, Lucas? Truly?"

"Put your foot on my boot, Lavinia," he said gently.

She complied, and Lucas lifted her easily to sit in front of him. "Hold on," he said, one of his arms coming around her to hold her in place. He urged the horse forward, and they rode for what Lavinia figured to be about a quarter of a mile before they stopped. There, on the side of the rode, was a weatherworn sign coming off its post with faded letters that read "Primrose Farm." She looked around for any sign of a farmhouse, but there was none.

Lucas clicked his tongue, urging Hector down a lane nearly hidden from the road by the surrounding overgrowth of sedge and grasses toward a small rise, shrouded in tall shrubbery and trees. As they neared the top, a derelict two-story brick structure came into view. Slates were missing from parts of the roof, leaving great gaping holes, and several windows were broken. The exterior was as weather-beaten as the sign that had led them here, its shutters and door in dire need of paint.

They made their way to the front of the building, and Lavinia saw that the door was, in fact, hanging from its hinges. Her sinking spirits plummeted into the vicinity of her toes. She and the others couldn't stay here even for a single night in order to allow Lavinia time to come up with an alternate plan for them all.

Lucas dismounted and put his hands on Lavinia's waist to help her down. She didn't look at him—couldn't, or she would break down completely.

The coach arrived much too soon and came to a lumbering halt behind them. "Oh dear," she heard Delia say. "Oh dear, oh dear, oh dear."

Hannah and Delia had descended from the coach, and they were both staring at the farmhouse in dismay, but poor Delia was shaking her head in disbelief, a hand clutched at her heart. Lavinia watched as her knees began to buckle beneath her. Mr. Grimes dashed over and caught her before she crumpled to the ground. Artie sprang from the coach at Delia's cries, stumbling, nearly falling before catching sight of the decrepit farmhouse and crashing to a halt.

Lavinia stood, the tableau unfolding around her as though she were in a play, her head buzzing. Her dear elderly friends' faces were contorted by shock, but Lavinia could only watch. She couldn't move a muscle.

She'd thought she had the solution for them all, but instead, she'd led them out of London toward . . . nothing.

Oh, what horrible predicament had she created for her poor friends? Here they were, in the middle of nowhere, facing a sodden farm as their only means of living. The dilapidated building didn't even have the dignity of being a house anymore. It appeared to have been converted into some sort of outbuilding intended for use by the farm laborers employed here—except there hadn't been any farm laborers for years, by the look of things.

Mr. Grimes led Delia to a fallen log, and she sat, ghostlike, her eyes closed, her face ashen while Hannah fanned her and Artie alternately paced about and patted Delia's hand, murmuring words of reassurance.

Lavinia rested her forehead against Lucas's chest, barely aware that at some point, she'd clutched his lapels like a lifeline. His hands were still on her waist. She might have collapsed if not for that.

"It's a sorry sight, and that's a fact," Hannah said from her position by Delia.

What an understatement, Lavinia thought.

Letting down Hannah was the worst part of it. Steady, reliable Hannah, who'd taken care of her for as long as Lavinia could remember. She'd been the constant in Lavinia's life. Hannah had changed her nappies and fed her and kept her safely away from her father's bawdy women and his drunken fits of temper and had comforted her when he'd died. Hannah, who'd sewn Lavinia's clothes and welcomed Artie and Delia when Lavinia had learned the troupe manager planned to sack them.

Hannah had always given Lavinia the sturdy support she'd needed. And Lavinia had failed her.

"Courage, Lavinia," Lucas whispered to her, his hands moving to her shoulders. "You are strong, and you will rise above this challenge. Of that I have no doubt."

"Oh, Lucas," she said with a sigh.

"Ho, there," a voice called out. Lucas's hands dropped away, and Lavinia saw a man on an old nag a ways off, waving his cap in the air as he approached.

Lucas waved in acknowledgment, which was just as well since Lavinia, despite having acted on and offstage her entire life, wasn't sure she could rein in her emotions and respond in a normal fashion.

"Don't get many visitors out this way," the man said, dismounting. "Got me curious-like when I saw the coach here back on the road. Thought I'd see if I could be of service. Name's Allard."

"Lucas Jennings, Mr. Allard, and this is Miss Lavinia Fernley," Lucas said, reaching out to shake the man's hand.

Lavinia smoothed her expression as best she could and turned to face Mr. Allard, extending her hand to him as well, despite the gloom that threatened to swallow her whole. "How do you do, Mr. Allard? I'm the new owner of Primrose Farm."

"Pleased to make yer acquaintance, ma'am," Mr. Allard said, removing his hat and bowing over her hand.

He was being utterly respectful toward her without the typical reaction she was so accustomed to. It was surprising and a relief. "I was recently informed I inherited Primrose Farm from my late great-aunt," Lavinia said, pressing forward. "A Miss Martha Harrison, my grandmother's sister."

"Indeed, Mr. Allard, we arrived here under the assumption that Primrose Farm was a working farm, not a derelict," Lucas added.

"Aye, that it was. Two hundred acres and a good piece of land, too, when it's drained proper-like," Mr. Allard said. "Been a few years though." He scratched his bristled chin in thought. "Five or six, I'm thinking."

Two hundred acres? And it hadn't been worked in that long a time? Lavinia didn't remember the solicitor mentioning its size or its condition in his letter to her. He'd been negligent in that regard, to say the least—not that Lavinia had thought to ask. But then, since it had apparently taken the solicitor time to find her father and then three more years after that to locate Lavinia after her father's passing, she supposed the man had tired of the whole business and had simply been glad to be done with it.

"Jennings, eh?" Mr. Allard said, turning his attention deliberately from Lavinia to Lucas. "There be Jennings hereabout, family of the Viscount Thurlby. You any relation?"

"His son, actually."

"Ah, well, ahem." He tugged deferentially at his forelock again. "Don't know the viscount personally, o' course. Fine family. Well respected hereabouts."

"Good to hear it," Lucas replied.

"Mr. Allard," Lavinia said, beginning to feel steadier. "What more can you tell us about Primrose Farm? Why was it left to decay in this manner? I can't imagine an elderly woman such as my great-aunt would have managed the farm on her own. She must have had a man of business. Why would that have ended upon her death?"

"Don't know the particulars, ma'am," Allard said. "What I heard tell was there was a falling out between what parties was involved, if you catch my meaning. People what worked the farm needed their income, and when the old lady died, the wages stopped, so they left. Couldn't legally work the farm and keep the profits, you know. And that was that. Sad, it was."

Why had Lavinia thought that Primrose Farm would be an idyllic cottage with a bit a land for growing vegetables? She hadn't even considered that the farm was more of a commercial entity than a family farm. Her education in these matters was sorely lacking.

She was a landowner with two hundred acres to her name—good heavens!—except the land had to be reclaimed and cultivated and the house restored, and the physical labor resources at her disposal included two retired thespians and a middle-aged seamstress and herself. She wasn't afraid of work, but she could hardly undertake all this on her own.

"If you'll excuse me, I'll be on my way. I'm off to see the wife," Mr. Allard said. "Time for luncheon, and then I'm back to work. You're welcome to come along, if you like. The missus is a good cook, and kind."

"Thank you, Mr. Allard, perhaps another time," Lavinia said, smiling and offering her hand again. "I'm sure we shall be great neighbors. In the meantime, my friends and I have plans that need to be made."

"Understood." He secured his cap on his head and walked over to remount his nag of a horse. "The missus and me are just down the way a bit and to the left, if you should need anything at all."

Lavinia had a sudden thought. "Mr. Allard, before you go . . ."

"Yes, ma'am?"

"Tell me about the people who worked the farm. Did you happen to be one of them?"

"Aye, ma'am," he replied. "Was foreman, in fact. I was fortunate to get on at a neighboring farm when things took a turn for the worse here. Others wasn't so lucky. Some has moved away. Others is making do." He coughed and looked away.

Lavinia was beginning to understand. "And by making do, are you suggesting they farmed some of my land in order to get by?"

"Won't say yes or no to that, ma'am, begging your pardon. They be good folks what was left in a bad way, is all."

"I see. Well, you may tell them the new owner of Primrose Farm has arrived, and hopefully things will be changing soon."

"Yes, ma'am, I'll do that, and a good day to you."

Lavinia watched him until he disappeared from view, then turned determinedly and studied the farmhouse. She had saved up a goodly sum of money in London, but not enough to see to the monumental task of restoring Primrose Farm.

She needed to think.

The first issue that needed to be addressed was lodging. That meant inspecting the house more closely. Perhaps there was a room or two that was habitable in a rustic sort of way . . .

She picked up her skirts and walked to the front door hanging precariously from its hinges. She could hear Lucas following behind her, his boots treading through the undergrowth.

"Careful, Lavinia," he said. "The house isn't safe."

Have you ever been backstage at a theater? she almost replied before remembering that she hadn't told him about their past yet. Backstage could be a chaotic place, with props and costumes here and there, furniture and set pieces stowed about. One grew used to such things.

He moved in front of her and opened the door, bracing it against the inside wall, and Lavinia followed him into the farmhouse. She marveled at how easily he'd lifted the large, wooden door. She'd felt that strength when he'd lifted her on and off his horse and had held her while she'd regained her composure. She'd felt his inner strength too, when he'd encouraged her.

Lavinia had never felt such strength, and to feel her burden lifted—even for that brief moment—had been as much of a solace to Lavinia as seeing the decrepit farmhouse had been a shock.

She allowed herself the brief luxury of imagining Lucas's strength as a permanent part of their lives—of her life. He was taller and broader than any man she'd ever met, and his utter maleness was apparent in his every breath and movement.

He was also kind.

Such thoughts would get her nowhere, however. She pulled her attention away from him and made herself focus on the situation around her.

* * *

Lucas surveyed the inside of the farmhouse, but his awareness was centered on Lavinia. His hands still tingled from the feel of her.

He had asked the coachman to delay following them for a few minutes, but that hadn't happened, much to Lucas's consternation. It meant Lavinia had had to struggle with her own reactions to seeing the place at the same time she'd had to assure her little band of travelers. Mr. Allard's arrival on the scene had been fortuitous, for he'd been able to answer at least a few of their questions.

He had no idea what resources she had other than the farm itself, but he doubted she troubled Delia and Artie with such details. Hannah probably had a better idea, but even then, Lucas suspected Lavinia kept her deepest troubles from Hannah. She was going to need someone to help her assess her options, he suspected.

Perhaps Lucas should be that someone.

He had dealt with calamity many times. If he could bring Anthony back from near death during their time in Spain, if he could arrange temporary shelter and procure food for officers, if he could learn to be a valet, he could help Lavinia through this immediate problem somehow.

Just inside the door was a moderately sized entry hall, with a stairway to the left leading upstairs. There was a good inch of dust and dirt everywhere—on the floor and covering each tread of the stairs that still remained in place. To the right was an open archway through which Lavinia passed and Lucas followed into what must have originally been the front parlor, although now it held only a battered, old desk and a toppled chair missing one of its legs, which was lying on the floor on the other side of the room. The windows were covered in grime, and one at the back of the room was broken, with only shards of glass hanging to its warped frame.

Owing to the marshy environment hereabouts, there had been water seepage, and the floorboards and lower walls were gray with mold and other unseemly things that thrived in dampness.

Lavinia exited the room, and Lucas followed. She said nothing, and he did nothing to disrupt the silence. He had nothing optimistic to say at the moment anyway.

Behind the stairs was a corridor that led to the kitchen—or what had been a kitchen. It had a large stone fireplace built to accommodate roasting large joints of beef, although the chimney would need to be thoroughly cleaned before attempting to build any fire in it at all. A large work area made of hardwood stood under more grimy windows and seemed in salvageable condition, if one ignored the fact that it was covered in vermin droppings.

He watched Lavinia lean over to peer through the windows; she was careful not to brush against the worktable or the droppings. Something had caught her eye, so he followed her gaze. Through the grime he was able to make out a large cistern used for collecting rainwater, the most reliable source of potable water here in the Fens.

A door leading outside was still intact on its hinges. Lucas threw the bolt and opened it, then walked over to inspect the cistern. Surprisingly, it was in fairly good condition but was full of murky water. It would need to be emptied and cleaned. Tiles along the roof on this side of the house had been laid in such a manner that the rainwater drained in a path that funneled into the cistern.

The farmhouse, with a little effort, could at least have water and fire available for setting up lodging. And this particular room had less rot along the foundation, which was more good news. An inspection of the entire foundation would be in order, but not today.

"I suppose I must attempt the stairs if I am to inspect the upper floor," Lavinia said, brushing at the dirt that had accumulated on her skirt during her inspection. Her gloves were dirty too.

"The stairs are in poor condition, Lavinia," Lucas said. "Let me inspect it for you."

"I won't turn down an offer for you to join me, Lucas," she replied. "But I intend on seeing everything for myself. I must, you see."

There was such earnestness in her voice. She was a determined woman who wouldn't be put off when her mind was made up, and he admired her for it. Very well; she would attempt the stairs. He would lead the way, then, for safety's sake. "I'll go first. If the treads can support my weight, they'll have no problem supporting yours."

"Excellent idea. Thank you, Lucas."

The first four treads were in solid condition, but the fifth tread was missing entirely, and the sixth was broken. Lucas easily stepped from the fourth to the seventh tread and then held out his hand to assist Lavinia.

The confounded woman surprised him yet again. She yanked her skirts up to her knees, clutching them in one hand, and then set her other hand in his, exposing a pair of very nice legs Lucas couldn't help but admire right along with her fortitude. She stretched a leg toward the seventh tread until she gained a bit of footing. Then she gripped his hand tighter, and he hoisted her over the two bad treads.

"That wasn't too bad," she said after puffing out a breath.

"That was the easy part." There were still a few treads that didn't look too damaged, but then there were two treads entirely gone and two broken treads immediately above them.

Lucas planted a foot on the first of the broken treads to test its strength, and the simple movement broke it loose, and it fell to the entry hall below them.

"That's not good," Lavinia said rather unnecessarily.

He moved his foot to the second of the broken treads and applied a little weight to it. His height enabled him to stretch the distance necessary with only minor difficulty; his concern was for Lavinia. She would have to put more force behind her effort to jump, which could dislodge the tread they were currently on. Or he could lift her, but their combined weight could also dislodge it.

Lifting her was the best solution. He was certain he could toss her safely up to the landing before he found himself slipping through a hole and breaking a leg or plummeting through the stairs altogether to the floor beneath. All in a day's work for someone who'd dug muddy, slimy trenches in torrential rain while serving as a soldier in Spain.

He tested the tread once more. It seemed to be holding, although it wobbled more than he would have preferred.

"Let go of my hand," he said.

"What? No!" she exclaimed.

"I'm going to lift you to the landing," Lucas explained. He should have been more specific in his instructions—especially considering the handrail was in as bad a shape as the rest of the stairs. "Simple as can be. Think of it as me lifting you up to sit on Hector's back."

"It suddenly dawns on me," she said, now squeezing his hand for dear life, "that we may reach the next floor and then not be able to come back down afterward."

At that moment, another loose piece of tread fell with a clatter. Her hand jerked in his.

"Not to worry; Artie will rescue us," Lucas said. Lucas grinned at her, hoping he'd allayed her fears.

Her eyes widened in response to his absurd words—and then it happened.

She squeaked.

The squeak turned into a giggle and then a full-throated laugh. She still clutched his hand, but he used her laughter as an opportunity for action. While laughing himself, he wrenched his hand free and grabbed her waist, turning her laugh into a shriek, and swung her up to the upper floor landing, where she tumbled into a heap on the dusty floor. Then he jumped over the last few stairs to join her on the landing, although he tripped over her foot as he did so and fell in a sprawling heap on top of her.

Pushing himself up with his arms, still laughing, he looked down at her. The tumble had knocked her bonnet askew, loosening her hair in such a way as to create a riot of red curls about her face. Her cheeks were pink, her eyes luminous, and she was altogether lovely . . .

Her laughter faltered.

"Goodness me!" a resonant voice exclaimed, echoing off the walls and through Lucas's brain.

It always amazed him that such a voice belonged to a petite elderly woman. He quickly rolled away from Lavinia and rose to his feet, still feeling rather dazed from the close proximity of Lavinia's enticing face.

"Delia!" Lavinia sat up, and Lucas assisted her to her feet, shaking his head to clear it. "Mr. Jennings and I have been inspecting the farmhouse and had a bit of a spill when taking the stairs." She brushed her hair from her face and then gave up and removed her bonnet, causing the rest of her curls to tumble down her back.

"If you say so." Miss Weston stood—more like struck a pose—just inside the doorway, and Lucas got the distinct impression that it was more for show than concern over what she'd observed—not that it had been anything but an accidental spill, Lucas reminded himself. He had not accosted Lavinia, nor had she made any overtures toward him.

Mr. Drake's head popped around the doorjamb, and then he came in to take his place next to Miss Weston.

"And now we shall inspect the upper floor," Lavinia announced in an authoritative tone. "I hope we're able to descend the stairs a little more gracefully than we ascended them just now," she added jauntily.

"I shall save you if that is the case," Mr. Drake said cheerily. "I'm sure there's a ladder or a rope around here somewhere that can be put to use."

"I told you so," Lucas murmured so only Lavinia could hear.

Lavinia threw her hand over her mouth to stifle her laughter and looked straight at Lucas. He coughed, trying to cover his own laughter. It was no use; they both failed, laughing until tears were running down their faces.

"I say, what's so funny?" the old man asked indignantly.

Hannah stomped into the entry hall at that moment. "It's a fine mess we're in to be sure, Livvy," she said, unaware of what had gone on before. "The coachman's wondering if he's to leave us here or take us elsewhere, considering the state of things. He's hankering to be on his way and wanting to be paid too. I'm not keen to see him take that carriage and leave us here, what with the house not exactly fit for human habitation."

That was quite a speech coming from Hannah Broome. Lucas wasn't sure he'd heard her sling that many words together at one time before. She was right though. Decisions needed to be made, and quickly.

Lavinia dabbed at her eyes, all the humor draining from her face. "True enough," she said. "Tell him I shall be along shortly."

She and Lucas quickly assessed the upstairs rooms, consisting of what originally would have been four bedrooms of varying sizes and a linen closet. They were empty and dirty, with several broken windows, and had been subjected to the elements in areas where the roof was missing. Fortunately, the rot wasn't beyond repair, which indicated the roof had developed holes only in the last year or two. It was a small blessing, but a blessing nonetheless.

Since Lucas was now familiar with which treads on the stairway were the most stable, he was able to maneuver himself partway down and then lift Lavinia over the trouble spots more easily. Mr. Drake's rescue was not needed after all.

Lavinia gathered her little band of travelers together in the main hallway while Mr. Grimes and Garrick lurked just outside the door, waiting for instructions. Drake had located an unbroken chair somewhere, and Miss Weston now sat in it. Lucas stood to the side of the room in the role of observer, allowing Lavinia to take charge. This was her affair to manage, not his.

"There's no reason to beat around the bush, my dears," she began. "It is entirely apparent that the house is not habitable, although nothing about the farm's current state was mentioned in the letter. I am dreadfully sorry I didn't think to find out more about Primrose Farm before we set out, only to face disappointment like this. If we'd stayed in London—"

"If we'd stayed in London, you'd still be battling old Hinchcliffe and fighting off Lord—"

"Hannah!" Lavinia said sharply, cutting her off. Lucas wondered again who this Hinchcliffe character was and what hold he had on Lavinia. And now Hannah had let slip that there was also a Lord Somebody-or-Other Lavinia had been fighting *off*. As in advances.

Lucas's blood heated with annoyance.

"Nonetheless," Lavinia continued before Hannah could say more. "We did leave London, and we are here now. We shall simply have to return north to Sleaford and take rooms until the farmhouse can be made habitable. I don't see any other solution. I shall hire laborers as soon as I can. One step at a time and we'll get there eventually." She looked around for agreement.

"Back the way we came, then, it seems," Miss Weston said, her frail shoulders collapsing in on themselves for the merest moment before straightening again. Miss Weston had struck the perfect balance of abjectness and resolve with her statement, Lucas thought abstractedly, arousing sympathy without adding to Lavinia's guilt. It had been a subtle yet artful performance, managed in the uttering of one sentence.

"Beggin' your pardon, Miss Fernley." Mr. Grimes stepped fully into the hallway. "I couldn't help but overhear the conversation. I'd like to remind you that our arrangement was for me to bring you here and for me to continue on my way south from here back to London. If you're planning to return north to Sleaford, we'll need to discuss things a bit."

"Yes, of course. I understand fully."

"I wish we'd thought to bring sandwiches," Mr. Drake said. "I'm feeling a bit peckish all of a sudden."

"I *did* bring sandwiches, Artie," Lavinia said. "And cheese and apples and jars of lemonade and water as well. I may not have had the foresight to realize the farmhouse would be in such a state, but I at least assumed there might not be a hostelry nearby to provide us with luncheon." The clenched fist she was hiding behind her skirts during her speech told Lucas she was nearing her wits' end, and he had to admire how well she maintained her composure and smooth tone so far. "Hannah," she continued, "I'm sure Mr. Grimes or his associate would be kind enough to help you fetch the basket from the back of the coach, as there is plenty of food for all. And after we've had the opportunity to eat, Mr. Grimes, we can discuss our travel arrangements, if that agrees with you."

"Aye, ma'am, it does, and thank you."

"I think we must avail ourselves of whatever stairs or floors suit our personal fancy. It shall be a picnic."

"Oh, how I adore a picnic!" Miss Weston said, clapping her hands at her breast.

"We'll be right back, then." Grimes tipped his cap and followed Hannah out the door.

Lucas suddenly had an inspiration—a thought that should have occurred to him sooner. But it hadn't dawned on him until this very moment, when the acuteness of his newfound friends' situation had become blatantly obvious. "If you would excuse Lavinia and me for a moment," he said to Miss Weston and Mr. Drake. "I wish to speak to her privately."

"You don't intend any more of that naughtiness I caught you at earlier," Miss Weston said with a shake of her finger.

"Delia!" Lavinia exclaimed. "There was no naughtiness. I fell and tripped Mr. Jennings in the process. Completely innocent."

Miss Weston, however, was looking at Lucas like a cat that had trapped a mouse. "It is as she said, Miss Weston," he replied as evenly as he could.

"If you say so," she said again, arching an eyebrow.

He was not going to convince the old woman of anything, so he gave up trying. He took Lavinia by the elbow and led her to the kitchen and away from listening ears.

"You mustn't put too much stock in Delia's comments," she said. "She can be fanciful at times."

"She has a vivid imagination," he said. And yet there *had* been that distinct moment of connection during their mishap that might have been discerned by the woman. "That is not why I want to speak with you though." He looked her fully in the eye. "Lavinia, I realize I have no right to interfere in your life. But as a bystander who has inadvertently fallen headlong into your affairs and as a gentleman trained from birth to help a lady in need, I would like to offer my assistance—"

"I am not a lady in need, Lucas," she said, interrupting him. "I have resources, and I am perfectly capable of taking care of myself and the others."

"Assistance with temporary lodgings, then, as I was about to say if you had allowed me to finish my sentence." Regardless of her words to the contrary, she *was* in need. "You have unlimited resources, then, do you? The money to lease rooms indefinitely while your farm of two hundred acres is restored and producing once again? The expertise to do this as quickly and efficiently as possible?"

She looked away.

"Lavinia," he said, gentling his tone. "You pressed me into service when you leapt upon me and called me husband. Do not refuse my help now when I offer it freely to you and your friends. Listen for a moment. I have a solution to the immediate problem of lodging—at the very least a temporary solution that will give you the time you need to make further plans."

She studied him intently, her expression a blend of curiosity and skepticism. But she hadn't silenced him, so he continued. "Primrose Farm is not far from my ancestral home, where I was intending to go before chance brought the two of us together, as you already know. In fact, we are at least as close to Alderwood in the south as we are to Sleaford in the north. We should be able to make it there within an hour or two. It is also in the direction Grimes already wants to travel on his return to London, heading south back to Stamford. He will not have to double back to the north and then south following the way we came, wasting his time and your money putting in extra miles. It works best for everyone."

"Everyone except your family, who are not expecting us," she countered. "We cannot simply show up there and expect a place to stay. We would be a huge imposition."

Alderwood wasn't the largest of estates and didn't have the most expansive manor house. And if all of Lucas's siblings and their families had gathered for his return, there would be little spare room available. There was no way to know. Regardless, he couldn't abandon Lavinia in an unfamiliar part of the country with only Miss Broome to assist her in herding Miss Weston and Mr. Drake about while she commenced restoring her farm.

"My family will be delighted to receive you all," he assured her, hoping it wasn't an outright lie. "Besides, my father is a landowner with connections throughout the county. Mr. Finch, his steward, has been with the family for years. I'm completely confident they would be willing to help, and their expertise will be invaluable as you make your plans."

She heaved a sigh. "Accompanying you to Alderwood is not what I would prefer to do, and yet I will concede that your reasoning is sound. As regarding the state of Primrose Farm, I admit I am out of my depths. Very well. We shall accompany you to Alderwood—for a brief stay, and only if I can see for myself that it is no imposition."

"Excellent." Lucas was surprisingly relieved that she'd agreed to his suggestion, not realizing until that moment he hadn't been looking forward to bidding her, or her friends, farewell.

"But, Lucas, I can't arrive at Alderwood looking like this. My dress is covered in dust and filth of a sort I don't wish to analyze too closely. My hair's a fright—"

"It appears we are both in need of some freshening up." He glanced at her traveling gown and then his own clothes. "I propose we continue south and take a room when we reach the town of Bourne so we can all make ourselves more presentable. How would that make you feel?"

"Better, thank you. If you're sure we won't be a bother . . ."

He belatedly wondered what effect Lavinia's arrival at Alderwood might have on his family. He was certain his newfound friends were actors, although he had yet to confront Lavinia about it. Bringing actors—who, in general, were considered to be of questionable morals and low social standing—as guests to his family home was highly scandalous. His parents were good, pious people, as was his brother Isaac, the vicar, and most of his other siblings as well.

It was too late now. His heart and good intentions had once again leapt before he'd thought through all the ramifications. But he couldn't be any sorrier now than he'd been when he'd stayed behind with a badly wounded Anthony in Badajoz after the bitter siege there had ended. His new friends' theatrical past would simply have to stay hidden.

"It's settled, then," he said. "Let's return to the others and inform them of the plan."

* * *

Lavinia spent the time they rode toward Bourne contemplating her farm, her finances, and her fellow travelers, and she came to the dispiriting conclusion that she'd been reckless. She'd been so intent on leaving Drury Lane and her life as Ruby Chadwick behind that she'd neglected significant matters that should have been obvious and had put her friends in a vulnerable position.

She twisted the ruby ring on her finger, the ring that never left her finger in public. Oh, but she wished the ring and its matching necklace and earbobs were made of real rubies rather than paste. She would sell them in a heartbeat. She had absolutely no idea what the costs of restoring Primrose Farm would be. It could potentially deplete most, if not all, of her savings.

They secured a room in Bourne, and she and Delia freshened up, with Lavinia taking extra care to make sure her appearance was demure and untheatrical. "The lord and lady won't have any interest in me," Hannah said, insisting on using the hour they were there to assist Lavinia and Delia with their dressing and grooming. "I look like a servant because that is what I am."

All too soon, they were back in the coach and on their way to Alderwood, where she would be introduced to Lucas's parents, the Viscount and Viscountess Thurlby.

"I shall tell these people I am your long-lost grandmama," Delia proclaimed. She'd long since recovered from her fainting spell at the farmhouse and had donned a light gray gown, her fluffy white hair twisted as best as possible into a topknot. She looked, as she always did, like someone's fairy godmother. "You're already like a grandchild to me, Livvy dear, if I'd ever had children who could give them to me. I shall say you and I were reunited in London after the death of your poor papa."

"And I shall be your father's loyal valet, who stayed by to protect you and the other ladies with my presence," Artie added. "I play the faithful servant very convincingly, I believe."

"You play the faithful friend excellently too, Arthur," Delia said. "You were a wonderful Horatio. I never saw a performance so moving." She dabbed at her eye with her handkerchief for effect.

Artie bowed his head in humble acknowledgment of her words, laying a hand on his heart. "That is a greatest of compliments, Delia, and I shall hold it close to my breast until my dying day," he said.

"You always have such enthusiasm for whatever roles you play," Lavinia said, interrupting their bout of mutual admiration. "However, a truthful approach is best, for all our sakes. To wit: Hannah has been my nurse since the loss of my mother, which is true. And you and Artie are longtime associates of my father and are my dear friends, which is also true. It is what we told Lucas, and it will suffice for his family, until we can make other arrangements for lodging." She tried not to think of the cost involved in taking rooms for them all and wished she had a better idea of how long it would take to get the farmhouse habitable.

"What if they ask, Livvy?" Artie asked. "What then? What are we to say? Our characters need a history."

"We aren't *characters*, Artie. We are who we are," Lavinia said. *But who is the real Lavinia Fernley?* she asked herself. She wished she knew. She was tired of playing roles, both on stage and in real life. "Turn the conversation away from the past, if possible. For example, I became acquainted with Lucas in London, and he invited us to his home for a visit. I won't tell them it was barely three days ago when we met."

"Ah, I see. I shall say you are a dear girl and *like* a granddaughter to me, then," Delia said with a nod. "That is the truth too, after all."

"And I am here as a family friend and gentleman escort to you ladies, providing aid and protection," Artie said, straightening in his seat. "That is true too."

Lavinia looked over at Hannah, who rolled her eyes. Lavinia turned to look out the window and bit her lip so as not to insult Artie's masculine pride.

From beyond the window, she could see Lucas on his horse, his face like granite. Studying faces came naturally to Lavinia—it had helped her hone her craft as an actress. She studied Lucas more closely. What would cause him to have such an implacable countenance, growing even more so the closer they got to Alderwood? He'd not hinted at bad relations with his family. He'd described them to her as hospitable and friendly.

What if they were anything but?

She looked away, her heart pounding as though it was an opening night at the theater. She tugged at her gloves and smoothed her burgundy skirt, then checked to make sure the ribbons of her bonnet were snug and arranged in a becoming style beneath her chin.

"You're fidgeting, luv," Hannah said.

Lavinia immediately folded her hands into her lap. It was ironic, really. She, The Darling of Drury Lane, who'd been hailed and applauded by London's elite, was terrified to be presented to Lucas's family—because they were a *normal* family.

And more than anything, she wanted to be normal.

Out the window, Lucas suddenly reined Hector to a halt and pointed. "There," he called. "Just beyond the trees. Alderwood."

Lavinia closed her eyes briefly to collect her wits before looking out the window to see his family seat.

"Oh," she breathed. Alderwood was a solid, two-story structure built of stone with cultivated gardens Lavinia could just make out through the trees. She'd driven past many stately homes in her travels with the theater troupe, and she was always struck by their size, the magnificent grounds, and her smallness next to them by comparison.

The coach, with Lucas leading the way, turned off the road to head down Alderwood's private avenue, bordered on either side by hedgerows. Long before she was ready, the coach slowed to a stop at the main entrance, and Lucas opened the door and set the steps in place. Lavinia descended first, her gloved hand in his. His face still looked like granite, but his lips were curved slightly at the corners in what might almost be considered a smile. It wasn't the most promising of sights, and Lavinia's pulse sped up again.

"Welcome to Alderwood," he said as Garrick arrived to assist Delia and Hannah from the coach.

The front doors blew open, and a young female burst through and down the steps toward them. "Lucas! Is that you? Oh, it *is* you! Finally, *finally* you are here!"

The girl, who looked to be about eighteen, flung herself into Lucas's arms and buried her head against his broad chest. "Oh, Lucas, how I've missed you!" Tears streamed down her cheeks.

"Rebecca," Lucas said simply, resting his head on hers and wrapping his arms around her, holding her close.

It was a sweet reunion between brother and sister, and Lavinia's heart ached. How would it feel to have a brother or sister and share a love like that?

Three other people came through the front doors and approached them. Two of them, a tall, lanky man of middle years and a short, plump woman,

Lavinia presumed correctly to be the Viscount and Viscountess Thurlby, Lucas's parents.

"Mama, Father," Lucas said, embracing his mother and shaking his father's hand as Rebecca moved to the side and dabbed at her cheeks with her handkerchief. "It's good to be home."

The other individual was a lady Lavinia guessed to be about her own age or slightly older. She was slender and graceful in her movements and perfectly poised—the epitome of what a young lady of quality should be. Her blonde hair was elegantly coiffed, her face a perfect oval. She was truly the perfect English rose.

When the English rose's eyes fell on Lucas, her expression changed to one of deep emotion. She moved closer and offered him her hand, which he bent over. "Lucas, dear brother," she breathed. "It has been so long. Welcome home."

"Thank you, Isobel," he said.

The woman had called Lucas her dear brother, and yet her eyes had been luminous with something that clearly spoke of a relationship different from what Lavinia had just observed between Rebecca and him.

Lucas stepped back from Isobel, his face once again like granite.

"You have brought guests with you," his mother said. "We did not anticipate you would be traveling in company with others, but if you are friends of my long-lost son, you are welcome here. Lucas, would you please make the introductions?"

"Of course, Mama," Lucas said with a tight smile. "Allow me to present Miss Delia Weston, Miss Hannah Broome, and Mr. Arthur Drake."

Artie made a deep theatrical bow, and the women each dropped into curtsies, with Delia curtsying so low Lavinia was afraid her knees would lock and she wouldn't be able to get up again without assistance. Lavinia was going to have to remind her and Artie once again to be subtler in their manners.

All eyes had turned to her now, and Lavinia felt a hum of expectation rise amongst them that was similar to what she had experienced each time she'd left her theatre dressing room to meet her admirers—except these people were not her admirers, and there was a look of outright disdain on Isobel's face.

Lucas's face was so rigid Lavinia was afraid it might crack. He looked from his mother to his father to Lavinia to Isobel and back to Lavinia. Lavinia hardly dared breathe, so intense was his gaze. And then it was as though the air shifted. Something in his eyes changed—a look of epiphany and defiance.

Lavinia stopped breathing altogether.

He extended his hand to her, taking hers in his own. "Mama, Father, Rebecca . . . Isobel," he said. "It is my great pleasure to present Miss Lavinia Fernley, my betrothed."

Chapter 10

It seemed to Lucas that the earth actually stood still—like the suspension of time a soldier experiences before pulling the trigger immediately following the command to fire. It lasted less than a fraction of a second, this stopping of time, and then Lavinia transformed before his eyes into a new Lavinia, a Lavinia who was his betrothed.

She was always a wonder to behold, with her radiant hair and arresting looks. He never tired of looking at her. She couldn't help but draw attention by simply being *her* wherever she went. But there, right before his eyes, her back straightened a bit more, her chin tilted slightly upward, and her mouth curved into the most poised smile he'd ever seen.

She hadn't looked at him in shock or given away his falsehood. Neither had her friends. Hannah had already assumed the role of servant and had retreated into the background. Mr. Drake stood stoically by, as though making such a pronouncement as Lucas had done was a daily occurrence. Miss Weston was smiling beatifically.

On the other hand, his mother's mouth was uncharacteristically open, his father's eyebrows had risen nearly to his receding hairline, Rebecca looked about to burst, and Isobel had gone pale.

All this happened in but a matter of seconds, although it seemed a lifetime to Lucas. He continued the introductions. "Lavinia, dearest, may I present my parents, the Viscount and Viscountess of Thurlby, my sister Rebecca, and my eldest brother, Thomas's, wife, Isobel."

Lavinia dropped into an elegant bow worthy of the court of the Prince Regent.

And the earth began moving again.

Rebecca squealed and dashed to Lavinia, giving her a bone-crushing hug and exclaiming how happy she was to be getting another sister while

Lucas's mother took his hands in her own and received his kiss. His father came forward to shake his hand and then bow over Lavinia's.

"We knew it was a match made in heaven," Lucas heard Miss Weston saying to his mother. "Did we not, Arthur?"

"Oh, indeed, indeed," Mr. Drake said, winking.

"It appears we have much to discuss," his mother said diplomatically, although if Lucas was to go by her countenance, he suspected the discussion would be a private one between him and his parents and could potentially occur at a rather high pitch. "You could have at least mentioned her in one of your letters," she added in a low voice for Lucas's ears only. "I feel rather thunderstruck."

His father's brows had nearly returned to their normal position on his forehead, which was a good sign, although he'd also gone somewhat serious after Lucas's announcement, which was not. "Lucas, if you'll point the coachman in the direction of the stables so Martin can see to their needs," his father said evenly.

"Certainly, Father."

"Come inside, Miss Fernley," Mama said, "and your traveling companions, of course, so you may rest and we can get better acquainted. Isobel, if you'd be so kind as to ring for tea. Rebecca, let the rest of the family know Lucas is home and we have visitors. They will want to meet their brother's . . . betrothed. This way, everyone. Miss Fernley." She led the way inside, the others following close behind.

Lucas took a deep breath and brought up the rear.

He'd done it.

The son who'd left university to enlist and had no wife and no career had not faced his family empty-handed after all; he had not arrived home with nothing to show for himself.

He'd presented his parents with something—something quite impressive, in fact. He'd arrived with a bride in tow—a spectacularly beautiful bride. It was all a big lie, of course, but he'd deal with that later.

Best of all, Lavinia and the others had followed his lead. Well, Lavinia would—she'd pulled the same trick on him at the White Horse in London just a few days earlier, and he hadn't even known her at the time. He'd followed her lead then, hadn't he? Of course, she would follow his lead—they all would.

Isobel, he'd noticed, had gone pale and utterly still when he'd made his announcement. What had she expected would happen when he finally returned home? That she would ignore what they'd shared and the unspoken attachment they'd formed before she'd gone and married Thomas and then expect Lucas would simply remain her forlorn admirer?

No, he would not be sorry he'd done this.

His father fell in step next to him as his mother herded the others toward the drawing room. "Welcome home, son," he said. "It's past time you returned to the bosom of your family. Your mother in particular felt great anxiety after you traipsed off to war, taking the King's shilling in Spain. It is good to have you with us again at last."

"I'm truly sorry for any worry I may have caused Mama, Father. I am one of the fortunate ones. Many mothers lost and are continuing to lose sons in the fight against Napoleon." It had been a close call for him on more than one occasion. "I'm here now at least, although I cannot say for how long. I must find the means to support myself."

"Yourself *and* a family," his father added. "As you apparently have found a bride-to-be." He was studying Lucas closely as he spoke those words.

"Indeed, Father, although we have yet to discuss a date for the marriage. It was important to return home and spend time with my family first."

"Quite prudent of you both, I must say." They stood next to the drawing room door while his mother led Lavinia to a small sofa and the others took the remaining available seats in the room. "She has quite dramatic coloring, does she not? Not the run-of-the-mill English beauty at all."

"Indeed."

"One might wonder where the two of you became acquainted. But I suppose London has a greater variety of young ladies from which to choose a bride than we do here in our modest little corner of Lincolnshire."

"I believe Lavinia would be considered a rare beauty even in London, Father. I feel very fortunate."

"I'm sure you do."

The arrival of Lucas's elder brothers, Thomas and Isaac; Isaac's wife, Clara; and their sister Susan interrupted them.

"Lucas!" Isaac cried, shaking Lucas's hand before pulling him in for a brotherly hug. "I was just telling Clara this morning that my faith was foundering on whether you'd actually arrive here before the week was up and we must return to the vicarage. No sooner spoken than proven wrong, by George!"

"Clara, you are a sight for sore eyes," Lucas said. "I hope you've been able to keep my brother sufficiently on the straight and narrow," he added jokingly.

"Considering he's the vicar, it hasn't been too much of a strain," she bantered back.

"It's about time you returned," Susan said in a low, slightly bored voice as he leaned in to kiss her offered cheek. "As you can see, I have long needed someone with whom to have a sensible conversation. I hope you have exhilarating stories of war and intrigue to share and gossip from Town to make me laugh."

Clara jabbed her good-naturedly with her elbow.

"I shall do my best," Lucas said, smiling.

"That is all one can ask."

Susan was just older than Lucas, and Isaac just older than Susan. As children, the three of them had been inseparable, and he'd missed them, he realized.

Thomas, the eldest, stood apart from the others, appearing aloof and much more serious than he'd been the last time Lucas had seen him. "Thomas," Lucas said after greeting the others. "It's good to see you."

"It is time you were home, Lucas. Past time," Thomas said.

"It appears you have brought guests with you," Susan said after peering into the drawing room. "Ah, and tea has arrived for us all. Excellent; I'm parched. You must introduce us to your friends, Lucas. They look . . . enchanting." She bit her lip to hide an amused smile.

He could only imagine what thoughts Susan might already entertain about Lavinia and her entourage, and under other circumstances, he might have found it amusing to hear her impressions, but not today. "I would be delighted to introduce you, Susan. Come with me, all of you, if you please."

They joined the others in the sitting room, and Lucas watched the faces of his siblings as he made the introductions. Isaac's eyes were as wide as saucers when Lucas introduced Lavinia as his betrothed, although he was polite enough, as was Clara. Thomas's eyes narrowed slightly before glancing at his wife to assess her reaction.

Susan, on the other hand, grinned widely. "Miss Fernley—Lavinia— *may* I call you Lavinia?—I believe we are going to become fast friends. I can feel it."

Lavinia smiled warmly, although Lucas had gotten to know her well enough in the past few days to detect a glint in her eye. "I think you are right . . . *Susan*," she replied. Lucas took a sip of his tea to hide a chuckle. His wily sister had asked to call Lavinia by her Christian name but hadn't offered the same courtesy in return. The redheaded minx hadn't let her get away with it.

Susan, for her part, turned back to Lucas. "Fast friends, indeed," she murmured and sipped her tea.

"Miss Weston, would you care for another tea cake?" his mother asked. "Mr. Drake?"

"I would, by all means," Mr. Drake said. "'What nourishes me destroys me.'"

His mother looked alarmed as she placed the cake on his plate. "Are you feeling unwell, Mr. Drake?"

"Not at all, ma'am, I assure you. I say, 'What nourishes me destroys me,' for I could simply die of bliss at its deliciousness."

"Marlowe," Miss Weston said. "Well done, Arthur. He was quoting Christopher Marlowe, you see, to express his enjoyment of your tea cakes, Lady Thurlby. I quite agree with him."

"What a relief." Lucas's mother said as she placed another cake on Miss Weston's plate. "Miss Broome?"

"No, thank you, ma'am." Miss Broome sat, looking like a fish out of water, her feet planted next to each other, her back straight, her hands clutching her cup and saucer.

"Such a lovely family you have, Lady Thurlby," Miss Weston said after she dabbed at some crumbs speckling her chin. "Family is a wonderful blessing, is it not? We were brokenhearted for our dear Lavinia when she lost her mother . . ." Miss Weston trailed off sadly.

Lavinia shot Miss Weston a glance and surreptitiously shook her head at her.

"Oh, Miss Fernley, how dreadful for you. I'm so sorry," his mother exclaimed.

Lavinia opened her mouth to speak—

"So you can imagine our distress," Miss Weston said, "when our dear, *dear* cousin lost her father too, and such tragic circumstances they were. But perhaps those particular details would be better shared on another occasion. Today is a day of reunion and celebration, after all."

Lavinia choked on her tea and set her saucer down, coughing.

"Are you all right, dear?" Miss Weston asked.

Lavinia glared at Miss Weston over the napkin pressed to her mouth as she continued to cough.

One wouldn't think a woman of advanced years would be inclined to stir things up, Lucas mused, but then, one would be forgetting it was Miss Weston one was talking about, who had already proven to be the unpredictable sort ever since she'd marched into his room while he was bathing.

Mr. Drake took up the reins now. "And so Delia and I and Hannah, of course, who has been our dear cousin Lavinia's nurse and companion all these years—have made it our calling to take care of our sweet girl since the loss of her parents, may they rest in peace." Mr. Drake raised his eyes toward heaven—Lucas didn't think Isaac the vicar could pull off such a look of piety—before casting his gaze serenely at the other persons present in the room.

"For that is what a family does, does it not?" Miss Weston said.

"Indeed," his mother said. "Well, we are certainly happy to have Miss Fernley and you all as our guests. Perhaps, now that you've had refreshment, you'd like to be seen to your rooms so you may settle in and rest for a while. Miss Fernley, may I rejoin you here in an hour's time so we can get better acquainted? It isn't every day a woman learns she is to be blessed with another daughter."

"Thank you, Lady Thurlby," Lavinia managed to croak, still suffering the effects of choking on her tea.

Lucas heaved a sigh of relief. They were dismissed—for now. And then a low voice spoke behind him.

"Lucas," his father said, "join me in my study, please."

* * *

"Cousins?" Lavinia said in a low, albeit piercing voice once she was alone with Delia, Artie, and Hannah in her assigned suite of rooms, consisting of a small sitting room and bedroom. She suspected it was one of the Jennings sisters' rooms and had been given to her as Lucas's "betrothed." "*Cousins?* What happened to staying as close to the truth as possible?"

"It didn't seem right, you having no family when there were so many of them," Delia explained unapologetically. "Besides, Lucas started it by announcing you as his betrothed. If you're going to be angry, you should be angry with him too."

"I *am* angry with him," Lavinia said. She refused to see the parallel of what he'd just done to what she'd done at the White Horse. That had been a roomful of strangers and had been intended only as a simple ruse for escaping. No one would have cared or remembered once they were gone—barring the possible exception of the Earl of Cosgrove's friends. Hopefully they'd been drunk enough to forget the incident.

What Lucas had done today was *not even close* to the same thing.

"Besides, Livvy, we *are* your cousins; I'm sure of it," Artie added. "We are undoubtedly related through some tiny distant branch on your family tree. There is such a strong theatrical connection, you see; it must be in the blood."

"Yes, well, if we go all the way back to Adam, I'm sure we'd find something," Lavinia retorted. "And you said I lost my mother, Delia, as though she died. She *left* us. *Left*. I have no idea who or where she is. Another untruth."

"Not at all, Lavinia. You lost your mother," Delia replied. "I cannot help it if they presumed she passed away. Isn't language a beautiful, artful thing?"

"Indeed, Delia," Artie piped up again. "As the Bard once said—"

"*Enough* of quoting Shakespeare, Artie! Enough of Marlowe and anyone else you intend to dredge up. We are not cousins, nor am I betrothed to Lucas—"

"A pity, that," Delia said with a sigh.

Lavinia fought for patience. "We are supposed to be starting a new life—no longer actors but *normal* people. *Normal!* And yet, what is the first thing that happens when we arrive here? We are *acting* again. Pretending we are family and I am Lucas's betrothed."

"That's Mr. Jennings's fault, luv," Hannah said.

"Truth be told, Livvy, I'd rather be here under the pretext of being your doting cousin than a friend of your father's," Artie said. "I never liked the man all that much."

Delia nodded in agreement. "Nor I. Artie's right, Livvy; you must see that. And don't worry; we are *consummate* actors, as you know, and will have them convinced of our familial attachment to you with no effort whatsoever on our parts."

Lavinia buried her face in her hands. "If I am to face his mother in one hour's time, I think I'd better lie down," she mumbled. "I'm going to need all the strength I can muster to get through that conversation convincingly. And then I am going to find Lucas and give him a piece of my mind."

Chapter 11

LUCAS WASN'T SURPRISED TO SEE that Isaac and Thomas had joined his father and him in the study.

Thomas immediately went to a side table and poured himself a healthy measure of brandy. "Anyone else interested?" he asked. No one was, so he replaced the stopper of the decanter and took a seat in one of the leather chairs near the fireplace.

"It is good to have you back home, Lucas," his father began after they were all seated. "Your brothers and I have a keen interest to hear about your experiences fighting Napoleon, but those are not topics for the tender ears of our ladies. Perhaps we should have allowed you some time at home before having this conversation. But I think it is altogether better that we discuss things now and put our questions to rest."

"We are anxious to know whether our brother returns to us whole," Isaac said.

"There have been others in the district who have returned to their families but are no longer . . . themselves," Thomas added. "That knowledge has had us concerned for your well-being. And when you were reluctant to return to Alderwood—"

"You feared the worst," Lucas said.

"We were *hopeful* you were well," his father corrected. "But we could not be certain until we saw you for ourselves."

"And now?"

"I am still hopeful," his father said.

"What can you tell us?" Isaac said. "I ask, not only to assure myself as your brother, but also as your vicar and spiritual advisor. I wish to be of service to you, if needed."

"Thank you, Isaac, but truly, I am well enough. Each man's experience is his own, and he must reconcile it within himself the best he can. Those who cannot reconcile it deserve compassion and support. No one who experiences war firsthand comes out of it unscathed. It changes him—and her—for better or for worse."

He stood and wandered over to the table with the decanter. He removed the stopper and sniffed the contents. Drink had deadened many of his friends' anguish, but Lucas himself had not found it effective. "We may speak at length about the honor of fighting for one's country and the glories that come with victory, but honor and glory come at great cost to the soldier. There is a brutality—" Lucas stopped speaking and replaced the stopper. Outside the study window, birds were singing. The sound seemed ludicrous.

"There is a brutality I would not wish to impart on any of you, for even to speak of it gives it continued life. Suffice it to say, I did my utmost to sustain life in the midst of so much suffering and death. I was blessed to find a friend in Lord Halford early on. We kept each other alive and in relatively good spirits for seven years. And when he was gravely wounded, I felt a need and obligation to stay at his side until I got him safely back to England and was assured of his continuing health."

"At the expense of your own family's concern for you," Thomas said.

"I knew I was well enough, Thomas, and I had been informed through letters that my family was well enough too. Should you have had me leave my friend and fellow soldier under such circumstances? Do you take issue with my judgment in the matter?"

"Of course, we don't," his father said. "Come, sit down, Lucas. We are merely trying to understand and assure ourselves."

"You are different," Thomas said.

"As are you," Lucas replied. "But then one would expect change after the course of seven years." He briefly fought temptation within himself and lost. "How is Isobel? She looks in good health." He shouldn't have asked or even spoken her name aloud. Thomas had learned of Lucas and Isobel's attachment after the nuptials, when Lucas had announced his enlistment in the army and the reason for it had become apparent.

"She is, thank you," Thomas said.

"And Clara, Isaac?" Lucas asked, hoping to cover his lack of discretion.

"Clara is quite well, although somewhat peaked these days. She is increasing again. Our fifth child."

"Four children already and another on the way. You're building nearly as big a brood as Mama and Father did."

"God willing," Isaac said. "The children are with Thomas and Isobel's two up in the nursery."

"Now that you have assured us that you are well," his father said, "perhaps you can enlighten us regarding your friends, among whom is a young lady you referred to as your betrothed."

Three pairs of nearly identical eyes looked fixedly at him, awaiting his response. Lucas's neckcloth suddenly felt tight, but he resisted the urge to tug at it.

"I am the luckiest of men to have had Lavinia accept my proposal of marriage," he began. "We met in London." He'd been in London for a few months now—plenty of time to meet a young lady, court her, and propose.

"Your letters to your mother never mentioned her," his father said.

"What man writes to his mother of such things?" Lucas responded.

"Good point," Isaac said. "I didn't write to Mama about Clara either."

"I was here at home when I proposed to Isobel and she accepted," Thomas said, "so I wouldn't know."

"What more can you tell us about her?" his father asked.

"She recently inherited a farm of two hundred acres."

"An heiress, eh?" His father nodded. "Well, that is something, at least. Land is always a valuable asset."

"Land is an asset when it's thriving and profitable, Father. Unfortunately, the farm has not been maintained the past few years, and there is a great deal of work to be done, so I shouldn't think of her as an heiress in the typical sense, and I didn't propose marriage to her based on that anyway."

"It would seem she has plenty of other assets from which to choose," Thomas said.

"Thomas," Father said reprovingly.

"Have a care, Thomas," Lucas warned, feeling protective and surprisingly possessive of Lavinia. "I have an affection for the lady."

"My apologies." Thomas stood and moved to lean against the fireplace mantel.

"But Thomas's comments raise an important concern, Lucas, if I may be allowed to speak freely on the matter," Isaac said.

Lucas waved his hand. "Fire away."

"Thomas's words illustrate something you must be prepared to deal with if you marry the lady." Isaac paused before continuing. "How shall I put this? Your Miss Fernley's looks speak more of sinner than of saint."

"She cannot help the features with which she was born, Isaac," Lucas said. "Any more than I can help that you and I—and Father and Thomas, for that matter—are over six feet tall and have varying shades of brown hair."

His father reached over and laid a hand on Lucas's arm. "True enough, son. Of course it is true. But that will not stop men from looking or women from wagging their tongues. And sadly, in our so-called genteel society, many men take mistresses at their whim. Even in marriage, your Miss Fernley may be considered fair play by men of lesser character."

"I understand fully and accept your counsel and thank you for it," Lucas said. "I shall bear it in mind. But I will not have Lavinia feel subjected to such judgment while at Alderwood." He locked eyes with Thomas.

"Of course not," Thomas said and sipped his brandy. "She will be welcomed with open arms. Just not too open, obviously." He set down his empty glass. "If you'll excuse me, I have a meeting with Finch. Duty calls."

"And I must check on Clara," Isaac said. He clasped Lucas's hand. "It's good to have you home at last and see for ourselves that you are well. I, for one, am greatly relieved." He followed Thomas out the door.

Once he and his father were alone, Lucas spoke. "There is one other matter I wish to discuss with you, Father, if I may," he said. "I would ask for your advice regarding Lavinia's farm. It is called Primrose Farm, ten or so miles north of here. Have you heard of it?"

"Primrose Farm." His father's brow furrowed in thought. "The old Harrison place? Haven't thought of it in years. That's hers now, is it?"

"Yes, and nobody has thought about it much, from the looks of it," Lucas said. "It's time someone did."

"I should have taught all my boys something of managing an estate, not just Thomas, despite the fact that I had only one estate and five sons who needed livings. I'll do my best to help you and your Miss Fernley with her farm. We can discuss it further tomorrow, and I'm sure Thomas and Finch would be agreeable to helping as well. In the meantime, however, I suggest you get reacquainted with your ancestral home," his father said, rising to his feet. "Go settle in and rest."

Lucas rose as well. "Thank you, Father. It is truly good to be home at last."

He went to his old room, which felt familiar and strange at the same time. He'd been a mere boy when he'd been here last. He was a man now—a man who'd seen more of the world than he wished.

He lay on his bed and propped his hands behind his head in thought. He still felt indignation on Lavinia's behalf over the comments his father and brothers had made, especially Thomas's ribald ones. Had she been subjected to such judgments her entire life? Had men always viewed her as easy prey? Had women always assumed she was a wanton and a threat? He dearly hoped not—but he also remembered how thunderstruck he himself had been when he'd seen her without her disguise for the first time. He'd had the good fortune of being introduced to her beauty incrementally, but even seeing her today in her burgundy traveling gown with her radiant hair styled atop her head had stopped him in his tracks.

Oh, no, he was not immune to her either.

He also hadn't missed the fact that Miss Weston and Mr. Drake had referred to themselves as her cousins this afternoon, when Lavinia had told him herself that they were associates of her father. Of course, Lucas had lied about his own relationship with Lavinia, so he wasn't about to judge.

It was time he told them he'd figured out that they were actors—Miss Weston and Mr. Drake definitely were, with her dramatic fainting spells and Drake's spouting Shakespeare and Marlowe every other minute. Miss Broome was decidedly *not* an actor; she looked as though she would crack into pieces if anyone looked at her for longer than a minute.

If the older couple were associates of Lavinia's father, it meant he'd been an actor. And if he'd been an actor . . . it was only logical that Lavinia had become one.

When he'd called her his betrothed this afternoon—well, *that* had been a moment to behold. She'd transformed from the Lavinia he'd come to know the past few days into a *lady*, a true lady of genteel birth and training. A remarkable transformation it had been.

Oh, yes, she was definitely an actress too.

He knew well enough that actresses were part of the demimonde. Decent people did not mingle with such individuals. He wondered what his parents—not to mention his vicar of a brother—would think if they were to discover the truth.

Chapter 12

LATER THAT AFTERNOON, LUCAS FOUND Lavinia and his mother in the sitting room on the south side of the house. It had always been his mother's favorite room. It was smaller than the drawing room, with furniture upholstered in a flowery fabric, and large windows that let in the afternoon sun. The conversation he'd interrupted had seemed congenial, even if his mother hadn't seemed quite her normal, effusive self. But at least he didn't sense any tension in the air, which was a good sign.

"Mama, with your permission, I believe I will steal my betrothed away from you for a while. I have scarcely seen her since we arrived at Alderwood, and I would like to show her the grounds. Would you care to join me . . . my dear?" In the nick of time, he thought to add an endearment.

Lavinia smiled at him with such adoration that Lucas's heart nearly stopped, and he very nearly believed what he saw before he remembered she was most likely an actress and was more than capable of playing the part of his betrothed. She was a very good actress, then, as believable as she'd seemed just now.

"I would like nothing better," she said.

"It's been lovely getting to know you better, Lavinia," Mama said. "Perhaps we can continue our conversation later."

"Thank you, Mama," Lucas said.

He offered Lavinia his hand as she rose to her feet, and they bid his mother adieu. Neither of them spoke as they walked; for his part, Lucas wanted to ensure that there were no eavesdroppers in their vicinity before saying anything.

They strolled through the house and outside to his mother's rose garden, and the air was heavy with the pungent fragrance of the summer blooms. He plucked a bud that was just beginning to open and offered it to her.

"Thank you," she said, brushing it softly under her nose before tucking it into the bodice of her dress. "I ought to be giving you a piece of my mind, calling me your betrothed—although it doesn't seem quite fair since it's precisely what I did to you, isn't it?"

"It was a spur-of-the-moment decision," he said. "I had no intention of speaking those words—I hadn't even thought them—and then they were in my mind and out of my mouth just that quickly. I'm sorry, Lavinia. In the meantime . . ." He reached into his pocket and removed a simple gold ring. "This isn't much in the way of betrothal rings, but at least it's not the monstrous thing you're wearing."

Lavinia removed the ruby ring that had been on her finger ever since Lucas had met her. His family would never believe he'd had the means to give her such a ring. Fortunately, it had been hidden under her glove when they'd arrived.

He slipped the gold band onto her finger, which fit well enough and would do for the time being.. "It's not much, but it's mine, and my family will recognize it, at least."

"We are going to have to find a way to end this so-called betrothal without any scandal, you know. I'm not sure how this is to be accomplished, but I feel strongly about it. Your mother has been gracious to me this afternoon. I'm quite sure I'm not what she had in mind when she envisioned you with a wife, but she has been kind and accepting nonetheless. I won't have her being hurt or embarrassed by any of this. And I'm sorry, too, for dragging you into my own troubles. I never intended for you to do more than get me safely out of the public room at the White Horse."

"It sounds like we're even, then."

She looked around her and lifted her face to the sky. "Oh, but it is lovely here, Lucas. Alderwood—well, a considerably smaller version of Alderwood—is what I had envisioned Primrose Farm being. I was terribly wrong on that score."

"Lavinia." He paused to choose his words carefully. "I spoke to my father about the work needed at Primrose Farm. He has offered the assistance of his steward, Finch, and my eldest brother. I thought to show them the farm tomorrow. They have the connections and knowledge that I do not, and it will give us the information we need to proceed with the repairs and restoration."

"I'm going with you, Lucas. Primrose Farm is mine and my responsibility."

"That's true, of course, Lavinia. However, through no fault of your own, my family considers you my betrothed, and, as such, when we marry Primrose Farm will belong to me."

She drew back at his words, as he'd known she would. "But we are not betrothed, Lucas. Primrose Farm is mine, and I must learn what I can if I am going to have any hope of survival, for me and for the others."

Her argument was sound, and Lucas felt guilty for creating this predicament for her. But this was something he could do to help her, and he wanted to help her and allow her respite from her troubles. "Lavinia, we intend to go on horseback. It is faster and will allow us to return sooner, which is better for everyone. You have already seen the farm, so there is no need for you to travel uncomfortably to see it all again when you can relax here with the others. And we wouldn't want to scandalize my father and brother by having my betrothed picking her way through rotting foundations, now, would we?" he joked. "What if I were to promise you that we will wait until we return to discuss our findings so you may be present?"

"Staying here to keep an eye on Delia and Artie is certainly wise," she conceded grumpily. "And I don't want to appear scandalous. My hair is scandalous enough."

He grinned. "Not scandalous. Glorious."

"Says you. Personally, I have discovered over the years that proper English ladies are born with golden hair, like your Isobel—"

"She is not *my* Isobel," he interjected—rather too sharply.

"I see," Lavinia said, and Lucas feared she did. "Golden hair," she continued, "and fair complexion make up the ideal proper English lady. Those features are *unpretentiously* lovely."

"Your hair reminds me of a time when I was in Spain. We were quartered in a small town, Anthony and I and a few of the officers, and we went to a bullfight. A man called a *matador del toro*—it means 'bull slayer'— waves a red cape and encourages the bull to charge at him. I don't know if it is the red color that draws the bull's attention, but it definitely held the attention of the crowd. I think your hair must be like that."

"It sounds like a dangerous dance that ends in the death of the bull and perhaps even the matador," Lavinia said. "I'm not sure I like the analogy, Lucas."

Thomas's earlier comments—and even the cautions from his father and Isaac—suddenly sprang to mind. Fearing he'd distressed her, he changed the subject. "I believe I have solved a puzzle, Lavinia. I have concluded that your Miss Weston and Mr. Drake are actors."

She paused for the barest moment before continuing. "What makes you think so?" she asked. "And, by the way, you may call them Delia and Artie, you know. Everyone does."

"Not Delia. She refers to Mr. Drake as Arthur."

"That's true." She smiled slightly. "It's really quite endearing."

"He's besotted with her, isn't he?"

"Yes. He always has been, I think. I'm not sure Delia realizes it; although, how she could miss it I can't begin to imagine. And your presumption is correct. They are retired actors, with long and storied careers. They were associates of my father, who was also an actor."

"But not cousins of yours, I'm guessing," he said with a smile.

"No, but just as dear."

They had crossed the lawns and were nearing a cluster of willows he'd played under as a boy—he and Isaac and Susan. Lavinia drew the fronds of the first willow tree to the side so she could step under the canopy. Lucas followed. "Delia was quite the rage in her day, from what I understand," Lavinia said. "She's small in stature but very powerful when she wants to be. She was quite the leading lady and even performed for the king."

"Indeed?"

"I saw her play Titania, queen of the fairies, in *A Midsummer Night's Dream* when I was very young. I—well, never mind. She was breathtaking—commanding the stage as a queen would, even a fairy queen. She truly seemed a fairy, and I wanted her to be, and I wanted her to have magic, to actually be able to change men to beasts and back again." She stopped speaking, and Lucas wondered about a little girl who longed for that particular magical wish. Didn't little girls wish for handsome princes or jewels and such?

She continued. "The others have told me about her performances as Desdemona and Ophelia, and apparently she was a very saucy Viola in *Twelfth Night*."

"I'm guessing Artie has similar accolades."

She actually grinned then, and Lucas's heart did a somersault. She'd looked so somber just a moment before. "Artie's specialty tended to be more comedic, although, personally, I think he always dreamt of being a leading man."

"How long have you been an actress, Lavinia?" he asked as though it were the most normal question he could have posed to her.

She was silent, and Lucas thought she would not answer, but finally, she spoke. "How long have I been an actress? Oh, Lucas, I have acted my entire life."

A simple reply, but one that held many layers.

Lucas intended to peel away those layers to the real Lavinia beneath them.

* * *

"You have been asking all the questions," Lavinia said, running the leafy fronds of the willow tree through her fingers. "It's my turn now."

"Fair enough," Lucas replied. "You may question me to your heart's content—after I ask you one more: Have you ever climbed a tree? These willows are some of the best climbing trees to be found. Susan and Isaac will tell you the same. You could frequently find one of us or all of us here when we were young."

Lavinia was wearing one of her best day dresses, having changed out of her best traveling gown, so she would feel presentable to the viscount and viscountess. What if she climbed the tree and her dress snagged on a branch and was ruined? Oh, but she'd never had the opportunity as a child to do something as utterly normal as climb a tree. The idea was incredibly tempting . . .

"The woody branches are low enough even for a child," Lucas said, apparently sensing her initial hesitation. "There is truly nothing to compare with climbing a tree. Children of all ages need to climb trees. It is where the worlds in their dreams become real."

Lavinia gazed longingly at the willow and at Lucas standing next to it, his hand propped against its solid trunk. There were four willow trees here that looked to be the same age and size, each of them with solid, sturdy branches near the trunk, beckoning to be climbed, and long, slender branches covered in feathery leaves that created a green curtain about them that waved softly in the breeze.

"I'm wearing one of my best dresses," she said. "If I tear it because I listened to you and ventured up into this tree, I shall consider it your fault and expect you to replace it with something equal or better."

He grinned at her, a lopsided one that was part rake and part little boy and altogether too charming for her own good, and extended his hand to her. "Deal. Allow me to assist."

Lavinia puffed out an exasperated breath, placed one hand in his and the other on the tree, and set her foot on a large knot in the trunk about three feet from the ground. Then she boosted herself up, with Lucas's help, setting her other foot in the spot where the trunk split into two sturdy branches. A couple of feet above that spot, the tree split again, and Lavinia decided to climb up to it as well. In for a penny, in for a pound, as the saying went.

"I'm right behind you," Lucas said. "I'll catch you if you fall."

Lavinia looked over her shoulder. With Lucas standing on the first split, his head was nearly even with hers. Oh, but he was a lovely man, with thick brown hair and clear hazel eyes, and Lavinia was drawn to him, but her growing attraction for him was alarming to her as well.

Ever since she'd reached her adolescence, men in every town the troupe had visited had tended to swarm her. At the age of ten it had been terrifying—the catcalls, the lewd gestures she hadn't understood, the money offered to her. Her father had at least been a marginally protective parent back then, shooing the riffraff away. "Livvy, my girl," he'd said to her on more than one occasion. "Your looks are your prized possession *and* your poison. Have a care."

As she'd gotten older, her father's dubious paternal instincts had dwindled as his need for drink had grown, and his advice had changed. "Livvy, my girl," he'd say—he'd always addressed her as "Livvy, my girl," come to think of it—"there's this toff I know. Good bloke, deep pockets. He'd take care of you, good care, mind, and it wouldn't do me any harm either. Think about it. Then your old papa wouldn't have to worry about you."

She'd heard variations of it in nearly every town they visited. If she hadn't had Hannah by her side all those years . . . She shuddered to think where she'd be now.

But she'd *had* Hannah, and Hannah had stood up to Lavinia's father when she was young and had stood by Lavinia when she had gotten older and had been strong enough to stand up to her father herself.

"Why don't you sit on this branch before you get so lost in your thoughts you fall out of the tree?" Lucas said to her. "Where were you?"

She'd been wishing she'd had parents like other children did, like Lucas and his siblings did, thankful she'd at least had Hannah. What would it be like to share part of herself with him?

Could she trust Lucas enough to tell him about her childhood? Her dreams?

It was a terrible risk. She could barely breathe, she felt such anxiety.

"You don't have to share anything you don't want to," he added gently. "If you'd rather simply sit and enjoy your first tree-climbing experience quietly, that is your choice to make."

There he was once again, acting honorably. Perhaps she could share part of the truth with him.

"I was thinking about my father," she said.

"Here, sit, and you may tell me about him, but only if you wish."

He assisted her as she maneuvered herself into a sitting position on the branch, her back against the trunk. He stood where he was and held on to a branch above their heads. The arrangement put their faces close together, nearly eye to eye.

"He was a handsome man," Lavinia began, "at least when I was a small child, he seemed that way to me. Tall—though not as tall as you—with deep auburn hair and gray eyes."

"That explains a few things," Lucas said.

She smiled wanly. "My hair is much redder than his ever was. He had beautiful hair. Thick and wavy, and he was forever brushing a lock away from his eyes. This one unruly curl . . . I imagine that is why my mother and all the other women, for that matter, were attracted to him."

"Your mother . . . ?" He left the unspoken question hanging in the air.

"I scarcely remember my mother. Hannah has always been more of a mother to me than she was. I recall blonde hair and the scent of lilies. Snatches of songs she must have sung to me. Kissing my cheek, asking me not to forget her." Lavinia rested her hand on her cheek and could almost conjure the sensation she'd felt back then. "I have forgotten so much. I'm sorry, Mama," she whispered.

"She loved you," Lucas said. He set his hand on her shoulder, offering comfort. How odd it felt to have a man touch her and know it wasn't because he wanted something for himself. Lavinia's eyes burned.

"She left me, Lucas. She could have taken me with her, but she didn't."

"Perhaps she had no choice."

"Her name was Sally. That's all I know about her. Just Sally. I don't even know if my father was married to her or not. He never spoke of her." She blinked away her tears and then turned to smile at him. Here, in the willow tree, with his face just inches from hers, she could see a scar, a fine white line that ran along his hairline near his forehead. His eyes, though hazel, were predominantly green. Clear, sober eyes that looked steadily back at her.

She had told him of her parents. It felt freeing somehow. But now she wanted to learn more about him. "We have spent all our time talking about me, even after you said I could question you to my heart's content."

"You have only to ask," he said.

"Good. Tell me about Isobel," she said. She'd wondered about Isobel since she'd witnessed the woman's reaction to Lucas's return.

"Isobel is my eldest brother, Thomas's, wife, as you already know," he answered simply.

She stared at him.

He heaved a sigh. "You're not going to let it go at that. Very well. As children, Isobel and I had an affection for each other that had grown—I mistakenly thought—into something more by the time I went away to university.

During my brief absence, she and Thomas formed an attachment and married soon after."

"Brief?"

"You don't miss anything, do you? Yes, brief. Shortly after their marriage, which occurred at the end of my first term at Cambridge, I enlisted in the army."

Isobel had quickly turned her affections from one brother to the other. A single university term was a mere few months. "She broke your heart."

He snapped a twig near his face and tossed it to the ground. "If so, it has mended."

"Has it?" she asked him softly.

He looked her in the eye. "Yes."

"Why did you choose to enlist when you could have asked your father to purchase a commission for you?"

"I was eighteen, nearly nineteen—a foolish young cub whose masculine pride had been hurt. I suppose I enlisted as a way to make everyone suffer guilt—'See the poor, hurt young man who is now mucking about in trenches and may be shot and killed, all because unrequited love has driven him to extreme measures.' I don't know. I didn't ask my father to purchase a commission for me because he would have talked me out of going, and I was determined to go. I think I also blamed my family for being complicit in Thomas's courtship of Isobel. It was all rubbish thinking on my part. I learned my lesson the hard way over the course of seven long years."

"Tell me about Spain," she said.

"It's difficult to appreciate the beauty of a landscape when one is on a long march. One simply concentrates on putting one's foot in front of the other." Before she could respond, he went on. "Spain is dry and hot. It can be dry and cold. And it can also rain torrents. I had my fill of all three. It is not like England in appearance at all, and I suppose, had I been there under other circumstances, I might have considered it exotically beautiful. But I cannot separate the place from the experiences I had there. At least not yet."

She reached out and ran her finger down the scar along his hairline. "Did you get this while you were there? Do you have other scars?"

"Yes." The word was nearly a growl that came from deep inside his throat.

Lavinia had flirted over the years; alienating male admirers wouldn't have been good for box-office receipts. She wasn't flirting with Lucas though; her questions were direct, as were his answers. She'd touched his scar impulsively, out of compassion, and doing so had made his experiences in Spain real to her. But the willow tree fairly vibrated now from the attraction between them. She didn't know what to do, having never allowed herself to feel attracted to any man. It had always been too dangerous before.

She mentally called on Ruby to help her out of her predicament. Ruby would lower her eyelashes and say some sighing, witty thing that would simultaneously encourage and deter the gentleman in question. But Ruby was nowhere to be found.

"Lavinia—" Lucas said, his voice still sounding deep and rough and doing something startling to Lavinia's insides.

"If I were younger," Lavinia chirped, interrupting Lucas, afraid of what he would say or do and of how she was feeling, "I would pull on a pair of breeches and climb to the very top of this tree." She tipped her head back to view the top of the canopy and then pointed. "See? To that branch. It must be a wonderful view up there. I would be able to see all of Alderwood, I daresay, and even to the village beyond."

"Not quite to the village. I know, because I've done exactly what you are suggesting on more occasions than I can count during my childhood and early youth. I wouldn't be at all surprised if Susan herself hasn't sneaked out here in a pair of our brothers' breeches to do the same." He paused. "Lavinia—" he began again.

"I knew I liked Susan, from our first introduction. And Rebecca too; she's such a lovely girl."

"I think so too. But before you begin to wax rhapsodic over each of my siblings and start listing all their qualities in alphabetical order—"

"I wasn't going to do anything of the sort. Don't be ridiculous. But I can't help but admire Susan, who is so clever; I quite like that about her, and Rebecca is sweet and gentle. And they have both been kind and welcoming since we arrived."

"I'm glad you feel that way," he said. "Lavinia—"

"What? What do you want?" she cried, unable to deal with the anxiety any longer. "Do you want to kiss me; is that it?"

His gaze dropped to her mouth at her words. "Well, yes, frankly, but—"

"Then do it! Get it over with!"

"*But*," he said with emphasis, "what I was going to suggest is that we spend some of our time alone here discussing how to proceed since my rashness has gotten us into a fix. And *what the devil* do you mean by 'get it over with'?"

She froze, her eyes glued to his face. He brought his free hand up, and she flinched and pressed back against the trunk of the tree. But instead of slapping her or grabbing her, as she'd half expected him to do, he laid his hand gently on her shoulder.

"Devil take it—you're as white as a sheet," he said, looking stricken. "You can't think I was going to . . . Lavinia, I would never strike a woman or assault one. *Never*. I'm appalled that you would think, even for a moment, that you were in any kind of danger with me. Have I not proven myself trustworthy to you so far? There have been plenty of opportunities for me to take advantage, if that had been my intent.

"And furthermore, when I said I wanted to kiss you, that was the truth. But even at that, I would never do so without your permission or your desire to kiss me back. I have *sisters*, for heaven's sake! If some man were to . . . to *any* of my sisters, I would call the bounder out, and my brothers would have to get in line behind me." He turned and stared out into the distance while he appeared to rein in his emotions.

"Lucas," Lavinia said once she had found her voice. "I've never kissed a man before."

He turned and looked at her skeptically.

"See? Even *you* believe I have a history with men. I can see it in your face."

"I don't know what you can see in my face. But I do know you have a history with men, and I don't believe it has been a particularly pleasant one. You reacted with fear just now. I saw that same look on the faces of the women and girls in Spain. War doesn't always make heroes. It frequently brings out the worst in people." He cupped her cheek with his hand, and she nearly wept. "Tell me, Lavinia, about these men."

"You're right. Must I say more? I have been kissed, Lucas, but I have never kissed."

"Where was your father when all of this was going on?"

"He was too busy at the pubs and bawdy houses to care, and when he died, I'm sorry to say, it was no great loss to anyone. Even me." She suddenly felt tired to the bone. The day had begun with such hope and had gone through such highs and lows since then. "Perhaps it is time to return to the house," she said.

"Very well. I'm truly sorry about the betrothal. Once again, you have been ill-used by a man without your consent beforehand."

"Oh, Lucas, I did the same to you, did I not? It would be the height of hypocrisy if I were to hold it against you. So, for the time being, I shall be your devoted betrothed. You have joined up with a band of actors, you will recall. We are as comfortable playing characters as we are at being ourselves." More comfortable, in truth.

He climbed down from the willow tree and then assisted her down, putting his hands on her waist and lifting her from the branches to the ground. "Come then, Lavinia. Let us return to the house and continue our charade."

"Lucas," she said before she lost her courage. There was one thing more she wanted him to know, needed to let him know, but Ruby Chadwick's flirtatiousness and wit were still not to be found anywhere. Only Lavinia remained—and she was terrified by what she was about to say.

"What is it?" he asked.

"I think I may want to kiss you. Sometime. But not today."

His eyes softened, and the corners of his mouth turned up. "I can wait," he said.

It was exactly what she'd hoped—no, *needed*—to hear.

She fell a little in love with Lucas then.

Chapter 13

THE FOLLOWING MORNING, LUCAS SET out on horseback for Primrose Farm, accompanied by Isaac and Thomas and Finch. Lucas had borrowed one of his father's horses so Hector could enjoy a full day of rest and grazing after so many days of travel.

The day was overcast, and Lucas suspected it might rain that afternoon. Hopefully they would be back at Alderwood long before that happened. He'd truly had his fill of rain and mud while in Spain. Rain and mud were rife with bad memories.

He located the ramshackle sign that pointed the way to Primrose Farm and led the others down the lane until they reached the farmhouse.

"Oh, dear me," Finch said from atop his mount.

"That's putting it lightly," Thomas added. "You certainly aren't marrying her for her inheritance, if that wasn't obvious already."

"Thomas, a little decorum, please," Isaac cautioned before Lucas could say anything himself—which was just as well, for he wouldn't have been as circumspect as Isaac had been.

Thomas smirked as he dismounted.

"Well, let's see what we're about here, then," Isaac said after he and Finch dismounted as well.

"There's a fellow not far from here, Allard, by name, who used to be the foreman," Lucas said. "I'm going to go find him. I expect he can shed some light on the situation for us."

"Excellent idea," Finch said. "Folks living nearby likely built their livelihood around this farm and would have been affected by its failure. Knowing how many people remain who could possibly be lured back would be critical information to have."

Lucas needed no more encouragement. He turned his mount and headed back to the main road and then followed the directions Allard have given them the day before, finding the cottage with no trouble at all.

"Mr. Jennings, it's an honor, sir," Mrs. Allard said once Lucas had explained who he was and why he was there. "Come in, come in." She ushered him into the cottage like she was rounding up a sheep that had strayed from the flock. She was plump and pretty in a round-faced sort of way, with an equally round-faced but wiggly toddler balanced on her hip. She seemed the type who would keep the more reserved Allard on his toes.

"Allard told me all about it yesterday. Such great news! I can't help saying how very thrilled everyone will be that something's to be done to make things as they was." She wiped some drool off the toddler's chin with the corner of her apron. "He's out back tending to the chickens. Have a seat, and I'll inform him he has company." She curtsied, nearly tipping off-balance due to the uncooperative toddler, and exited the room.

Lucas propped himself on the edge of a fairly worn chair, unsure if it would fully support his weight. The room was shabby but still felt homey and welcoming, with a braided rug Mrs. Allard had undoubtedly made herself covering the floor and freshly cut flowers sitting cheerily in an earthenware pot on the table.

Allard arrived shortly thereafter, drying his hands on a towel before reaching out to shake Lucas's hand. "Welcome back, sir! I'm that pleased to see you again so soon. I've asked the missus to bring in some refreshment— or would you care to take luncheon with us?"

"Neither, thank you. I'm wondering, Mr. Allard, if you can spare an hour or so of your time. I've brought two of my brothers and our steward to inspect Primrose Farm for Miss Fernley, and I wonder if you might join us and fill in the gaps of our knowledge as it relates to the history of the place and those who worked there."

"I'd be only too pleased to do so, sir. I shall saddle up my horse and join you there in, say, half hour's time?"

"Excellent. Bid your good lady goodbye for me." He tipped his hat and left.

Locating Allard hadn't taken long at all, and when Lucas returned to Primrose Farm, he found Finch still poking around the exterior of the farmhouse. His brothers were inside the main parlor—in deep discussion about Lucas's betrothed and her farm.

"I take your meaning, Thomas, but I'm certain she's an altogether fine person, once one gets to know her," Lucas overheard Isaac say.

"I, for one, am appalled," Thomas replied. "The only asset Lucas is getting from this marriage is the woman herself, and if he wanted her so badly—as I'm sure he and many other men do—he should have set her up discreetly with her own household, not proposed to her and introduced her to Mama and our sisters. It's utterly insupportable. Isobel was in such an ill humor last night, I could scarcely tolerate it."

"Clara was shocked at first, I will confess, as were we all," Isaac said. "And that hair of hers *is* rather brazen. But—"

Lucas had heard enough. He stalked away from the farmhouse, hands clenched, teeth grinding, working with all his might to bring his anger under control. If he confronted his brothers the way he was currently feeling, he'd end up using his fists rather than his intellect. It was what he'd been required to do for the past seven years—fight, battle, do damage to the enemy. Protect the innocent.

Except they weren't the enemy; they were his brothers—decent men with decent lives and wives and families. If they believed such things about Lavinia, what must lesser men assume about her?

If her father were alive, Lucas would beat the man to a pulp, as he was still sorely tempted to do to his brothers at the moment.

I have been kissed, Lucas, but I have never kissed.

Those words had spoken volumes.

I think I may want to kiss you. Sometime. But not today. The innocence he'd seen in her face when she'd spoken those words to him—they had not been the words of a wanton, although they had succeeded in thoroughly seducing him.

He would do all in his power to defend her and her honor.

Thankfully, Allard arrived on his nag shortly thereafter. Lucas hailed Finch and introduced him to Allard, and then the three of them joined Thomas and Isaac inside the farmhouse. Over the next few hours, they explored the property, and Finch took copious notes. Lucas kept himself at a distance most of the time, unsure he'd gained enough control over his emotions. Every time he looked at Thomas, in particular, he felt violent.

"Are you well, Lucas?" Isaac asked, taking him aside while Allard was showing Thomas and Finch the old wind pump workings. "You seem out of sorts, and yet you were in high spirits when we set out."

"I'm well enough."

"Are you sure? It really seems to me that something is amiss."

"I'm well enough, Isaac," Lucas said more firmly. "Let us be about our business and return home, shall we?"

He walked away from Isaac and arrived at the wind pump in enough time to hear Allard and Finch discussing what parts would be needed to get it back into operation. "That's one thing settled," Finch said cheerfully, oblivious to the tension in the air. "Mr. Allard also assures me that there are enough men in the area to make quick work of restoring the farmhouse at least. They were all employed here, and Allard knows them well."

"Aye, good men and lads, they are," Allard said. "All I need is the word and the work can begin."

"Excellent," Lucas said. "I have assured my betrothed, Miss Fernley"—he shot a disparaging glance at Thomas—"that I would apprise her of our findings before any plans are put into action. I'll get word to you within the next day or so."

All four men looked perplexed by Lucas's words. "Begging your pardon, but what precisely do you mean?" Finch asked. "I was under the assumption that we were to begin work immediately."

"What he means," Thomas said, "is that he is being led around by the petticoats of a—"

"Allard, Mr. Finch, will you excuse us?" Lucas said, interrupting his brother before he could say anything more.

Allard and Finch had enough sense to excuse themselves and leave.

Lucas kept his eyes on Thomas until he was sure Allard and Finch were beyond earshot. "I will have your apology," he said. "Yours too, Isaac."

"For what?" Thomas asked, locking eyes with him.

"What do you think? Petticoats? Brazen? Discreetly setting Lavinia up in her own household? I would have your apologies!"

Isaac's face had turned beet red. "I'm sorry you overheard that exchange, Lucas. It was just talk between brothers, truly. But surely you realize Miss Fernley's looks have a remarkably, uh, *singular* effect on others. Regular people need time to . . . adjust." He seemed to be stumbling over his tongue in his search for the right words. "I'm truly sorry, Lucas."

"It's your turn now, Thomas," Lucas said.

Thomas drilled him with his eyes. "I apologize for speaking in an unflattering manner *in private* about someone who is a guest of my parents in their home. *My* home. I shall do my best in future to keep my opinions to myself. That is your apology."

"That is no apology. What right have you to judge her in such a manner on such short acquaintance? Was her dress immodest in any way? Was her bearing? Her speech?"

"Not at all," Isaac assured him. "Quite the opposite. Isn't that right, Thomas?"

"I daresay the woman could be completely hidden under draperies and she would still look—"

"Thomas," Lucas said in warning.

"Never mind. I take your point, little brother. I shall refrain from speaking about the lady and will allow that I have no cause to judge her on such short acquaintance," Thomas said.

"Excellent," Isaac said, looking relieved. "I believe we have what we need and can return to Alderwood; don't you agree, Lucas?"

"For now," he replied, his words holding a double meaning. Lucas was in no way satisfied with Thomas's words, but they would have to do for the time being.

They spotted Finch and Allard standing near their horses at the front of the house in an animated discussion about the renovations that would soon begin.

"Ah, Mr. Jennings, sir," Allard called to them as they approached. "Me and the guv here are in agreement about how to proceed, if that meets with, er, your lady's approval. I can get some men started on the farmhouse straightaway, and once we get the parts for the wind pump, we can get that up and running too. It's too late to be starting regular-like planting, but if we're lucky, we might get a few quick-growing crops into the ground."

"Mr. Allard is very enthusiastic," Finch said. "We have yet to discuss the costs involved, however. But he's right in that if we can get some acres drained and planted posthaste, there may be enough income brought in from that to offset the initial costs of restoring the house, at least. And that gets things off to a good start."

"I will take a good start where I can find it," Lucas said. "We all will, won't we?" He looked over at his brothers. He hoped the meaning of his words wasn't lost on them.

* * *

Lavinia wasn't sure what to do with herself. The previous day had been exhausting, but she'd lain awake most of the night nonetheless, knowing that Lucas would be returning to Primrose Farm early that morning and she would be left to carry on the charade without him for most of the day.

She'd risen later than she'd intended as a result, certain Lucas's family held to country hours, and berated herself for the reflection her lateness might have on Lucas. She'd washed and donned the most demure day dress she had, a simple muslin with a high neckline and no flounces, then she'd brushed and twisted her unruly curls into a knot at the back of her head.

She should go downstairs and face Lucas's family. But she wasn't ready to do that quite yet.

She removed a small notebook she kept in the false bottom of her jewel case. Anything she'd been given of worth from her admirers she'd sold to jewelers or pawned and had added the money to her carefully invested savings. In order to appease her conscience, she'd always declined any such gifts, only accepting something if the gentleman was stubbornly insistent—and then she'd made it clear that it was a *gift*, not a quid pro quo in expectation of receiving sensual favors.

She had watched her father and his women enough as a girl—the countless occasions she'd seen him wander off with one to a local pub after rehearsals or performances, his returning home the following morning to sleep off too much drink, stinking of stale perfume and gin. He'd at least had enough decency not to bring the women under their roof—whatever roof it had happened to be in whatever town they were staying. Lavinia suspected he'd known Hannah would have shooed him and his light-o'-love out the door with a heavy broom if he'd done so.

Lavinia had not known what a light-o'-love was back then and had been jealous of the women and the attention her father had given them.

That had changed when she'd turned thirteen, following a performance in Newbury of *The Babes in the Wood*. Lavinia, despite her impending womanhood, had played one of the orphaned children left abandoned by the wicked uncle in the wood. It had been a good role with actual spoken lines, the first role in which Lavinia had played a significant part rather than appearing as a background performer of some type. She'd been flattered to have been chosen and had gone into rehearsals with a great deal of enthusiasm. Her father had seemed pleased too.

Opening night, however, Lavinia had discovered the hard way that the actor playing the wicked uncle was, indeed, wicked, when he took her aside and whispered in her ear the kinds of delights they might share together during the duration of the run.

Lavinia hadn't known what he'd been talking about; she'd known only that she hadn't wanted any part of what he'd been suggesting. The incident had actually helped her performance during the run of the show, for she'd truly been able to convey total repugnance toward the wicked uncle onstage as well as offstage. After that, Hannah had stuck to her side like a stern governess wherever she went.

By the time Lavinia's father had died, she'd had her fill of opportunistic men and their coarse intentions.

Shaking off her gloomy memories, she opened her notebook and studied the numbers written within, trying to imagine how much of her hard-earned savings she would need to spend on Primrose Farm before she and the others could at least move in. She was not comfortable here at Alderwood, despite the polite hospitality being offered. She was not comfortable being here under false pretenses.

She added the columns to check her sums, then added them again and then again just to be sure. There was really no way for her to determine what the expenses would be, not until Lucas and the others returned. She had no experience whatsoever with which to even venture a guess. She wished she'd gone with them despite Lucas's gentle insistence that she remain behind.

Her calculations did nothing to clarify the situation, and really, she was simply avoiding the inevitable—leaving her room and joining the family downstairs.

She closed the notebook and tucked it back into the false bottom of the jewel case, then returned the case to the wardrobe. She peeked at herself in the mirror, patted her hair to make sure her pins were securely in place, and then straightened her back and lifted her chin before leaving her room.

It was time for Lavinia, betrothed lady, to make her entrance in this little farce.

"Oh, good. There you are. I was just about to send a servant up to check on you." Lucas's sister Susan stood at the bottom of the stairs watching Lavinia as she descended to the main floor. "Where are the others?"

"Still asleep," Lavinia said, hoping her voice sounded convincingly cultured. No one had commented to the contrary yesterday, so that was a good thing. "Delia and Artie aren't used to country hours. They may not show themselves until after noon. Hannah is usually an early riser, like myself, but I suspect she was more tired than usual after yesterday's travel. I thought to let her sleep."

They reached the breakfast room, a cheery, intimate space with windows that let in the morning sunshine. "Please ask Cook to arrange for hot cocoa and toast to be sent up to our guests' rooms in an hour," Susan said to the footman, who stood inside the door. He nodded and left. "There you go, Lavinia. You are not to worry about your cousins and friend. Now, please help yourself to whatever you wish at the sideboard."

"Where is the rest of the family?" Lavinia asked as she dished eggs and sausage onto a plate. She and Susan were the only two here.

"Father has broken his fast already and is inspecting the grounds since Finch accompanied Lucas and Isaac to your farm. Mother rarely eats breakfast, preferring tea and toast in her room when she wakes, but she should be joining us shortly. Rebecca—"

"Rebecca what?" Rebecca herself asked as she entered the room.

Susan dished eggs and toast onto her plate and set it on the table across from Lavinia, who had seated herself. "Rebecca is a wonderful baby sister of whom I am inordinately fond. And if I know my sister well—and I do—she can usually be found wherever there is anything new and exciting taking place." Susan raised her hand to the side of her mouth. "And you, Miss Fernley," she said in a stage whisper, "are definitely new and the *most* exciting thing to happen to this family in longer than I can remember."

"That is true," Rebecca said, dishing up a plate of food for herself. "Most of the excitement in the family occurs far away from Alderwood, and I must beg Mama to tell me what my brothers and sisters write in their letters. To have you and Lucas here, to watch your love and betrothal unfold, is a delicious dream." She plopped into the chair next to Lavinia as Susan poured tea for each of them.

"Rebecca really is a clever girl." Susan sighed dramatically. "Although you would never know it from her overly romantic declarations. Please do not wax rhapsodic over the ecstasies of love, Rebecca. Not while I'm eating, at least."

Lavinia sipped her tea to cover her smile.

"Susan is a self-avowed bluestocking, you know, Miss Fernley," Rebecca said.

"Please call me Lavinia, if you would. What is a blue—"

"Oh, that's smashing! I should love for you to call me Rebecca, above all things. A bluestocking is a lady who prefers books to men."

Susan rolled her eyes. "That's rather an oversimplification of the word," she said.

"Susan has always been *exceedingly* clever," Rebecca continued. "Even more clever than James, who is a solicitor in Lincoln and was always at the top of his class."

"James?" Lavinia asked.

"Yes, James, our brother," Susan said. "I know, there are a lot of us to keep track of. You'll get used to it."

"Right. James." Lavinia needed to be a bit more careful about what she said.

Rebecca giggled. "James was here for an entire week a fortnight ago, expecting Lucas to arrive, but he had to go back to Lincoln. Pressing business, he said. And now you're here. Oh, I wish he could have stayed. It's so *exciting* that you are here; I can scarcely contain myself. Lucas, home safe from the war and *betrothed*, no less. What fun!" She clasped her hands to her breast.

"Our Rebecca was disappointed about not having a Season this year, you see," Susan explained. "But you shall have a Season next year, Rebecca, now that Lucas is home. I'm sure of it. *If* you really want one, that is."

"Oh, Susan; you *know* I do."

"Yes, darling, I do—as long as you remember that London Seasons aren't always what they're cracked up to be. They can be terribly dull. I know mine was."

"There are sights to see, of course, and the gentlemen and ladies look elegant in all their finery," Lavinia added. "But one can grow tired . . ."

The sisters both looked at Lavinia with interest when her words trailed off. Lavinia had mingled with members of the *ton*, it was true, but certainly not in the same way a young debutante would have been introduced to London Society. "I merely find the country a refreshing change from London at present," she explained while she gave herself another mental talking to. "I imagine we can find tediousness in day-to-day living no matter where we are."

They seemed to accept that answer, thankfully.

"How did you and Lucas meet?" Rebecca asked, propping her chin on her hand in preparation, no doubt, to hear a romantic story for the ages.

Lavinia took a bite of eggs and chewed slowly and swallowed before answering. "I saw him across a crowded room," she began. She would let them imagine what kind of room it was—she certainly wouldn't tell them it was the public room of the White Horse. "He was tall and handsome," that was true, "we spoke briefly," also true, "and then he took me for a stroll," at her pleading insistence—out of the public room and up to his room so she could avoid being spotted by the Earl of Cosgrove's cronies.

Rebecca sighed. "And was it love at first sight?"

Susan raised an eyebrow in anticipation of Lavinia's answer.

What to say?

"Oh, good. Here you are, Lavinia." The Viscountess of Thurlby swished into the room at that moment, rescuing her from having to answer a difficult question. "I can see Lucas's sisters have been taking good care of you."

"Indeed, Mama. She has been telling us how she and Lucas met," Rebecca said.

"That is a story I should like to hear sometime," Lady Thurlby said, pouring a cup of tea and sitting next to Susan. "You must promise me, Lavinia. But at present, we have other matters to discuss. Yesterday afternoon, I wrote to Lucas's other siblings, James and Martha and Simon. I was hopeful when Lucas returned to England that we could all be together, but he felt the need to stay at his wounded friend's side, and now Martha will have to remain home until after the baby arrives. But I expect James and Simon to arrive shortly after they receive my letters, if they know what's good for them. Perhaps Lucas has already had occasion to introduce you to Simon, since he has been in London."

"No, ma'am. I am looking forward to the pleasure." Lucas had never mentioned any siblings whatsoever during their journey. And Lucas's brother Simon was living in London? That was a complication she hadn't anticipated in agreeing to come to Alderwood.

"In the meantime, I think we should begin planning the wedding. You can never start too soon for these types of occasions, I always say. Have you begun calling the banns? Are you planning to marry in London or here at our own St. Alfred's, with Isaac officiating? Oh, wouldn't that be lovely, having Lucas's own brother perform the nuptials. He hadn't been ordained yet when Thomas and Martha each married. Susan, I shall need you and Rebecca, along with the servants, helping with the cleaning and cooking, you know— we are not above such honest work here in the country, are we, girls?"

"Yes, Mama, er, no, Mama," Rebecca said, apparently unsure which question she was answering.

"Ma'am, meaning no disrespect, but your son and I have not precisely settled on a marriage date," Lavinia said. "Perhaps it would be well to wait for Lucas to discuss the matter. He was most anxious about returning home and spending time with all of you after his long absence—and assisting me with Primrose Farm, of course. Those were the priorities, you see, and so I am perfectly content to remain betrothed for the time being." Trying to stay as close to the truth as possible and wrack her brain for the proper demeanor and etiquette she'd observed over the years was beginning to give her a headache.

"He hasn't suggested a wedding date yet? You have more patience than I do," the viscountess said. Then her expression cleared. "No matter. We shall begin the preparations regardless. And we shall have an evening of entertainment for our closest neighbors and friends once James and Simon arrive so that you may become acquainted with everyone and they with you."

"That would be lovely," Lavinia said. Oh, but her head was beginning to ache in earnest. What had Lucas gotten her into?

"It would seem a meeting has been going on, Clara, and we were not invited," Isobel said as the two of them entered the breakfast room.

"There was certainly no meeting I was aware of," Susan said. "I have merely been breaking my fast, as I do every morning. How about you, Rebecca?"

"The eggs are particularly good today, Isobel," Rebecca replied.

"I haven't seen that day dress before, Isobel," Lady Thurlby said. "Is it new?"

"I have been saving it for a special occasion. And what can be more special than the arrival of a new sister-in-law?" She smiled at Lavinia.

Ah, her smile. Lavinia had perfected that particular smile when she'd played Beatrice in *Much Ado about Nothing*—sweet, with just enough acid dripping from it to warn of potential danger. "I'm honored you would think my arrival a special occasion. What a beautiful shade of blue. Very becoming."

"Yes, indeed, it is very flattering, Isobel," Lady Thurlby said. "But I thought—" She glanced at Lavinia. "Well, never mind what I thought."

Isobel dished food onto her plate and took a seat next to Rebecca. Clara took a single slice of toast.

"How are you feeling this morning, Clara? Better, I hope?" the viscountess said, attempting to change the conversation. "Clara is in the family way again," she explained to Lavinia.

"Not really," Clara said.

"Your color is much improved," Lady Thurlby said.

"It's the dress."

Poor Clara. The day dress of soft-pink muslin she was wearing did flatter her, despite her being a bit under the weather this morning.

The viscountess patted her hand. "Did you get any sleep last night, dear? That's it, isn't it? You were in the nursery most of the night again."

"Samuel is cutting a tooth, and Mrs. Wynn can't see to him and keep up with all the other children come morning," she replied.

"The dress is a lovely choice, and I'm sure it is one of your favorites when you are feeling well," Lavinia said. "May I offer to help with the children? I know Hannah would be delighted to help as well."

"That's really not necessary, Lavinia," Lady Thurlby said. "You have other responsibilities to see to, and Mrs. Wynn is a very capable nurse."

"Lavinia had been telling Susan and me how she and Lucas met and fell in love," Rebecca interjected rather unnecessarily.

Isobel set down her fork.

"I would dearly love to meet the children, Lady Thurlby, and I'm sure Mrs. Wynn would appreciate having a brief respite," Lavinia said, wishing to avoid the subject of love, especially with Isobel present. "Lucas would enjoy getting acquainted with his nieces and nephews too. Perhaps he will join us when he returns."

Clara's eyes brightened at the idea, and the change to her countenance was remarkable.

"Good point," Lady Thurlby said. "Very well, then. Between Lavinia and her friend, they should be able to handle your combined six for an hour or so later this afternoon, eh? Clara? Isobel? Better yet, I will join you, Lavinia. An hour or so with the children would be delightful."

"Thank you, Lady Thurlby," Lavinia said.

"Oh, I wish we could join you, but Susan and I have promised to make calls in the village."

"Indeed," Susan said. "I daresay the calls could wait for a different day, were it not for the fact that Mrs. Smith's nephew is visiting from Cambridge and Rebecca would like to be introduced before he vanishes."

"Oh, Susan!" Rebecca poked her in the arm.

"Thank you so much," Isobel said, offering the same acidic smile to Lavinia that she had before. "Sadly, I won't be able to join you either."

Lavinia smiled back at Isobel with more treacle than acid. She loved children, and spending time with them was sure to be a welcome diversion from everything else that was going on. "If you'll excuse me, I shall go inform Hannah of the plans for later." Besides, it was getting to be late morning, and she wanted to be sure Delia and Artie were not off wandering on their own, weaving tall tales about Lavinia's childhood to all and sundry.

And then she was going to lie down with a cold compress on her forehead. If only for a minute or two.

Chapter 14

LUCAS AND THE OTHERS ARRIVED back at Alderwood around four o'clock, dusty and tired, but Lucas wanted to find Lavinia straightaway and let her know what they'd learned. A more detailed meeting with Finch could wait until tomorrow, but he knew Lavinia would not want to wait until tomorrow to hear the news, nor did he want her to wait.

He was also anxious to know how his "betrothed" had coped with his family during his absence.

As they dismounted and handed their horses over to the grooms, they could hear shrieks and squeals coming from somewhere nearby.

"What is that infernal noise?" Thomas asked. "Has someone set the pigs loose?"

"I do believe they're children, Thomas," Isaac said. "Ours, no doubt."

Finch bid them farewell and returned to his office, leaving the three brothers to investigate.

As they rounded the corner of the house, Lucas spied six children of varying age and size prancing about beneath the large oak tree not far from the house, laughing and playing—with Delia and Artie, of all people. He blinked to make sure he was seeing things correctly. Seated on blankets in the shade nearby were Clara and Lavinia, who were clapping and laughing along with the children. Hannah was shooing one little scamp who'd strayed from the group back toward the other children, and Lucas's mother stood nearby watching the spectacle. She spotted them and walked toward them.

"Where is Mrs. Wynn?" Thomas asked in a demanding tone. "And what in heaven's name do you call *that*?" He pointed toward the raucous group.

"I call it perfectly acceptable childlike behavior, Thomas," their mother replied. "You were a child once yourself, you may recall. We decided to give Wynn an hour to herself; heaven knows the poor woman has earned it the past few days. Lavinia offered to play with them all, and her elderly cousins were more than thrilled to join in the fun."

She glanced over her shoulder, drawing Lucas's and the others' attention back toward the children. Artie was dancing in a most awkward fashion to the song Delia was singing, though it was barely audible over the shrieks of laughter the children were making as they watched Artie and mimicked him.

"I must say, Lucas, your Lavinia's cousins are a singular pair," Mama said. "I'm not quite certain what I make of them. Despite the fact that the children are being highly entertained, there is something unnerving about seeing an elderly man down on his hands and knees, braying like a donkey."

Thomas's eyes looked as though they might pop from his skull at their mother's comment. Isaac snorted and covered his mouth with his hand to avoid laughing outright.

"Braying like a donkey?" Lucas managed to ask with a nearly straight face.

"Yes. He reenacted a fable about a man and a boy and a donkey. I believe your Edmund portrayed the man in the story, Thomas. Isaac Junior was to have played the boy, but Mary felt it unfair that all the parts were being played by males, so we adapted."

"Edmund did *what*? Did Isobel agree to this?"

"Now, Thomas, don't be so stuffy. Sometimes I think Wynn can be overly strict. Children need to play."

"Play, yes, Mother. Some vigorous exercise, especially for boys, is an important part of a child's daily regimen, but in an orderly fashion, with other children, not with decrepit old men who pretend they are donkeys."

"Well, yes, that was somewhat of a shock, but he wasn't actually *playing* with Artie, Thomas. It was *a play*—not so dissimilar as doing charades with one's friends for an evening's entertainment. I recollect plenty of instances during your own childhood when you were a pirate king or a musketeer or some such—you and Martha and James were always coming up with escapades of that sort. Delia and some of the girls were fairies at one point this afternoon, and she made a most wonderful witch, too—just scary enough to delight the children. Lavinia herself played the good fairy that rescued little Annabel from the witch. Annabel thought it great fun and asked to be rescued again."

"Is that right, Annabel?" Isaac said, reaching down to pick up the little girl who'd wandered over when she'd seen her papa. "You were rescued from the witch by a good fairy?"

The rosy-cheeked cherub pointed at Delia and grinned. "Bad witch. Funny."

Lucas looked at Annabel in wonder—his niece. Samuel was the baby in leading strings, and the young girl who looked so much like Clara must be Mary, with Isaac Junior standing next to her. Isaac and Clara's children.

Isaac, only four years Lucas's senior, had four children already. Four. And another on the way.

The boy with light-brown hair, who was plucking grass and tossing it at everyone, must be Edmund, then, and sitting next to Lavinia was his little sister, Sarah.

Thomas and Isobel's children.

Little golden-haired Sarah looked exactly like Isobel had at that age. Lucas was flooded with bittersweet memories. Sneaking into the stable with Isobel to play with newborn kittens. Pulling off their shoes and stockings to splash about in the lake that lay between their parents' properties and ending up completely soaked. Hiding from Isaac and Susan—and Simon, who was three years their junior. A shared first kiss.

He and the others walked over to the oak tree to join the happy little group. Artie's comical dancing had ceased, and another story was underway.

"And so the beautiful little princess grew and became even lovelier with each passing day," Lavinia said, narrating. Delia—the beautiful princess in question—swished her skirt and picked daisies, humming softly.

"But one day, while her parents were busy, the princess decided to explore the castle. In a small room she'd never noticed before, she spied an old woman spinning wool. 'How delightful!' the young princess exclaimed—" Delia clasped her hands to her bosom at Lavinia's words—"'May I try?'

"'Of course, dearie.' The woman cackled." Lavinia's own voice cackled as she spoke the words. "No sooner had the princess reached for the spindle, but she pricked her finger on it and immediately fell into a deep sleep, as did everyone else in the castle." Delia's outreached hand jerked, and then she collapsed into a heap on the ground.

"Gracious, I hope she'll be all right," Lucas's mother whispered to him behind her hand. He was about to remind her she hadn't actually fallen into a hundred years' sleep when she continued. "She's an old woman; she could break a hip doing something like that."

"Many years passed," Lavinia told the children in a hushed voice. "And all around the castle, huge briars sprang up, growing thick and thorny and dangerous, until the castle itself all but disappeared from view, and the people in the village forgot about its existence and the royal family and beautiful princess who'd lived within its walls."

Everyone was transfixed; the silence around them profound—it seemed to Lucas that even the songbirds had stopped to listen to Lavinia's tale.

"And then one day, a hundred years later, a handsome prince decided to hunt in the woods nearby." Artie rose to his feet, suddenly appearing for all the world like a young prince as he pantomimed aiming his invisible bow here and there and shooting invisible arrows. He'd been sitting off to the side, and Lucas had completely forgotten he was there, so engrossed he'd become with Lavinia's words. "He spied the castle and remembered the old tales that had been told of a sleeping beauty within a sleeping castle. 'I must see for myself if the stories are legend or true,' he declared. He slashed at the brambles that seemed nearly alive and fighting against him in his quest."

Artie slashed and slashed again at Lavinia's words. "I will not give up!" he cried. "Help me fight the brambles. Lend me your strength!"

"You can do it, handsome prince!" Mary cried while the others clapped and encouraged him to be strong and keep battling through the thickets. Edmund and Isaac Junior leapt up, followed quickly by Mary, and joined Artie, slashing with their own make-believe swords.

"After one final slash, the prince made it to the castle. He broke down the door"—Artie pantomimed this remarkably convincingly—"and climbed the stairs to the very top. And there he spied—"

"A hundred-year-old crone, from the look of things," Thomas murmured under his breath.

"The most beautiful woman I have ever seen is asleep here," Artie pronounced with reverence.

"He tried to awaken her," Lavinia said. Artie gently nudged Delia's shoulder once and then again. Her arm, which had been resting on her chest, slid limply off to the side. "But to no avail. In sadness, he watched her as she slept."

"Wake up, Deela," Annabel cried, clutching Isaac's shoulders tightly.

Isaac kissed her cheek. "Don't worry, poppet. Keep watching."

"Suddenly," Lavinia's voice rose with excitement, "the prince remembered an important part of the tale of the sleeping castle—that only a handsome prince could awaken the princess by offering her a kiss."

The boys groaned.

Artie went down on bended knee. "Beautiful princess, forgive my rashness, but for you to awaken, I must kiss you." He leaned over, propping himself with one hand so he didn't lose his balance and fall in a heap on top of Delia, which would ruin the dramatic effect completely, and placed a gentle kiss on her lips.

It was the sweetest of kisses, Lucas thought. His lips had barely touched Delia's, but there had been a tenderness that had transcended mere playacting.

Well, of course it had. Lucas had already noticed Artie's affection for Delia—but what was completely obvious to him now was that Artie *loved* Delia. Loved her deeply.

It made the story that much more poignant.

Delia's eyes opened, and she blinked several times. "Ah, my handsome prince! I have been waiting for you," she exclaimed, smiling radiantly at Artie.

Did she have an affection for him as well?

"I certainly hope your betrothed's *cousins* hail from different branches of the family tree after a kiss like that," Thomas murmured.

Lucas shot him a glare.

"And I have found you," Artie said. He maneuvered stiffly to his feet and then assisted Delia to hers.

"They fell in love," Lavinia said triumphantly. "And were married soon thereafter. And they both lived . . ."

"Happily ever after!" the children crowed.

"In a way," Lavinia said, holding up a finger to silence them. "For they lived *fully*—through sickness and sadness and good times and difficult ones. But in so doing, they found happiness of the very best kind, for they grew together in their love for each other for the rest of their lives. The end."

Everyone clapped—even a begrudging Thomas—and Artie and Delia gave several elaborate bows to their enthusiastic audience, as Lucas suspected they had done at the conclusion of every performance they'd ever given for the past half century.

As he applauded the performance, Lucas reflected further upon Lavinia's concluding statement about the prince and princess growing together in their love for each other through happy and difficult times. She'd been raised in the theater, where fantasy was acted out on stage every evening, where people went to escape sickness and sadness and difficult times and imagine fanciful lives beyond their own. And yet, her own mother had left when Lavinia was little more than Annabel's age. Her father had done little for her as her parent after that. Her version of "happily ever after" was utterly plain—but would be of great worth to someone who'd never experienced it.

With the aid of the ever-gallant Artie, Lavinia rose to her feet and took a modest bow herself before being thronged and hugged by all the children, except Edmund and Isaac Junior, who stood awkwardly by as boys of that age generally did. Lucas couldn't take his eyes off her. She seemed relaxed and happy in a way he'd not seen her before. She was beautiful.

Well, *of course* she was beautiful. That was blatantly apparent to any-one who cast eyes on her. She was extraordinarily so.

But this was different.

This was a beauty that came from within her and made her luminous. She was not of this earth, nor from any fairy tale she might have shared with the children this afternoon.

She was heavenly.

Her eyes caught his, and he hardly dared breathe. She smiled at him—first with her eyes and lips and then with her whole countenance. *My angel,* he thought. *Mine.*

He crossed to her and bowed low over her hand, leaving a prolonged kiss there. "My beautiful Lavinia," he murmured, "what an honor it is to have you in my life."

He meant every word, and he realized with urgency that he must find a way to keep her in his life, to make the betrothal one in truth.

* * *

"I understand from Thomas that I missed a rather extraordinary theatrical performance this afternoon," Isobel said at dinner as soon as everyone was seated. Delia and Artie had asked to take their meals in their rooms so they could retire early, their antics entertaining the children having thoroughly worn them both out, and Hannah had opted to join them. "I'm sorry I missed it. I had already heard from the children about it. They were quite enamored by it all, from what I understand. I must congratulate you, Lavinia."

"Thank you," Lavinia replied demurely, taking a sip from her goblet. She was still feeling shaken from the look she and Lucas had shared after the last story. His eyes had burned with an intensity that had made her heart pound. It was similar to looks other gentlemen had given her over the years—but also completely different.

He'd looked at her with passion, but a passion that went beyond phys-ical attraction to a higher plane. It was at once exhilarating and terrifying.

"I, for one, was enchanted," Clara said. "I wish you had been there, Isobel. And Susan and Rebecca too."

"Nothing of note ever happens around here except when we have appointments in the village we are obliged to keep," Rebecca said, dipping a spoon into her soup and blowing gently to cool it before taking a sip. "The chestnut soup is divine, Mama."

"I believe Cook added bacon to the recipe this time," Lady Thurlby said.

"Perhaps you can be persuaded to do an encore performance for those of us who weren't there," Viscount Thurlby said, directing his comment to Lavinia.

Lavinia looked at Lucas, which was a mistake. Her insides trembled again.

"Perhaps tomorrow evening, Father, with your—and the others'—permission," he said, his eyes never leaving hers. "Tonight, I should like to spend some time with my betrothed showing her the portrait gallery."

"Be warned, Lavinia," Susan said as the main course of pheasant and vegetables was served. "There is a horrid picture of Lucas there—the only image we had of him before he left for Spain. You wouldn't recognize it as him unless you were told. I dare you to not laugh when you discover which one it is out of the many fine Jennings men hanging on the walls there."

"It's not so bad," the viscountess said.

"It's terrible, Mama," Lucas replied. "One might think it was painted upon my return from war, having become disfigured in battle."

Lady Thurlby waved her hand at him in dismissal. "They exaggerate, Lavinia. While I will concede it isn't the best likeness—"

The viscount coughed, making Lucas laugh.

"Nonetheless, it looked enough like him for me to feel comforted that I had something to remember him by should—" She stopped speaking abruptly and looked down at her lap.

Everyone paused while she collected herself. After a moment, she sniffed and dabbed at her nose, and then raised her head to continue. "I'm beyond relieved that you are returned to us, Lucas, when so many mothers lost and continue to lose their sons in this cause. Now, enough of my foolish sentiment. What did you learn on your inspection of the farm?"

"Perhaps that is a conversation suited to another time, Alice," the viscount said.

"For we'd much rather discuss the latest frills on this year's fashions," Susan said with perfectly placed irony.

"I was directing my question to *Lucas*, who, rather than spend his first full day here in the bosom of his family, *left* us once again to return to this Primrose Farm," Lady Thurlby said, her earlier tears gone, her eyes gleaming.

"You will have noticed that our mother is not fearful of speaking her mind," Lucas whispered to Lavinia.

"Thank goodness for that," Susan whispered, overhearing his words.

"It's no wonder you haven't found a husband," Thomas tossed into the hushed conversation.

"You're quite correct, Thomas," Susan said more loudly. "But it isn't for a lack of offers, you'll recall."

"*Primrose Farm*," Lucas said, pitching his voice above Susan's, "can be brought into good shape incrementally, we concluded, Mama. The priorities are to get the farmhouse habitable for my bride and me"—he glanced at Lavinia—"and gradually bring the acreage into full use. Any other details, I will refrain from sharing until I have discussed them with Lavinia, as I promised her I would."

"How unusual," Isobel said, "for a woman to wish to know the details that accompany the running of an estate. I, for one, am grateful I have Thomas to see to such tedious things—with Father Jennings, of course. And Finch's invaluable assistance."

"I understand your point," Lavinia replied, hoping she wasn't about to say something better left unsaid. She looked adoringly at Lucas, as was her role to perform, also hoping it would mitigate her next comment. "But Primrose Farm, for the time being at least, belongs to me. And since any work that must proceed must have my signature attached, I prefer to sign my name with full knowledge. Lucas and I are in full agreement on this." Lavinia wasn't going to make a friend of Isobel with her comment, but it couldn't be helped. It was the best answer possible without blurting out that the betrothal was all a sham.

Isobel looked at Lavinia with a feigned admiration Lavinia was able to see straight through. "How perfectly brave of you. Lucas, you have found a true gem. I'm so relieved."

Thomas and Lucas shared a look then that spoke volumes. Did Thomas know he'd stolen Isobel from his brother? He must. And Lucas had told Lavinia he'd gotten over his feelings for Isobel, but had he? The shared look suggested they had unfinished business.

Lavinia's presence here had somehow made things worse for everyone.

"I am curious about the individuals in the portraits I'll be viewing later," she said, hoping to take the conversation into more genial areas. "Perhaps you all can tell me about them so I'm prepared when I meet them face-to-face."

"Excellent idea," Viscount Thurlby said, giving her a look of approval, which surprised and pleased Lavinia. "My favorite portrait is of Edmund Jennings, first Viscount Thurlby, for whom our little Edmund is named. He was rather pivotal in these parts during the Glorious Revolution and the ascension of William and Mary to the monarchy. A colorful character, from what I've read. But I believe you will enjoy yourself much more, Lavinia, if

Lucas tells you of the rest of his ancestors when you are actually able to put a face with a name."

"And with that introduction, we ladies will depart," Lady Thurlby announced. She rose, and Lucas's sisters and sisters-in-law followed suit. "Do be sure to ask your cousins if they will provide a small encore performance for us tomorrow evening, after they have rested? Such quaint people they are. Miss Weston in particular seems almost familiar to me for some reason."

"Thank you, Lady Thurlby; I shall," Lavinia said.

"Come, then, Lavinia," Lucas said, rising to his feet as well. "It is time for you to meet the rest of the family, so to speak."

Chapter 15

THE PORTRAIT GALLERY AT ALDERWOOD was a long, narrow room on the top floor of the manor house, in the opposite wing of the private sleeping quarters. Its walls were lined with paintings of varying sizes, some in gilded frames, others in ornately carved wooden ones. Lavinia was enthralled by the sense of history the room held and envious of its homage to family.

"Here is Edmund Jennings, the first Viscount Thurlby, whom my father mentioned," Lucas said, pointing out one of the larger portraits in the room. The gentleman depicted wore a long, dark wig and was elaborately dressed in an embroidered jacket.

"I don't see much family resemblance," Lavinia said, studying the painting closely. Now that she and Lucas were alone, she could relax and step out of character for a moment.

"Nor would you," Lucas replied. "Sometime during the mid-eighteenth century, the viscountcy passed to a second cousin—the gentleman over here, in fact"—he pointed to a particular portrait—"and has continued unbroken from father to son ever since."

"Yes, I can see the resemblance now."

"Going back to the first viscount, however, according to family legend, he became a wealthy man through farming and sheepherding and supported Parliament financially during the Glorious Revolution."

"I don't know much about such things," Lavinia said. "I'm afraid my education is lacking when it comes to the particulars of England's history—unless it's covered in one of Shakespeare's plays, that is. And I doubt those are entirely accurate. But I should like to learn."

"You're exceedingly clever, Lavinia, and I have no doubt you would soon be an expert in whatever you choose to study if one were only to put the right books in your hands. Let's concentrate on more recent history for the time being, shall we? Over here is the seventh Viscount Thurlby, with his first wife and their son, my grandfather." Lucas proceeded to share tidbits of his grandfather's life, but Lavinia kept repeating the compliment he'd given her in her mind. He'd called her exceedingly clever. No man had ever said such a thing to her. Any compliments she had ever received had revolved around her appearance and had merely been a means of gaining her favors.

Oh, she wanted to believe he had meant the words.

"Lavinia?" he asked, breaking into her thoughts. "What is it? What's troubling you?"

"Nothing, truly," she answered, smiling up at him. "Perhaps being surrounded by so many of your ancestors conjured up ghosts of my own."

He took her by the hand and led her to a sofa between two windows. He did not let go of her hand. "Tell me of these ghosts. Allow me to help, if I can."

And there it was again—a kindness toward her that seemed genuine and not self-serving. "I'm not sure I can explain myself so that you will understand."

"We can't know that for certain until you try."

Her lungs felt constricted, so dearly did she want his kindness to have a pure motive but unwilling to unburden her heart to him quite yet. "I envy you your family—both living and dead." She gestured about the room. "This room is filled with riches, Lucas. A heritage that has helped define who you are. And you have parents and brothers and sisters who love you and rejoice that you have returned to them."

"I'm not certain they all—"

"Even Thomas loves you, Lucas, although he is hurting and angry and unsure how to resolve things with you. He is aware that Isobel has not cut all the silken threads she wove around you when you were young. It wasn't as troubling to him while you were gone, I suspect, but now that you are back, he is afraid he has a rival."

"He has no rival."

"Does he not?" she asked softly. "You have told me this is so, and yet something still remains between you and Isobel."

He stood and walked a few paces away before turning to face her. She feared she had angered him. "Very well," he said. "You speak of ghosts; Isobel and I have ghosts too. Mine came from the shock of a first love betrayed when it encountered temptation—hers, not mine. Perhaps I flattered myself in thinking her attachment was equal to mine, although I had no reason not to believe the words of love she spoke to me. The simple reality is that Thomas is the heir, not me. Someday she will be a viscountess.

"Thomas knew of our friendship and perhaps even our attachment but chose to court her anyway, and she chose to accept. I do not blame either of them for their choices any longer. But they are choices that must be lived with. If anything remains unresolved, it is on their part, not mine. I wish them only happiness together."

"And yet, when she came out of the house to greet our carriage, you suddenly had need of a bride, did you not? One, if I may speak so boldly, with an appearance that might put the beautiful Isobel in her place?"

He turned away from her. "I arrived here with *nothing*, Lavinia," he said. "Nothing. No living, no wife, nothing to account for all the years I'd been away. Oh, I had managed to save some earnings, due to the generosity of my friend, Anthony. Pittance compared to my brothers, who completed their university studies and are gainfully employed in positions worthy of their status as gentlemen. Even my youngest brother, Simon, has completed his studies."

"Your mother thinks you saw him during your time in London."

"I couldn't. I couldn't leave Anthony, who still had much healing to do after our return from Spain. Afterward, I simply . . . couldn't."

He returned to her and sat, taking her hand in his. "I'm ashamed, Lavinia. Because of my pride, I pulled you into a lie and took advantage of you for my own purposes. I received a letter from Isobel, encouraging me to return home. It was an entirely decent letter, I suppose, and yet it made me feel . . . small . . . as though I, who had impetuously enlisted in the army, had not gotten over her properly, while she had moved on. I was angry." He kissed her hand. "I am no better than any of the other men you have encountered in your life. I intend to right this wrong I have done to you."

"But not yet, I think," Lavinia said. "You have only just arrived home, Lucas. If you were to confess to your family now, I worry it would damage your relationship with them, and they only just got you back. I wouldn't for the world want them to think ill of you. No. It is better to proceed as we are for a little while longer, and in the meantime, we will get Primrose Farm livable. I must have a secure place for my friends, you see. Once Delia and Artie and Hannah and I are there, you can inform your family that I ended our betrothal. Or better yet, I will write a letter you can share with them, so they can see it for themselves and conclude that I was the one who ended it." She blinked back sudden tears that threatened to escape. "Tomorrow, you and Finch will fill me in on the particulars of repairing the farmhouse. There. That is our plan. I believe it is the best one, for everyone's sakes."

"I can't do that to you, Lavinia." He brushed a lock of hair from her face, nearly undoing her resolve.

"Think, Lucas. How will your family perceive the others and me if you tell them I am not your betrothed? We all went along with it."

"But only so I would not be embarrassed. They will understand."

"They will reach the conclusion that we are not who we claim to be, and they will be correct. You will have exchanged a gently raised bride and her eccentric relatives and friend for three actors and a costume maker. Your family is respectable, Lucas. We are not."

"You are utterly respectable and honorable in my eyes, Lavinia. Delia and Artie are a trifle eccentric, I'll grant you, but also kind, and Hannah is true and loyal. My family *will* understand." He cupped her cheek with his free hand. "Lavinia," he said softly.

"Yes?" She could barely utter the word.

He brought his face close to hers, close enough that she could feel his breath mingle with hers, and her heart quickened. "May I kiss you?" he asked.

"Yes," she whispered.

His mouth found hers.

Lavinia had never experienced such heaven. He gave of himself and, at the same time, received from her, never taking. Eventually, and far too soon, he drew back and simply held her. He demanded nothing, not even her words, and for that she was relieved and exceedingly grateful. She couldn't have found the words to express what she was feeling.

They remained that way for several minutes before Lucas finally spoke in a barely audible voice. "I watched the war in Spain turn men into animals," he said. "War is a terrible business for everyone involved, but it is the women and children who suffer most, I think."

He rested his head against hers. "I witnessed firsthand, Lavinia, what women are subjected to by selfish, unthinking men. It angered me. I resolved even further to be a champion of the gentler sex. My brothers and I were reared to respect womanhood and motherhood by our father, who has always loved our mother. I have sisters and nieces, and I would do violence to any man who ill-used one of them.

"I desire you, Lavinia; I cannot lie. But I also care deeply for you. I have feared that you have been subjected to such ungentlemanly treatment. And yet I have done the same by pulling you unwittingly into my ruse."

"It is not the same, Lucas," she said. "It is not nearly the same."

"It is to me," he whispered. "And I will make it right. I promise you that."

She raised her head. "Lucas, will you kiss me again?" she asked.

"Gladly," he said.

And then he pressed his lips to hers and said no more.

* * *

The following morning, Lavinia sat through a wholly uncomfortable meeting with Lucas, Thomas, Mr. Finch, and Viscount Thurlby. Isaac, she'd been informed, had ridden out early to his vicarage on some church business and would be back later that day.

If Lavinia hadn't already known that her insistence on being part of the proceedings wasn't a huge breach of propriety, the meeting would have swiftly clarified that particular point.

Before Lavinia had entered Viscount Thurlby's study, Susan had pulled her into a small anteroom. "Don't let them bully you. You are clever and learn quickly. I have observed this about you in the short time you have been with us at Alderwood. And until you marry my brother, the property is yours. They will huff and puff—especially Thomas and Finch—and make you think they are the noblest of gentlemen, freeing you from horribly unladylike undertakings, but you must hold your ground."

"I'll do my best, but they are at the advantage in that they understand such things. I have no experience with restoring a farm."

"I daresay none of them have had the actual experience of restoring a farm themselves." She'd squeezed Lavinia's hands. "Now, go remind them you are a woman of property to be taken seriously. If anyone can do that, it's you."

"Thank you, Susan."

An hour later, Lavinia wasn't so sure Susan's confidence had been well placed.

"You were brilliant," Lucas said as he escorted Lavinia from the study to a sitting room and ordered tea.

"Hardly," she replied. Mr. Finch had begun the proceedings by outlining each project that would need to be undertaken, followed by its estimated cost. At the mention of each project by Mr. Finch, Thomas had gone into a detailed description for her benefit in what Lavinia considered a patronizing tone. She had observed that during his pontifications, he'd occasionally shot pointed looks at Lucas, which had suggested to Lavinia that Thomas, as heir to Alderwood, knew of such things in fine detail, but a former soldier couldn't begin to comprehend the complexities of land stewardship, nor could his betrothed, ignorant female that she was.

"I repeat: you were brilliant, Lavinia. I am personally resolved to remain respectful of your abilities if ever we have occasion to disagree in the future. You were utterly dignified, you would have put a duchess to shame with your impeccable manners, and yet you managed to ask the most salient questions at just the right moments. I wanted to stand and applaud you in more than one instance."

"I've had enough applause in my day, Lucas. And I didn't precisely endear myself to Thomas, did I? He thinks me impertinent. But it is *my* farm and my home now, so if I must be impertinent, I shall. But so many *details*, Lucas! My mind is a blur."

"And that is precisely why I suggested Finch make a copy of his notes for you. He should have thought of it beforehand and done it already."

A serving girl arrived with tea, and Lavinia poured them each a cup after she left. "This afternoon, I will write to my banker and arrange for the necessary funds to be made available so work on the farmhouse can begin," she said after she'd poured milk into her cup of tea. "Would you like milk? Or sugar?"

"No, thank you. As to the funds, Father is going to put them up so work can begin today. Allard is already busy talking to carpenters and the like and is just waiting for word. We can send a message to him this afternoon."

"Oh, no, Lucas! I will not have your father paying for it. I won't be beholden to him in that way, especially since he is playing host to us under false pretenses. I simply can't—don't you see? We will have to wait for the funds. It should only take a day or two."

"Lavinia, be reasonable. My father is not doing this to curry favor, except, possibly, with me. Perhaps he missed me while I was gone; who knows? At any rate, this wasn't a declaration of orders; it was an offer. A sensible one I urge you to consider."

He finished off his tea and set the cup and saucer on the table. "Come," he said, standing. "A distraction is what you need. How about a nice stroll in the garden and some fresh air?"

"I should like that," she said. "You're right—a distraction would be just the thing I need to clear my mind."

"There's a particular spot not far from the formal gardens that is so breathtakingly romantic that a young lady cannot resist kissing the gentleman she is with—at least that is what I have been told."

"Indeed?" she asked, biting her lip in order to stay serious.

"I can only relate what I've heard on the matter," he said solemnly. "It may be exaggerated rumor."

"Exaggerated rumor."

"*Or* it might very well be true. I think we should investigate the matter for ourselves. What do you think?"

He was flirting with her, and she was flirting with him. Flirting had only ever been a tool in her arsenal for keeping men off-balance, not a playful means of expressing her attraction to someone.

His eyes twinkled merrily as he waited for her response.

Oh, but he was lovely—strong and capable and handsome, and she was attracted to all those things about him. Her trust in him was growing stronger. It made her feel less alone and vulnerable and, unexpectedly, more *real*. It was a step toward discovering who Lavinia Fernley, the woman, was.

She placed a finger to her lips in feigned deep thought. "Such a curious location *should* be studied carefully, if for no other reason than to dispel or confirm its claim. Unsuspecting people might wander into this spot and find themselves in complicated attachments that were not of their intent. We should indeed investigate."

He grinned and crooked his elbow out for her to slip her arm through. "I was hoping that was what you were going to say."

"Indeed?"

"I am a hopeful man," he said.

Oh, she was in trouble—deep, deep trouble, she thought as she strolled with him through the house and along the formal gardens to a secluded spot that was indeed pretty but much like the rest of the landscape. But because she was with Lucas, it was as breathtakingly romantic as he'd claimed it would be, and she had to concur with the rumors, for she indeed kissed him willingly, and there was no hesitation on his part either.

His arms enveloped her and felt both secure and freeing. She closed her eyes as her hands explored the strength of his arms and shoulders and the softness of his hair, by contrast, while his lips sought hers over and over again. His face was still smooth from his morning shave, and he smelled of soap and warm amber. Lavinia closed her eyes, and for the first time, she allowed herself to revel in the arms of a man. An honorable and caring man.

His lips eventually parted from hers. "We must return to the house now, my dear," he said softly. "I will not have your reputation remarked upon, even if I am allowed time alone with my 'betrothed.'" He kissed her again and gazed into her eyes, and Lavinia could not look away. "I must take you back while I am still in control of my wits. You are even more beautiful than usual, if that's possible, when you look at me like that."

"How am I looking at you?" She had no idea what he saw.

"I daren't say. I will let you figure that out on your own. Come, Lavinia. Let us return. We have a farm to restore and a wedding to pretend to plan."

She put her hand in his, and they walked back to the house.

Chapter 16

LUCAS AND LAVINIA HAD SCARCELY entered the house when one of the servants informed them that his lord and ladyship were awaiting them in the drawing room. When they arrived there, they saw that Isaac had returned, and he had James in tow. Thomas and Isobel and Clara, Susan, and Rebecca were there as well.

"Look who I discovered on the way back here," Isaac said cheerily. "Told him it was too late to change his mind and turn around now that I'd spotted him."

"I had no intention of turning around, not when I had your assurance that our wayward brother had actually shown his face at Alderwood this time. Hello, Lucas," James said, shaking Lucas's hand before pulling him into his arms for a brotherly embrace. "Welcome home."

"It's good to be home," Lucas said. Lavinia was standing quietly to the side, and he drew her next to him, feeling more than a trifle possessive after their tête-à-tête in the garden just moments before. "Allow me to present my future bride, Miss Lavinia Fernley of Primrose Farm. Lavinia, my brother James."

James bowed elegantly over her hand, his eyes fixed on Lavinia's face, as smitten as any man who encountered Lavinia for the first time. "A pleasure indeed, Miss Fernley. Perhaps you can be persuaded to forget this old warhorse and be induced into matrimony with a different Jennings brother."

Lavinia smiled at James's flirtatious comment. Lucas, by contrast, felt poised for battle.

"I see no 'old warhorse,' Mr. Jennings, but only the most honorable man I have ever met," Lavinia replied. "Any efforts on your part to direct my interest elsewhere would be utterly in vain."

"High praise, Lucas. You are a fortunate man. Alas, my heart is broken." He threw a hand dramatically over his heart.

"I'm sure it will mend," Lavinia said with a twinkle in her eye.

"But certainly you must be tired from standing, Miss Fernley," James continued with a smoothness that he must have honed as a barrister speaking before judges.

James extended his arm for Lavinia and led her to a spot on the settee next to Rebecca, then took a seat on the chair next to her. Lucas wandered over and stood by the fireplace, resting his shoulder against the mantel, trying to act as indifferent as he could when his instincts were yelling, "*Get away from her; she's mine*" at top volume. James was a handsome devil; some—like their outspoken sister Susan—might even say he was the most handsome of all the Jennings brothers—not that what a sister said about such things typically counted for much.

Except that right at this moment, it did.

James was speaking softly to Lavinia, Lavinia chuckling in response, and Lucas strained to catch bits of the conversation, even though he knew he was behaving like a jealous boor. James must have said something witty, blast his brother to Hades and back.

In the first place, Lucas thought grumpily, one would think a brother one hadn't seen for seven years would rate higher than the said brother's betrothed—however dazzling she may be. In the second place, one might also think said betrothed, however fictitious the betrothal might be, would be a little more . . . clingy, for sake of a better word, following a half hour of highly enjoyable kissing with said faux-betrothed.

Susan wandered over. "Lucas, you won't believe what I've just seen. Come with me over to the window, and I'll show you. It's quite remarkable."

He was deuced unwilling to be that far from Lavinia while she was still in the clutches of his brother, but he begrudgingly pried himself away from his sentry post and followed Susan over to the window. She gazed out at the formal gardens, so he followed suit.

"I don't see anything I haven't seen a thousand times before," he grumbled.

"That's because you're not looking in the right direction," she said.

"Then why don't you tell me more specifically where it is you wish me to look?" he snapped. His mother turned and glanced at him with alarm. "Apologies, Mama," he said. Thankfully his voice had been low enough not to register on anyone else.

"Oh, Lucas, you are in such a bad way," Susan said with a knowing smile on her face. "I have seen the most incredible thing—you have only to look inwardly to see it yourself. I see a brother who suffered so much from unrequited love he could not see past his feelings toward a happy future. And now—*finally*—that brother is in love with someone else. I believe I can stop worrying about you now. I was more concerned about that than your ability to survive on the Peninsula, although I would never have said such a thing to Mama."

"In love?" He was barely willing to entertain such a thought, especially after what had happened with Isobel. Attracted to Lavinia, yes. Cared for her, yes. A bit possessive at present . . . But in love?

"And she loves you too," Susan said. "But of course she does, or why else would she have agreed to marry you? You have little to offer a bride beyond your charming self."

He stared at her.

"And," she continued, "if you were being observant at the moment rather than jealous and petulant, you would have seen that your fair bride's back has straightened, her chin has lifted, and her airs have become all genteel perfection. She has not looked so proper and untouchable since the day she and her friends arrived here with you, before she knew any of us. I daresay she is tolerating James's attention, but that is all."

"Tolerating?"

"Just *look*, Lucas."

He turned so he could discreetly watch the two of them converse. James was thoroughly entranced by Lavinia; Lucas could see it in his face. Lavinia, however—

Devil take him for a fool.

Lavinia was precisely as Susan had said. The changes in her demeanor wouldn't be apparent to anyone who didn't know her well, but Susan was clever and observant, so she had seen it too, and it had taken her to shake him loose from his jealous reaction—and fear.

For it *had* been fear. Fear that he'd lose the woman he loved to another brother. Again.

Susan had been right about that too—he did love Lavinia.

What a mess he'd created for them both.

* * *

A few days later, Finch informed Lucas that he'd received word from Allard. Repairs on the farmhouse were proceeding well: the stone foundation had been thoroughly inspected and its weak areas reinforced, as well as the original framework. They were beginning the repairs to the roof, with new shingles scheduled to follow, and the carpenters had begun work on the stairs. The house would be ready for habitation within a week's time, give or take a few days, depending on the weather or any other unforeseen event.

Cash transfers from Lavinia's bank had arrived the previous day; she had insisted on repaying Lucas's father herself. Lucas had accompanied her as she'd approached his father in his study. He'd been very gracious to her, for which Lucas had been grateful, although he'd pulled Lucas aside later in the day and had questioned her odd insistence—his words—in repaying him thus.

"We all agreed she would reimburse me, although soon enough, the two of you will be wed and I would consider it a moot point," his father had said. "It is something that can be addressed easily enough in the marriage contracts. There was really no need for her to be part of it when you could have dealt with it easily enough for her. I sometimes wonder at her, Lucas, I must tell you."

Marriage contracts, Lucas had thought. That was going to be trickier to deal with than pretending to set the wedding luncheon menu with Cook.

"And those relations of hers, Lucas! They're agreeable enough, I'll admit, very likable and quite entertaining—that encore performance they gave us the other evening was better than I expected. But they are lacking the discretion one usually expects in the elderly. Just the other day, I actually saw Mr. Drake in the park doing *cartwheels*, of all things, with Edmund and Isaac Junior. I'm not opposed to the *boys* doing such antics, but to see *Mr. Drake*—his movements were inelegant, and I was deathly afraid he was going to dislocate his shoulder or something equally dreadful. It was most peculiar, watching someone his age going feet-over-head that way, over and over again. Edmund and Isaac Junior thought it a lark, but I must wonder at the old man's antics."

"Hmm," was all Lucas could think to say.

Before dinner that same day, Lucas's mother had said something similar to him about Delia. "Miss Weston is a curiosity, Lucas, although she seems a dear lady. I am doing my best to keep an open mind. Just this morning, however, she complimented me on my marriage and lovely family—and then proceeded to ask me how I'd managed to *snare* your father. *Snare!* Her word. As though I hadn't the qualities to earn your father's affections otherwise. I have chosen to think she merely wished to hear our love story since we are all in a betrothal state of mind, what with you and Lavinia. But I was rather taken aback, I must say."

"Perhaps we can chalk it up to the idiosyncrasies of old age," he'd suggested.

He'd had no intention on either occasion of saying to his parents, "Please forgive Delia and Artie their oddities. They're actors, you see—have been all their lives. They know nothing else."

Today, with the arrival of Allard's letter, Lucas had an excuse to get out of the house for a while and away from his parents' questions. He wanted to see the progress at Primrose Farm for himself. He also needed time to think. The ride would do him good. Before he left, however, he needed to tell Lavinia what Allard had said in his letter. She would want to know, and she would wonder at his sudden departure.

He found her in his mother's favorite sitting room, where the ladies had congregated. His mother and Clara and Isobel were busy with their needlework. Susan sat next to the window and was reading a book; she had always loathed sewing of any kind. Rebecca sat at the small pianoforte located in the corner of the room, with Lavinia standing nearby, turning pages for her. Rebecca had always had a gift for music, and it was a pleasure to hear how accomplished she'd become while he was away.

He stepped inside the room and quietly closed the door behind him and then listened and watched as Rebecca filled the room with the sounds of Mozart. Every so often, she nodded slightly and Lavinia turned the page in response.

Delia was listening to the music with her eyes closed.

Soon the piece came to an end, and everyone, including Lucas, applauded. "Well done, Rebecca," his mother said. "You are improving nicely under Mr. Burnhope's instruction."

"Thank you, Mama. I like Mr. Burnhope exceedingly well. He is extremely good at explaining the heart of the music to me in a way I understand." She pulled another piece of music from the small stack sitting next to her. "Do you know this song, Lavinia? It is one of my favorites."

"I do," Lavinia replied.

"Will you join me?"

"It would be my pleasure." Her eyes fluttered briefly in Lucas's direction.

Rebecca played the introduction, and Lavinia began to sing.

Lucas liked her voice immensely. She had a fine voice, true of pitch, and she seemed comfortable singing before the others, which, undoubtedly resulted from her experience in the theater. But her voice wasn't extraordinary—at least, not like her physical beauty was. And that made her voice absolutely perfect for her.

Midway through the song, she stopped. "The melody is rather high for me in this key," she said.

Rebecca stopped playing. "You do seem to be more of an alto," she said. "Can you sing harmony? Isobel, come sing the melody with us. You're a soprano. A vocal duet will be such fun!"

Both ladies froze.

Isobel moved first. She calmly set her needlework aside and stood, straightening her skirt before crossing the room to stand next to Lavinia. The others set their needlework in their laps so they could watch. Susan closed her book.

Isobel nodded at Rebecca to begin.

Rebecca played the introduction again, and Isobel began singing the melody Lavinia had just sung. Isobel's voice was superior to Lavinia's, having taken voice lessons throughout her girlhood.

On the second phrase, Lavinia added her voice in harmony. Their voices blended well, and soon they were sensing each other's musical nuances—or so it seemed to Lucas, untrained as he was.

Much too soon, the song ended, and there was a moment's pause as everyone savored the music before breaking out into enthusiastic applause.

"Oh, well done, well done, all of you!" his mother cried, clapping.

"That was the prettiest thing I've heard in an age," Clara said, dabbing at her eye with her handkerchief. "Sorry. Don't mind me. I'm a watering pot these days."

Delia sighed gustily.

Lavinia and Isobel shared a look—Lucas held his breath—and then they smiled at each other. It was the slightest of smiles, true, but it was, perhaps, the beginning of reconciliation. And with that shared look, Lucas realized he no longer envied Thomas or harbored resentment toward Isobel. He wanted peace with them. He was no longer in love with Isobel—and most surprising of all, he realized he probably hadn't been for a long time.

Pride could make a man do foolish things.

It was time for him to congratulate them on their performance. He crossed the room. "What a visionary you are, Rebecca, as well as being so much more accomplished on the pianoforte than I remember. Asking these two to perform together was brilliant."

Rebecca beamed at him, and Isobel and Lavinia turned to acknowledge his compliment. "Thank you, Lucas," Rebecca said. "Perhaps Susan isn't the cleverest of your sisters after all."

"I heard that," Susan called from across the room.

Rebecca giggled.

"Isobel, Lavinia, you were enchanting," Lucas said. "No one would ever know you had never sung together before. Brava to you both."

Isobel's eyes traveled from Lucas to Lavinia and back again. "Thank you, Lucas," she said, smiling. "That is generous of you."

"Yes, thank you, Lucas," Lavinia said, her eyes glowing. "It was a privilege to sing with such a gifted vocalist as Isobel."

"It was a joy to hear you sing once again, Isobel. You have a great gift, you know, one I enjoyed even as a boy. Now, I'm afraid I must steal Lavinia from you, if you'll excuse us," he said.

Isobel's face fell slightly, but she recovered nicely. "But of course. Lavinia, it was truly a pleasure. Perhaps we can sing together again soon? I would enjoy it very much."

"I would like nothing better," Lavinia replied.

Isobel nodded, and Lucas led Lavinia from the sitting room to the corridor beyond. "I am leaving for Primrose Farm. Allard has written. The farmhouse should be habitable by sometime next week. I wish to inspect the work and discuss the next plans with him."

"Oh, I wish I could go with you, Lucas. I'm interested in seeing the work being done for myself."

"In time, Lavinia, all in good time. Next week will arrive soon enough."

"When it is habitable, my friends and I will be returning there to live," she said as though to put him on notice. "We cannot remain guests here in your parents' home when we will have a perfectly suitable home of our own in which to stay."

"I understand." He was already aware of what the information in Allard's note had implied. The farmhouse's completion meant Lavinia would be gone, and they would have to proceed with their plans to end their feigned betrothal.

He kissed her hand and bid her farewell with a heavy heart.

* * *

"Ho, there, Lucas," James called as Lucas walked toward the stable to get Hector, who was saddled and ready for him.

He turned and held his hand to his eyes to block the overhead sun. James was striding toward him, and not far behind him were Thomas and Isaac, with Finch bringing up the rear. "I thought I might ride with you to this little property you'll be gaining by marrying that delectable heiress of yours, and then this lot decided they ought to tag along. Doesn't anyone have anything better to do around here than gallivant up and down the countryside?"

"*I* am not joining you today," Finch said indignantly. "For *I do* have work that needs to be done. I am merely giving Lucas the banknotes for funding the next work projects. Here you go." He handed the notes to Lucas with a dramatic flair that would have made Artie proud before returning the way he'd come.

They all watched him go before looking at each other and breaking into laughter.

"Four brothers back together again, eh, Lucas?" James said. "It wants only Simon and the set would be complete. Is he returning home, by any chance?"

"If he's not here within the next day or two, our mother will probably petition the Home Office for his speedy apprehension and return," Isaac said.

James laughed. "That does sound like Mama."

"Did you not see Simon during your time in London, Lucas?" Isaac asked.

"I'm sorry to say I did not," Lucas replied. He'd intended to travel to Primrose Farm alone, but spending the afternoon with his brothers would do him good—despite the guilt he was now feeling over his avoidance of Simon while he'd been in Town.

"Probably just as well," Thomas said. "Simon has some wild oats to sow, and I'm not sure he's done sowing them yet or that Mama will like what she sees if and when he does arrive home."

"I had no idea," Isaac said, his brow wrinkled in vicarly concern. "I would have done something before now had I known."

"Which is precisely why the little bounder chose to write to me over the past year or so and not you, Isaac," Thomas replied.

"He's not as bad as all that, surely," Isaac said.

"We all sow our wild oats in one way or another," James said, looking slightly bored at having to explain this to Isaac. "Lucas went off to play soldier. Thomas and I did as much reveling as studying while at university. Simon merely has the fate of being the youngest of five brothers and must exceed our accomplishments—both bad and good—in order to find his place amongst us. He'll be fine."

"I hope you're right," Isaac said. "I never felt the need to sow any oats."

"We *know*," James said in a dramatically exasperated tone, making the other brothers laugh.

"You were born pious, Isaac," Thomas added. "We were always concerned you were going to confess our boyhood pranks to Father and we would get a birching as a result."

Isaac shrugged with mock modesty. "'Tis true. I was the most perfect of all our parents' sons."

"And still are to this day," Lucas said. "As you remind us on a regular basis."

"Pride must be the reason you have not entered sainthood yet," James said wryly. "As soon has you have developed humility regarding your perfection, I shall contact the Archbishop myself on your behalf."

Isaac laughed.

"Now that we've settled all that, are we allowed to join you on your errand this afternoon or not, Lucas?" James asked.

"Do I have a choice in the matter?" Lucas said.

"No."

"Then, by all means, I welcome the company."

Chapter 17

LAVINIA RETURNED TO THE SITTING room and resumed her seat, picking up the small square of embroidery she pretended to work on when doing needlework was socially called for. Hannah had always done any of their necessary sewing, although she'd taught Lavinia enough basics to muddle along.

Delia picked up her own neglected needlework, stared at it, and tossed it aside. "I never could understand the great interest women take in poking needles and thread into fabric day in and day out."

"It has something to do with wanting clothes to wear," Hannah said.

Susan and Rebecca burst out laughing. Lavinia might have thought the exchange humorous, but she was still reeling from the fact that they'd be moving to Primrose Farm the following week. In a week's time, she would have no more reason to see Lucas, and she would be the one to cry off the betrothal in order to protect his gentlemanly honor.

"I *know* it's required for having clothing, Hannah," Delia replied. "But how many cushions and pillows and such can a person cover with embroidery before one goes completely mad?"

"I agree with you wholeheartedly," Susan said, earning a glance from Lady Thurlby. "Which is why I chose to read this afternoon."

"I don't mind sewing. I'm making a few new things for the baby," Clara said.

She held up the tiny gown she was working on, and Lavinia's heart felt a new pang. She'd never considered having children before. For so long, her life had consisted of mistrusting and avoiding men and merely surviving. Now she had the opportunity to have the normal life that she'd never thought possible.

A husband and a baby . . .

"That's so precious," Delia said, admiring the tiny gown. "I never had children. Never married either. Some people don't realize what's right in front of them until it's too late." She looked directly at Lavinia. "That is why I'm so delighted our dear Lavinia has found her perfect match in your son, Lady Thurlby. When Arthur and I first heard of their betrothal, we were beside ourselves with joy. Were we not, Hannah?" She turned her fairy queen gaze on Hannah.

Hannah glanced at Lavinia before replying. "You and Artie were very enthusiastic," she said.

Lavinia bit her lip.

"As we still are," Delia said, nodding with satisfaction. "When I see the love these two young people share, it fills my soul with a bittersweet longing, but I shall rejoice in knowing they will be sharing something wondrous and beautiful that I wasn't privileged to have." She sighed dramatically.

Of course she did.

Lavinia wanted to take her from the room and throttle her—if she didn't think it might break every brittle bone in Delia's body. She was laying it on too thick. There was something in that little speech of hers, with its poignant tone of regret—especially when she knew full well the betrothal wasn't real—that was intended to turn the screws even tighter.

"Were you ever in love, Miss Weston?" Clara asked.

"Oh, yes," Delia said, staring off into the distance like any accomplished thespian would. "Thoroughly, deeply in love. But things don't always turn out as we'd wish, now, do they? We must *reach* for love when it is *right before us*."

And there it was.

That little wisp of an exasperating woman was bound and determined to make Lavinia's fake betrothal a real one since fate hadn't granted her with her own happy ending. Bless her little interfering heart.

"I've been so impressed with how the children have taken to both you and Mr. Drake," Lady Thurlby said as she rethreaded her needle. "The boys especially seem rather keen for his company."

"Arthur has always enjoyed the company of children," Delia said. "They have such wonderful imaginations, you see."

"Mr. Drake does seem rather imaginative—I daresay I've never seen the like from a grown man before," the viscountess said.

Hannah snorted and bit off the end of her thread with her teeth.

"I must confess I was rather uncomfortable with his . . . antics . . . at first," Isobel said. "Even yesterday my little Sarah wasn't sure what to think when he pretended to be a bear and charged after Edmund and Isaac Junior, roaring with his arms outstretched, when the children were outside for their daily constitutional. Of course, according to Sarah, the boys thought it great fun and created some sort of invisible bear trap to catch him."

"I wondered where he'd gone," Delia said thoughtfully. "The children. I should have realized."

"Is it a good thing, do you think, for a grown man to cavort with children in such a manner every day?" Clara asked hesitatingly. "The children seem delighted, but is it something they should encounter with such regularity? Isaac recalls imaginative escapades with his brothers—playing pirates and explorers and such—but not with his father, although I know Father Jennings spent quality time with his children. I am trying to understand."

"I shall speak to Artie," Lavinia said. "He should have consulted with both you and Isobel before imposing himself upon the children and Mrs. Wynn. Wouldn't you agree, Delia?"

"I've never had to consider it from a parent's point of view—all I can say is that I've known Arthur Drake for nearly fifty years, and in all that time, I've never known a kinder man whose greatest delight is making others happy, especially children."

"I'll speak to him," Lavinia said again when it appeared Delia's speech hadn't entirely reassured Isobel and Clara.

"Thank you, Lavinia," Lady Thurlby said. "I'm sure the others would agree that the *occasional* theatrical or imaginative playtime, with their mothers' prior approval, would be entirely acceptable. There. That is settled. Now, if you'll excuse me, I have some things to discuss with Cook regarding the betrothal party we've arranged for next week."

The other ladies dispersed soon after the viscountess left the sitting room, leaving Lavinia alone with Delia and Hannah.

Hannah stood and shut the sitting room door before turning to Delia. "What you done is beyond the pale," she scolded. "It's bad enough our poor Livvy here was pulled into this betrothal nonsense, nice as Mr. Jennings is, but you talking about love and 'sharing something wondrous and beautiful,' as you put it, like it's a real thing between them two—well, that's taking it too far."

"We were to keep as close as possible to the truth, Delia," Lavinia added. "I care about these people. They are going to be hurt and embarrassed when the truth comes out. I don't want to make it any worse." Especially for Lucas. Oh, especially for him.

"As far as I'm concerned, the betrothal *is* the truth," Delia said. "He said the words, didn't he? I've seen the looks he gives you—and you give right back to him. I'm an old actor who's seen more than my share of good acting in my day—some so convincing it looks as real as I'm sitting here—but Lucas isn't an actor, dearie, and I've been reading his face like a book ever since we met up with him back in London. He looks at you different than all the other gentlemen did—and you know he does.

"You're a fine actress yourself, Livvy, but I can see what's in your eyes too. You don't fool this old woman. I know that look. I've felt that look—" Her voice caught. Seasoned actress that she was, she shook off her real emotions and continued on—and Lavinia's heart broke for her. "Love is a precious thing, Lavinia. Too precious to waste. I should know." She stood and straightened up, looking like the grand lady of the stage she'd been for so many years. "Now, I believe I shall go to my room and lie down for a while." She turned to Hannah next. "If you love this girl of ours even half as much as Arthur or I do, Hannah Broome, you'll convince her that what I said is the truth." She turned and marched out of the room, as grand an exit as any she'd ever made onstage.

"Don't say anything, Hannah," Lavinia warned.

Hannah folded her needlework and placed it in her sewing basket. "I don't need to," she said. She rose and kissed Lavinia on her forehead. "Because she's right—at least when it come to Lucas Jennings. I never seen a man what's treated you with such respect."

"And that's precisely why I won't force him into a betrothal, Hannah, or allow Delia and Artie to force the issue," Lavinia said. "I won't repay his kindness that way. I can't."

"That's as it should be, but it's a sorry thing too. For I want you to be happy for once in your life, and I think you've found a man who has finally seen that you're as beautiful on the inside as you are on the outside. And that's a rare thing, Livvy. A rare thing, indeed."

* * *

It had felt good spending time with his brothers at Primrose Farm, Lucas thought as he handed off Hector to the stable boy. Now it was time to clear the air with Thomas—and with Isobel too. The few conversations he'd had with either of them since returning home had been uncomfortable. Except for yesterday.

Spending time together, reminiscing and playfully badgering each other as they had done as boys, had felt like old times, and it seemed to Lucas that it might also have worked to soften the edges of the prickly subject that was Thomas's marriage to Isobel.

Mr. Allard had done a fine job supervising the laborers repairing the farmhouse. It wasn't difficult to imagine it being ready for occupants within the week. Considering its dilapidated state a mere few days ago, Allard and his men had worked something of a miracle.

A miracle that would take Lavinia away from him.

He and his brothers had discussed Lavinia on the way to and from Primrose Farm. They had been brimming with questions about her: Where did they meet, where was she from, where did that *hair* come from, what could she possibly see in *him* (that particular question had come from James), and did he worry that others would assume she wasn't *modest* enough (that tactfully worded question had come from Isaac)?

Lucas had kept his answers brief and to the point: they had met in London (without telling them when or how), her family at least partly hailed from Lincolnshire (pointing to Primrose Farm as evidence), she obviously had good taste (that one in response to James's question), and she'd been given her glorious beauty from God, so God-fearing people should not be inclined to judge her based on it (that one in response to Isaac).

"You're one lucky devil," James declared to Lucas as they walked toward the house. They had lagged behind the two other brothers.

"You think so?" Lucas replied, knowing he alone understood the irony in his words.

"Yes, I do. You survived seven years in the army and on the Peninsula, which, I understand, is a remarkable feat in itself. You have an absolutely stunning bride-to-be, who appears to be quite devoted to you—and *only* you, although, with looks like hers, she could have her pick of any man."

"Agreed," Lucas said.

"How she managed to escape London with you before finding herself scooped up by some wealthy nabob or duke is a mystery I think many gentlemen would find intriguing. Me included."

James's phrase "managed to escape" made the hairs on Lucas's neck stand on end. James was so near the truth that Lucas wondered for a moment if his barrister brother had gained inside knowledge about Lavinia in some clandestine manner. And how ludicrous was that? As though James could have known beforehand that she was even here. Ridiculous.

"As I was saying," James continued. "You land a gloriously beautiful bride, who also happens to be an heiress, after surviving years of war as an enlisted man, to boot. I think, perhaps, you are the most successful Jennings brother of us all—or at least the luckiest. And still a relatively young buck too. Quite unfair."

"You wish to marry?" Lucas asked. James had always been so academically driven and focused on his career that Lucas thought his older brother would never allow time for a wife and family.

James shrugged and whacked some mud from his boot with his crop. "Not in the immediate future, no. Too many professional duties to attend to at present. But when I see my other brothers—and now you, too, in such happy circumstances . . . it makes a man think."

For the merest of moments, Lucas wondered if he should tell James his secret regarding his betrothal. It would have been nice to discuss it with him, unburden himself a bit, and feel he had a family member who had his back when he finally confessed the truth about the betrothal. But he wouldn't put Lavinia and her friends at risk, so any thoughts he had of confiding in James died a quick death.

James, and everyone else, would find out soon enough. It was going to feel like a very short week, Lucas suspected.

* * *

As Lucas headed toward the stairs on his way to breakfast the following morning, he could hear that someone had just arrived at Alderwood. The arrival of a person or persons this early in the morning could mean only one of two things: either his brothers had gone out for a morning ride without him, which he doubted—one of his brothers surely would have invited him along—or Simon had finally arrived, with or without the Home Office's intervention on their mother's behalf.

Indeed, it was his little brother handing over his hat and gloves to a manservant when Lucas arrived in the entrance hall. More precisely, it was his *younger* brother in the entrance hall—there was nothing *little* about Simon Jennings anymore. He was at least at tall as Lucas, slender, and had a darker shade of hair than any of the other brothers. There was only three years between them in age, which was nothing at all, especially when compared to

Thomas, who was nine years Lucas's senior. But Simon had always been the baby brother, a lad of but sixteen years when Lucas had enlisted.

Lucas himself had been not quite nineteen at the time, but had felt ages older than Simon back then—he'd had a term at university and had been dealing with a broken heart. They were adult things, to Lucas's way of thinking, that had made the gulf in age between Simon and himself seem even wider.

Amazing what a few years could do to a man's perspective.

Lucas came down the stairs quickly and crossed the hall to him. Why hadn't he felt an urgency to meet up with his brother in London? He felt the urgency now, now that he was here. "Simon!" he said, his hand outstretched.

Simon turned away from the manservant, and Lucas came to a halt. Simon hadn't simply grown up—he'd aged. Lucas had seen his expression on countless soldiers and officers. It was the world-weary look of someone who'd seen too much and considered himself hardened to it. His eyes were bloodshot, his welcoming smile more of a smirk. "Well, if it isn't my soldier brother, home alive and well," he said, shaking Lucas's offered hand.

"As you see, and I thank God daily for that small kindness," Lucas said.

"Kindness." He chuckled. "Indeed. God's kindness."

"Mama and Father will want to know you've arrived." Lucas signaled to the footman, but Simon forestalled him.

"There's plenty of time for that, don't you think? Come." He gestured toward a small anteroom next to the main drawing room. "Let's get reacquainted first, shall we?"

Once inside, Simon shut the door and leaned against it, shutting his eyes. "Excuse me," he said. "I left Stamford rather early this morning, and I need a moment to get my bearings."

What Simon meant, without saying it, was that he'd been reluctant to return home, not unlike Lucas had been, and had stayed in Stamford—barely twelve miles away—rather than continue the journey last evening. And judging by the redness of his eyes and his unsteadiness, he'd whiled away his time there drinking and who knew what else until the wee hours of the morning.

He'd at least found the wherewithal to wash and dress properly. There was no tavern stink about him. But he didn't fool Lucas, and he wouldn't fool the rest of the family either.

Lucas locked the door and placed a hand on Simon's shoulder. "Come and sit, before you slide to the floor. I'll ring for some breakfast to be brought here. I haven't eaten, so no one will be the wiser. You need food in you."

Simon shook off Lucas's hand. "I'm not in that bad of shape," he said. He crossed to the nearest chair and sank into it with a groan. "And I don't want any food."

"Well, I do." He stepped out into the corridor. "You—I don't know your name, sorry," he said to the same manservant who'd taken Simon's things. "If you'd please fill two breakfast plates and bring them here. And keep this between us, if you will."

"John, sir, and yes, sir."

"Good man." He went back into the anteroom, leaving it open the barest crack so he'd hear the man's return. It wouldn't do to have him juggling two plates on a tray while trying to get into a locked room.

"Heard you were back on English soil, y'know," Simon said, his eyes still closed. "Word got round that you'd kept the Earl of Halford alive when he should have died. Very commendable."

"He'd done the same for me before. It's what soldiers do when they aren't actually killing people."

Simon croaked out a laugh at that, although Lucas hadn't really intended it to be funny. "I suppose that's true enough."

"I should have called on you while I was in Town, Simon. I have no excuse, except to say I was looking after my friend, who was still rather unwell, and I—"

Simon waved his hand. "Enough, Lucas. I wasn't in a mood to be called on by family, even by my soldier brother, or I'd have called on you myself."

A subtle clearing of a throat at the door let Lucas know the manservant had arrived with the food. Lucas opened the door for him, and the man set the tray on the table in front of Simon before excusing himself.

"It smells awful," Simon muttered, grimacing, his head falling back against the chair again.

"Nevertheless, it will help you get over what ails you."

"It'll only help me cast up my accounts on Mama's carpet," Simon said.

Lucas was hungry and not inclined to wait, so he picked up a knife and fork and began cutting into the generous slice of ham on his plate. "Here, start with some toast." He handed a square of buttered toast to Simon, who nibbled on it gingerly. After Simon had eaten a few bites, his color began to look less gray, which boded well for the carpet. "Mama's letter said you arrived here betrothed. I must say, I'm anxious to meet the young lady."

Lucas stopped chewing.

"Not once did I hear any rumors of you being betrothed while you were in Town," Simon added, taking another small bite of toast.

"I doubt I'm the sort of person London society spends much time gossiping about," he said. He reminded himself he needed to act normal and not make assumptions about what Simon did or did not know. He sliced off more ham.

"That's true, although, as your brother, I did attempt to find out about you a time or two. Curiosity, you know. When I did, it was mostly talk about your friend the earl's surprise betrothal to that girl from the country, and that was that."

Lucas began to breathe a little easier.

"At any rate," Simon continued, reaching for another square of toast since he'd managed to eat the first square and keep it down. "I was much too busy with my own *affairs*"—he chuckled—"to worry all that much about yours. You must have returned from war eager to ensure your immortality by producing progeny to have found a willing bride so quickly, especially since you're still a relatively young man. Now, James—*he's* the one Mama ought to be carping at." He sighed. "Sorry. I shouldn't say such things about Mama; I know she means well. But she keeps writing me these *letters*. Most of the time, I just ignore them. But James is thirty-one, devil take it. If anyone deserves to get letters from Mama reminding him of his duty, it should be he."

"I think he's inclined to pursue that route in the not-too-distant future, although he says he is too busy with professional duties to marry right at the moment."

"That *is* news. Well, well. Any prospects? Lovely young ladies from Lincoln dying to marry a man who's always busy with his so-called 'professional duties'? James was always the one who seemed most keen on excitement, if you were to ask me, despite his intensity in school. I can hardly believe he spends his days molding away in a wig and ceremonial gown before a judge. It seems to go against his basic nature."

Lucas smiled. "I hadn't thought about it that way. And, no—no prospects as of yet, at least no one he's mentioned."

"Well, I'll believe it when I see it when it comes to James." He'd finished the second square of toast by this time. "You know, Lucas, I'm feeling somewhat better after your hounding me to eat the toast. I'll try a few of those eggs and see how they sit."

"Good." Lucas scooped some eggs onto a plate for Simon. "And if all else fails, I'll grab Mama's decorative urn over by the window and have it over here in a trice."

Simon turned to look in the direction of the urn, then grabbed his head with both hands and moaned.

"Shall I grab the urn?" Lucas asked, setting the eggs down just to be on the safe side.

"No, just give me a minute for the room to stop spinning. It might actually be an improvement for the urn if I were to use it though. I never could understand what Mama saw in the ugly thing."

Lucas chuckled and handed the plate of eggs to Simon. Even in the aftermath of a night of carousing, Simon still managed to keep his wit. "When we're done here, I'm taking you to your room so you can sleep. You can make your grand entrance this afternoon."

"That's the best idea I've heard yet. Many thanks, brother."

Simon ate the eggs and successfully kept them down, then Lucas helped him circumvent the rest of the family and got him to his bedroom. "Sweet dreams, baby brother," he said before shutting the door to Simon's room.

Simon shot him a withering look.

Lucas was enjoying being home with his family. He really should have come sooner. He'd delayed only a few extra weeks, true, but he could feel his guilt over the matter returning to nag at him again.

He forced it back. Enough of guilt. And enough of feeling inferior to his brothers and their accomplishments. Lucas had made his choices. He could not undo them; his life was what it was. It was time for him to look to the future and choose again.

It was past time.

* * *

After sneaking Simon up to his bedroom so he could sleep off his inebriation, Lucas went to the breakfast room in search of Thomas and Isobel.

They were not there, however. "Sarah had a nightmare last night and was inconsolable," Rebecca explained as she delicately separated the yolk from her coddled egg and proceeded to eat the white part only. "She dreamt her mama and papa were fighting, and poor little Sarah would not believe them when they told her it was just a dream and that everything was all right."

"I see," Lucas said. And he did see—more than Rebecca herself did, for she'd been but twelve when Lucas had left for the army. She may have known about his and Isobel's youthful attachment, but she would have assumed it was ancient history by now.

But the tension between Thomas and Isobel in the wake of Lucas's return had been evident in both their faces. Little Sarah must have sensed the emotions of the adults, and it had given her nightmares, poor thing.

He pictured the little girl. His niece. She was the spitting image of her mother—delicate, blonde, and blue-eyed. The perfect little English rosebud. He was relieved to discover he did not feel the slightest prick of regret that she was not his and Isobel's daughter.

Lucas made his way to the nursery and briefly introduced himself to Mrs. Wynn, who was busy with Isaac and Clara's four children. The elder two were working on their letters, and the younger two stacked blocks and knocked them over, laughing and beginning the process all over again.

Thomas and Isobel were at the other side of the room. Isobel was seated in a child-sized chair at a child-sized table that Lucas remembered from his own days in the nursery, reading a story to Edmund and Sarah, who were seated on either side of her. Thomas sat in the window seat nearby, which was the only spot in the nursery that could accommodate Thomas's height.

Isobel stopped reading when Lucas walked toward them.

"May I beg a moment of your time? Thomas? Isobel?" he asked in a low voice so as not to disturb the children at the other end of the nursery.

Isobel glanced at Thomas. "Of course," Thomas replied. "Edmund, Sarah—Mama and I are going to speak to Uncle Lucas for a few minutes. We shall leave the book right here so Mama can finish the story when we return."

The children looked at Lucas and then scampered off to join their cousins, little Sarah appearing to have gotten over her nightmare satisfactorily. Thomas and Isobel followed Lucas out into the corridor and then to a nearby room where they would have privacy while they conversed.

When they were all seated, Lucas spoke. "I believe it is time to clear the air," he began. "Time to speak openly about the past so we may go forward with open hearts and clear consciences into the future."

"I will start, then," Isobel said.

"No, my dear, let me," Thomas interrupted. "Lucas, I knew of your attachment to Isobel. I was twenty-nine and Father's heir, and in my arrogance, I thought myself a more worthy match for her than you and didn't hesitate to court her as a result. It was wrong of me, and I blamed myself when you left in bitterness and enlisted in the army. Every day over the long seven years you were in Spain, I expected a letter to arrive announcing your death. I think I became resentful to you over that guilt I felt—odd as it may seem."

"It is my turn, Thomas, my dear," Isobel said, laying her hand on Thomas's arm. "I have always loved you dearly, Lucas. You know that. I even thought myself in love with you for a time. But you were always . . . braver . . . than I. I enjoyed our frolics here in the safety of the parks of Alderwood, but I think I always sensed that your soul was much more daring than mine. I longed for security and steadiness, and I quickly saw that Thomas had those qualities. I fell in love with him. Had I known the pain it would cause you, I would have done things much more differently. All the same, I do not believe I would have married you, dear though you were to me—for Thomas was and is the husband of my heart."

"And while I was arrogantly proclaiming myself a more suitable match for Isobel back then," Thomas added, "I will ruefully agree with Isobel that I am less inclined to face risk and challenge than you. I hope that doesn't count against my manliness."

"Oh, Thomas," Isobel said. "You are *such* a dear man."

Lucas nodded thoughtfully. Was it really just that simple? Now, in this moment, he could hear their words and understand and accept them. Seven years ago, he doubted he would have. They could have talked for hours, explaining themselves over and over, and he would not have heard what they were telling him.

"I was hurt by both of you," he said. "I felt horribly betrayed. My home here at Alderwood no longer felt like my home with you here, married to Thomas. I think perhaps you are right, Isobel; I think there is an element of my character that longs for challenge, although I don't think I realized it back then. Enlisting was a rash thing to do and demonstrates clearly a willingness to take risks. I could have gone back to Cambridge and simply kept my distance from Alderwood, but I set out to do something utterly dangerous. Perhaps I intended to make you all suffer. Perhaps I wanted you to await that letter that never arrived, Thomas. I do not know. By then, I was too busy learning how to stay alive to think about such things. When I arrived home this time, it was with hurt pride and nothing more."

"I'm so glad to hear this, finally," Isobel said, tears blossoming in her clear, blue eyes. "I told Thomas I felt I must write to you and explain that you were loved and wanted here at home, and he agreed. But you didn't write back."

"I misunderstood the reasons behind your writing," Lucas said. "Let us leave it at that."

She smiled and nodded, dabbing at her eyes with her handkerchief. "And then when you finally arrived home, it was such a shock to hear you announce your betrothal to Miss Fernley. We were all shocked at the news, quite frankly.

She seemed so, I don't know—*excessively* beautiful. It seemed utterly wrong somehow, and I'm afraid I felt a bit protective of you, perhaps even possessive. But as I have gotten to know her, I can see how loyal she is to those elderly cousins of hers, and she also seems to have the same ability to face challenges that you have. She is a better equal to you than I ever would have been."

The children were knocking over the blocks and laughing, and Lucas gazed at them with fondness. "You have a beautiful family," Lucas said. "Edmund and Sarah are fortunate to have you both. Perhaps one day, I will be as blessed as you are."

"That day appears to be looming large on the horizon," Thomas said.

"One can hope," Lucas said. He stood. "And now I will leave you to finish reading your story to your children."

"Thank you, Lucas," Thomas said, rising to his feet and shaking Lucas's hand before pulling him into a tight hug. "And welcome home, at last."

Chapter 18

"THAT FARMHOUSE OF YOURS IS going to need a woman's touch now that repairs are underway," Lady Thurlby said to Lavinia as she took her on a tour of Alderwood. She'd been going into detail about the responsibilities that would be Lavinia's as mistress of her own household. "The girls and I would be only too willing to go with you into the village to look for fabrics and colors. Those men doing the repairs will slap on a coat of paint in some drab color they find at hand if we don't act quickly. Paper-hangings, draperies, carpets . . ."

Furnishings for the house had moved near the top in priority. They would need beds and wardrobes and washstands and dishes and cooking utensils and tables and . . . the list went on and on. And they would need those things to begin arriving by next week.

Lucas met them on the landing as Lavinia and Lady Thurlby rounded the corner of the corridor. "There you both are. I've been looking for you."

"We've been busy," the viscountess said. "I have been instructing Lavinia on the management of a household. You need to sit down together sometime soon and talk about furniture for the farmhouse. There is much to be done before Primrose Farm becomes a home for the two of you, from what Thomas and James have told me."

"I am always willing to set aside time for Lavinia, Mama," Lucas said. "I am entirely at her disposal."

The look he gave Lavinia melted her heart and a good deal of her resolve.

"Come," he said, extending an arm for each of them. "Everyone is waiting."

"Everyone?" Lavinia asked as she slipped her hand into the crook of his elbow. "Waiting for what?"

"Goodness! Has Simon arrived? And without my knowing it," the viscountess said, taking his other arm before they descended the stairway. "That
bounder. It's about time. One would think London was halfway across the
globe considering how long it took my two wayward sons to arrive from
there."

"I apologize profusely for my own procrastination."

"Apology accepted. But just barely."

Lucas leaned over and kissed his mother on the cheek, and Lavinia
lost a little more of her heart to him.

Lavinia discovered when they reached the drawing room that "everyone" included the entire family, minus the children. Hannah, Delia, and
Artie were also there.

Simon Jennings stood in the midst of them.

The first thing Lavinia noticed about him was his striking resemblance
to James, although his coloring was darker than his brothers; Susan was the
only other sibling who had the same dark hair as he. He also had an air of
dissipation and ennui about him that robbed him of the vitality he should
have had as a young gentleman, especially considering the fact that, according to Lucas, he was a year younger than Lavinia.

"Lavinia, may I present my youngest brother, Simon? Simon, my betrothed,
Lavinia Fernley," Lucas said.

Simon turned to acknowledge Lavinia and stopped, an arrested look
on his face.

Lavinia attempted to ignore his expression and extended her hand to
him. He bowed over it. "It is an honor to meet the lady who has captured
my brother's heart," he said. "And such a *rare* beauty she is too." He smiled—
rather wickedly, it seemed to Lavinia.

His eyes narrowed, and Lavinia's heart raced. He was studying her too
closely. Had he recognized her? Had he been one of the countless young
bucks who'd stood on the floor of the Orpheus Theatre nightly, clapping
and cheering for Ruby Chadwick as she'd performed in breeches onstage?
Was he about to share her secret with Lucas's entire family? She struggled to
maintain her composure.

"Have we met before?" he asked.

"No, sir." She should say something more, keep the conversation from
stalling and giving him time to think, but in her panicked state, her mind
was a complete blank.

"You must be right, although I could swear . . ." He paused and Lavinia held her breath. "Well, brother dear, you must tell us how you managed to convince such an exquisite female to marry you. I'm sure James and I would both appreciate some pointers."

"I said virtually the same thing to him, Simon," James said. "Except for the pointers part."

"It's no great mystery," Lavinia said, knowing she must be her most convincing self right now. She looked at Lucas. "He is the kindest and most noble man I have ever met, and sharing my life with him would be the greatest honor I could ever hope to have."

Lucas's gaze burned intensely at her words.

"You're sure it's *our* Lucas you're talking about?" James asked.

"Oh, I think that's lovely," Delia said from her spot on the sofa next to Artie. "Such words of *devotion*; pure declarations of the heart. Don't *you* think so, Artie?"

"'Love looks not with the eyes, but with the mind; / And therefore is winged Cupid painted blind,'" he replied.

"Ah, yes, indeed," Delia said. "*A Midsummer Night's Dream*," she added in explanation, for the sake of the others in the room. "Shakespeare says it so well when the *rest* of us are lacking the words for ourselves." She stared flatly at Artie.

The corner of Simon's mouth twitched upward.

"I adore Shakespeare," Isobel said, a statement that seemed to startle everyone. "Well, I do. I read it quite often when I was a girl, didn't I, Lucas?"

All eyes turned expectantly in Lucas's direction.

"You were always dragging a book with you wherever we went," he said, shrugging. "I never paid much attention to what it was."

"I didn't know you liked Shakespeare," Thomas, who was standing close to the chair in which his wife was seated, said. "You've never said anything to me about it."

"Well, I wouldn't now, would I? I found my Romeo and have no need for any another."

Thomas smiled warmly at Isobel and laid his hand on her shoulder. Lavinia prayed Isobel's words meant that she, Lucas, and Thomas had made amends.

"I prefer the Good Book, myself," Isaac said. "'Who can find a virtuous woman? / for her price is far above rubies.'" He smiled and patted Clara's hand, making her blush.

"Quoting Song of Solomon there, Isaac?" Simon asked with a smirk.

"Simon," Lord Thurlby warned. "There are ladies present."

"Many pardons, Papa." Although the smirk was still present on his face.

"Proverbs, actually," Isaac said.

"I would have you sit by me, Simon, so we may chat," Lady Thurlby said, patting the cushion next to her on the settee. "I have missed you, you unruly child. I want a full accounting from you."

"She won't be getting a *full* accounting if the state I saw him in this morning is any indication of what he's been doing," Lucas whispered to Lavinia as Simon took the spot indicated next to his mother.

"What is London like, Simon?" Rebecca asked, sitting forward in her seat. "I suppose I could have asked you the same question, Lucas. But you spent most of your time with your friend at his residence. Simon has been to balls and routs and operas and the like, and I daresay he has met many important people."

Mentioning opera hit a little too close to home for Lavinia's peace of mind, especially when Simon once again glanced at her with narrowed eyes.

"Apparently the Earl of Halford and the Marquess and Marchioness of Ashworth are not important people by my baby sister's standards," Lucas said.

"That's not what I meant, silly, and you know it," Rebecca replied archly.

"I know precisely what you meant, Miss Jennings," Artie, of all people, said. Lavinia closed her eyes and waited for the non sequitur that was surely to proceed from his mouth. He took a deep breath in preparation—

"You haven't the *faintest idea* what she's talking about," Delia blurted out, fanning herself with such vigor that her fine white hair looked like a dandelion puff about to take flight in the wind. "Such utter nonsense, Arthur. She speaks of *romance*—dashing young men and elegant ladies and flirting and stolen kisses."

"I know that," Artie blustered. "I will have you know I am entirely well versed in—"

"'Cupid is a knavish lad, / thus to make poor females mad.'" Delia, not Artie, was the one quoting Shakespeare this time in a singsong voice, no less, effectively shutting Artie up with her words, along with the rest of the people in the room.

Artie turned purple with indignation. "If you wish to speak of madness, madam, then I would have you recall a certain time in Bristol—"

Hannah cleared her throat forcefully, and Artie shut his mouth, looking disgruntled. Delia lifted her chin defiantly and folded her hands in her lap.

Bless Hannah for doing something to stop Delia and Artie before it got any worse. Their banter, while dramatic, was usually of an amiable nature, but Delia's impetuously flung words in particular had held a sting. Lavinia glanced around the room, her anxiety nearly at a breaking point. Rebecca's mouth was gaping open, as were Clara's and Isobel's. Susan was fighting laughter behind her hand; Lady Thurlby was not laughing at all—a single eyebrow arched sufficiently to declare her point of view. Lord Thurlby and Lucas's brothers—except for Simon—looked utterly confounded by what they'd just witnessed.

"You were speaking of important people, Rebecca," Susan prompted.

"Was I? I have forgotten," Rebecca replied.

Simon locked eyes with Lavinia—and then he winked.

Her heart sank. He'd thought her familiar but hadn't placed her; Delia and Artie's verbal jousting with their generous quoting of the Bard had supplied the missing piece of the puzzle.

She deliberately turned away from the others while they attempted to revive the stalled conversation and took hold of Lucas's arm. "May we leave, please? I'm feeling unwell all of a sudden," she whispered.

"Of course." He studied her face.

"Please don't let the others know," she said. "I don't wish to alarm anyone."

He nodded. "Mama," he said, "now that we've officially welcomed Simon home, I beg you will excuse Lavinia and me," he said. "We have wedding matters to discuss."

"Wedding matters, indeed," James remarked. "Oh, that I had such delicious matters to attend to myself."

"James, really!" Lady Thurlby exclaimed, frowning at him. "Certainly you may, Lucas, but have a care that these matters are discussed in public so that propriety is maintained."

"Of course, Mama," Lucas said. "I wouldn't have it otherwise." He nodded his farewell to his parents and the others and escorted Lavinia from the room, his brothers still quietly chuckling behind them over James's last remarks.

Lavinia didn't care.

* * *

"What is it, Lavinia? What's troubling you?" Lucas asked when they arrived at her bedroom door. He opened his arms wide, and she stepped into them and leaned against him. She was so wary of men, and for her to express this level of trust toward him now spoke volumes. He wrapped his arms about her and rested his chin on her head, waiting for her to answer.

"I was wrong when I told you we should wait to tell your parents there is no betrothal," she said softly. "Delia and Artie simply cannot behave as anything other than what they are. You would think actors would be the most capable people of carrying out a fiction. But they must spout Shakespeare and behave as caricatures using the broadest gestures—what other man do you know who would play the dragon to Edmund's St. George?"

Lucas thought about it. "I might—if it were my own son asking." A son with curly red hair and clear gray eyes. Or a daughter. Or both. His and Lavinia's children.

She heaved a sigh, and Lucas savored the warmth of her breath against his cheek. "Oh, Lucas, you wonderful, terrible man. Just when I resolve to take my friends and myself away from here at the soonest possible moment, you say something like that and I am undone. But the truth will come out. It's inevitable. I've never seen Delia in such a state as she was just now. I don't know what's gotten into her lately, but she isn't her usual self. I hope she isn't ill, but at her age, who can know for certain? Regardless, she or Artie are bound to let something slip, and then we will have to face your family and tell them they have been harboring *actors*—"

Lucas shuddered theatrically. "Actors, good heavens. I am shocked and dismayed."

She leaned back in his arms enough to look him in the eye. He wanted to kiss her and had a devil of a time keeping his eyes from wandering to her lips.

"Lucas, be serious," she said. "We actors think we are fine enough folk, but you know that to others, especially an aristocratic family like your own, we are entirely beyond the pale. I will not be able to bear the looks on your family's faces when they discover the truth—especially your parents. Your mother has taken me under her wing and led me upstairs and downstairs, teaching me"—she choked on her words—"teaching me what I need to know to run my own house. She has been kind and accepting of me when I know how reluctant she was at first. Oh, Lucas!" She collapsed against him, and Lucas held her, feeling the weight of his guilt. He had thrust this encumbrance upon her. Her little ruse at the White Horse had been nothing compared to the demands he'd made on her and her friends in order to spare his pride.

He was ashamed of himself.

He continued to hold her quietly outside the door to her room. "Don't worry, love," he said. "We'll sort it out. All will be well, I promise you. Trust me." He couldn't bear to let go of her, so he simply held her until he felt the tension in her body begin to subside.

"I don't think either Delia or Artie said anything that was beyond what my family has come to expect from those two," he said. It dawned on him, in retrospect, that Lavinia's upset was rather extreme for what had occurred in the drawing room. "Is there something else troubling you of which I'm unaware? You can tell me, you know."

She turned sad eyes on him and shook her head, giving him a weak smile. "Nothing, really, beyond the realization that my past will inevitably find me no matter where I go. We need to tell your family the truth before they learn of it some other way. We must do it soon, Lucas."

"And we will. You're right: they must know. But today they will be celebrating Simon's return, and we will let them have that celebration. And tomorrow my father has business in Peterborough that will keep him from home most of the day. I will arrange for us to meet privately with my parents two days hence, then, and we will tell them the truth together." He placed a soft kiss on her mouth. "Now, rest and cease worrying. Promise me?"

"Yes. But, Lucas—"

"What, my love?"

"You think all will be well when we tell them, but it has been my lifelong experience that they will not take kindly to having played host under false pretenses. Actors are a motley group, from the most talented and respected thespians in the country to the vagabonds hiring on for bit parts, and everything in between, and most are not accepted in genteel society. You already know this. So I am warning you—your family will not accept our confession well."

"I hear what you are saying, Lavinia, but I also know my family. I know their ability to forgive and accept."

"As you were able to with Isobel and Thomas?"

She'd landed a worthy blow with her question, and it deserved a truthful answer. "My family is better at forgiveness than I am, but I am learning. I allowed my pride to blind me to the truth. We have made peace with each other."

"Truly, Lucas?" she asked, her eyes wide and searching.

"Truly. So for now, I ask that you trust me—or, at the very least, trust that my family's goodness is greater than mine."

She nodded. "Very well. I will try."

"That is all I ask."

Hannah was lumbering down the corridor toward them, so their time together was at an end, for now. "Hannah," Lucas called out to her, "I have given Lavinia orders to rest, as she claimed to be feeling poorly, and now I may be assured that you will see my orders are carried out."

"I was more than glad to see you two leave. It gave me all the reason I needed to get out of there and find some peace and quiet—wait, you're feeling poorly, luv?" she said, a look of concern on her face. "You do look peaked, after all. Are you ill?"

"No, Hannah, I'm not ill, but I do think perhaps a lie-down will do me good."

"I will look forward to seeing you both at dinner, then," Lucas said, relinquishing her into the care of Hannah—and there was no one he trusted more to take care of his beloved Lavinia than Hannah Broome. "Rest well, my love."

* * *

"He called you his love," Hannah said to Lavinia the minute the door closed behind them.

"I heard what he called me," Lavinia replied. "Help me unlace this corset, if you would, please."

Hannah unfastened the back of Lavinia's dress and began loosening the corset. "Men don't use that word lightly, Livvy."

Lavinia had nearly cried when Lucas had used the endearment on her. "Men say whatever suits them, Hannah," she replied. "Lord Cosgrove said it several times, and he's not the first, as you well know." She slipped her arms out of the sleeves of her dress, letting the garment slide to the floor. The corset soon followed. "Ah, what a relief. Now I can breathe."

"Lucas isn't like them others," Hannah said. "Step out of that dress so I can get it off the floor before the wrinkles set in; there's a good girl."

Lavinia did as she was told.

"He's a fine man, I've come to see," Hannah continued. "Oh, he's not above a lie or two—that's clear enough—but that's the worst sin I've seen in him so far. He lied to help my Livvy girl, now didn't he? It were wrong him lying and calling you his betrothed when you aren't, but just perhaps it was wishful thinking on his part."

"It wasn't wishful thinking, Hannah. It was pride. He loved Isobel, and she married Thomas instead."

"Well, he don't love her now; that's plain enough for anyone to see. Up on the bed with you."

Lavinia dutifully crawled onto the bed and plumped the pillow under her head until it felt comfortable.

"As far as I'm concerned," Hannah continued as she fussed about the room, "he's twenty times the man Lord Cosgrove is, earl or no earl. You could do a lot worse than Lucas Jennings, Livvy."

"That's high praise, coming from you. And I will go one further: I will confess that Lucas is the best man I have ever known."

Hannah stopped fussing and turned to face Lavinia. "I should have taken you away from that ne'er-do-well of a father of yours—and let him do his worst to me to try getting you back. But I didn't, and that's the sad truth of it, and I will never forgive myself."

"Hannah." Lavinia stretched out her hand to her dear friend. "I will not hear you berating yourself in such a way. You are as dear to me as though you were my real mother, for you are the mother who raised me and took care of me and protected me from harm. If it weren't for you, I would be— well, I can't bear to think what would have happened to me. I love you dearly, Hannah."

"Oh, Livvy," Hannah said, sitting on the edge of the bed and stroking Lavinia's hair back from her forehead. "And I love you, my sweet girl. It would do my heart good to see you settled with a decent man at your side. Primrose Farm is a blessing we never expected to have, but it will be a lot of work. It would be that much more of a blessing if you had someone who matched your strength by your side, helping you."

"You match my strength."

"It's not the same, luv."

Lavinia sighed. "I know. But he is not mine to have, Hannah. Day after tomorrow, Lucas and I will be meeting with his parents and explaining everything to them. And then you and I and Artie and Delia will prepare to leave Alderwood." Hannah's fingers were working their magic, and Lavinia found herself becoming drowsy.

"That makes me sad, for you and for him," Hannah said. "Now, sleep, dearest. Perhaps in your dreams, you'll find the way."

"The way where?" Lavinia mumbled, nearly asleep.

"The way to love," Hannah said.

Chapter 19

AFTER LUCAS LEFT LAVINIA WITH Hannah, he went to his room and pulled out the notes he'd gotten from Finch regarding the repairs to Primrose Farm and the costs that would be involved as a result. It made a certain amount of sense, Finch had explained, to bring only a few acres into production at a time. It would minimize the outlay of expense; the income made could then be used to help cover the costs of rebuilding the farmhouse and bringing more acres into production the following year, and so on and so forth until all the acreage of Primrose Farm was once again producing.

The alternative was to get the entire farm into production during the upcoming year. They could plant a few acres of fast-growing crops now in order to recoup some expense with its harvest. In the meantime, the rest of the land could be drained and prepared for next spring's planting. This was the best way to proceed, as far as Finch was concerned, and Thomas and Isaac had agreed.

It made the most sense to Lucas too—except for the cost involved. He didn't doubt that Lavinia had funds. She'd given him a banknote written for a generous amount just the other day. How much more money she had beyond that, he couldn't say. It wasn't his place to ask her for her personal financial details. If their betrothal were real, he'd be entitled to such information; it would have been addressed in the discussions of their marriage contract.

He looked over the notes again, adding a column of numbers here, subtracting there. Labor, seed, drainage, pumps. Times acreage. What crops yielded the best return when sold. What crops had the fastest growing seasons. Acreage set apart for raising livestock, particularly sheep. The amount of land sheep required.

Information Finch had shared and Lucas was trying to digest.

If one were to ask Lucas how to dig a trench or walk twenty miles in torrential rain—or take the life of a Frenchman intent on taking his own— *that* information Lucas could recite in his sleep. How to clean a rifle. How to treat a wound.

He went over the notes and numbers until they began to blur before his eyes. There was no way to decide on the right solution for the farm without all the knowledge, and he didn't have the knowledge that was key here: the amount of available capital.

Lucas knew how much money he himself had. He'd been one of the fortunate ones during his years in the army, and he had saved as much of that income as he'd been able. On its own, it was almost enough to fund the first plan regarding Primrose Farm, the conservative one that would take years to implement.

If he and Lavinia were to combine assets . . .

The idea knitted well with the other thoughts that had been constantly in his mind the past few days, namely, getting Lavinia to agree to a betrothal in truth. He knew she trusted him more than any other man. But did she trust him—or, more to the point, did she *care* for him—enough to give up her independence to him in marriage? A wife's property became her husband's upon marriage, and that would make Primrose Farm his. He had two days to find out the answers to those particular questions.

He felt restless. Perhaps he'd take Hector out for a nice run.

When Lucas arrived at the stables, he was surprised to see Simon there preparing to mount one of their father's horses.

"Simon, have you had enough of the family already that you must leave before you've even been here a day?" he said, somewhat amused.

Simon settled himself easily atop the horse; he'd always been a natural horseman, even as a boy. "Not at all, Lucas," he said, grinning. He looked much better now than he had when he'd arrived early this morning. "I am merely riding to the village to post a letter. Thought I'd tell a friend where I'd gotten to so he doesn't have the authorities dredging the Thames looking for my body."

"Your little joke isn't that funny, Simon," Lucas said.

"I suppose not. Blame it on the hammer pounding on the anvil in my head, although it's much improved since this morning, thanks to you."

"Would you care for company on your ride?" It wasn't what Lucas originally had in mind when he'd left his room, but spending time with his rebellious younger brother seemed a good way to fill what was left of the afternoon.

"Thank you, but not this time," Simon said. "Don't worry—I shan't get lost; I still remember the way to the village. I'll be back in time for supper."

"Away with you, then, and post that important letter of yours. I wouldn't want people frantically searching the Thames for you when you're safe in the bosom of your family."

"Indeed." He nudged his horse down the lane and then turned back. "That's quite a bride you've got, Lucas. I daresay her looks are one of a kind—that hair, that figure. That face of hers."

"Her heart is just as beautiful, Simon. More so." Simon's words annoyed Lucas. "I am the most fortunate of men," he added, even though that fortune depended on how persuasive he could be over the next two days.

"You are certainly that. I imagine there are many gentlemen of my acquaintance who would agree with you." He gave the horse a flick with his crop, and then they were gone.

Lucas briefly wondered at Simon's cryptic words, and then they were forgotten as he gave Hector free rein and let the fresh air clear his mind for the next few hours.

* * *

It was the day Lavinia and Lucas were to speak to his parents. Lord Thurlby had spent the previous day in Peterborough, and Lavinia had exhausted herself acting as though all was well, keeping a keen eye on Artie and Delia and helping Lady Thurlby with wedding plans. Lucas and his brothers had ridden to Primrose Farm once again, reporting back at supper on the progress of the farmhouse and fields.

This morning, Lavinia took her time eating breakfast—if one could call the few bites she'd managed to swallow "eating"—so she could be alone in the breakfast room with Delia and Artie when they arrived later, as had been their routine. She needed to warn them to pack their bags. She'd decided during what had been a sleepless night that if Primrose Farm was indeed ready for them by next week, she could afford for them to stay at the inn in Sleaford for the few remaining days until then. She and Lucas were to speak to Lord and Lady Thurlby this afternoon, at which time Lavinia would make her apologies, take dinner in her room, and leave with her friends first thing tomorrow morning.

Her heart was heavy.

By the time Delia and Artie arrived for breakfast, the room was essentially empty, every family members' whereabouts accounted for as they all went about their routines as usual. Soon the entire family would learn that Lucas's betrothal to Lavinia was a lie.

"I'm telling you, Delia, I didn't mean it the way it sounded." Artie's voice preceded him into the breakfast room. "When I said you were like an egg, I meant it as a compliment. There's no reason for you to be upset over such a little thing."

"Do you hear a magpie squawking, Lavinia?" Delia said as she entered the room, flicking a disdainful hand in Artie's direction. "Such noisy creatures, magpies, don't you think? They squawk and squawk, making a ruckus that drowns out the songbirds and giving people headaches with their noise."

Oh dear. Whatever it was that had these two longtime friends pecking at each other in such a way had apparently not resolved itself yet.

Artie pulled out the chair next to Lavinia for Delia to sit in. "Let me fetch you some tea, Delia," Artie said, being as solicitous as he could possibly be. "And then I shall fill a plate for you. A bit of toast and some eggs—"

"Not *eggs*, Arthur, unless they are *coddled* eggs. For you know *we eggs* are best when treated delicately. We like to be coddled."

Lavinia looked at Delia in surprise at such an ill-natured comment; she wasn't acting like herself at all.

"Here's a nice cup of tea, Delia, just the way you like it, with milk and sugar," Artie said, setting the teacup in front of her. "Piping hot too." He didn't wait for a reply but went back to the side table to fix a plate of food for her.

"I'm tired," Delia murmured to herself.

Lavinia wasn't sure now if she should tell them they'd be leaving tomorrow. "I don't understand this talk of eggs. What is going on?"

"Here you go," Artie said too cheerily, setting a filled plate in front of Delia. "Toast and some nice grilled kidneys—no eggs of any kind, you'll be happy to observe, and some herrings. Just the thing, eh?"

"The magpie told me I reminded him of an egg. I'm an *egg*, Lavinia," Delia said, ignoring the plate in front of her.

"Now, Delia," Artie said.

"Why an egg, Artie? Of all the things to call someone, it seems an unlikely choice," Lavinia said, trying to understand what was going on.

"But I *like* eggs, you see? Coddled eggs are very fine, you know, but they need proper care. Boil an egg, you can take it with you anywhere. It's handy food that way. Small—doesn't take up much space. Very convenient.

Add a pinch of salt—you've got yourself a nice enough meal. But then you *must* boil them, see, if you're to take them along with you. Can't otherwise, else the shell will crack open, and then it's a mess you've got."

"Like coddled eggs, because they aren't all hard inside," Delia said. "Too much of a bother, coddled eggs are. Like me. I need coddling, apparently, or else I am a bother."

"Now you're putting words in my mouth, Delia. You're not a bother. I said no such thing. You were the one who pointed out *coddle* and *coddle*, not I. An egg is a very fine thing."

"It's always in the words, Arthur. It's always in the words. The murderers in *Macbeth* called Lady MacDuff's son an egg, and then they killed the poor lad."

"Delia, eggs can be good as well, you know, if one would only take a moment to understand the *intent*—"

"'Some Cupid kills with arrows, some with traps,'" Delia said, ignoring Artie's plea.

A manservant discreetly cleared his throat, and a still confused Lavinia turned her head to acknowledge him. "I was instructed to give this to you." He handed her a folded note.

"Thank you." She unfolded the note and read it. It was from Lucas, informing her that the meeting with his parents had been arranged and apologizing that he was unable to deliver the message in person. "The meeting is set for this afternoon. It is done, then," she said quietly.

"Meeting?" Delia asked, turning sharply to look at Lavinia, as did Artie.

"Yes. Lucas and I decided to tell his parents the truth before it goes any further. I think it best that we pack our things, the four of us, and return to Sleaford tomorrow until Primrose Farm is ready for us next week."

How two people could wilt in the space of an instant, Lavinia didn't know, but Delia and Artie managed it.

"I see," Delia said so softly Lavinia could barely hear her. She'd gone alarmingly pale at Lavinia's words.

"We are on the move again, eh? Well, that's what we old thespians are used to doing," Artie said, mustering a shred of fortitude. "Delia, you must eat more than one bite of kidney, you know. We have a farm to run starting next week. Eat up; there's a good girl."

Delia took another small nibble and set her fork down. "Arthur, I—" she managed to say. And then she collapsed, sliding off her chair and crumpling to the floor.

Chapter 20

"DELIA!" LAVINIA CRIED AS ARTIE rushed over from the other side of the table. She knelt over her elderly friend, caressing her face. "Delia, can you hear me? Speak to me if you can."

Delia was unresponsive.

Lavinia patted her hands and then patted her cheeks and then patted them more vigorously. She peeked under one of Delia's eyelids—what she expected to find she wasn't sure, but all she saw was a rheumy eyeball staring at nothing.

"Smelling salts," she muttered. "Why I've never thought to carry smelling salts, I'll never know."

"Delia," Artie cried, kneeling by her and taking one of her hands in his. "She's only fainted, right, Lavinia? She's only fainted. I told you to eat more kidneys, Delia. Oh, what to do, what to do!"

"Artie, go get help. Quickly! She still isn't responding."

He dashed from the room, and once he was gone, Lavinia put her mouth next to Delia's ear. "Come on, Delia. It's time to end this."

No response.

"If I find out you are up to something, I will be extremely upset. It isn't fair to put Artie through this. Or me and Hannah either."

One of Delia's hands lifted slightly, her eyelids fluttered, and . . . that was it. Nothing more.

Lavinia's insides felt leaden. Delia could not be ill. She *couldn't*. But what if she was? And what if Lavinia's own skepticism had kept Delia from getting the help she needed in time? She kept caressing her friend's dear, familiar face; they had gone through so much together. She should not have told them they'd be leaving Alderwood when it had been obvious that Delia was not her usual self this morning; it had placed too great a strain on her.

Lavinia would never forgive herself if Delia did not pull through.

"What has happened?" Lady Thurlby exclaimed as she rushed into the room, followed quickly by Lord Thurlby, Lucas, and Artie.

Artie dashed back to Delia's side, dropping to his knees again. "Wake up, Delia," he said, patting her hand frantically. "Come on now; there's a good girl. Wake up. Please wake up."

Delia didn't move.

"John, fetch Doctor Ellis," Lord Thurlby told the manservant who'd delivered Lucas's message to Lavinia earlier. "Tell him it's urgent."

"Yes, milord."

Lucas placed a hand on Artie's shoulder. "Let's take her up to her room," he said gently. "She'll be more comfortable there."

"Yes. Right." Artie reluctantly moved out of the way, and then strong, sure Lucas crouched down, took Delia carefully into his arms, and rose to his feet. Delia hung limply, like a rag doll. Lady Thurlby gave swift orders to a maid to have Delia's bed prepared for her. Lucas carried her from the breakfast room and up the main stairway, with Artie and Lavinia trailing behind, creating a somber procession to Delia's room.

Hannah came out of her room as they passed by. "What's going on?" she asked, and then she blanched when she noticed Lucas carrying Delia. "What has happened?"

"We were in the breakfast room, and she fainted," Artie explained, his voice cracking. "But she won't come around. We tried and tried to wake her, Livvy and I did, but she won't come round!"

"Oh, Hannah!" Lavinia threw her arms around Hannah in a desperate hug. "What are we to do?"

"There, there, luv," Hannah said, patting Lavinia's back. "Let's go be sure our Delia's settled in proper-like, shall we?"

When Lavinia and Hannah got to Delia's room, Artie was pacing back and forth outside the door, tearing at his hair, while Lucas stood nearby with his hands clasped behind his back. Delia was visible through the doorway, lying as still as a corpse on the bed.

How quickly the day had changed, Lavinia thought. One moment she'd been concerned only with having her friends ready to leave Alderwood; now she was frantic that one of them might be dying.

When Lavinia's father had died, she hadn't felt like this. The lessons she'd learned from her father had been bitter ones, and his passing, as unfortunate as it had been, had been more of a relief to her than a sorrow.

But losing Delia, despite her advanced years . . . Delia was clever and delightful and had brightened their lives during the time she and Artie had been with them.

She would be greatly missed.

Oh, she mustn't think this way, Lavinia chided herself, clutching her waist and fighting back the tears that threatened to fall—she mustn't presume the worst. The doctor would arrive soon, and he would explain everything and assure them all would be well. And all *would* be well. It *must* be.

She and Hannah quietly entered Delia's room. The maid had carefully tucked a coverlet around her and was now adjusting the curtains at the window to dim the light. "Anything else I can get, miss?" the maid quietly asked Lavinia. "It's right sad to see Miss Weston like this. Such a sweet one with the children, her and Mr. Drake, and kind to the rest of us too."

"Thank you," Lavinia said. "I think you've done everything you can for now."

The maid bobbed a curtsy and left.

Hannah placed a small wooden chair next to the bed. "Sit, Lavinia. You look about as pale as poor Delia here."

Lavinia sat. The maid had set Delia's hands on the coverlet, one atop the other. She looked like she'd been laid out for a funeral.

"It's my fault, Hannah," Lavinia murmured. "I told her and Artie about leaving Alderwood, and then this happened. I should have known better. Delia hasn't been herself the past few days. I should have realized it and said something different or waited or—oh, I don't know—but *something*."

"Don't go blaming yourself, luv." Hannah laid a comforting hand on Lavinia's shoulder. "Delia knew we was going to Primrose Farm sooner or later. She's small, is our Delia, but she's a fighter. Actors have to be. You know that as well as anyone."

Lavinia gazed sorrowfully upon Delia's still form. "I hope you're right, Hannah. Oh, I hope you're right."

* * *

"What in blazes is it taking the doctor so long to get here?" Lucas muttered. "He should have arrived by now. Sit, Drake; you're going to wear out the carpets with all that pacing."

The old man sat. He began wringing his hands. His breathing escalated. It was driving Lucas mad, sitting here, doing nothing, watching Artie when what he wanted to do was go to Lavinia's side. Unfortunately, he couldn't—he and Artie had to keep vigil outside Delia's room.

Lucas's frustrations, however, were nothing compared to the agony Artie was going through. The poor man was beside himself with worry. If Lucas hadn't already figured out how much Artie loved Delia, it would have been obvious to him now. Lucas sighed. "Never mind. Pace if it makes you feel better," he said.

Artie immediately popped up out of the chair and proceeded to pace again.

Lucas dropped his head into his hands and shut his eyes—at least this way he could block out the back and forth, back and forth of Artie's movements.

"Right this way, Doctor Ellis," Lucas's mother said from farther down the corridor.

He and Artie both heaved an audible sigh of relief. Lucas rose to his feet.

Dr. Ellis, whom Lucas had never met, was a relatively young man with a kind face. Lucas wanted to trust that he could actually do something to restore Delia to her prior good health, but he'd seen enough sawbones and quacks in Spain that he held little faith in doctors of any kind. It had frequently seemed to Lucas that more of his friends had died from complications after being seen by a surgeon than had died in actual combat.

"My son Lucas and Mr. Drake," Lady Thurlby said, presenting them to the doctor. "Lucas, Dr. Ellis was a godsend when he set up practice here after old Dr. Vickers passed."

"Delia's in here," Artie blurted out. "Can you help her?"

"I shall do my best," Dr. Ellis replied.

Dr. Ellis entered Delia's room. Lucas, his mother, and Artie clustered just inside the doorway to watch. Lavinia stood and moved out of the way, and Hannah moved the chair Lavinia had been sitting in so the doctor could examine Delia.

He felt her forehead, listened to her heart, raised her eyelids one at a time to look at her eyes—all the things physicians always seemed to do when evaluating the health of a patient. He seemed respectful in his approach, for which Lucas was grateful. Lavinia and Artie—and probably Hannah too—would have attacked the man, teeth and claws bared, had he been the least bit severe in his methods.

He listened to her heart again.

"Hmm," he said.

"What is it?" Lucas's mother asked.

"I'm not sure," Dr. Ellis replied. He tapped his chin in speculation. "Her heart is weak, certainly, but not unexpected, considering her age. She has no fever that I can detect. We could try bloodletting and see if she improves—"

"No bloodletting!" Artie cried. "Delia hates blood, even when it isn't real—" His mouth snapped shut.

Lucas's mother looked at Artie curiously, but the doctor only shrugged. "I'm not generally an advocate for bloodletting myself. I've been exploring the use of herbs in my practice, but that is a discussion for another day."

"No bloodletting," Artie said again.

"As you wish," Dr. Ellis said.

"What has caused her condition?" Lavinia asked.

"I'm not sure. It would help to know how she seemed before the onset of her illness."

Lavinia looked at Artie before answering the doctor. "She hasn't been herself lately at all," she said. "Delia is usually so happy, so engaging. But the past few days, she has seemed a bit . . . off. Irritable. And Delia is never irritable. Quite the contrary."

"Not like herself at all," Artie added. "I was beginning to wonder if I could say a word to her without it being the wrong one."

"Hmm," Dr. Ellis mused. "Obviously something is amiss for her to be in this unresponsive state." He thought for a moment, watching Delia closely. "With your permission, I would like to examine the patient more thoroughly. I would ask you to remain with me, Lady Thurlby, for propriety's sake."

"Of course, Dr. Ellis," Lucas's mother said.

Dr. Ellis nodded.

The others exited the room, and Dr. Ellis quietly shut the door behind them. Lucas led Lavinia to the chair he'd been sitting in earlier and sat in the one next to it, taking her hand in his. It felt cold to the touch.

Artie, not unpredictably, began pacing again. Hannah, to Lucas's surprise, placed her ear next to the door. "I can't hear nothing—no rustling of bedclothes, nothing to indicate what that doctor fellow might be doing," she reported to the others before giving up.

"Oh, Lucas, I can hardly bear it," Lavinia whispered. "What if we lose her? What will poor Artie do without her? They've been friends for decades."

"We will pray that doesn't happen, my dear, but if it does, we will honor her life as best we can and we will be there for Artie and share his grief."

Several minutes passed, and finally, Dr. Ellis again opened the door, and he and Lucas's mother joined them in the corridor. His mother had her handkerchief pressed to her mouth, and she turned away from the group, which seemed rather alarming to Lucas. He hoped it wasn't an indication of worse news to come.

"After having thoroughly examined Miss Weston and consulted with Lady Thurlby, I'm afraid I have nothing more to say to you regarding Miss Weston's medical situation at this time," Dr. Ellis said. "My suggestion is to be patient and wait. The rest is up to Miss Weston."

"There's nothing more you can tell us? Nothing at all?" Lavinia asked, rising to her feet. Lucas rose as well and stood behind her, resting his hands on her shoulders.

"Perhaps a day or two more will provide answers," Dr. Ellis said. "In the meantime, there is nothing else I can do. You have leave to call upon me at any time, should her condition change." He nodded to Lucas's mother. "I can find my way out, Lady Thurlby."

"Thank you, Dr. Ellis. We are grateful to you for your time," she said and seemed much more composed now than when she'd exited the room. "But I will accompany you, nonetheless. There are a few questions regarding Miss Weston's care I wish to discuss with you."

He nodded to her in acknowledgment, and the two of them proceeded down the corridor to the front of the house.

"I'll sit with Delia," Hannah volunteered. "I'll just go get my sewing basket first."

"*I* intend to sit with her," Artie declared. "I don't plan to leave her side for a single moment."

"We shall *all* take shifts so that someone is with her at all times," Lavinia stated decisively. "I will not have you wearing yourself out with your vigilance, Arthur Drake. I couldn't bear it if you were to get ill too."

"You'll need food and sleep if you intend to stay strong for Delia's sake," Lucas said in the calm, firm tone he'd frequently had to use with Anthony on the worst days. Lucas could see the same type of agitation now in Artie, poor fellow.

"You can stay with her first, then, Artie. I'll come back later," Hannah said.

Without further ado, Artie rushed into Delia's room.

For the rest of the day, someone remained at Delia's side—mainly Artie, which was no great surprise, although he did allow himself short periods of time away from her, with Hannah or Lavinia keeping vigil in his place. Even his mother sat with Delia a few times during the day and evening, as did Lucas's sisters when they arrived home.

The meeting Lavinia and Lucas were to have had with his parents didn't happen, the concern for Delia's welfare taking precedence.

"I shall sit with her later this evening," Clara said at supper after she and Isaac and the children had returned to Alderwood. Lavinia was sitting with Delia, and Hannah had asked to take supper in her room so she could eat quickly and keep Lavinia company. "I feel so dreadfully sorry we were not here to help earlier."

"You must save your strength for your children and the babe you are carrying, Clara. I will go up after supper so Lavinia can rest, and I shall read aloud to Delia this time," Susan declared. "Perhaps she will hear the words in her sleep, and it will help her awaken."

"Take care you select something with lively prose, then, not one of James's stuffy legal texts," Simon said with a grin.

"A little more tact, if you please, Simon," Lucas said. He glanced at Artie, but the poor man was lost in his thoughts and hadn't heard the flippant remark.

"No slight was intended," Simon said. "My apologies." He lifted his goblet and drained it, then signaled the footman for more.

"In case you're wondering, I left my stuffiest texts at my office in Lincoln," James said. "As I'm sure Isaac left his stuffiest sermons at the vicarage."

That was James's subtle way of telling Lucas he was overreacting to Simon's small jest, but Lucas didn't care—he could still see the grief etched in Lavinia's face, to say nothing of the anguish Artie was feeling.

"I shall keep you company, Susan," Rebecca said. "And you can borrow one of my books, if you like—perhaps one of Mrs. Radcliffe's novels?" she added hopefully.

"I would love your company, little sister," Susan said. "But perhaps we should select something less Gothic than Mrs. Radcliffe for Miss Weston under the circumstances."

"I hadn't thought of that, but you're right. Perhaps some poetry, then," Rebecca said.

The footman stepped out of the dining hall to answer a subtle knock at the door and then returned and made his way swiftly to their father. "Excuse me, milord, but there's a gentleman just arrived, wanting to speak to you." He presented a card on a salver. In a lowered voice, he added, "Despite the lateness of the hour, he insists he will not leave until he is seen. He's in the drawing room."

Lucas's father picked up the card and read it.

"Who is it, Thurlby? Don't leave us in suspense," Mama said.

"We have an illustrious visitor, Alice. The Earl of Cosgrove, of all people. I wonder why he should be calling, especially at this late hour. I've never even met the gentleman. I cannot imagine he has urgent business— with me or anyone else in Lincolnshire, for that matter." He dabbed at his mouth with his napkin and set it on his plate. "John, you may tell the earl I shall be with him presently."

Simon had gone still at the mention of the earl, and then drained his goblet a second time.

What did Simon know? Lucas wondered. Simon was the only person at the table other than himself who'd spent any time in London, where the Earl of Cosgrove resided most of the year, and Lucas had no connection to the earl, nor did Anthony. Cosgrove, while liked well enough by most of his peers, was also rather notorious for his dalliances with widows and actresses . . .

The food in Lucas's stomach congealed all at once.

For there was another person here at Alderwood with connections to London. Not to mention her three traveling companions as well.

I have been kissed, Lucas, but I have never kissed.

Oh, Lavinia.

"Come, Alice, let us go welcome our guest and see what he is about."

Lucas rose so quickly that his chair nearly toppled over behind him. "I would like to go with you, if I may, Father," he said.

"Very well; I don't see why not," his father replied, looking curiously at him as he stood and walked to the other end of the table to assist Mama from her chair. "Anyone else? Perhaps we should set a place for him here in case he's hasn't dined yet this evening." He nodded at the footman, who immediately left the room.

Lucas followed his parents from the dining room, down the corridor that seemed infinitely too short a distance, toward the drawing room, where the Earl of Cosgrove apparently waited impatiently for . . . Lucas didn't know precisely what. But he knew with horrible certainty that it had to do with Lavinia, so he used this all-too-brief span of time to prepare to face the enemy, as he had done endless times before in Spain.

Whatever Cosgrove intended, Lucas would face it and prevail—no matter what.

* * *

At first glance, the Earl of Cosgrove seemed like many noblemen Lucas had met during his time at university and through his association with Anthony.

Lucas, however, was used to evaluating his enemies more thoroughly—their intellect, their guile, the details of their physical appearance. It may not provide all the information needed when preparing for battle, but it narrowed the chances for failure. And Lucas was quite sure he was facing an enemy.

Lord Cosgrove was nearly as tall as Lucas but more slender and a good decade older than Lucas's own twenty-six years. The earl's riding clothes were of the latest style, his blond hair trimmed with precision. His boots fairly shone, even after what would have been a lengthy ride up from London, so fine was the polish on them. He would cut a dashing figure as he made his way on horseback through Hyde Park, Lucas thought.

"Welcome to Alderwood, Lord Cosgrove. Allow me to present myself," Lucas's father said. "I am Thomas Jennings, Viscount Thurlby, and this is my wife, Alice, Lady Thurlby. Perhaps you have met my son Lucas."

"I have not had the pleasure, although I have heard of him as of late," the earl replied.

Lucas bowed respectfully to the earl's nod of acknowledgment.

"Please, be seated. Would you care for a drink?" Lucas's father said as his mother sat on the sofa. "Or perhaps you would like to join us for supper. We would be only too happy—"

"Lord Thurlby," the earl said. "The reason for my arrival here is best shared only with you and your son, no offense to Lady Thurlby intended. But as she is here and I have no wish to stay any longer than is necessary, I shall get right to the point. It is my understanding that you are in possession of something that belongs to me," the earl said.

Lucas's father knitted his brows. "I'm sure I don't know what you mean. I did travel to Peterborough yesterday about a new venture I'm considering. Are you an investor? I was sure I knew who they all were."

"I am *not* an investor," the earl said impatiently. "Do you think I would travel *all day* to discuss something as undignified as a business venture? Hardly. I have people who do such things for me. No, this is of a more personal nature."

Lucas's mother, who'd seated herself on the settee during this exchange, straightened at the earl's condescending words.

Lucas's father simply looked at the earl with benign curiosity. "I'm sure I can't begin to imagine what you're talking about, although you seem to presume that I do, for some reason. Please sit, my lord, and we will sort this out."

Lucas's pulse had been increasing steadily as he listened to the conversation like he had as an infantryman waiting for the command to fire. There had been something troubling Lavinia; she'd warned him, but he hadn't understood.

My past will find me no matter where I go.

Lucas wandered over to the side table, poured himself a bracing drink, and downed it in one swallow.

"I received word that you have a young woman staying with you at present," Cosgrove said.

"That is true. She is betrothed to our son," Lucas's father replied.

"My felicitations," the earl said with no little sarcasm. "However, a young lady happened to slip through my fingers at the same time your son seems to have found himself betrothed, despite her claims to having been betrothed for years."

"Years?" his mother asked, looking at Lucas.

"Ah, it is as I expected, then. It is my belief that your son has taken what belongs to me."

"What are you implying, Lord Cosgrove?" his father asked.

"I am not *implying* anything. I am speaking plainly of my *chère amie*," the earl said impatiently. "My mistress, if you wish me to be even more blunt." He fingered his quizzing glass, its jewels flashing garishly in the candlelight.

"Language, sir," Lucas's father warned. "I will not allow a virtual stranger, regardless of rank, to speak in such a manner in my home, or indeed make such accusations. You will choose your words carefully. Alice, I would have you leave the room so we gentlemen can talk."

"I rather think not," Mama replied, every inch the viscountess. "Lord Cosgrove, you are entirely mistaken. There is no *chère amie* of any sort here at Alderwood. The very idea. My son would never bring such a woman as you describe to dwell under our roof."

"If that is the case," Cosgrove said, "it should be no hardship for me to see the young woman in question and discern for myself if my assumptions about her identity are correct." He turned to look straight at Lucas. "A few questions, if you will oblige me, about this betrothed of yours. By any chance, is she excessively beautiful? Does she possess the figure of a goddess?"

Lucas refused to answer, his jaw clamped tightly shut.

"A mouth as red and ripe as cherries? Eyes like silver?"

Lucas only glared at the earl, his hands clenched as though his rifle were in them, loaded and ready for use.

"And is her hair long and luscious and *sinfully* red? The sort of hair a man dares only dream about?" The earl's voice rose in crescendo with each question he posed.

"Cosgrove, you will cease speaking about her in this way," Lucas growled, fairly vibrating with rage.

His mother gasped, her hand flying to her mouth.

"Lucas, what is going on?" his father asked.

"And would her name be *Ruby Chadwick*?" Cosgrove boomed.

Wait, what?

Lucas drew back in utter shock. Ruby Chadwick? Who in blazes was *that*?

His parents, next to him, exhaled loudly in relief. "Well, there you go. There's no Ruby Chadwick here, I'm afraid," Lucas's father said with an edge to his voice. "It would appear your journey was all for naught. Good evening to you, my lord."

Cosgrove saying a name other than Lavinia's had been wholly unexpected. Lucas's mind, however, was now awhirl with snatches of conversations and observations about Lavinia since he'd met her. Could there be *two* such extravagantly beautiful redheaded females in England? Of course. But would both of them have left London within the past few days, headed to Lincolnshire?

Not likely.

And then a particular card game he'd joined at the Hissing Goose before leaving London and the discussion regarding Ruby Chadwick that had accompanied it flashed through his mind.

"I have ridden a long way, Lord Thurlby," Cosgrove said. "I must insist upon remaining until I have seen your son's betrothed with my own eyes and am satisfied that she is not Ruby Chadwick, The Darling of Drury Lane."

Lucas was quickly coming to the conclusion that Ruby Chadwick and Lavinia were one and the same—the descriptions were too similar to think otherwise. He needed to warn her. "I'll go get her," he said.

"I think not," Cosgrove snapped. "I won't have you telling her I'm here and having her run off again. Ring for a servant, if you please."

Lucas's father crossed to the bell pull. "Please send for Miss Fernley, John," he said when the footman arrived.

"Yes, milord." He left, closing the door behind him.

Cosgrove had called her The Darling of Drury Lane; Lavinia and her friends were all actors. The puzzle pieces were falling swiftly and neatly into place. But was she Ruby or Lavinia? Which was the real woman?

Far too soon, the door reopened and Lavinia entered the room and then stopped short.

"Hello, Ruby," Lord Cosgrove said.

Chapter 21

THE EARL OF COSGROVE STOOD in front of Lavinia in all his resplendent glory. Tall, blond, richly dressed, and with elegant manners—to the uninformed, he appeared the perfect nobleman, the consummate gentleman.

Lavinia saw a toad.

"Let me introduce you, shall I?" he said as he approached her, his voice tinged with smugness. "Lord and Lady Thurlby, Mr. Jennings, allow me to present my *chère amie*, Miss Ruby Chadwick, The Darling of Drury Lane, known throughout London for her lively onstage performances, frequently while wearing breeches. She's very popular, as you might expect, especially among the gentlemen."

"An *actress*?" Lucas's mother gasped. "In *breeches*?"

"Alice, truly, I think it best if you leave the room. More to the point, I'm ordering—"

"Fiddlesticks," his mother replied. "If you think I'm leaving Lavinia—Ruby—whatever her name is—alone in here with you three, you're sadly mistaken."

"Thank you, Lady Thurlby," Lavinia said.

"Don't be thanking me yet," she said. "I'm not about to leave you without a chaperone in a room with three men, not in my house—although if you are who Lord Cosgrove claims you are, I doubt it will affect your reputation one way or another. An *actress* known for wearing *breeches*, in my *home*. I can scarce believe it. No, I'm staying because I fully intend to hear what all this is about."

"What this is about, Lady Thurlby, is the scandal that was about to descend upon your family," Lord Cosgrove said. "Nothing more and nothing less. Fortunately, I have arrived to spare you such humiliation." He smirked, and if not for the fact that Lucas and his parents were present, Lavinia would have slapped his loathsome face with all her strength. But she was not blameless in this disaster, so she could do no such thing.

"You may outrank me, Cosgrove, but do not by any means mistake me for a fool," Lord Thurlby said. "You have already shown your motives to be less than noble."

"Pious country sensibilities. How tedious," Cosgrove said, bringing his jeweled quizzing glass to his eye so he could look down on Lucas and his family with haughty scorn.

Lavinia stood as straight as she could, calling upon all the most courageous roles she'd ever played to guide her demeanor and give her strength: Portia, Cordelia, Joan of Arc. "I have nothing to say to the Earl of Cosgrove, Lord and Lady Thurlby," Lavinia said, head held high. "I am more than willing to explain myself to the rest of you, however."

"Did you know Miss Chadwick's *affections* are highly sought after?" Cosgrove drawled. "She's a prime article, as should be plain to see. Since I no longer need disguise my motives here, I will tell you straight: I consider her to be mine. Bought and paid for."

"Good heavens," Lord Thurlby muttered.

"I am not the only one who has pursued her, you know. Lord Anston, Lord Wetheral, Sir Robert Mattersey . . . the Duke of Worthing . . . have all sought after her quite ardently—*and* extravagantly. There are others I could name as well. Shall I?"

"Alice, leave the room this instant," Lord Thurlby practically yelled.

Lucas's mother ignored him and turned to Lavinia. "I took you into my home, into my *heart*, thinking my son had finally found love and a purpose in his life. But you have lied to me—to all of us—the entire time. How could you do this to us?"

Her words cut deeply. Lavinia, wracked by a day of grief and worry over Delia, thought she could take no more. But she must, for Lady Thurlby's words were entirely true.

"Come, Ruby, it is time for us to go," Cosgrove said with bored impatience. "There is nothing for you here; you are deluding yourself if you think otherwise. I commend you for your ingenuity in slipping out of my sight and out of London. Well done." He gave a slow clap. "You like applause, don't you? Now take your final bow, and let us be gone from here."

Lavinia looked at Lucas. She saw only too clearly the shock and confusion in his eyes. "My name is Lavinia Fernley," she said to him. "And I refuse to go anywhere with the Earl of Cosgrove. If you wish me to leave, I will, but I will *not* go with him."

"Stop this infernal nonsense, Ruby," Lord Cosgrove said. "You have cost me a pretty penny, *chère amie petit*, and I have no intention of leaving here without you after all the trouble and inconvenience you've put me through. You cannot actually believe you will be happy in such rustic surroundings. The idea is appalling. Your life is in London, with me, under my protection. It is time you accepted that fact."

"My name is Lavinia Fernley," she repeated more firmly, this time to Lord Cosgrove. "I created the character who was Ruby Chadwick. She served me well, but she is gone. I no longer need her."

She turned to Lady Thurlby. "Your son and I are not betrothed, milady, and I am truly sorry for the deception we created surrounding it. The meeting we were to have had with you and Lord Thurlby this afternoon was to tell you the truth and explain everything."

"Apparently not everything," Lucas said.

Stung by his words, Lavinia turned on him. "You wish I had taken you aside on such short acquaintance and told you of every man who has flirted with me backstage, made an overture, offered me a jewel? To what end? Lord Cosgrove is merely the latest in a constant stream of gentlemen with ungentlemanly intentions, although he is certainly among the most vile—"

"Watch your tongue," the earl growled.

"I will *not*." She turned deliberately away from Cosgrove to face Lucas and his parents. "I am not the earl's *chère amie*, despite what he wishes you to believe. And while it is true that I was offered gifts from some of my admirers, I always made it very clear before accepting that they should expect no favors of any kind in return. These so-called gentlemen are never so direct as to call their gifts 'inducements,' although that is certainly what they are—lures to dangle in the hopes they may secure a female plaything.

"I have no interest in these men. I *despise* them." She looked over her shoulder and shot a venomous glare at the earl. "I despise *you*. Oh, no, I will *not* be going anywhere with *you*, Lord Cosgrove, not now or at any time in the future. I own my own property, you see, far away from London and Drury Lane, and I will have my own life there, a *normal* life, away from you and men like you."

She took a deep breath. "And now, Lady Thurlby, if you'll excuse me, I will go pack my things so I may leave in the morning. I only pray you will take pity on my friend Miss Weston and Mr. Drake too, for I doubt he will leave her side, and allow them to stay under your roof until I can secure arrangements for them to join me. If I may beg that one favor of you, I will be forever in your debt. Thank you for allowing my friends and me to share your home and your family. You are extraordinarily blessed in the family you have. I hope you know that."

She dropped into a deep curtsy—there was still enough actress in her to want to make a grand exit—and then she left the drawing room. She took the stairs with all the dignity of Joan of Arc, knowing she would fall apart the moment she reached her room. Lucas's siblings would be hearing what had happened soon enough from Lucas and his parents, and Lavinia was relieved that she would at least be spared from seeing the shock and dismay on their faces.

Oh, Lucas.

Her heart was broken. He hadn't defended her, hadn't pursued her after she'd left the drawing room—that was what hurt the most. She'd told him more about herself and her past than she'd told anyone, save Hannah—the only *man* she'd told, certainly.

It only went to prove what she'd known her entire life, she reflected as she entered the safety of her bedroom and began packing her belongings into her trunk—that trust was a hard-earned thing, a rare commodity. Perhaps she hadn't told Lucas about her past as Ruby Chadwick, but he'd betrayed her by accepting the Earl of Cosgrove's distorted version of the truth so readily.

She sat on the bed and covered her face with her hands, unable to hold back the flood of tears any longer.

* * *

It took all of Lucas's fortitude not to dash after Lavinia, pull her into his arms, apologize profusely for his momentary shock, and tell her how brilliant she'd been in confronting the Earl of Cosgrove—she'd thoroughly outranked the man with her magnificent, virtuous defiance of him. She'd been a duchess, a queen.

He would go to her soon. He must tell her how proud he was of her and how much he loved her—for he *did* love her, thoroughly and completely.

There was still the Earl of Cosgrove to deal with, however, not to mention a significant amount of explaining he owed his parents and siblings, who were currently gathering in the entrance hall and looking on with curiosity.

"It would seem one particular young lady is not for sale this evening," Lucas told Lord Cosgrove.

"Nor would it ever have been allowed, not in my house," his father added. "You have worn out your welcome, Lord Cosgrove. Good evening to you."

"Allow me to escort you from the premises," Lucas said, gesturing toward the door.

But with his family gathered in the entrance hall, it immediately became apparent that the earl wasn't about to leave quietly when he had an audience at his disposal.

"What a fine group we have here, Mr. Jennings," Cosgrove said. "Siblings, I presume? I'm sure your parents are as pleased as punch with the lot of you. Which one is Simon, pray?"

Everyone turned in surprised unison to look at Simon, who looked like a trapped animal seeking escape at the earl's words.

"Ah, Simon—*may* I call you Simon? I had planned on giving you two hundred fifty pounds tonight—half of the reward I'd offered for information leading to the whereabouts of Ruby Chadwick. I already gave the other half to your friend—what was his name? Woodhouse, Woodhull, something like that. Anyway, the one who showed me your letter."

"George Wootton," Simon mumbled.

"That's it. Wootton. Well, I was close."

"I don't want any money."

"That's good to hear, Simon, because I don't intend to give you any. Since I already paid two hundred fifty quid to your friend Mr. Woodley, not to mention incurring the added expense of traveling all the way to Lincolnshire, of all places, only to discover that my little bird of paradise refuses to return with me—"

"Bird of paradise?" James asked.

"You will cease referring to her in such terms," Lucas hissed at Cosgrove.

"She has found herself a champion, it seems." Cosgrove pulled on his gloves and took up his hat and cane from the table nearby. "Sadly, I have no intention of battling you to the death or any other such nonsense over a mere female, Mr. Jennings, no matter how delectable she may be. I have wasted enough time and money on her already." He tapped his hat into place. "I bid you all a good evening and her a good riddance. Enjoy the scandal that is about to erupt in your midst. May it provide you hours of entertainment."

Lucas followed Cosgrove to the door and then outside as a gathering fury built within him. He had no intention of letting the earl have the final word. "A moment, Cosgrove, if you please."

The earl's coach stood nearby, the groom ready to open the carriage door.

Lucas approached Cosgrove until he stood toe-to-toe with the man. "Allow us to understand each other: Ruby Chadwick is no more. The disappearance of the actress who was the so-called Darling of Drury Lane is a mystery that will remain unsolved. Do you take my meaning?"

"Jennings, you are an utter bore. I cannot imagine what she sees in you."

"Do you take my meaning?" Lucas growled, leaning menacingly into the earl's face. Only the discipline instilled in him during his years in the army kept him from wrapping his hands around the man's throat and choking him to extinction.

"Perfectly," Cosgrove drawled.

Lucas watched the earl enter his coach and continued watching until the coach had traveled down Alderwood's private lane to the road and disappeared from sight before he turned and entered the house. There were questions to answer and discussions to be had.

And then he would go to Lavinia as quickly as he could.

* * *

Lucas reentered the house to find everyone talking at once—excepting Simon, who had moved away from the others, and James, who had wandered close to Simon—presumably to keep him from bolting, which is what he appeared to want to do.

"Lucas, I think it is time you told us what is going on," their father said. "Into the drawing room, if you please."

It was not to be a private interview, however, as siblings and spouses queued up and followed Lucas and his parents into the room. James poured brandy for all the men—a mere splash for Isaac and a generous measure for Simon, who was looking pale.

"You're all wondering at the Earl of Cosgrove's pronouncements just now, no doubt," Father began.

"Rebecca, perhaps it's best if you aren't here," Mama said, interrupting. "This discussion is likely to be unsuitable for delicate feminine ears."

Their father looked at their mother in amazement. "Alice, sometimes your logic truly baffles me."

"I'm eighteen, Mama, and not so delicate as all that," Rebecca said. "I keep company with Susan, after all."

"While that is true enough, Rebecca, I would not have our parents think I am filling your mind with radical philosophies or wanton suggestions," Susan retorted.

"Susan, the very idea," Mama said. "Very well, Rebecca. Move over, Isaac; I want Rebecca to sit by me so I may cover her ears during the conversation should the need arise."

"Mama, really!" Rebecca exclaimed. "I know what a bird of paradise is. Isaac gave a Sunday School lesson about that very thing only a few weeks ago."

"Isaac? In *Sunday School?*"

"It was the woman taken in adultery, Mama. Repentance, you know. 'Go and sin no more.' Not the same thing at all, Rebecca," Isaac said.

"*What* bird of paradise?" James asked. "And *who* is this Ruby Chadwick the earl was talking about?"

"For a barrister, you can be rather dim sometimes," Susan said, earning a scowl from James.

"It would seem our fair Lavinia is known in London by the name of Ruby Chadwick," Father said. "I'll let Lucas explain."

And Lucas did. Over the next hour, he told them what he knew—of his initial encounter with Lavinia at the White Horse and her public claim that he was her husband, at helping her find her friends and his decision to accompany them to her farm. "Our encounter with Lord Cosgrove this evening has helped fill in some of my gaps of knowledge: that Lavinia had been performing on Drury Lane under the fictitious name of Ruby Chadwick and had become something of a sensation. I was not interested in London social life while I was seeing to Anthony's health and, therefore, had not heard of her."

"Apparently *you* had though, Simon," James said. "What was your part in all this?"

"I meant no harm—truly, Lucas," Simon said, looking beleaguered. "But you must understand that for the past several days, all the talk in Town had been about Ruby Chadwick and her sudden and mysterious disappearance. There was speculation and gossip of all kinds—kidnapping, ransom, murder. A fellow couldn't go anywhere and not hear about the popular actress who performed breeches roles and what could have happened to her.

"And then I showed up here only to discover my brother's betrothed, of whom none of us had any prior inkling, was none other than Ruby Chadwick herself. It was laughable, really. I wrote to Georgie to tell him my discovery so he could share in the joke. I'd heard Cosgrove had offered a reward, but that wasn't my reason for writing Georgie. Truly, Lucas."

"And yet a young man of modest means could surely make good use of a few hundred pounds, I daresay," Lucas said, unconvinced. "Especially one who has been busy being a man of leisure. Leisure can be expensive, can't it?"

Simon dropped his gaze to the floor. "The money was tempting; I can't deny it, I'm ashamed to say. It was mostly for laughs though, Lucas. Now that I've gotten to know Lavinia better, I see what a mistake it was."

"But Cosgrove referred to her as a bird of paradise too," James said.

"You seem fixated by that term, James," Susan said.

"Susan, hush," Mama said.

Susan merely smirked at James, who glared back at her.

"She was not, nor has she ever been such a thing, James," Lucas said. "Do you recall your introduction to Lavinia? What was your first impression?"

"Ah, I understand. She's a deuced attractive woman, to be sure. One would have to be dead not to notice. I imagine there have been too many men like Cosgrove who've had less than honorable thoughts where the fair Lavinia is concerned."

"Precisely. As a result, she has an extremely poor opinion of men and has since she was very young."

"I find all of this fascinating, setting aside the bird of paradise part, of course," Susan said. "Becoming Ruby Chadwick protected Lavinia while also creating a career for herself. Very resourceful, if you were to ask me. Clever."

"I shudder when you speak of such things as careers, Susan," Mama said. "It seems so . . . I cannot find the right word."

"*Exciting?*" Susan offered. "*Challenging? Inspiring?*"

"*Unladylike* was more what I was looking for."

"Back to the issue at hand," Father said. "Rather than hosting Lucas's betrothed and her cousins and friend these past few days, we have taken a band of actors into our midst."

"One of whom wears breeches," Mama said.

"Two if you include Mr. Drake," Susan added with a wink.

"You are not taking this seriously enough, Susan," Mama scolded. "Breeches on a woman—the very idea is shocking. The neighbors would be scandalized if they were to find out."

"I can't see why, Mama," Susan said. "Women have the same appendages as men—arms, legs, and so forth. Why a woman can't don a pair of breeches and be considered modest defies logic. The legs are entirely encased in sturdy fabric. Now, bare a woman's bosom in the latest fashion—"

"Oh dear." Mama's hands flew to cover Rebecca's ears.

"Enough, Susan. We must return to the point. It's getting late," Father said. "We still have a problem to resolve here. Miss Fernley and her friends have lied to us the entire time they have accepted our hospitality, and regardless of what anyone thinks, our neighbors will not look kindly upon this if it were to reach their ears. We have the family name to uphold. We are pillars of the community. As personable as they have all been, we have a duty to think the ramifications through thoroughly before we can proceed. Miss Weston's recent illness only complicates this further."

"If I may say something," Isobel said, speaking for the first time. "For reasons of my own, which are no secret to anyone, I was concerned when Lucas arrived with a bride in tow. Concerned and protective. Thomas and I felt a heavy burden of guilt when Lucas enlisted, you see. I have observed Lavinia closely, and I find her to be clever and kind and even genuine, which, of course, seems an odd thing to say at this particular moment in time. But I see how she looks at Lucas—when she thinks no one is looking. So I, for one, am inclined to forgive who or what she was before she arrived at Alderwood. If she loves Lucas and will make him happy, she has my blessing."

"I echo the words of my wife," Thomas said.

"Thank you, Isobel, Thomas. That means a great deal to me," Lucas said. "You will recall, Father, that it was *I* who announced we were betrothed. I hadn't said anything to Lavinia beforehand—devil take it, I'd barely had the thought spring to mind before I'd blurted it out. To allow me to save face here at home, Lavinia and her friends followed my lead—even though they'd left their acting lives behind them in London. I take full responsibility for the deception.

"I do not know who Ruby Chadwick is. I never met her. But I do know Lavinia Fernley. I know her very well, in fact. I have seen her devotion and her courage and her strength. She is truly the most beautiful woman I have ever met, for she is beautiful inside and out. I have also discovered that I love her." He'd never voiced the words aloud, hadn't even spoken them to Lavinia yet, and here he'd blurted them out to his entire family. What a blundering fool he was! And yet they'd felt delicious rolling off his tongue. "I love her," he repeated. "But she intends to leave Alderwood tomorrow with Hannah to spare us the scandal and humiliation should her past follow her here again. I do not want her to leave."

"But what is to be done?" Mama asked. "She is who she is, Lucas. Can a leopard change its spots?"

"No, Mama, a leopard cannot, as we learn from the book of Jeremiah," Isaac replied. "But Miss Fernley and her friends are not leopards; they are people. And people can change, can they not? Or else there is no hope for any of us."

"Lavinia is determined to make a new life for herself and the others at Primrose Farm—"

"A daunting task for anyone, considering what we brothers observed when we visited the place," James said. "But for a young woman such as Miss Fernley? It will take a great deal of fortitude for her to be successful, especially with that entourage of hers."

"I wish to help her," Lucas said. "I wish to marry her and make a life with her at Primrose Farm. The problem of her past has a simple solution, but only if all of you are willing to support it. With the permanent disappearance of the actress Ruby Chadwick, any concerns regarding actresses or breeches or scandal can disappear along with her. Lavinia is free to be Lavinia now. I hope you will all be willing to accept her as such and help me convince her to make our betrothal one in truth."

He looked around the room, from sibling to sibling to his parents, trying to read their expressions as they pondered his words. Having their support was essential if he was to convince Lavinia to marry him. If his family still had misgivings about her, there was no hope to be had.

It was Clara who spoke first. "Oh, Lucas," she said, a lone tear rolling down her face. "How moving your words are! Of course we will support you—and Lavinia too. And here I am, crying again."

"Come, love, let me take you upstairs," Isaac said. "You and our growing babe have had enough excitement for one day and need to rest. I am in agreement with Clara, Lucas. You have our support."

"I may have to speak to her privately about the breeches first," Mama said. "But you have my support as well. I have found myself rather attached to the girl. When I first saw her, I thought she would be intolerable to be around with those looks of hers. But she is kind, as Isobel remarked upon, and not proud at all."

"Thank you, Mama," Lucas said. "After the earl's visit tonight, I fear it will not be easy to convince her. I need you all on my side if I am going to succeed in this." He needed to go to her tonight, right now, to assure himself that she was all right after the confrontation with Cosgrove. "In fact, if you'll excuse me, I would like to go to her now."

"Whatever I can do to help, Lucas, you have only to ask," Simon said.

"What of you, then, Father? What is your opinion on the matter?" Lucas asked.

His father was silent for a moment, studying Lucas, before he finally spoke. "It has been my observation that Miss Fernley has been a gracious and well-mannered guest while staying at Alderwood. I also found this evening to be especially enlightening. If her handling of the Earl of Cosgrove is any indication, she is a young lady of courage and conviction. And I daresay her friends are no more peculiar than old Brumby and his wife down in the village. You have my blessing."

"Thank you, Father," Lucas said.

"It appears we are all in accord, Lucas," Father said. "We are at your service—but I fear the real convincing will have to come from you."

"I agree, Father, and thank you. Thank you all." Lucas excused himself and took the stairs two at a time to reach Lavinia as quickly as he could.

Chapter 22

LAVINIA SPLASHED WATER ON HER face and blotted it dry with a towel, then studied her reflection in the oval mirror on her washstand. She had to look calm and steady when she spoke to Hannah and Artie, whom she'd left at Delia's side when she'd been summoned to the drawing room by Lord Thurlby. The reflection that stared back at her from the mirror wasn't very convincing, but it would have to do.

She patted a few loose strands of hair back into place and straightened her skirt, praying that no one would be in the corridor when she left her room so she could slip into Delia's room unnoticed. She needed to let the others know about the Earl of Cosgrove's arrival at Alderwood and the resulting confrontation before they learned about it from someone else—a member of the family or, heaven forbid, one of the staff. Hannah and Artie deserved to hear about it from her.

She quietly unlocked the door and turned the knob—and the door flew open, nearly knocking her over in the process. Lucas slipped in and shut it behind him.

"You cannot be in here," Lavinia hissed. "Your family has been scandalized enough this evening. I will not add to their discomfort by having their son discovered alone with me here in a private tête-à-tête." She swung the door open wide and pointed. "Out. Now." She was sorely hurt by his mistrust and inaction down in the drawing room, effectively leaving her on her own to face Lord Cosgrove and his insinuations.

"Fine," he said, pointing as well. "We shall have this conversation in the corridor, then, but we shall have it. After you, Lavinia."

She marched out of her room, relying on anger to get her past her grief, and then whirled about to face him. "Say what it is you have to say, Lucas, so I may get back to my packing."

He shook his head at her, which only succeeded in fueling her anger further. "You are waiting for the rest of the list, no doubt. The men who sought my favor. *Favors*, to be more precise. Let me think"—she tapped her chin—"Sir John Ewell, Lord Bromley—"

He placed his fingers over her mouth, effectively silencing her. "Hush, Lavinia. Don't do this to yourself. I confess I was shocked to discover there was one more rather *large* secret you had kept from me, *Miss Ruby Chadwick*, but it had more to do with the fact that I thought I had gained your trust and yet you had kept an important part of yourself from me."

She pushed his fingers aside. "You left me on my own to face that horrid man in front of your entire family. I felt so alone and exposed, Lucas, like I'd been stripped bare by his words."

"I'm sorry for that," he said. "It was rather difficult to get a word in edgewise. But you were absolutely brilliant, like a virtuous, fiery goddess. I got rather caught up in the performance. It took every fiber of my being to keep from dashing after you when you left, but I had to make sure Cosgrove left with certain understandings in place. I also wanted to explain what had been going on to my family—and to let them know that the deception surrounding our betrothal was of my doing. That it was *my* fault, not yours."

He was so close, so close, and then his arms came about her. "I must tell you something," he whispered in her ear, his cheek resting against her own. She shut her eyes. "A confession, I'm afraid. I am impetuous at times—perhaps you've noticed—and I said something to my family tonight I should have spoken with you about first."

"What?" she whispered, caught up in the warmth of his body, fighting the enticing sense of security it gave. There was such power in intimacy, true intimacy. He had not even so much as kissed her, and yet the feeling of oneness with him nearly overwhelmed her with its sweetness.

"I told them I love you, for it is true. But I should have told you first. I love you, Lavinia Fernley, with all my heart. Please don't leave." He dropped to one knee, and Lavinia looked into his eyes and saw truth there. "Marry me. We shall work together to make Primrose Farm thrive, and we shall live as regular people—or we will return to London so you may be The Darling of Drury Lane if that is your choice. Only marry me—the sooner, the better."

Oh, but it was tempting.

Could one learn to trust after so many years and so many poor examples warning her against it? Could she trust him? She dearly wanted to, but there was so much at stake.

She knew what she had to do.

He closed his eyes and brought her hand to his mouth for a kiss.

"Lucas," she whispered. "I trust you more than I have ever trusted anyone, save Hannah. You said you spoke impetuously to your family. I cannot afford to be impetuous."

"Lavinia, please—"

She cradled his face with her hands and made him look her in the eye. "I must have time to consider. I am not saying no; oh, please don't think that, for I love you too. Oh, I do love you. But I need time. My father—"

"I understand, my love." Lucas rested his forehead against hers. "Your father has much to account for with his Maker. I will be patient—and hopeful. I ask only that you remain here, where I can court you in earnest."

She kissed him with her entire being, wrapping her arms around his neck as he held her tightly in his arms. "Lavinia," he whispered, drawing back and looking at her with the eyes of a hungry lover, but this time Lavinia knew it was love that fueled the passion, not merely passion alone. "We must stop ourselves, my dearest love, or I will be riding off to obtain a special license this very minute. I'm hopeful your enthusiasm means your answer will eventually be yes." He kissed her one last time and then took a deep breath. "You were going somewhere when I arrived at your room, I believe."

"Yes, I was going to tell Hannah to pack her things." She kissed him and then kissed him again.

"But you won't tell her that now, surely?" he murmured.

"No. But, I still must let Hannah and Artie know what happened. They need to know."

"Then I will accompany you to Delia's room, if I may. Poor fellow, Artie; it breaks my heart to see him this way. He barely leaves Delia's side, even for a moment."

"I feel so helpless. It's been longer than twenty-four hours, and she's barely made a flutter. What if she doesn't wake up?"

He caressed her cheek. "Then we will do what has to be done, my love. We will stay by her side until the end, we will be there for Artie and for Hannah, and we will grieve together."

They arrived at Delia's room and saw the door had been left open a crack. Inside, Delia lay still as death in her bed. Hannah sat nearby, a single candle providing illumination while she did her sewing. Artie was slumped in a chair by Delia's side, his head on his chest, quietly snoring.

"He finally gave out," Hannah whispered, setting her work aside. "I didn't have the heart to leave him."

"I'll take him to his room," Lucas said.

"He'll only wake up and insist on staying if you try. Better he stay here and get what sleep he can," Lavinia said. Hannah nodded her agreement.

"Very well." He laid a soft kiss on Lavinia's cheek. "I will bid you good night, then, my dearest Lavinia. I must retire to my room, as I expect to do a great deal of praying tonight—that should make Isaac happy to hear, don't you think?"

Lavinia smiled. "Spare a few prayers for Delia while you're at it."

"I will—and for Artie too. He and I both know how it feels to wait while the women we love keep us in terrible suspense." He kissed Lavinia one last time and nodded to Hannah. "Good night to you both." And then he was gone.

"Seems I missed something important while I was up here keeping our Artie company," Hannah murmured.

Lavinia crossed to where Hannah was seated and knelt on the floor next to her, then laid her head in Hannah's lap. "He loves me, Hannah, and heaven help me, I love him. He has asked me to marry him—in truth this time. And I am sorely tempted."

"Of course you are, luv." Hannah stroked Lavinia's head. "'Tis only to be expected."

"But what am I to do? If I marry him, Primrose Farm will be his, and if he proves as untrustworthy as every other man I've ever met, we will have nothing."

"Do you really think him the sort to do such a thing? And what's all this about 'every other man' being untrustworthy? You've only to look across this very room to see one of the most devoted men there is."

"Artie, yes; he's a dear. And yet, for all his devotion, he's never declared himself to Delia, has he? He's never asked to marry her. They've known each other for years, and he's never spoken the words."

"Artie's never felt worthy of our Delia, luv. Delia Weston—my, but she was a grand lady in her day, Livvy. Nearly as popular as your Ruby Chadwick, she was. Artie was a fair success himself, never quite the leading man, although he always had steady work doing lesser roles, but nothing like our Delia. Very few compared to our Delia back then.

"So there's Artie for you—as fine an example of a devoted man as you could ever hope to find. And from the looks of things around here, there's another devoted man or two—Mr. Isaac and Mr. Thomas seem to fit the bill, not to mention his lordship himself. They have wives what seem content enough, if you was to ask me."

"Hmm," Lavinia said.

Hannah gently patted Lavinia's head, like she'd done so often when Lavinia was a child. "Now, luv, if you'll excuse me, I think I'll be off to my bed. You should too. Artie will be well enough, asleep as he is, here at Delia's side."

Lavinia lifted her head from Hannah's lap and stood, and Hannah rose from her chair and picked up her sewing basket. "You must do what you feel is right, and only you can answer that, luv. You can take a risk for a chance at happiness and find you made a mistake, or you can hold back out of fear and never know what you could have had. But I'm guessing right now, Artie's wishing he'd chosen differently."

* * *

Lavinia did not sleep a wink. She tossed and turned, she plumped the pillows, and then she tossed and turned some more. Her head was full of thoughts that plagued her all during the night:

Livvy, my girl, your looks are your prized possession and your poison. Have a care.

Forget marriage, my sweet. It'll never happen. Be practical instead.

All will be well, I promise you, love.

Trust me.

Several hours later but long before dawn, feeling restless and uncomfortable, she got out of bed and pulled on her dressing gown. She may as well sneak down to Delia's room and make sure Artie hadn't toppled out of his chair at some point during the night.

She lit a candle and tiptoed down the corridor. All was dark and quiet; the house was asleep. Apparently, she was the only one who wasn't.

She listened at Delia's door for a moment or two before turning the knob and quietly opening the door a few inches.

And then she stopped.

Artie was kneeling on the floor next to Delia's bed, holding one of her hands in his and speaking softly to her, unaware that he now had an audience in Lavinia. "Delia, if I could go back and do it all again, I'd tell you how I feel. I swear on bended knee I would," he declared in a heartbreaking whisper.

He rested his head on the bed, not letting go of her hand. Delia, illuminated by the light of the moon shining through the window, looked like a sleeping angel. Artie sobbed quietly. "'Is there no play, / To ease the anguish of a torturing hour?'" he said and sobbed again, his bony shoulders heaving.

Even in grief, the dear man must quote Shakespeare. How like Artie it was to do so.

"Come back to me, Delia," he went on. "I love you, my sweet girl. Always have. And I don't think I can bear it if you leave me without knowing how I feel. Please come back to me. Please. Oh, Delia." He sobbed some more.

Lavinia quietly shut the door and returned to her room. She'd intruded on a private—even sacred—moment, for what was more sacred than pure love? But she could not be sorry for her intrusion. It had been a gift, and her heart was full.

She had her answer.

Chapter 23

LAVINIA AWAKENED WITH A START. Someone was shaking her—rather vigorously too. When she opened her bleary eyes, she saw to her surprise that it was Rebecca, of all people.

"Lavinia, you must wake up! Quickly!" Rebecca cried. "Oh, good, you're awake now. Hurry! Here, put this on." She grabbed Lavinia's dressing gown and tossed in on top of her while Lavinia struggled to sit up.

"What is going on?" she said, still trying to get past the fog of sleep. She was going to need a nap later in the day, she was sure of it. "I think I'd prefer to dress."

"There's no time! You must come at once."

"Is she awake? Oh, good, you *are* awake. You simply won't believe what has happened!" This was Susan, who had burst into Lavinia's room like she'd been shot from a cannon.

"Then tell me," Lavinia said with a touch of impatience. She would have been in a perfectly good mood after the decision she'd finally made in the middle of the night if she hadn't been jarred awake so suddenly.

"You must see for yourself," Susan said, pulling her to her feet while Rebecca began threading Lavinia's arm through the sleeve of her dressing gown.

"I can do that myself," she said, tugging the sleeve from Rebecca's grasp and sliding her arm through it. And then she realized there was more commotion coming from outside her door in the corridor.

Delia! Lavinia thought, panicking. *No!*

She brushed away Rebecca's hands as the girl fumbled to button Lavinia's dressing gown. "Truly, I'm awake now, Rebecca. I can manage on my own."

"Here are your slippers. Quickly!"

Fighting back tears, she hurried with the sisters toward Delia's room. There was already a small cluster of people gathered outside the door. Lucas came toward her and took her hands in his.

"Lavinia," he began—

"I must see her!" she cried. "Oh, my dear, sweet Delia—"

"Yes?" a familiar voice from within the room called.

Lavinia looked at Lucas, her brow furrowed in confusion.

"Lavinia, is that you?" the voice called out again.

Lavinia's heart began to race. She turned, letting go of Lucas, and walked as though in a trance toward the bedroom door. She pushed it completely open and blinked . . .

There sat Delia. Sat. In the bed. As wide awake and alive—*alive*—as she could possibly be, a beaming Artie sitting proudly in the chair next to her, where he'd been holding vigil for the past twenty-four hours, give or take the few times Lady Thurlby had been successful in prying him away.

A maid scurried past Lavinia, carrying a tray of hot chocolate and scones, from the looks and smell of it, and set it on Delia's lap.

"She's hungry," Artie said triumphantly.

"Well, she would be," Susan retorted. "She's the size of a hummingbird and hasn't eaten in over a day."

"I don't understand," Lavinia said, shaking her head, then crossing to Delia's bedside and embracing her. She felt so thin and frail. "Oh, my dear, you have come back to us! We were so worried!"

"There, there, now, dearie. 'All's well that ends well,' as the playwright wisely said." Delia patted Lavinia fondly before taking a bite of scone. "Would you care for a scone, Livvy? Artie?"

"No, thank you," Lavinia said, still feeling a bit dazed.

"I would," Artie said.

Lavinia wandered back over to Lucas's side. "We all took turns sitting by her bedside," she whispered. "She never moved, never smiled. *Nothing.* And now she's wide awake, acting as if nothing had even happened."

"Mama sent for the doctor. Perhaps he can shed some light on the situation."

Lavinia nodded and then grabbed Lucas's arm. "Where is Hannah? I must tell Hannah."

"I sent one of the maids to wake her," Susan said. She and Rebecca were still in the doorway, with Isobel and Clara standing behind them. She remembered now that Lucas's brothers—*all* of them—and his father had also been in the corridor when she'd arrived. They'd all had smiles on their faces, as had Rebecca and Susan when they'd awakened her. If she'd but noticed, she could have spared herself a great deal of anxiety, especially considering how truly radiant Delia currently looked. She was nowhere near death's door.

Artie suddenly popped out of his chair. "Excuse me, Delia, my dearest love. I shall be right back." He bowed with a flourish and kissed the hand she held out for him. It was all accomplished with such pageantry that Lavinia wanted to laugh—if she hadn't wanted to cry.

"Lavinia, Lucas, I hope you will congratulate us on our good news. Delia and I are to be married." He looked about to burst his buttons with pride.

"What?" Lavinia asked, although it was more of a rhetorical question; after what she'd observed in the middle of the night, it seemed only natural that something like this would have occurred between the two of them, finally.

"No surprise there, sir," Lucas said. "A hearty congratulations to you both. I'm so pleased Delia has made such a remarkable recovery."

"You must hear the entire story," Artie said. "Delia, we must tell these two our story, don't you agree?"

"Of course, Arthur dear, but it might be better to wait just a bit. For Hannah, you know, and perhaps we can include Dr. Ellis too."

"Good idea! Splendid idea! Oh, it is such a *grand* story, Livvy. Such a wonderful day it is!"

Artie blew a kiss to Delia and then strutted out the door to share his news with Lucas's family. He could hardly contain himself, so joyful he was; Lavinia couldn't help but smile. She could hear the hearty congratulations and backslaps from Lucas's brothers and the well-wishes of his sisters and sisters-in-law—for both Delia's return to health and the announced betrothal.

Lady Thurlby arrived with the doctor at nearly the same time Hannah arrived. They joined Lavinia, Lucas, and Artie in Delia's room and closed the door behind them. "Lord Thurlby has sent the rest of the family about their business. They have heard the news and given you their congratulations, I am sure." She gestured toward Delia. "Here is our patient, Dr. Ellis, looking as fit as ever, as you can plainly see." Lady Thurlby said, a twinkle in her eye.

"I hope you can explain what has happened," Lavinia said. "Delia's recovery is nothing short of miraculous."

"I know precisely what has happened. I was able to diagnose her correctly yesterday when I was here."

"What do you mean?" she asked.

"I knew there was something amiss, and my private examination quickly confirmed my suspicions."

"Indeed," Lady Thurlby said, fighting back a smile.

"And it worked, Dr. Ellis, as I told you it would," Delia said, beaming.

"*What* worked?" Lavinia asked, feeling as if an entire conversation was eluding her.

"Why don't *you* tell them?" Dr. Ellis said, smiling at Delia.

Delia straightened up against the pillows and shot a victorious look at Artie. "Sleeping Beauty, that's what," she said.

Lucas began to chuckle.

"Sleeping Beauty?" Lavinia repeated. *Sleeping Beauty?* And then it suddenly dawned on her. She turned and glared at Delia. "I knew it! You little schemer." She shot an accusing look at the doctor. "And you are telling me you *knew* she wasn't unconscious? That she was *acting*? And you didn't *tell* us!"

Dr. Ellis smiled. "Miss Weston is a most charming and persuasive patient, Miss Fernley. She is also ticklish. It was easy enough to uncover her deception when I examined her more thoroughly, but then she begged Lady Thurlby and me to keep her secret for a little while. It seems she'd had a reluctant suitor for several years now and felt it was time to give him a push. Congratulations, by the way, Miss Weston, Mr. Drake."

"Thank you, sir!" Artie said, reaching over to pump the doctor's hand in a vigorous handshake. "I am the most fortunate of men."

Lucas was laughing so hard tears were streaming down his face. "Well done, Mama. Conspiring with Delia and Dr. Ellis in this. I commend you!"

"I recognized Miss Weston, shortly after your arrival at Alderwood," Lady Thurlby explained. "I thought she looked familiar, and I eventually recalled that I had seen her onstage during my first Season in London. Lady Macbeth, she was back then. Wonderful. But it was all so many years ago, it took me awhile to sort it out."

"Thank you for the compliment, Lady Thurlby," Delia said before taking a bite of scone.

"I did inform your father, I would have you know, Lucas, although the secret will remain between him and those of us in this room, if you please. And it was quite a chore, even if it was for only a single day and night. Mr. Drake was most insistent about staying with Miss Weston at all times. I could barely coax him out of the room so the poor woman could eat and use the necessary on occasion."

"My sincerest apologies, Lady Thurlby," Artie said.

Lady Thurlby waved her hand in dismissal. "Quite all right. It all worked out rather well in the end, and it was great fun to be in on the deception. I haven't enjoyed myself so much in years."

Lavinia felt dizzy and confused—and slightly queasy—as though she'd taken a blow to the head. "You knew you were playing host to actors all along, then? But what of the scandal it could have caused the family? What of that?"

"I knew I was playing host to the great Delia Weston, acclaimed actress and leading lady of the London stage, and her rather eccentric relatives. I did *not* know until Miss Weston feigned her illness that Mr. Drake was not a relative but a reluctant suitor. And I *definitely did not* know you were an actress who starred in breeches roles, Lavinia."

Lavinia blushed at the mild set down before remembering she was still angry. "I cannot dismiss all of this quite so easily as the rest of you seem to be doing. You had us—me—terrified, Delia. Why are you not angry at what Delia did, Artie? I believe I have been good to you. I deserve more of an explanation than this."

"And you shall have one," Delia said.

"Indeed, you shall, Livvy," Artie added. "And it is a *grand* story, Livvy. You will not be disappointed."

* * *

Lucas put his arm around the back of Lavinia's chair and rested his hand on her shoulder, hoping it would offer her support. She seemed to be in a bit of a daze.

Artie cleared his throat, gaining everyone's attention.

"As a young lad, I always dreamt of being onstage," Artie began. "I was most fortunate in that my parents, while poor, insisted upon educating their children, which is why my sister and I could read. I still remember the first time—"

"Best skip over the childhood parts, Arthur, or we'll be here until supper," Delia interjected.

"Understood, my dearest."

Lucas bit his lip to avoid laughing.

Artie cleared his throat again. "Once there was a beautiful lady, the fairest in all the land, and the leading actress of her age."

"This is going to take forever," Delia said. "I believe I shall give it a try, Arthur."

"As long as I can still add in my bits," Artie said.

"Certainly. As you may have guessed," she said, directing her words to the others in the room, "I have felt an attachment for Arthur Drake for many years, and I thought he may have had a similar attachment to me."

"Oh, I did, I did," Artie insisted.

"But try as I might, I simply could not get him to speak his heart. I tried everything I could think of."

"What do you mean?" Lavinia asked. "What did you try?"

"Oh, you know." Delia fluttered her hand in the air. "Rehearsing love scenes together, for example, or feigning injuries, like the one during the carriage accident on our way out of London."

"But you were hurt," Lucas said. "I could tell you'd been hurt."

"A bit," she conceded. "But not very, at least not as much as I led you to believe. I'm an excellent actress, if you haven't noticed by now. I was at my wit's end—and then the lovely children here asked for a story."

"Sleeping Beauty," Lavinia said.

"Exactly. Well, a couple of old thespians can't simply *tell* a story, now, can we? We must *act*, so I was the sleeping princess, and Arthur was my prince. And he kissed me . . ." She paused dramatically. "But it didn't change *anything*! Even after that most romantic of kisses, Arthur still did not declare himself to me."

"I think we can fill in the rest of the story," Lucas said. "You allowed life to imitate art: you pretended to be dying; your hero, distraught that he may actually lose you, declared his love; and then, as required by the fairy tale, he awakened you with a kiss."

"This time it worked," Delia answered triumphantly. "And I was not *pretending*, Lucas. I was *acting*. There is a big difference."

"What I don't understand is *why*?" Lavinia said. "Why this elaborate deception when you are always so direct with people and Artie has been your devoted friend for so long?"

"Why, indeed?" Delia replied, looking straight at Lucas.

Lucas shifted in his seat.

"Because we are afraid of the pain the truth may hold," Delia said, answering her own question. "You see, I am not Delia Weston any more than you are Ruby Chadwick, dearie. My real name is Minnie Hopgood."

"It *is?*" Artie said, his initial shock turning into excitement. "Why, mine is really Johnny Grimmett! Ho, *ho*, my dear! What a fine coincidence! I had to change my name, you know, for who wants a leading man named Johnny Grimmett, I ask you?"

"I never felt equal to a man named Arthur Drake," Delia—Minnie—said, clasping her hands to her breast. "But I *can* be the equal of a Johnny Grimmett."

"It appears we are two of a kind, a couple of sparrows who have pretended all these years to be swans. 'A heaven on earth I have won by wooing thee.' And while I will apologize on behalf of my dear Delia—or would you prefer Minnie?"

"Delia. I haven't been Minnie in a while."

Artie—Johnny—nodded his approval. "I do hope you will forgive her, Livvy, for she has given me the most splendid gift a man who has devoted his life to the theater could ever hope for. I have seen many great performances over the years—thrilling, moving, wonderful performances—but I have *never* seen such convincing acting in all my life until now. And she did it all for *me!*"

"Here, here," Dr. Ellis said.

"True love, indeed. We've gotten a taste of our own medicine, have we not?" Lucas said quietly to Lavinia. "But would you look at Artie's face?"

The elderly man had finally won the woman of his dreams, and Lucas had rarely seen anything so beautiful.

* * *

For several minutes, everyone congratulated the ecstatic couple. Eventually, Dr. Ellis took his leave, Hannah went to her room to get some rest, and Lady Thurlby left to consult with her housekeeper.

It was as good a time as any, Lavinia thought, to resolve a little matter of her own. She laid a hand on Lucas's arm as they left the room, immediately drawing his attention.

He smiled at her. "What a couple of characters they are!" he said. "I'm not sure what names we address them by now though. Is she Delia or Minnie? Is he Arthur, as Delia calls him, or Artie or Johnny? When they marry, I suspect they will have to do so under their real names. I wonder what Isaac would have to say about that?"

"I'm sure he'd agree with you." Now that the moment had arrived, Lavinia found that her carefully thought-out speech had fled. "My guess is that they will go by Artie and Delia, since that is who they have been for decades."

"You're undoubtedly right," Lucas said.

Lavinia swallowed.

"Was there something else?" he asked, his eyebrows raised in question.

"Yes. I—" Her heart was racing, and she was having difficulty breathing. "I am terrified, Lucas," she whispered. "But I have discovered that, after all, there are a few honorable men in the world, and you are one of them. And, heaven help me, but I am willing to take a risk on love . . . if you are."

He closed his eyes as if in benediction. "Thank God." And then he took her hands in his and kissed each one and then kissed her. "It seems we have a real announcement to make to my family, then."

"Yes," she agreed. "And a confession."

"Amen," he said.

* * *

That evening at dinner, after everyone was seated at the table and toasts had been made to Delia and Artie, the newly betrothed couple, Lucas stood. "There is more news to share," he said, raising his voice in order to be heard over the convivial noise in the room. When everyone had quieted down, he continued. "I must come clean to all of you. After my time in Spain, my pride got the better of me, and rather than return home empty-handed, I announced to you all that I was betrothed to this remarkable woman." He gestured toward a radiant Lavinia, who was seated across the table from him. "She and her friends were gracious enough to go along with my deception and spare me the humiliation of confessing my lie so soon upon my arrival home. But I, for one, have learned my lesson."

"Something about pride going before a fall?" Isaac suggested, earning a few laughs.

"And honesty being the best policy," Lucas said. "The happy reality is that despite my failings, Lavinia has looked beyond them and has agreed to marry me in truth. She is to be my wife. I am the happiest of men."

"Second happiest," Artie crowed, making everyone laugh as they all once again raised their goblets in a toast.

"Happiest," Lucas said to Lavinia.

And then they ate and talked and enjoyed being a family together with friends, and afterward, he and Lavinia joyfully accepted hugs and good wishes from everyone.

Epilogue

THREE WEEKS LATER, TWO COUPLES stood at the altar of St. Alfred's Church of the village of Lower Alderwood. It was three weeks because the elder of the two brides had always dreamed of a traditional wedding, so the vicar of St. Alfred's, the Reverend Isaac Jennings, by name, had been instructed to have the banns officially read and published.

The younger of the two grooms would have preferred to ride all night long in a rainstorm if necessary to procure a special license and marry his bride the following day, but it was not to be. He found the patience required during the three weeks before his wedding by doing hard physical labor at the farm his beautiful bride was bringing with her to the marriage. It would be their home, and he intended it to be the sort of place where a man and his wife, together, could build a prosperous life and provide for a family.

Lucas had great confidence that they would be prosperous. He and Lavinia had both endured hardships and made mistakes, but as a result, they had also learned that they were strong and could face the challenges that would come. For challenges inevitably would come; such was the nature of life.

St. Alfred's wasn't a large building, and it fairly overflowed with family and friends. Lucas's mother and father sat on the front pew, and all of his brothers and sisters and their spouses and children filled several more pews, Hannah with them. Only Lucas's sister Martha, who had given birth to baby Abigail the previous week, they'd learned in the letter that had arrived only yesterday, wasn't here to join them on this occasion, nor were her husband, Albert, and their other two children, Bertie and little Joseph, and they were sorely missed.

Dr. Ellis was here, as were several of the good villagers of Lower Alderwood.

One of the great surprises and delights for Lucas was the arrival of his best friend, Anthony, and his wife, Amelia, along with the Marquess and Marchioness of Ashworth.

"For we must join in the celebration of the gentleman who brought our son home from war at great personal expense," Lady Ashworth had said upon their arrival at Alderwood the day before.

"Precisely, my dear," Lord Ashworth had echoed.

"Congratulations to you both," Amelia had said. She'd hugged Lucas and then she'd hugged Lavinia. "And now I'm going to steal your future wife, Lucas, so that we may get acquainted and become fast friends."

"All of London was set on its proverbial ear over the disappearance of a rather popular actress," Anthony had then observed once the ladies had gone off together to explore the parks at Alderwood. "And then the most curious thing happened—Lord Cosgrove, who was the sure bet for acquiring the lady's favors, according to White's betting book, left town, supposedly to retrieve his prodigal lady love, but he returned the following day declaring the woman didn't exist. Can you imagine?"

"Quite remarkable," Lucas had said.

"Indeed. You know, I happened the see The Darling of Drury Lane perform once, not long after our return from Spain."

"Did you? You never mentioned it."

"It was one of those rare times my valet forced me from my home but refused to accompany me. Best valet I ever had too, although my current one is improving sufficiently enough to keep on."

"Glad to hear it."

"The actress in question was remarkably talented, as I recall. Wore breeches during the final act. Not the first actress to do so, if you know the history of London theater, but still rather daring of her. I found the performance . . . impressive." He'd looked about. "Beautiful country, Lincolnshire. Flat though. Green, but flat."

"Indeed; that's what lowlands tend to be. Perhaps you would like to visit Primrose Farm one day soon and offer some advice now that you're a wealthy nobleman and not a captain in the army. You may have learned something useful in the meantime."

"I believe I will take you up on your offer. Too bad that actress disappeared. Drury Lane hasn't been the same without her, from what I hear."

"Most unfortunate."

Anthony had smiled knowingly. "I think you would have found her most appealing."

"I have no doubt at all that you are correct."

And now she was his wife, Lucas thought as he slid the ring on her finger.

* * *

"I don't understand what could possibly be such a big mystery that I couldn't even visit my own farm for three weeks," Lavinia said as their carriage rolled north from Alderwood. "You promised we would work together to create a home at Primrose Farm."

"And we certainly shall," Lucas replied. "I left the interior completely in your hands, if you'll recall."

"Except that I couldn't even supervise any of it because of your so-called mystery," she said. "Your mother has spent more time at the farm than I have."

"Think of it as preparing your bridal suite, my love. We are poor, you know, and must economize, so no extravagant travels to far-off lands for us. Allow that I wanted Primrose Farm to look like more than an empty house when I brought my bride to it."

Lord Thurlby, who had requested Lavinia call him Father, had offered his gig to Delia and Artie, who, naturally, had made plans of their own for the next few days. Hannah had been invited to stay at Alderwood, with Susan and Rebecca promising Lavinia that they would attend to her and keep her company.

Lavinia looked around her, remembering the first time she had traveled this road, taking in the scenery and wondering what Primrose Farm would be like now. It seemed a lifetime ago. She and Hannah and Artie and Delia had not known what they would find, but Lavinia had been ready to do whatever it took to leave London and the likes of Lord Cosgrove and others of his ilk behind.

"I was never so proud of you as when I heard how you stood up to the earl," Hannah had told her not many days after Delia's little ruse, when it had dawned on Lavinia that she hadn't shared that particular nugget with the three of them after everything else that had happened.

Indeed, facing the earl openly had given Lavinia a peace of mind she wouldn't have had otherwise, she was sure.

"We're nearly there. Close your eyes," Lucas said.

Lavinia smiled and closed her eyes.

Lucas kissed her rather thoroughly. "I don't think I shall ever tire of kissing my wife."

She laughed.

After a quarter mile or so, she sensed the carriage turn onto the lane that she knew led to Primrose Farm, and then it eventually rolled to a stop.

"You've been a very obedient wife so far," Lucas said. "So I will praise you for it, because I'm no fool, and I don't expect you will always be so obedient, despite the vows you took earlier today. Let me help you." He opened the carriage door and put down the steps, then guided her as she descended from the carriage. "Thank you for trusting me," he said. "You may open your eyes now."

She opened her eyes.

There before her was the two-story brick farmhouse she remembered— its shape and size. But it was not the same at all, for now the brick exterior was clean, and the doors had fresh paint, as did the shutters that hung alongside new, clear windows, and there were new shingles on the roof. It was utterly normal and completely wonderful.

Lavinia loved it.

"Now, walk with me, if you will, Mrs. Jennings, past these trees. Can you see? Over there." He pointed.

She looked in the direction where he was pointing, and saw two small stone cottages standing side by side. "A home for the new Mr. and Mrs. Grimmett, and a home for Hannah. I asked her, you know, before we began building, if she would like a cottage of her own, and she said yes— so long as she can visit us from time to time."

"Foolish woman," Lavinia said, blinking back tears. "You would think we'd sent her all the way to India rather than down a small lane."

"She is special to me, Lavinia. She kept you safe and gave you the confidence and the courage you needed to survive all these years, my clever, wonderful girl. How grateful I will always be that an old crone tumbled into my lap and proclaimed me her husband. For now I am."

"And I am your wife," Lavinia said. "Lucas, do you suppose any of the trees on our property would be good for climbing?"

"I believe so. Why?"

"Because I think climbing trees and breeches might go together quite well. What do you think?"

He grinned at her. "I couldn't agree more."

"It's a good thing Ruby Chadwick gave hers to me, then, isn't it?" And then she laughed and dashed off toward the house, Lucas chasing after her, for there was a new house to explore without falling through the stairs and new adventures to be had and a new, normal life to be lived.

And a love to be savored for a lifetime.

About the Author

KAREN TUFT WAS BORN WITH a healthy dose of curiosity about pretty much everything, so as a child she taught herself to read and explored the piano. She studied composition at BYU, graduated from the University of Utah in music theory, and was a member of Phi Kappa Phi and Pi Kappa Lambda honor societies. In addition to being an author, Karen is a wife, mom, grandma (hooray!), pianist, composer, and arranger. She likes to figure out what makes people tick, wander through museums, and travel, whether it's by car, plane, or paperback.